BIO-STRIKE

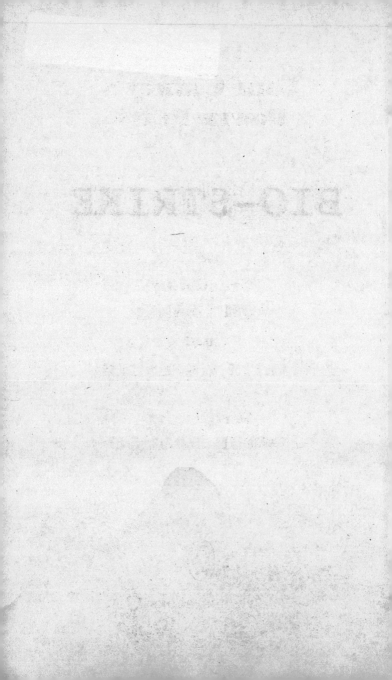

Tom Clancy's
POWER PLAYS

BIO-STRIKE

Created by
TOM CLANCY
and
MARTIN GREENBERG

Written by
JEROME PREISLER

PENGUIN BOOKS

PENGUIN BOOKS

Published by the Penguin Group
Penguin Books Ltd, 27 Wrights Lane, London W8 5TZ, England
Penguin Putnam Inc., 375 Hudson Street, New York, New York 10014, USA
Penguin Books Australia Ltd, Ringwood, Victoria, Australia
Penguin Books Canada Ltd, 10 Alcorn Avenue, Toronto, Ontario, Canada M4V 3B2
Penguin Books India (P) Ltd, 11 Community Centre,
Panchsheel Park, New Delhi – 110 017, India
Penguin Books (NZ) Ltd, Cnr Rosedale and Airborne Roads,
Albany, Auckland, New Zealand
Penguin Books (South Africa) (Pty) Ltd, 5 Watkins Street,
Denver Ext 4, Johannesburg 2094, South Africa

Penguin Books Ltd, Registered Offices: Harmondsworth, Middlesex, England

First published in the United States of America by Berkley Books 2000
Published in Great Britain in Penguin Books 2000

1

Acknowledgments

I would like to acknowledge the assistance of Marc Cerasini, Larry Segriff, Denise Little, John Helfers, Robert Youdelman, Esq., Tom Mallon, Esq.; the wonderful people at Penguin Putnam Inc., including Phyllis Grann, David Shanks, and Tom Colgan; and Doug Littlejohns, Kevin Perry, the rest of the *Bio-Strike* team, and the other fine folks at Red Storm Entertainment and Holistic Design. As always, I would like to thank Robert Gottlieb of the William Morris Agency. But most important, it is for you, my readers, to determine how successful our collective endeavor has been.

—Tom Clancy

ONE

AMERICAN CITIES RUN BY THE CLOCK. THIS IS TRU-
est of the largest and busiest, where the minute hand
impels people through their routines without room for
pause. The sleep-demolishing clatter of a five A.M. trash
pickup, a breakneck dash to the subway, back-to-back
conferences noted in a desk planner, business luncheons,
happy hours, and more commuter sprints—these are distance markers on the constricted urban fast track, a daily
marathon of appointments and schedules where it is only
an apparent contradiction to say even the unpredictable
occurs at predictable times.

It was largely because of its precise adherence to
schedule, its tidal inflow and outflow of humanity, that
the New York Stock Exchange was chosen to be ground
zero for the northeastern seaboard of the United States,
the epicenter of an explosion that would be neither heard
nor felt by the thousands of souls it overtook, yet was
potentially more catastrophic than a full-scale nuclear
assault.

Inconspicuous as the weapon he was carrying, the man in the dark blue suit walked past the statue of George Washington in Federal Plaza to the impressive Greek Revival building on Wall Street amid a swarm of traders and clerks eager to make the opening bell. A tobacco-leather briefcase in his right hand, he climbed the broad outer stairs, passed under the stone pediment with its sculpted gods of finance and invention, and strode through the entrance onto the main trading floor. Once inside, he continued moving with the flood of conservatively dressed men and women as they pushed toward the brokerage booths, trading posts, and banks of phone and video monitors that linked the Exchange to the national and foreign market networks.

Scanning the room, he discovered an unoccupied phone stall, jostled toward it, placed his briefcase on the floor near his feet, and lifted the receiver.

His hand on the hook, he randomly keyed in a number and pretended to make a call.

He would stand there waiting until the time was right.

A few moments later, the bell rang out from the platform, and the nation's most powerful engine of commerce jolted into high gear. The buzz of voices around him became an enthusiastic clamor, the loud outcries of stock auctioneers carrying up to the vaulted ceiling, tantalizing their bidders like bright flashes of gold and precious gems.

He felt sure that no one was paying attention to him. He was invisible in his conformity, to all eyes just another securities professional touching base with his office as the early quotes hit the board.

The silent phone cradled between his chin and shoulder, he leaned down and pushed a catch beside one of the briefcase's combination locks. The latch did not snap open. Nor had that been his intent.

Still bent over the case, he heard a low sound issue from its side panel.

Hissssss.

Like a venomous snake.

The device was patterned after the modified attaché cases once found by authorities in the compound of Japanese *Aum Shinrikyo* terrorists, the same extremist cult responsible for the 1995 Tokyo subway attack that killed a dozen riders and left over 5,000 people grievously injured from exposure to sarin nerve gas. Like the *Aum*'s delivery system, it had been contrived from a small aerosol canister, a battery-operated handheld fan, and a nozzle running to a camouflaged vent in the shell of the briefcase. His single improvement to their original design was the lock-catch triggering mechanism, which eliminated any need to raise the lid and reduced his chances of drawing unwanted attention.

Lifting his case, the man in the dark blue suit hung up the receiver and stepped back into the crowd. Someone immediately shouldered past to take his place at the phone, scarcely noticing him. *Good,* he thought. In the general commotion, the expulsion of aerosol couldn't be heard. He had only to wind his way around the room a bit, insuring the agent was spread throughout, and his job here would be finished. His targets would do the rest with their scrambling between appointments, their five-o'clock cocktail gatherings, their close-packed bodies on homebound trains and buses. Mingling with coworkers, casual acquaintances, and friends, kissing their wives and hugging their children, going around and around in

3

relentless, cyclical patterns of high-speed movement, they would very effectively do the rest.

Soon he left the Exchange and turned onto Broad Street, the canister in his briefcase emptied of its unseen contents. In his mind, he could still hear the noise from the vents: *hissssss*.

The memory raised the hairs at the back of his neck. He'd been guaranteed there was nothing to worry about, and the assignment had paid handsomely enough to help compensate for any lingering anxiety. Still, he was glad to be outside the building, and he welcomed even the thick, unseasonably warm air of Manhattan in fall . . . knowing he hadn't really left anything behind. Not anything that couldn't follow him.

If what he had released wasn't already out there on the street, it would be.

Soon enough, it would be everywhere.

The Air Tractor AT-802 turboprop is a mainstay of the agricultural aviation industry and a common sight in the sky above central Florida, a region that accounts for almost 70 percent of the nation's total citrus production. Aboard the plane is an 800-gallon hopper that may contain any of a wide range of fertilizers, herbicides, pesticides, and fungicides. Pumps beneath the fuselage drive the chemical from the hopper into wing-mounted booms equipped with either special nozzles, in the case of liquids, or spreaders, in the case of solids, for spraying the vast groves of orange, grapefruit, lemon, and lime trees.

On this particular morning, an AT-802 launched from a grass airstrip west of Clermont for a spray run with something worlds removed from the products normally used by ag pilots. To prevent its degradation in storage and transport, the material had been lyophilized, or freeze-dried, into an ultrafine, whitish powder that resembled confectioners' sugar to the naked eye. The particles were then embedded in tiny granular spheres composed of a biodegradable organic compound, increasing their stability and ensuring a controlled and uniform rate of release. Perfectly smooth and free-flowing, the microcapsules rolled virtually without friction and would not acquire electrostatic charges that might make them cling to objects on which they alighted, enabling secondary dissemination of the agent in breezes kicked up by weather, the wings of birds, or the tires of a Mack semi whipping down the interstate.

Its manufacturer had wanted only the best and obtained it at the cost of millions, knowing his clients would find the product irresistible, and confident of an impressive return on his investment.

The crop duster banked to the southwest now, maintaining a low altitude, flying across the wind. At his controls, its pilot could see the trees spread out beneath him, row after row seaming the fields to the extreme limit of his vision, their heavy green crowns jeweled with orange and yellow fruit that would soon be harvested, packaged, and shipped from coast to coast. On his panel were state-of-the-art GPS and GIS displays mapping the acreage to be covered in exact coordinates, displaying a stream of real-time data about outside environmental conditions, monitoring every aspect of his dispersal unit's operation. According to the instruments, a meteorological inversion had kept a band of cool air close to the ground today, ideal weather because it would prevent the powder from drifting off target with warmer, rising air currents.

He buzzed over the groves, once, twice, and again, a vaporous swath trailing from his wings with each deliberate pass. The aerosol hung in the blue, billowed in the blue, marked the blue with wide, white, parallel stripes that gradually scattered and bled into a light, milky haze.

Then—gently, softly—it settled to earth.

A Boeing 747 wide-bodied jumbo jet can carry over 400 passengers on an international trip, seating as many as 10 abreast, far exceeding the capacity of other commercial airliners. For Steve Whitford this had been so much a mixed blessing that he found himself happily awaiting his layover as his flight taxied to a halt in Sydney.

While he had gotten the last available booking on that flight at the very last possible minute—and supposed he should have been too thankful for the seat to bemoan the absence of leg and elbow room—Steve had little doubt the plane would have burst open like an overstuffed tube of Pillsbury cookie dough had they tried squeezing even a single additional body aboard. At a spindly six feet four—with most of that beanpole height stacked from hip to shin—he was willing to admit his opinion might be a tad prejudiced, but he would have argued its worthiness, nonetheless. *Higher than himself can no man think,* hadn't some famous philosopher said that once upon a time?

Good lawyer that he was, Steve never missed an opportunity to cite precedent.

". . . like to thank those of you who are visiting Australia or going on to connecting flights for choosing our airline. For those continuing to London with us after the stop, please feel free to stretch your legs and enjoy the airport's restaurants, shops, and other amenities. . . ."

Steve unfastened his seat belt, slid into the aisle, and took the flight attendant's advice, stretching, massaging the small of his back with his knuckles. His achiness and complaints aside, he had to admit that there were worse things in life than rubbing up against his neighbor in the window seat.

He glanced over at her, an appealing blonde of about thirty in a sort of retro hippieish outfit consisting of a peasant blouse, hip-hugging bell-bottoms, and big, round red earrings like three-dimensional polka dots. At forty-four, Steve could recall an era when clothes of that type hadn't been so, well, *form-fitted*, as if they'd come straight out of a chic fashion designer's showroom.

Not that she didn't look good in them. In fact, he'd been very aware of *how* good she looked the moment they boarded the jet in Hong Kong, and had tried striking up a conversation with her soon after takeoff. Just chitchat, really, while he'd checked her finger for a wedding band—a quick glance verified there wasn't one—and tried to assess whether she might be inclined to pursue a more intimate dialogue at some later point in time. He'd told her his name, that he was an attorney who had been in Asia doing some patent and licensing work for a Massachusetts-based toy manufacturer, and that he was about to take a few days' R and R in London before returning to the grind. She, in turn, introduced herself as Melina, no surname given and none asked, her English subtly laced with an accent he couldn't associate with any particular nationality. It was kind of exotic, that name, especially hanging there *exparte,* so to speak. With a whimsy peculiar to the solo traveler, he had speculated that she might be an actress or pop star.

At any rate, she'd been reserved but pleasant, responding to his comments on the weather, their runway delays, and the lousy airline food, not revealing much about herself in the process. When he thought about it, she seemed almost secretive . . . although it was likely he was coming off too many days of legal gamesmanship to be a reasonable judge.

Steve got his travel bag out of the overhead stowage compartment, figuring he'd find a restaurant, eat a halfway decent meal, then maybe slap some cologne on his face in the rest room to freshen up for the next long leg of the transcontinental haul. He'd batted around the idea of asking Melina to join him and was still undecided. Why necessarily take her reticence as a snub? It was understandable that a woman flying alone would be cautious toward some strange guy talking her up. Besides, he couldn't see anything inappropriate in a friendly invite.

He stood looking at her from the aisle. Still in her seat, she'd reached into her purse for a pen and a paper bag with the words *Gift Shop* printed on it in frilly silver lettering, then slipped some postcards out of the bag. It appeared she meant to stay put during the layover . . . unless he could persuade her to do otherwise.

He took a breath and leaned toward her. "Excuse me," he said. "I was wondering if you'd like to join me for a cup of coffee, maybe grab a quick bite. My treat."

Her smile was polite, nothing more, nothing less. "Thank you, but I really have to fill these out." She placed the postcards on her tray table. "It's the kind of thing that can slip right by."

"Why not bring the cards along? A change of scene might inspire you to write better. Or faster, anyway."

The cool, unchanging smile was a rebuff in itself,

making her clipped reply superfluous. "No, I think I'll stay right here."

Steve decided to do some face saving. They would be sitting together for another seven hours or so once the plane got back in the air, and he didn't want the situation to get awkward.

He nodded toward the postcards in front of her.

"Guess you do have a fair-sized stack there."

"Yes." She looked at him. "You know how it is with obligations. They're like little plagues on my mind."

Steve stood looking back at her. *Sure, whatever you say*, he thought.

He told her he'd see her later, turned back into the aisle, and filed toward the exit with the other debarking passengers.

She waited, her eyes following him until he stepped off the plane. Then she rapidly got down to business.

She removed the top of her pen and dropped it onto her tray beside the postcards. The ink cartridge was metal, with a small plastic cap above the refill opening. She twisted the cap to loosen the cartridge, slipped it out of the pen, and put the bottom half of the pen beside the other items on the tray.

Little plagues, she thought. A choice of words the man who was both her employer and her lover might have appreciated, though he surely would have disapproved of her speaking them aloud.

Her thumb and forefinger tweezered around the cap, she separated it from the cylindrical cartridge with an easy pull. Careful that no one was watching, she held the cartridge away from herself, turned it upside down, and tapped it with her fingertip. A powdery white substance sprinkled out and immediately dispersed in the cabin's cycling air. On newer commuter jets, maximum-efficiency filters might have trapped a significant amount of the contaminant, but she knew the aging fleet of Boeing 747s used ventilation systems that would suck it in and recirculate it with the plane's oxygen supply.

Entering the respiratory tracts of the aircraft's crew and passengers, the microscopic capsules would release the dormant presences within them. Transmitted from person to person, airport to airport, and city to city, spread across nations and continents by their hosts, these unsuspected invaders would aggressively do what they had been created to do.

They would incubate. They would multiply. And they would smolder until fanned into inextinguishable wildfires, outbreaks that would burn scouring rings around the world.

Now the blonde woman checked her watch and decided it might be best to move on.

She extracted a replacement ink cartridge from her purse, loaded it into the pen, then put her stack of blank postcards back into the gift shop bag. Returning the pen and bag to her purse, she recapped the empty ink cartridge and dropped it into her sweater pocket for later disposal. When she noticed that a few specks of powder had landed on the surface of her tray table, she blew them off with a little puff of breath. They wisped away into the artificial air currents of the cabin.

She nodded, satisfied. Her business was concluded.

Folding back her tray table, she rose from her seat and slid into the aisle. The plane was empty except for a handful of passengers and one male flight attendant near the exit, and she smiled at him as she left the plane.

He smiled back, a touch admiringly.

She passed through the jetway into the terminal and glanced up at the monitors listing arrivals and departures. Her next flight was slotted for departure in just over two hours. It would be the seventh and last, and she knew better than to believe the number was coincidence. No, it was without question a demonic fancy. A conceit of the fiend to whom she had given herself willingly, needfully, body and soul.

Little plagues. Seven, and then some.

She was tired, even exhausted, from crisscrossing the globe. But she had dispensed almost her entire supply of the agent and, after the jog into Frankfurt, would be through with the remainder.

Meanwhile, she could find a place to relax for a while and possibly have something to eat. As long as she was careful to stay clear of her latest seatmate, why not?

There was a comfortable margin of time left before she had to be at the boarding gate.

Sight being its only faculty, the eye trusts what it sees. Striving always to keep us on a steady path, it will often slide past the out of place to turn toward the familiar. This makes it easily fooled.

A business-suited investor in Manhattan's financial district. A crop duster winging over open farmland. An airline passenger filling out postcards to kill time during a layover. All are sights that fit and belong. And all may be something other than they appear, camouflage to deceive the willing eye.

In San Jose, California, a municipal street sweeper brought the aerosol payload through the target zone, dispensing it from an extra spray reservoir aboard its heavy steel frame. It whooshed along Rosita Avenue, amber cab lights strobing, circular gutter brooms whirling, wash-down nozzles deluging the pavement with water as the lab-cooked agent jetted from its second tank.

An everyday part of the urban scene, the sweeper barely scratched the surface of people's awareness: It was a minor inconvenience, a momentary hiccup in their progress through the morning. Motorists shifted lanes to get out of its way. Pedestrians backstepped onto the curb to avoid its rotating brooms, raised their conversational pitch a notch or two as it swished past, and otherwise ignored it.

They breathed invisible clouds of aerosol and never attributed the slight tickle in the nose or scratchiness at the back of the throat to anything more harmful than stirred up sidewalk grit. They scattered the microscopic particles with their shoe bottoms, ferried them on their skin and clothing, and sent them out along countless routes of transmission with the money they exchanged for newspapers and lattes.

Their eyes seeing nothing amiss, no disruption in the orderly and ordinary course of their lives, they went on to their workplaces without an inkling that they had become carriers of a wholly new and insidious type of infection—many of them heading north on Rosita toward the high, sleek office spire that was the famed main branch headquarters of UpLink International, far and away their city's largest corporate employer.

Hardly by chance, the street sweeper kept moving in the same direction.

When Roger Gordian's daughter telephoned him on her way home from the courthouse, he didn't know what to say. No matter that the proceeding's outcome had been a foregone conclusion or that he'd had months to prepare for the news. No matter that he was used to talking to business leaders and heads of state from everywhere on earth, often under hot-button circumstances that required quick thinking and verbal agility. Julia was his daughter, and he didn't know what to say, in part because almost everything he *had* said to her these past few months had proven to be exactly the wrong thing, leading to more than one inexplicable skirmish between them. Gordian had found himself having to consciously resist feeling like the parent of an adolescent again, prepared for every word he spoke to come back at him and explode in his face. That would have been thoughtless, unfair, and corrosive to their relationship. Julia was a remarkably competent thirty-three-year-old woman who'd led her own life for many years, and she deserved better than stale, fatherly programming from him ... difficult as that sometimes was.

"It's over, my divorce is final," she had told him over her cellular. "The paperwork's signed, and I should be getting copies in a couple of weeks."

That was four long seconds ago.

Five, now.

His stomach clutched.

He didn't know what to say to her.

Six seconds and counting.

His watch ticked into the silence of his office.

Gordian was not by disposition an introspective man. He saw his mind and feelings as fairly uncomplicated. He loved his wife and two daughters, and he loved his work. The work less. Though for some years it had consumed a greater share of his time than it should have, and the family had felt bumped to the sidelines. His wife, in particular. He hadn't realized, then, how much.

At first there was so much to be done, a decade of struggle building his electronics firm up from the ground. The importance of being an earner, a provider, had been fostered in him early in life. His father had died before the term *quality time* was coined, but it was doubtful Thomas Gordian would have been able to grasp the concept in any event. He'd been too busy adding thick layers of callus to his fingers at the industrial machine plant where he had pulled a modest but steady wage from the day he'd turned sixteen and quit high school to help support his depression-stricken family. For the elder Gordian, bringing home a paycheck was how you *expressed* your love of family, and that dogged blue-collar sensibility had taken deep root in his only son, enduring long after he'd returned from Vietnam and, with the help of loan officers and a handful of farsighted investors, purchased a limping, debt-ridden San Jose outfit called Global Technologies for the giveaway price of twelve million dollars.

The rewards of his gamble far exceeded Gordian's hopes. In less than a decade, he turned Global into a Silicon Valley giant with a slew of tremendously successful defense industry patents. One after another, the contracts started coming in, and Gordian had worked harder than ever to keep them coming. He had used the technological windfall from his development of GAPS-FREE advanced military reconnaissance and targeting equipment to propel his firm to the leading edge of civilian satellite communications, and rechristened it UpLink International.

He had earned. He had provided for his loved ones. He had made more money than he would ever need.

And so he'd gone ahead and found a new reason to keep working.

By the time his corporation went multinational—and Fortune 500—in 1990, Gordian's thoughts had slung outward to pursue what his wife usually referred to as The Dream, based upon an idea as straightforward as his personality: Information equaled freedom. No lightning bolt of originality there, perhaps, but his real inspiration had been in how he'd set out to draw concrete results from the abstract. As head of the world's most extensive civilian telecommunications network, he'd been in a position to bring people access to information, a currency with which he could buy better lives for untold millions, particularly where totalitarian regimes sustained themselves by doing the very opposite—choking off the gateways of communication, isolating their citizens from knowledge that might challenge their strangleholds of oppression. History had shown that radical government change nearly always followed quieter revolutions in social consciousness, and the old axiom that democracy was contagious seemed no less true for all the times it had been used as a political cheer line.

Again, Gordian's triumphs went far beyond his expectations—but, ironically, the signals Ashley was sending from home about her own unhappiness weren't getting through the bottleneck of humanitarian goals he'd continued to pursue. Not till she'd compelled his attention with words he would remember for the rest of his days.

"I know that everything you've accomplished in the world makes a huge difference to people everywhere. I know it's your calling, something you have to do. What

I don't know is if I'm strong enough to wait until you're done."

Her words, those shattering, unforgettable words, had forced him to look into a deep mirror and see things about himself that were difficult to accept. Far more importantly, they also saved his marriage.

He had been luckier than he'd even realized at the time.

"Dad, you still with me? I'm on the highway ramp and it's pretty noisy—"

"Right here, hon." Gordian tried to pull his thoughts together. "I'm just glad the worst of the ordeal's behind you and that you can get on with your life."

"Amen." She produced a sharp laugh. "You know what happened when we were leaving court? After everything we've been through, all the legal sniping, all the *ugliness,* he asked me to have lunch with him. At this Italian place downtown we used to go to sometimes."

Her voice dropped abruptly into silence.

Gordian waited, his hand tight around the receiver. That laugh—so harsh and humorless—had startled him. It was like hearing a thin pane of glass suddenly crack from extreme cold.

"I guess," Julia finally said, "we were supposed to toast to our future as born again singles over wine and pasta."

Gordian heard the creak of his office chair as he changed position. *He,* common noun, had once been referred to by name: Craig. Her husband of seven years. It was still unclear what had pulled them apart. The divorce petition Craig had filed cited irreconcilable differences, no elaboration. Over the months she'd been staying with her parents, Julia had occasionally talked about their long separations because of his career, about her loneliness when he was away on the job. He was a structural engineer, freelance, though most of his recent assignments had been for the big oil companies. His specialized niche was the design of fixed offshore drilling platforms, and he'd often spent many weeks on-site, overseeing construction. One month it was Alaska, the next Belize. His absences surely contributed to their problems, but Gordian suspected there had to be more. If Julia was the one feeling neglected, why was it *Craig* who'd wanted out? Gordian hadn't pushed for answers, however, and Julia had offered very few on her own to either him or Ashley. She had claimed there was no infidelity, and they were trying to take her at her word. But why had she been so guarded with them? Were the reasons too painful to share? Or might Julia herself still be in the dark?

Gordian shifted in the chair again. "What did you tell him?"

"Nothing. I was too incredulous," she said. "But wait, it gets better. While I was staring at him, really dumbstruck, he leaned over and tried to kiss me. On the lips. I turned my head soon as I realized what he was doing, or *trying* to do, and it landed on my cheek. I had to stop myself from wiping it off. Like a kid who gets a wet one from some ancient aunt or uncle she hardly knows."

"And then?"

"And then he backed off, wished me luck, and we went our separate ways. God, it was just so awkward and squirmy."

Gordian shook his head.

"An overture toward putting the bad feelings to rest,"

he said. "Ill-advised, inappropriate, and without any grasp of how you'd be affected. But I suppose that was his intent."

"He wanted the greyhounds as part of the settlement, Dad. If I hadn't been the one to sign that contract at the adoption center instead of him, giving me ownership in black and white, he'd have taken Jack and Jill away from me. *There's* an overture I won't forget."

Gordian strove to come up with a response. In the end he could only echo his own previous comments.

"It's behind you now, Julia. You can move on. Let's be glad for that."

Another significant pause. Gordian heard car horns squalling at the other end of the line. He wished she hadn't insisted on going to court alone, wished she weren't driving unaccompanied—not being as distressed as she sounded.

"Better go, traffic's a mess," she said. "I'll be home in time for dinner."

But it was barely nine o'clock in the morning, Gordian thought.

"There are quite a few hours between now and then," he said. "How are you planning to fill them?"

There was no answer.

He waited, wondering whether she'd heard him.

Then, her tone suddenly brittle: "Did you want a complete schedule?"

Gordian raised his eyebrows, puzzled. His fingers tightened around the receiver.

"I only meant—"

"Because I can pull over at the nearest *Kinko's* and fax something over for your approval."

Gordian made a gesture of frustration into the empty

18

room. His stomach went from bad to worse.

"Julia—"

"I'm a grown woman," she interrupted. "I don't think you need a full rundown of my comings and goings in advance."

"Julia, hang on—"

"See you later," she said.

The connection broke.

Blew it, Gordian scolded himself. *Somehow, you blew it again.*

And try as he did to see where he had gone wrong, he could not.

He simply could not.

Many stories below on Rosita Avenue, a street sweeper shot past the building as Gordian's employees began to arrive for the commencing workday, but the clamor of its equipment would not have impinged upon his thoughts even had it reached the heavy floor-to-ceiling windows of his office. From where he was sitting, alone at his desk, the dead, silent telephone still clenched in his hand . . .

From where he was sitting right now, the rest of the world seemed immeasurably far away.

TWO

IN THE CENTER OF LA PAZ, ON THE MAIN THOR-
oughfare that descended from the heights to the modern
business district, one could look up beyond the rows of
exhausted little shacks on the canyon wall to where three
of Illimani's five snow-capped peaks took a great bite out
of the Andean sky. It was a sight that none who visited the
city could forget, and that even indigenous Aymara Indians, with their blood memories of the Incas as encroach-
ing newcomers, viewed with awe and respect.

The National Police Corps vehicle and its motorcycle
escort headed southeast on Avenida Villazón to its wide
fork less than a mile past the Universidad Mayor San
Andrés, then bore left onto Avenida Aniceto Arce toward the Zona Sur. Nuzzled deep within the canyon in
Calocoto and other suburban neighborhoods, sheltered
from the cold sting of high-altitude winds, the city's affluent lived behind high gates in exaggerated chalets and
sprawling, tile-roofed adobe mansions constructed in deliberate imitation of Hollywood cinematic style.

In the police car's backseat, the lean, ascetic man in first officer's dress had ridden most of the way with his eyes downturned, a bony hand on the satchel beside him, his lips moving in a nearly constant whisper. He had looked out the window only twice—the first time, by simple chance, when they had passed Calle Sagárnaga, crammed as always with customers of the Witches' Market. There at the outdoor vendors' stalls were charms, potions, powders, and fetuses carved from the wombs of llamas for their alleged luck-bringing properties, their dessicated skin pulled tight over unformed bones, forcing them into contortions that resembled, or perhaps preserved, a state of final agony. There, indigent chola mothers, wearing traditional bowler hats and shawls, walked beside women of means in Parisian and Milanese vogue, a rare mixing of classes in this city, fear or reverence for pre-Christian deities being perhaps all they had in common. There, *yatiri* witch doctors eyed the crowd for potential clients, estimating their worth in bolivianos or U.S. dollars, cannily deciding how much might be charged to read their fortunes or work fraudulent magic on their behalf.

The car's single passenger had frowned disapprovingly. He spent much of his time among the poorest of society and knew they reached out to the ancient superstitions in ignorance and desperation. But the moneyed, well-educated elite, what was their reason? Did they think to apportion their faith like cash in separate bank accounts, placing small deposits in each, giving their full trust to no god while hoping to prejudice the will of all?

As his escort had left Calle Sagárnaga behind, remaining on the boulevard that traced the subterranean flow of the Choqueyapu River to the city's outskirts, he'd briefly looked out his window again, his eyes going to the slum housing on the face of the mountain. At first glance it seemed an insult to the divine scheme, heaven and hell inverted, those in the bowl of the earth living without need, those on the heights needing for everything. But that was to ignore the more sublime visual message of Illimani in the background: its sharp white peaks at once reminders of God's soaring majesty and a warning that He had teeth.

Bowing his head again, the passenger addressed his inner preparations for the next thirty minutes, fingers spread atop the satchel, quietly reciting the prescribed lines of verse from memory.

Now his car swung over to the right side of the road, slowed, and turned gently into a circular drive. Ahead and behind, the flanking carabineers throttled down their motorbikes. At the end of the drive he could see the large gray hospital building rising above a handsome lawn with tiled walks, shaded benches, and a glistening multitiered fountain that drizzled off wavery rainbows of sunlight.

The Hospital de Gracia was the newest and best-equipped medical facility in Bolivia. The physicians recruited for its staff held model credentials. Like the luxurious homes in its surrounding neighborhood, it had been built and financed with money from the illicit cocaine trade and was affordable only to those of high status and privilege.

How ironic, then, that the patient admitted under absolute secrecy ten days ago had vowed before the nation to eradicate the cartels and to apprehend and prosecute the mysterious foreigner called *El Tío*, who had unified them in his recent ascendancy.

The man in the *officiales* uniform plunged deeper into his recitation, his lips fitting comfortably around the Latin.

"Averte faciem tuam a peccatis meis, et omnes iniquitates meaas dele . . ."

Turn away thy face from my sins, and blot out all my iniquities . . .

"Cor mundum crea in me, Deus, et spiritum rectum innova in visceribus meis . . ."

Create a clean heart in me, oh God, and renew a right spirit within my bowels . . .

"Ne proicias me a facie tua, et spiritum sanctum tuum ne auferas a mei."

Cast me not away from thy face, and take not thy holy spirit from me.

The motorcade pulled into a wide space that had been left vacant in front of the hospital's main entrance, the carabineers lowering their kickstands to dismount. One of the lead riders came around back and opened the door for the passenger. Lifting his satchel off the seat by its strap, he let himself be helped from the car. He could almost feel the eyes watching from other vehicles around the parking area, peering at him through tinted windows.

It was to be expected, he thought. *There would be a great many secret police.*

He climbed the stairs to the hospital entrance with his head still slightly bent and the carabineers on either side of him, sensing their unease as he continued giving whispered utterance to Psalm 50, the Miserere, one of the preliminary invocations for the dying.

"Libera me de sanguinibus, Deus."

Deliver me from blood, oh God.

A somber delegation of hospital officials and white-coated doctors met the visitors in the lobby and guided them toward the elevator bank with a minimum of formalities. A pair of soldiers in gray green fatigues were posted at the head of the corridor. They held submachine guns and wore the insignia of the Fuerza Especial de Lucha Contra el Narcotráfico, the military's elite anti-narcotics task force.

The soldiers hastily checked the small group's identification papers and motioned them into an elevator. A third FELCN guard stood at the control panel. He pressed a lighted button, and they hurtled up three floors.

Moments later, the elevator doors reopened, and they started toward the intensive care ward.

Humberto Marquéz, the vice-president-elect, was waiting in an anteroom. He stepped toward the man in the officer's uniform and gave him a firm handshake.

"I thank you for your swift response to our summons," he said. "And for your tolerance of the rather unusual security measures we've had to adopt in bringing you here."

"Would there had been no cause for any of it."

"Indeed." Marquéz ushered him inside. "Our coalition government is bound together by a fragile thread. If news of why you've come leaks out before I can meet with old rivals whose differences were just lately reconciled . . ."

"That thread might well begin to fray even before you are sworn into office. I understand." The man placed his canvas bag on a low table beside the doorway. Though the committee of doctors and hospital officials had entered the room with him, he noted that his police escort had stayed respectfully out of earshot in the hall. "Please, tell me of his condition."

Marquéz did not reply immediately. An attorney by background, he possessed an automatic verbal restraint that had served him well since his entry into politics. His manner formally polite, his frame as tapered as his dark gray suit, he nodded his chin at one of the doctors.

"As the one in charge of this case, Dr. Alvarez, it is perhaps best that you address such questions," he said.

The doctor looked from Marquéz to the uniformed man.

"The *presidente* is semiconscious and on a ventilator," he said. "I hope you will forgive any impropriety, but let me be direct in my advice: Omit whatever rites you can, for time is short."

The visitor kept his eyes on the doctor for two or three seconds. Then he nodded silently. What more was there to say?

He unbuttoned the officer's blouse he'd been given to conceal his black clerical shirt, shrugged it off, and draped it neatly over the back of a chair. His other vestments were in the satchel with the articles he would require for the sacrament. He opened the bag and began arranging them on the table.

"Un momento, Padre Martín. Por favor."

He glanced over his shoulder at the doctor.

"Yes?"

"It pains me to interfere. But we have safety practices regarding apparel. Protective clothing must be worn in the ward."

"Such as?"

"Latex gloves and a gown are standard. As is a filtration mask."

Martín raised his eyebrows. "Has the *presidente*'s illness shown itself to be communicable?"

"The *presidente*'s illness is still undiagnosed."

"That was not my question."

Alvarez exchanged a glance with him.

"No additional cases of infection have been reported," he said. "To my knowledge."

"Then I will follow the directives of the church. And, God willing, leave here with my good health."

The doctor's hand went up in a forestalling gesture. But it was the troubled look in his eyes that gave Martín pause.

"Listen to me, please," he said. "I have witnessed much suffering in my years of medical practice, but when I go home to my family, it is pushed from my mind. That is how I cope—or always have in the past." He hesitated. "The affliction that has taken hold of *Presidente* Colón is a mystery. Ten days ago he was admitted for examination after complaining of symptoms associated with the common flu. Aches and pains in his joints. Some feverishness. Mild gastronomic discomfort. But there is nothing common about his illness. What I have watched it do to his body, its rapid acceleration . . . I cannot escape the thoughts and images. They will often come upon me suddenly as I put my arms around my wife or look into the faces of my two young sons. And when it does, I am afraid for them. *I am afraid*."

Martín looked at the doctor steadily, appreciating his frankness. It had seemed a difficult thing for him to step from behind his wall of clinical detachment. But Martín had not changed his mind.

"Our callings revolve around mysteries of a different nature, my friend," he said after a few seconds. "You must come to terms with yours, and I with mine. As each of us deems fitting and necessary."

They were quiet for a while, Alvarez's eyes shifting to one of the administrators. Martín watched him get an almost imperceptible nod. Then the doctor turned back to him and sighed.

"Very well," he said resignedly. "I will bring you to the ward."

The president-elect's room was segregated from the rest of the intensive care ward and guarded by more FELCN troopers. Alvarez led Father Martín quickly through the security check and then down a long hall to its door.

As they reached it, Martín thought he heard noises from inside. The rasp of something scuffing against fabric, followed by a series of unrhythmical thumps. He waited beside the doctor, listening, and heard the sounds again.

He gave Alvarez a questioning look.

"The spasms can be violent," Alvarez explained. His voice was muffled by the particulate mask covering the lower half of his face. "We've applied restraints to prevent his injury or the interruption of life support."

He reached for the door handle, but Martín lightly touched his wrist to stop him.

"Wait," he said. "I need a moment."

He moved in front of Alvarez, conferred the ritual blessing upon the entryway, and, because there was no one to respond, gave answer in his own quiet voice.

"May peace reign over this place."

"It will enter by this route."

His prayer completed, Martín pushed open the door himself. His missal and a neatly folded white stole were tucked under the crook of his arm. A burse hung from a cord around his neck, its front embroidered with a large red crucifix. Strapped over his right shoulder was the canvas bag holding his candles, holy water, and a communion cloth, the latter brought in the event Colón proved able to receive the Host.

Martín entered the room. Inside, oxygen hissed through soft rubber tubes snaking from the artificial ventilation unit into the patient's nostrils, then down behind his tongue into the pharynx. A female nurse stood at the foot of the bed, a clipboard in her gloved hands. A bouffant cap, mask, and isolation gown hid all her features except her eyes, which were visible through a pair of clear goggles. They were large, brown, pretty, and full of the same profound distress Alvarez had confided in the anteroom.

Martín looked at her for a second, then turned to the man he had come to see.

He was either unconscious or asleep, the lesions on his eyelids, cheeks, and lips showing in angry contrast to his waxen pallor. His blankets had been turned down to free his bare right arm for the intravenous drip lines. Patched with a scarlet rash, it was all taut skin and knobby bone, reminding Martín in an awful way of the mummified llama fetuses at the *Mercado del Hechicería*. Three fingers of each hand were enclosed in open-mesh tubes to the second knuckle, the tubes connected to a strap looped around the bed frame. The blemishes on his wrists were dark and cuff-shaped.

"The finger restraints have been effective in reducing his skin trauma," said Dr. Alvarez, standing behind Martín. "Any pressure causes blood to well up through the pores. We call it pinpoint bleeding. You can see the bruising that resulted from our use of conventional restraints earlier on."

Martín's eyes were still on the bracelets of discolored skin around Colón's wrists.

"Yes," he said. "I can see."

A stand beside the bed had been cleared in advance of his arrival, and he stepped over to it now, donning his stole, taking the candles out of his satchel. Checking that they were secure in their holders, he mounted the candles on the stand and lighted them with a match. From his burse he extracted the pyx containing the wafer and put it on the bed stand in front of the candles. He covered this with the communion cloth and genuflected.

Rising from his knees, Martín reached into the satchel for the holy water, went around to the foot of the bed, and sprinkled the dying man according to the points of the cross—once to the front, once to the left, once to the right. His lips moving in prayer as they had in the police car, he performed further consecrations of the room with his sprinkler, extending it toward the walls and floor around him. At last he turned and shook droplets of holy water over the nurse and Dr. Alvarez.

He was walking back around to the bed stand when Colón went into another convulsion. All at once, his lips peeled back from his gums in a kind of rictus. The muscles of his neck and jaw began to quiver. A gargling sound escaped his mouth, his chest heaving and straining, the hiss of the ventilator growing louder as his demand for oxygen increased. He arched off the mattress, his right knee springing up to mound the blanket, his foot thrashing from side to side like a captured animal.

Martín gripped his missal closer to his chest and turned to Alvarez.

"Is there nothing you can do?"

The doctor shook his head. "The seizures are unpleasant to watch, but they will pass." He was observing the life support monitors on the wall. "We give him muscle relaxers. Otherwise, it would be much worse."

Martín wanted to turn away, but in his mind that would have been an act of selfishness and thus an abdication of his responsibility. In this room, charity was reserved for the dying.

He saw Colón's right hand sweep across the linen sheet, jump stiffly into the air, then pound down on the mattress several times: *rasp, thumpthump-thump*. When the arm jerked, it pulled his intravenous lines up over the safety rail, but the finger tubes and strap had sufficiently restricted its movement to prevent the lines from tearing loose.

The spasms diminished after less than thirty seconds, his withered arm falling over the rail, dangling there limply for a moment until the nurse came around to readjust it at his side.

Martín stared down at him. His cheeks felt too hot, then too cold in the air-conditioning. He could hear the intake and expulsion of his own breath over the hiss of the ventilator.

He ordered his legs to move him toward the bed.

"Señor Colón," he said in a low voice. "It is Father Martín."

There was no acknowledgment.

The priest leaned over the deathbed. The sores on Colón's face were crusted with yellowish discharge. Martín could smell ointment on him and, underneath, the far more unpleasant odor of infection.

"Do you remember our discussions?" he said. "We

have had many of them, about many subjects. About faith. And strength."

He thought he saw Colón's eyes twitch under their closed lids.

"Now we will ask God's grace, and find renewed strength in our unity with his spirit," he said. "You and I, together—"

Alvarez stepped forward. "Father, he is much too weak."

Martín shot a hand out behind his back and waved him into silence.

"*Mi presidente,*" he said. "Can you take Communion?"

A moment passed. Colón's eyes flickered more rapidly. And then one of them opened and fastened on Martín.

Its white was swimming in blood.

Martín's cheeks flushed hot and cold again. He realized they were wet with perspiration.

"Are you able to receive Communion?" he repeated, trying to smooth the tremor in his voice.

Colón strained to answer, managed nothing more than a croak.

"Enough," the doctor protested. "He mustn't be—"

This time Alvarez fell silent without any urging.

Colón had declared his wish with a weak but unmistakable nod, his red eye never leaving Martín's face.

Martín turned to the bed stand, knelt before it a second time, and lifted the communion cloth off the pyx. If the heart of Alberto Colón was weighted with sin, he would have to unburden himself before God almighty; it was not humanly possible for him to give confession in his present state.

Moving to the bedside, Martín put the communion cloth under the dying man's chin and recited the *Confiteor*, offering penance in his name, pleading for his absolution from worldly sin: *"Mea culpa, mea culpa, mea maxima culpa."*

When he had finished his petition, he took the Host from its receptacle, blessed it, and brought it over to Colón.

"Try to swallow," he said. "If you have difficulty, a sip of water might help."

Colón stared at him with his one open eye, the iris uncannily bright, as if all the passion and will that had gained him the presidency—an office he had won in a free election against a powerful league of corrupt influences—was blazing through it.

He produced a groan of effort. Then his cracked lips slowly parted.

The odor of sickness on his breath was even stronger than it had been coming off his pores. Crops of raised, purplish lesions marched across his tongue and palate. His front teeth were smeared with blood where it had leaked from the rim of his gums.

The wafer between his thumb and index fingers, Martín bent to put it in his mouth . . . and that was when everything inside him stalled.

He stood there, rigid, his hand inches from the dying man's mouth.

Those ulcers on his tongue. Open. Weeping fluids.

Martín was unable to budge.

Unable to touch him.

What was it Alvarez had said to him in the anteroom?

"I cannot escape the thoughts and images . . . and I am afraid."

The priest felt a cutting shame. His resolute dismissal of the doctor's admonition came back to him now as self-mockery.

I am afraid.

His forehead beaded with sweat, he averted his eyes from Colón long enough to place the wafer on his tongue. But he could not keep his hand from shaking or drawing quickly back, and as he gave utterance to his prayers of viaticum, they seemed to fall away from him, or he from them. The disconnection was like nothing Martín had experienced before. It was as if he were slipping into a dark hole, some forsaken inner recess where all words of faith dissolved into empty silence.

And though he would spend much time trying to convince himself otherwise, right then, betrayed by his fear, praying in secret anguish, Martín knew for a dreadful certainty that his fall had only begun.

THREE

ROLLIE THIBODEAU FELT HIS TACKLE JERK HARD AS the giant sea bass erupted from the bay, its spiny dorsal fin raised like a mainsail, foam spraying off its mottled flanks.

He braced himself, his feet planted apart, knowing he couldn't afford to give the fish any slack. His heavy line stretched taut. The stand-up rod bent in his hands, and its butt pressed into his abdomen. He tightened his grip, his harness straps digging into his shoulders, the muscles of his arms straining against the drag of the line.

Then something gave out inside him. It was less a sensation of pain than a sudden buckling weakness between his stomach and groin. His feet slipped forward over the *Pomona*'s deck, and he saw the gunwale come closer. Three, maybe four inches, but that was enough tow for the bass. It rushed straight up out of the water, plunged with a tremendous splash, and then broached again, its wide gray head whipping ferociously from side to side.

Vibrating like a bowstring across its entire length, the line snapped just behind the wire leader.

The bass flailed backward, away from the stern of the motor yacht, Thibodeau's hook still buried in its gaping jaw. For a charged moment it was completely airborne. Its scales seemed to darken and lighten in patches as its great body undulated in the sunlight. Thibodeau guessed it was between five and six feet long.

He was shouting imprecations at the creature as it smacked down into the water, rolled over, and dove beneath the surface, its tail churning up a small spiraling wake before it torpedoed from sight.

Winded, his face red with exertion above his short, brown beard, Thibodeau tossed his rod disgustedly to the planks and leaned over the rail.

"Damn," he grunted. And kicked the gunwale. "God-*damn!*"

Megan Breen stared at his back for a few seconds, then shifted her eyes to Pete Nimec over to her left. Both had raced up behind Thibodeau to cheer him on when the fish struck.

Nimec mimed a basketball handoff. *Ball's in your court.*

She looked at him another moment in the crisp, off-shore breeze, a thumb hooked into the hip pocket of her Levi's, her thick auburn hair blowing over the shoulders of a tailored leather blouse.

Then she shrugged and stepped closer to Thibodeau.

"It happens, Rollie," she said. "Everybody has a story to tell about the one that got away."

He turned abruptly from the rail.

"Non," he panted, shaking his head. "I had it beat."

"Seemed to me that it was full of fight."

"You don' know!" he said. His cheeks and forehead went a darker shade of red. "Doesn't matter if that thing was twistin' like a demon in holy water. It was tired out, *and I shoulda had it!*"

Her eyes sharpened.

"Cool down, Rollie," she said. "They call what you were doing *sport*fishing for a reason. It's supposed to be an enjoyable activity."

He shook his head again, took a deep breath, then released it.

"Ca marche comme un papier de musique," he said. "All right, everythin' goin' smooth, jus' got me a little frustrated." He looked embarrassed. "My big mouth ain' caused no trouble between us, eh?"

She regarded him steadily.

"No," she said. "No trouble."

"Then I think I'll go below, pack away the damn rod, an' enjoy the boss's luxury accommodations."

She nodded.

Thibodeau bent to pick up the angling rod and then strode off across the hundred-footer's deck, passing Nimec without a hint of acknowledgment.

Nimec came to stand beside Megan.

"I've never seen him act like that before," he said. "You?"

"No," she said, watching Thibodeau climb down into the stairwell under the vessel's flying bridge. "And we've been friends a lot of years."

"You think it was his tug-of-war with the fish that got to him, or the one with Ricci at the meeting?"

"Maybe both. I'm not sure." She sighed, her gaze drifting toward the vessel's prow. "Speaking of our other global field supervisor, he appears to be in a mood of his own."

Nimec turned to look. His serious face visible in profile, Tom Ricci stood gazing out over the water.

"I have to wonder if the cooperative arrangement we worked out for those two wasn't good chemistry," he said.

"Almost seven months down the road seems kind of late for us to second-guess our decision. We have to *make* it good." She put a hand on each of his shoulders. "Your guy," she said, "your ball."

Nimec let her aim him toward Ricci and shove him off.

Tall, lean, and dark-haired, his angular features several sharp cuts of the chisel from handsome, Ricci kept staring across the water through his sunglasses as Nimec approached.

"The ragin' Cajun get over losing the big one?" he said, moving not at all.

Pete stood next to him, his arms crossed over the rail.

"Didn't think you were paying attention," he said.

Ricci remained still.

"Old cop habits," he said. "I pay attention to everything."

They were quiet. Some yards aft, Megan had settled into a deck chair, reclining it to bathe in the afternoon sun, her long legs stretched out in front of her. Ricci tilted his head slightly in her direction without seeming to take his eyes off the water.

"Those Levi's, for example," he said. "They say snug jeans are out, baggies are in. Convinces me they haven't seen snug on Megan Breen."

Nimec smiled a little.

"Got you," he said.

They stood viewing the calm blue iridescence of the bay in silence.

"There's been a ban on landing giant bass since the eighties," Ricci said after a couple of minutes. "Thibodeau would've had to let it swim, anyway."

"The payoff's in the catching, not the keeping."

"Let me hear you argue that to the fishermen I knew up in Maine," Ricci said. "Funny thing, you won't find one of those guys who'll ever describe the sea in terms of its beauty. For them it stands for waking up in the cold before sunrise and long hours hauling nets on damp, leaky tubs. But it's the source of their livelihood, and there's a different kind of appreciation for it."

Nimec looked over at him. "I'm not sure what you're getting at."

Ricci leaned forward over the rail.

"Me neither, exactly," he said, shrugging. "I'm an East Coast boy, Pete. Grew up ten minutes from the Boston shipyards. I've always thought of the Atlantic as a workingman's ocean. Might not be reasonable, but to me the Pacific coast is catamarans, blond surfer dudes, and blonder *Baywatch* girls."

"Ah," Nimec said. "And you think you might be constitutionally unsuited to temperate waters, that it?"

Ricci started to answer, hesitated, then slowly turned to face him.

"I wasn't looking to get into it with Thibodeau at the meeting," he said at last.

"Nobody said you were."

Ricci shook his head.

"That's not the point," he said. "What anyone did or

didn't say isn't important to me. I don't *need* that kind of bullshit."

Nimec's expression was reflective.

"Agreed," he said. "The question is how you choose to handle it."

Ricci stood in the breeze, his shirtsleeves flapping around his sinewy arms.

"I don't know," he said. "Everybody who was at the meeting . . . except for me . . . has been with Gordian for years. You've all got similar ideas about what Sword ought to be. You're all used to sticking to certain operational guidelines. You *developed* them."

"Sounds to me like you've already decided you don't fit," Nimec said. "Or can't—or won't."

Ricci looked at him.

"I'm trying to be realistic," he said. "Come on, Pete. Tell me you don't have your doubts after what happened today."

Nimec thought about it. Sword was the intelligence and security arm of his employer's globe-spanning corporation, its title derived from a reference to the ancient legend of the Gordian knot, which had defied every attempt at unraveling its complicated twists and turns until Alexander the Great cast subtlety aside and split it apart with a definitive stroke of his blade. This illustrated Roger Gordian's own no-nonsense attitude toward the modern day problems that might jeopardize his interests, utilizing country-specific political and economic profiles to help anticipate the vast majority of them before they became full-blown crises, and tackling the unpredictable emergencies that cropped up to endanger UpLink personnel with the most highly trained and well-equipped counterthreat force he could assemble.

Every twelve months before the happy distractions of the Thanksgiving and Christmas holidays kicked into high gear, Gordian gathered Sword's leadership aboard his yacht for a sort of informal year-end review and free-wheeling blue-sky session, an open forum at which they could examine the organization's recent accomplishments and shortcomings, evaluate its current state of preparedness, and hopefully reach a consensus of opinion about its future direction.

This year's roundtable, however, had produced less in the way of common understanding than acrimonious confrontation, at least between two of its key participants.

The session had convened before lunch amid the plush carpeting and rich mahogany furnishings of the *Pomona*'s spacious main salon. Besides Nimec, Megan, Ricci, Thibodeau, and Gordian himself, it had been attended by Vince Scull, UpLink's chief risk-assessment analyst, freshly returned from a long stint in the South Pacific, where he'd been scouting out locales for new satellite ground facilities and had very noticeably added inches to his belly roll, as well as a tiny but expert helical tattoo to the back of his right hand that, he explained, had been applied by a Malaitan tribeswoman as a lasting souvenir of their acquaintance.

Scull had kicked things off with an endorsement of French Polynesia as a potentially excellent site for a monitoring and relay station, scarcely needing to refer to his copious notes while offering detailed facts and figures about the country's natural and industrial resources, trade statistics, governmental structure, etc. After taking several questions about his recommendation, he had moved on to a broader overview of UpLink's international standing.

Given his deserved reputation for crankiness, Scull's sanguine tone was remarkable.

"All in all, we can knock wood," he'd said in summation, rapping his fist twice against the tabletop. "It's been peace and quiet since that nasty affair last spring. There hasn't been a single territorial or ethnic flare-up anywhere we've committed our resources that couldn't be defused before it got out of hand, thanks as much to our company's pull as diplomatic massages. And lots of places that were giving me worries about their internal stability have managed to avoid the coups, genocidal bloodbaths, even your garden variety power plays that usually bite us in the ass." He had smoothed an errant strand of hair over his increasingly bald pate. "Take Russia as a for instance. With our old *drook* President Starinov resigning and the nationalist opposition coming on strong again, I figured we might be looking at payback for helping him hang onto his Kremlin office suite awhile back. But what we're worth in jobs and cash inflow seems to have gotten us past any vendettas."

"And your forecast?" Gordian asked. "I'm talking about Russia *and* elsewhere."

Scull shrugged. "Nothing lasts forever, I guess, but I don't see any major blips on my screen, bumps on the road, pick your favorite metaphor. Name a spot on the map that hosts an UpLink bureau or is linked to our satcom net, and you'll see people with a better quality of life. And not even the most balls-on tyrant wants to be known as the Grinch who'd mess with prosperity. Goes to show free market democratization works, folks."

"And that the fear of political backlash is a viable

substitute for conscience with most heads of state," Megan said. She glanced at Scull. "You'll notice, Vince, I made my point without a single mention of the lower anatomy."

Gordian smiled thinly.

"I'm pleased in either case," he said, sipping from a glass of Coke.

More discussion had followed across a range of subjects. How was the Sword hiring drive in India going? In South Africa? Where were they in terms of testing that new firearm developed by the nonlethal weapons division? The implementation of intranet software upgrades? What about those negotiations with Poland? And the possible ramifications of the sudden death of Bolivian president-elect Alberto Colón? The tragedy of it went beyond his youth. His humanitarian values and aggressive challenge to the minicartels had promised to spark a regional trend and led to preliminary talks with UpLink about joint commercial initiatives with his country. What were the prospects for those efforts without Colón at the young administration's helm?

And so on and so forth. At noon they broke for a lunch of cold poached salmon with hollandaise, and capers and cucumber salad, freshly prepared in the *Pomona*'s galley, brought in with decorum by a pair of adept servers, and eaten with corresponding appreciation.

It was not by chance that they had waited until after their meal to bring up the previous spring's sabotage of a NASA space shuttle carrying UpLink orbital technology, and Sword's presumably connected encounters with paid terrorists in southern Brazil and Kazakhstan—the "nasty affair" to which Scull had alluded. A number of major issues surrounding those events remained unresolved, and Gordian had wanted everything else on the agenda out of the way so they could devote the latter half of the meeting to them without digression.

The empty dishes carried off, he'd turned his penetrating blue eyes toward Rollie Thibodeau.

"Okay," he said. "Any progress to report?"

Thibodeau pursed his lips.

"Some," he said. "Got to do with *Le Chaut Sauvage*."

Nimec would later recall seeing Ricci tense with something between edginess and anger at Thibodeau's mention of the tag he'd given the terrorists' otherwise nameless field commander, Cajun French for "The Wildcat." A man who had twice eluded their efforts to capture him, the second time after tearing away from Ricci during a fierce hand-to-hand struggle at the Baikonur Cosmodrome.

"Up till a few days ago, we didn't have anythin' would give us a firm lead on him," Thibodeau had continued. "Was plenty for guesswork, though, startin' with what we knew about that American botanist in Peru got kidnapped and ransomed for seven million back in '97. He say the guy callin' the shots with the narco-guerrillas who did the snatch was tall, blond, an' light-skinned, body like a weight lifter. Ordered him returned to his family minus both eyes."

Gordian shook his head in horror. "Making a positive ID by the victim close to impossible, if any of his abductors were ever captured," he said. "The cold-blooded logic certainly fits our man."

Thibodeau nodded. "Ain't the worst of it, either. Word out of the Sudan was that someone with the same looks headed up mercenary extermination squads in the south, part of the country they call the triangle of death. This'd be two years ago, when the civil war heated up. Wiped out entire villages hostile to the radicals in Khartoum. Men, women, children, the old an' sick, wasn't no difference to him." He scowled. "Son of a bitch ain't just cold-blooded. Be a monster."

"And he gets around," Nimec said. "Remember the Air Paris flight that was hijacked in Morocco last year? Another hostage situation, another large payoff. The Algerians who took responsibility threatened to start killing the children first and convinced the authorities it wasn't a bluff. They were provided with a private jet as a condition of the hostage release, flew off to an unknown location, and got away clean with twenty million francs. Or *mostly* clean." He leaned forward. "This one has a silver lining, Gord."

Gordian had waited.

"The hijacker giving the orders never removed his stocking mask on the tarmac outside the plane. But inside with the air-conditioning down, no ventilation, it was another story," Nimec said. "Take one guess how he was described by the passengers who saw his face when the mask came off."

Gordian looked at him. "Blond, light-complected."

"And a heavy lifter," Nimec said, nodding. "Definitely *wasn't* Algerian, spoke with an accent that might've been either Swiss or German." He paused. "I prepared a brief on the incident when it happened, but because we didn't have any involvement, it had kind of escaped my mind. Then I came across my thumbnail on the computer while reviewing data for our own investigation, and got to thinking the blond guy responsible might be the same guy we're after. So I went back into the files and out popped the most crucial detail as far as we're concerned. Namely, a French ambassador being held on board managed to get a photo of him when he wasn't paying attention. He was so traumatized, it was months before he remembered the film and had it developed."

Gordian had raised his eyebrows.

"Did you actually see a copy of the photo?"

"Not then, I didn't," Nimec said. "But thanks to Rollie, I have."

Thibodeau minimized this accomplishment with a wave of his hand.

"Couldn't beat Pete's source for the info, a unit commander in the Gendarmerie National crisis intervention team at the airport," he said. "Only trouble was that he gave it off the record and uncorroborated. No GIGN official would admit there was a snapshot for a couple reasons. One, they're supposed to be the best, and it embarrassed 'em that the hijackers escaped. They wanted to save face, make it harder for competin' agencies to run 'em down before they did. Two, the ambassador got scared, pulled strings to make the picture disappear. Figured the terrorists might take revenge on him or his family if it was ever used as evidence in court and they found out who took it. I was in his spot, maybe I'd feel that way, too."

"Tell me how you got hold of it," Gordian said.

Thibodeau shrugged. "The ambassador ain't the only one has contacts. I called in an IOU with somebody in Europol, who did the same with somebody else. Like that, *soit*. Took a while for anything to shake. Then one morning last week, I turn on my computer, and there's the photo attached to an encrypted E-mail. Right away I recognize our man from that airstrip in the Pantanal, but I punch up the satellite image the Hawkeye-I got of him just to be a hundred percent sure. Forwarded the pair of 'em to Ricci, since he actually seen him up close."

Gordian glanced across the table at Ricci.

"And?"

"It's him," Ricci said. "No question."

Gordian looked thoughtful.

"Got another thing in the works," Thibodeau said into the momentary silence. "Might turn out to be important, gonna have to see."

Gordian gave him his attention. "Let's hear it," he said.

"Wasn't no small favor I used up with that friend of mine, but my whole nest egg," Thibodeau said. "Besides wantin' the picture, I asked to tap into Europol's database of known terrorists. Took longer for him to swing that, but he say it could happen any day. I'm gonna run every at-large be a general match for *Le Chaut Sauvage* through that new Profiler system the techies been workin' on, see if we get any hits."

"The software's designed to recognize suspects hiding behind full-face masks or disguises, even ones who've had plastic surgery, by comparing digital file images with each other and a checklist of hard-to-alter physical characteristics," Nimec said. "When it started to look like the Europeans might open up for Rollie, Megan and I became mildly optimistic about getting some cooperation from domestic security agencies. We've been trying to convince them to let us input their intelligence tech."

"Any luck?"

"CIA's my albatross," Nimec said. "I'm still being routed through channels."

Gordian glanced at Megan. "What about the FBI? Have you gotten in touch with Bob Lang in D.C.?"

She nodded. "He's sympathetic to my request, and I seem to be making headway." A shrug. "We've arranged a face-to-face meeting for early next week."

"Try to goose him along," Gordian said. He jotted a notation on the yellow pad in front of him. "Meanwhile, I'll place a call to Langley. We should stick to our game plan, at least as far as this aspect of the probe's concerned—"

"That isn't close to good enough."

In retrospect, Nimec guessed Ricci's interruption had surprised him less than the fact that he hadn't spoken up much sooner. He'd been at constant odds with his colleagues over how the probe was being handled and had expressed his unhappiness to Nimec on a multitude of occasions.

Gordian turned toward Ricci, as had Nimec and everyone else in the room.

"What bothers you about it?" he asked in a level voice.

"I was asked to join this team because you wanted somebody to help retool it, make it more proactive, not tinker with the status quo," Ricci said. "That was what I heard when I got the hiring pitch, anyway. And here we are talking about putting in phone calls to the Euros and feebs."

Gordian regarded him steadily a moment.

"You believe we should be doing something different," he said.

"A whole lot of somethings," Ricci answered. "I think

we need a special task force on the job twenty-four/seven. I think it should have a separate command center with the capability to send rapid deployment teams after the people that hit us in Cuiabá and the Russian launch site. I think we have to be willing to dig them out from under rocks, pull them out of the trees, whatever it takes, wherever they're laying low or being protected. They killed our people without provocation, and we've lost months that should have been spent running them down. We have to go on the offensive."

Silence.

Gordian kept his eyes on him. He opened his mouth to speak, closed it. Rubbed his cheek.

"Well," he said. "You certainly aren't on the bubble about this." He rubbed his cheek again. "I just wish you'd come to me with your feelings sooner."

Ricci merely shrugged, but it was obvious to Nimec why he hadn't. Whatever their disagreements, he and Ricci had been friends for many years. For Ricci to approach Gordian directly would have meant going over his head, and Ricci's sense of personal loyalty would never permit that.

After a brief pause, Gordian looked around the table.

"Anybody like to comment?"

Thibodeau was quick to gesture that he did. Maybe too quick, Nimec would think in hindsight.

"We gotta be realistic," he said, frowning. "Never mind the drain that kind of manhunt would put on our resources. Be hard enough gettin' approval to patrol our ground facilities in foreign countries. By whose sanction we gonna have armed search teams operate across borders?"

"Our own," Ricci said at once.

Thibodeau's frown deepened.

"That might've washed when you was a city cop lookin' to haul some gangbangers off the street, but not when you got to abide by international rules of law," he said. "We can't be goin' anywhere we want, doin' anythin' we please."

Ricci had fixed him with a sharp look.

"Like when you got yourself shot to bits playing Wyatt Earp in Brazil, that right?" he said.

The sudden tension in the room was palpable. Thibodeau stiffened in his chair, glaring at Ricci with open resentment and hostility.

"Knew plenty of tough guys in 'Nam," he said. His voice was trembling. "They either gave up their attitudes or choked on 'em."

Ricci said nothing in response. He sat absolutely still, his face impassive, his eyes locked on Thibodeau's.

Nimec hadn't been sure what was going on between them but had felt deep down that it had little to do with their differences over the investigation. There had been scarcely a moment to think about that, however. He'd been afraid Thibodeau would lunge at Ricci and was watching him closely, preparing to haul them apart if that happened.

Fortunately, it never did, thanks to Gordian's intervention. He had made a loud business of clearing his throat, breaking into the strained silence.

"I believe we should call it an afternoon, spend some time enjoying the fresh air," he'd said in a deliberate tone.

Thibodeau had started to reply, but Gordian cut him short.

"Meeting adjourned," he said, abruptly rising from his seat. "Let's try to relax."

And that had about finished it, or at least discouraged the hostilities from boiling over on the spot. And here Nimec stood topside two hours later, Ricci beside him at the rail, both men staring contemplatively into the blue distance.

What was Thibodeau's problem, exactly? he thought. Why had Ricci provoked such blistering rancor from him, the Fish That Got Away notwithstanding? Pete had always known Thibodeau to be a grounded, fundamentally reasonable man, and it was hard to reconcile that with his mercurial outbursts. His mind once again insisted that the root cause of his behavior was as yet unspoken and unknown . . . which got him *where* insofar as being able to keep the show he and Megan had scripted from folding?

Nimec wasn't quite certain—more or less standard for him lately, he supposed—but it had struck him that maybe part of the answer could be found in his recollection of another meeting, one that took place at UpLink's corporate headquarters just over a half year earlier and ended on a note very unlike the crashing discord of today's grand finale. It had been three, four days after Ricci had returned from his mission in Kazakhstan, something like that, and he'd joined Nimec, Megan, and Gordian to confer about the troublesome loose ends they'd been left to grapple with. At that point, their spirits had been anything but high, and it had been Ricci's thoughts on the affair that had helped to bring them around.

Nimec glanced over at him now, remembering.

"Small steps, that's how you count your gains," he

said quietly. "Those words sound familiar?"

Ricci didn't move for several seconds. Then he turned toward him, the faintest hint of a smile on his face.

"Yeah," he said. "Familiar."

"It's solid advice," Nimec said. "I can't think of a better way of saying you ought to give things a chance to work out."

Ricci grunted and studied the water again.

"Assuming for a minute that I would," he said. "If Thibodeau shoves, from now on, I'm shoving back harder. That bother you?"

Nimec shrugged.

"Whether or not it does, I'd be willing to carry it," he said.

Ricci gave no comment, just leaned forward with his elbows on the rail.

"The bay's pretty this late in the afternoon," he said after a long while.

"Yeah," Nimec said. "It's how the sun hits the swells when it dips toward the horizon."

"Just sort of glances off their tops, makes it look like they're sprinkled with a few zillion gold flakes."

"Yeah."

Ricci looked over at him.

"I'll stick around, Pete," he said. "For now."

Nimec nodded, and this time it was his turn to smile a little.

"That's about all I can ask," he said.

A distancing from consequence salves the betrayer's guilt. Do not look toward crime and politics for examples; that facile sense of remove is bait for the waiting trap, and we've all heard the excuses in our ordinary lives. The woman next door that leaves the cat behind on moving day—van's here, have to go, who'd have thought the dumb thing would wander off for so long after she let it out? The family man enjoying a peccadillo with his secretary after office hours—his wife's happily provided for, bought her an expensive gold bracelet last week, and he's sure his kids prefer their computer games to hanging around with dull old Pop.

Remove any act from a broader context, and one can become convinced it means nothing. You see how easily this happens? Just close the eyes to cause, look away from effect, and walk on down the road.

Alone in Roger Gordian's office at UpLink in San Jose, Don Palardy told himself it was only a few hairs he was taking.

Only a few hairs, what was the terrible crime?

White cotton gloves on his hands, he stood behind Gordian's open desk drawer and used a tweezer to pull a strand from the comb in one of its neat compartments. He carefully dropped it into his Zippit evidence collection bag and then plucked two more from the teeth of the comb, dropping them into the plastic bag as well.

As head of the sweep team that performed weekly electronic countersurveillance checks in the building's executive offices and conference rooms, Palardy had no concerns about being discovered in an awkward or compromising position.

He knew that Gordian was at the yearly blue-water conference and would not be walking in on him today. He knew that he wasn't being observed through hidden spy cameras first and foremost because it would have been he, Palardy, or one of his subordinates who performed their installation, had Gordian ever requested it—

and he had not. Moreover, Palardy had carried into the room with him the broad-spectrum bug detector known in his section as the Big Sniffer—a twenty-thousand-dollar device that looked like a somewhat larger-than-standard briefcase when closed, and that was now opened and unfolded on the floor to reveal a microcomputer-controlled system of radio, audio, infrared, and acoustic correlation scanners, the output of which was displayed on LED bar graphs or optional hard-copy printouts. Among the Big Sniffer's package of advanced tools was a Very Low Frequency receiver sensitive to the 15.75 kilohertz frequency emitted by the horizontal oscillators of video cameras. And the VLF detector was neither beeping nor flickering, which indicated none had been located.

Alone and trusted here in the office—safe from "surreptitious intercept," as it was known in the trade—Palardy slid the evidence bag between his thumb and forefinger to seal it, dropped the bag into a patch pocket of his coveralls, and pushed the kneehole drawer shut.

The deed done, he plugged the cable of his boom detector into its socket in the rear of the Big Sniffer and went about his routine sweep with due diligence. Taking care to avoid the antique Swiss bracket clock he so admired, moving the mop-shaped antenna across the walls of the office, Palardy probed for the harmonic signals of tape recorders, microphones, and other passive and active bugs. Had he found anything amiss, he would have been quick to disable it and report his findings to his higher-ups in Sword security.

Don Palardy considered himself a decent and caring man, though not without human frailty. Had he found an expensive piece of jewelry on the carpet here, a missing cuff link or tie clip studded with diamonds, he would have returned it to his employer, regardless of how much taking it with him would have helped with his debts.

All he had taken were a couple, three hairs.

Since Brazil, he'd gotten very good at rationalizing away his transgressions.

FOUR

BAJA PENINSULA, MEXICO
OCTOBER 31, 2001

THE TUNNEL WAS ABOUT TEN FEET DEEP AND RAN for two miles toward the United States under the sagebrush desert midway between Tijuana and Mexicali. Its southern opening was accessible through a trapdoor in the rear of a barnyard storage shed. Its northern opening was a small cleft in the hillside at the bottom of an arroyo within eyeshot of the California border. The old tales said it had been dug by Jesuit priests wishing to secrete away a portion of their abundant wealth—alleged to have been gathered through outlawed trade with pirates and Manila galleons—when the jealous Spanish crown ordered its confiscation in 1767. Over 230 years later, it remained a busy conduit for smuggling operations, although the clandestine traffic was now in narcotics and illegal immigrants bound for America. "The occasion makes the thief," went the Mexican saying.

Tonight, some thirty yards from the tunnel's northern entrance, two stripped-down, lightweight all-terrain vehicles and a dusty old Chevrolet pickup sat hidden from

Border Patrol agents by a carefully arranged screen of manzanita and chamiso. The truck's windshield had been blown out, and broken glass was sprayed all over the hood and interior. Both men inside were dead, slumped backward in their seats, the woven upholstery soaked with blood and chewed to ragged scraps by the fusillade of bullets that had passed through and around their flesh. Their pants were drawn down over their ankles, their severed genitals stuffed into their gaping mouths. Each of the lifeless ATV drivers had been shot, mutilated, and left sitting in an identical fashion.

Above the blind of shrubbery that surrounded the vehicles, a dozen men were positioned on sandstone ledges along the east and west walls of the gulch, the four-by-fours in which they had arrived from Tijuana parked at a distance. They carried Mendoza bullpup submachine guns with tritium dot sights and lamp attachments. On the outcropping nearest the tunnel mouth was a wiry, dark-skinned young man with a neat little chin beard and coal-colored hair swept straight back from his forehead. He stood flattened against the slope in a toss of shadows cast by the dim light of a quarter moon. Beside him on the rock shelf was a can-shaped metal object with a thin telescoping antenna on top. His weapon against the leg of his blue jeans, he studied the tunnel mouth from his elevated vantage, not suspecting that he, too, was being observed.

Higher up the arroyo's western slope, Lathrop crouched behind a wide slab of rimrock, his mouth slightly open, his upper lip curled back, almost seeming to sniff the air as he watched the men below with intense fixation. It was an attitude queerly resembling the flehmen reaction in cats—the detection of airborne trace molecules with the Jacobson's organ, a tiny, exceedingly acute sensory receptor in the roof of the mouth that, like the tailbone, remains vestigial in humans, and whose function is something between smell and taste, endowing the feline with what is often taken for a sixth sense.

Lathrop had held an affinity for cats since childhood, was fascinated by their ways, owned three of them even now—though this was in all probability nothing but coincidence with regard to his own flehmen, of which he was altogether unconscious.

Calm, motionless, wholly focused in on his surveillance of those below, Lathrop watched from his solitary position of concealment. His face was daubed with camouflage cream. He had on lightweight black fatigues and tactical webbing with a .40 caliber Beretta in a hip holster. Lying beside him on the ground was his SIG-Sauer SSG 2000 sniper rifle. The firearms had been brought only as a precaution. If he were forced to use either of them, it would mean he'd botched the whole setup.

Peering into the eyepiece of his miniature DVD camcorder, Lathrop switched it to photo mode and made a minor adjustment to the night-vision scope coupled to its lens.

He'd have a lot of extra material on disk before he was finished, but better that than to take the chance of missing something important. Anyway, whatever was nonessential could be edited out when he input the digital images to the wallet-sized computer on his belt.

"Okay, Felix, let's do it with feeling," Lathrop whispered under his breath.

He zoomed in tightly on the bearded man and pressed the Record button.

• • •

Guillermo hated going into the hole. Hated entering a shed piled with swine feed to lower himself onto a precarious wooden staircase that creaked, swayed, and buckled with each downward step. Hated the stifling heat inside by day, the miserable cold by night. Hated the low roof pressing down overhead, forcing the tallest men to stoop as they walked. Hated the close dirt walls, crudely shored up in places with wood and concrete but still looking as if they might collapse around him without warning. Hated the skitter of rodents and insects in darkness so thick you could almost feel it pouring over your skin, smothering you like black sludge. Perhaps more than anything else, though, he hated the fetid odor of sweat, unwashed clothing, and bodily wastes that permeated the narrow tunnel despite the swamp coolers used to pull fresh air through ventilation shafts along its entire length.

He hated going into the hole, yes, hated every moment of every passage he'd made through its cramped, stinking twists and turns, but he knew with an absolute certainty that without it he'd never have lasted a decade, more than a decade, in an occupation that had put many behind prison bars in a fraction of that time. It was because of the hole that he'd had unmatched success at eluding the border patrols, because of the advantage it gave him over the competition that the Salazar brothers had turned an ever-increasing volume and diversity of trade his way. There were dozens of coyotes on the peninsula to whom *Los Reyes Magos de Tijuana* granted their blessing and protection, but Guillermo was sure that none besides himself would have been entrusted with this latest bulk shipment, sixty kilograms of high-quality black-tar heroin, worth a fortune on the *norte-*

americano wholesale market. And while the job was far riskier than others he'd carried out for them in the past, it was also less work than having to hustle together enough people who could afford his thousand-dollar-per-head fee to make a border crossing worth the trouble. Most often he was booking agent and conductor rolled into one. Tonight, the train had been filled prior to his involvement, and he had merely to bring it up to the line to receive his payment from Lucio Salazar.

Un coyote, sí, Guillermo thought reflectively. This was the popular label for a smuggler of human beings and contraband, and he was well aware not all its connotations were flattering. Fast, canny, and dangerous, wise to the lay of the land, the creature was also an opportunist that scavenged its meals wherever and however it could. *Sí, sí, why take shame in it?* The environment Guillermo inhabited tolerated moralists poorly, and he much preferred survival to becoming a righteous casualty.

His flashlight shining into the gloom now, he moved through the tunnel ahead of the Indians who had backpacked the heroin from Sonoma—thirty-five villagers by his hasty count, none older than twenty, most teenagers, perhaps a third of them girls—the youthful couriers themselves followed at gunpoint by a half dozen of the Salazars' *forzadores,* their enforcers. It made for, what, fifty people, give or take, double the number he'd brought down with him on any previous run, easily double. *Madre Dios,* he hoped these walls could withstand the tread of all those feet.

Imagined or not, the increased danger of a cave-in during this particular run only worsened Guillermo's usual state of unease. As, he supposed, did the rifles being leveled at the *niñas*. One of them in particular, a pretty fourteen- or fifteen-year-old, had reminded him of his own angelic daughter, who was about her age and had hair that was the same length, that even fell over her forehead in an uncannily similar way . . . though he wasn't willing to let their resemblance lead him to any exaggerated assumptions. The government was fond of propagandizing that the Salazars had turned remote villages in the *Gran Desierto* and further south across the Sierra Madres into armed camps and sources of slave labor. But why did that portrayal make no mention of the abominable conditions that the inhabitants had endured before their "occupation," of families starving in shelters pieced together from the remnants of cardboard boxes until the Salazars arrived and replaced them with permanent dwellings? Which alternative left them better off? Guillermo didn't know, hadn't enough information to form a balanced opinion, and at any rate, it was truly none of his affair. The train was not his. He had only to mind his business and guide it along toward *Estación Lucio*, as it were. And collect.

Guillermo rounded an abrupt bend in the path, widening the variable focus of his flashlight. It revealed countless overlapping footprints in the earthen floor, some of them fresh, others little more than faded scuffings that were probably generations older than he was.

Then the conical beam glanced off a heap of scattered rubble that Guillermo recognized as a trail marker of sorts. He was nearing the last portion of the underground march. In another fifty, sixty yards, the tunnel would ascend to its exit on the western side of the arroyo, where Lucio's men would await him with their transport vehicles. Guillermo would have a short rest as they loaded up, and then it would be back into the hole for the return trip with the villagers and *forzadores*, tiring work for the fittest of men—and the growing paunch above his belt was conspicuous evidence he had never been especially good at self-maintenance.

Guillermo continued on for another fifteen minutes or so before the ground began to rise, and the tunnel's stagnant atmosphere was relieved by a stream of fresh air from outside. Soon afterward, he noticed a wash of spectral moonlight through the break in the rock face that opened into the gully.

He increased his pace despite his weariness, impatient to reach it.

Felix Quiros had been patient. Resisting any impulse to act prematurely, he had waited for several breathless moments after Guillermo appeared from the tunnel's entrance, waited until the long line of mules had filed into the arroyo behind the stupid fucking *cabrón,* even waited until all but a few of the Salazar *forzadores* had emerged—which was to say, until he was positive that the entire shipment of heroin had been carried out— before he reached a hand down to the radio detonator's transmitter unit on the ledge beside him.

Then, with a quick tug on its antenna to be certain it was fully extended, he flipped the device's firing switch.

Inside the tunnel, its receiver sent a jolt of current through the wires leading to the multiple TNT satchel charges that Quiros and his men had planted along the final yards of the passage, covering them from sight with stones and loose earth.

The explosion was virtually instantaneous. It clapped and rolled through the arroyo, shaking its very walls, a fantastic claw of flame and smoke lashing from the tunnel's entrance. Debris pelted from the spiky edges of the fireball like meteors, buffeting the *forzadores* who had been last to exit the tunnel as its sides came tumbling down in a cascade of blasted rubble, slamming some to the ground.

Felix aimed his bullpup at Guillermo and opened up on him, taking him out with a rapid volley that knocked him onto his back, his legs jerking and kicking, his hands on his spurting chest. Felix poured several more rounds into him and, when he finally stopped moving, began to rake the bottom of the gully with fire, raising little geysers of sand and pebbles into the air, fanning his weapon from side to side even as his men did the same from their own perches. Screaming in pain and terror, the helpless young mules were cut down where they stood, some crawling on the ground under their bulky loads in futile attempts to reach cover.

Meanwhile, the handful of stunned *forzadores* who remained on their feet had begun blindly triggering their own weapons at the outcrops, but they were easy, exposed targets for the scissoring barrage from the ambush positions.

The men on the slopes continued to lay down fire until all movement in the gully had ceased. Paused in the echoing, smoking stillness. Reloaded. And on Felix's signal chopped out another sustained hail of bullets, emptying their magazines into the sprawled bodies below, making sure every one of them had been left a corpse.

The slaughter had taken less then ten minutes from beginning to end.

• • •

Lathrop kept recording for a while longer, wanting to catch a scene of Felix and his men as they descended into the arroyo for the scag. They worked fast, cutting the straps of the dead couriers' bundles with folding knives, then tearing them from their backs and gathering them into a single huge mound. While this was going on, a few of Felix's *hombres* split off from the rest and went scrambling toward the north end of the gulch, presumably to bring the vehicles they'd use to haul away their score.

Lathrop considered waiting for them to return, maybe taking a shot of them in the process of loading up, but rejected the idea almost immediately. He'd got Felix hands down for the killings and the snatch, got what he needed from A to Z. Why push the envelope? Sometimes there was a temptation to make too much of a game out of things. He knew his weaknesses and had to be careful about giving in to them. No way a guy in his position could afford that.

Not unless he wanted to join Guillermo and those other victims who'd come out of the tunnel with him in the great hereafter.

Carefully detaching the night scope from his camcorder, Lathrop put both back into their cases, shouldered his weapons, and silently retreated into the darkness.

FIVE

"ANY SUCCESS CONVINCING LANG TO PAY FOR HIS chits?" Nimec asked, and held up his punch mitt.

"You're starting to sound like Roger." Megan threw an off-balance left jab that barely nicked the padded leather.

"Shit," she muttered, winded. Her face was glistening with perspiration.

"Let's go, keep your rhythm."

"We've been at this for almost an hour, might be a good time to call it quits—"

"Uh-uh."

"Pete, I'm bushed. It isn't coming together for me this morning, and I still have to get showered for work—"

"What I hear, you were tired in Kaliningrad when you took down an armed assailant. Way *before* you started these lessons."

"I had no choice then."

"You don't now, either," he said, sidestepping to the right. "Breathe deep. And stay *on* me!"

Megan opened her mouth and swooped in some air. Keeping her left foot in front of her right, she pivoted toward him and took another shot. It landed more solidly, closer to the white target dot in the center of the mitt.

"Better," he said. "Again."

Her fist snapped out, caught the edge of the dot.

"Again! Keep that arm in line with your lead foot!"

Her next punch was precisely on the spot.

"Good," Nimec said. He stepped in closer, pressing her, flicking the mitt past the side of her cheek. "Cover up, I could've nailed you right there. And what do you mean 'like Roger'?"

Megan raised her arms, tucked her chin low to her collarbone. Her hair pulled back in a tight ponytail, she was wearing a white sweatband around her head, a white tank top with an Everlast logo in front, black bike shorts, and Adidas sneakers.

"I mean that you're both assuming Bob feels he owes us," she said.

Bob, Nimec thought.

"Doesn't he?"

"I think he thinks we're even."

"With regard to what? The time we saved a nuclear sub from being hijacked with the President aboard? Or found out who did the Times Square bombing after his people got steered down the garden path?"

Megan let his question ride, bouncing on her knees to stoke her energy. They were in a regulation fight ring on the top level of his San Jose triplex condominium, the entire floor a sprawling rec/training facility that included, in addition to the professionally equipped boxing gym, a martial arts dojo, a soundproofed firing range, and an accurate-down-to-the-reek-of-cigarette-butts-awash-in-beer reproduction of the South Philadelphia pool hall where the blush of youthful innocence was slapped off Nimec's cheeks by the harsh red glare of neons when he was fourteen or so. Megan had never spoken to him about that period of his life at any length, never gotten the gist of why he looked back on a past that included being the junior member of a father-son hustling team, a borderline juvenile delinquent, and, by her standards, a victim of child exploitation—what else would you call being kept truant from school to hold a cue stick in a dive full of chronic gamblers?—with such obvious fondness. Whether this was because her own upbringing was so different from his, she couldn't really say for sure, but Ridgewood, New Jersey, might as well have been worlds away from downtown Philly, and while she'd taken courses on Old and Middle English at Groton prep, there had been nary a mention of draw, follow, left, or right English in the offered curriculum.

She concentrated on her workout now, measuring Nimec with repeated flicks of her outthrust fist as he continued side-shuffling to her right, protecting the outside margin of the defensive circle he'd taught her to imagine around herself.

"Back to Lang," he said. "We have to utilize the NCIC database if we're going to get the intelligence we need."

"And his inclination is to ask the director to okay us," she said. "Right up to the highest classification levels."

"Up to," he said.

She nodded.

"But not including."

She nodded again.

"That won't cut it," he said. "Your average uniformed cop can input the overall system from his prowl if it's got an onboard computer. I want Lang to arrange for unrestricted access."

Nimec lifted both mitts in the air. She threw a one-two combination, followed through with a straight left, and blocked another swipe at her head without surrendering any canvas.

"It gets sort of complicated," she said. "National security's foremost with him."

Nimec looked confused.

"He doesn't trust us?"

"I didn't say that."

"Then complicated *how?*"

"I'd rather not explain it right now."

She saw his frown of confusion deepen.

"Leave it alone, Pete. I'm flying to D.C. again in a couple of days. We'll see what Bob's got to say."

Nimec looked at her a moment.

Bob again, he thought.

Then he gave a little shrug and shifted direction, dropping his right mitt to take an uppercut. Megan swung and made only glancing contact.

"You pulled that one. Again."

She brought her arm up smoothly, throwing her shoulder into the blow, and felt the satisfying impact of her fist thumping the leather dead on.

"Okay, that was perfect. Relax a minute," he said, coming to a flat-footed halt. "Now listen, this is important." He patted the middle of his rib cage with his mitt. "A guy comes at you, here's where you hit him. Do it hard and clean, and it'll collapse his diaphragm, doesn't matter how big he is. And he won't have expected it from a woman. People who don't know how to fight will generally make the same mistakes. They either aim for the nose or chin, which aren't easy to tag, or the gut, where there's more muscle, fat, whatever sort of insulation, than anywhere else." He lifted the other mitt to the side of his neck, just below the ear. "If you don't have an opening for the upper body, and you think you have the reach, you'll want to pop him right here. At the pressure point. Got it?"

"The chest or the neck," Megan said, the words spaced between long gulps of breath. She brushed a trickle of sweat from her eye with her glove. "You've told me that at least a dozen times."

"Reinforcement's never hurt anyone I've trained." He wiggled the mitt in front of his ribs. "Quick, let me have some—"

"Pete—"

"And we'll be through for today."

She let him have some.

Ten minutes later, they were outside the ropes, towels draped over their shoulders, their T-shirts splotched with perspiration and clinging to their bodies. Nimec went over to his supply locker, put away his target mitts, then helped Megan to unlace her gloves.

"There's another item of business we need to discuss," he said, hanging the gloves on a peg inside the locker.

"Concerning?

"Ricci's brain flash about establishing RDTs," he said. "I've been mulling it over and feel it ought to be done."

Megan stood undoing her hand wraps, her open gym bag on a bench against the wall behind her.

"I agree," she said. "Provisionally."

"Your provisions being . . . ?"

"It would have to be on an experimental basis and subject to constant review. And I'd want everybody on board. Meaning Gord *and* Rollie." She looked at him. "You seem surprised, Pete."

Nimec shrugged.

"You didn't seem too enthused about the suggestion when it was offered," he said. "I figured I'd run into more resistance."

Megan considered how to respond. She finished removing the linen wraps, wound them up neatly, then turned to the bench and dropped them into her bag.

"Ricci's aptitude isn't anything that I question," she said finally, looking back at Nimec. "I just don't enjoy his contentious solo flier routine. And sometimes I need to be where he *isn't* to get past it."

Nimec shrugged a little, his hand on the locker's open door.

"Sounds like some kind of solution, anyway."

"You could call it that," she said. "I think of it as keeping my sights on the bigger picture."

He gave her a questioning glance.

"Whoever attacked us in Brazil last spring killed a lot of our people and would have caused even more destruction . . . would have been able to blackmail every country on earth . . . if we hadn't gotten in the way of their plans," she said. "Put me in our enemy's shoes, I'd be carrying one serious grudge. And the thought of not being ready if and when it's acted upon worries the hell out of me, Pete."

He kept looking at her for several long seconds and then swung the locker door inward. It shut with a dull, metallic clang.

"Makes two of us," he said.

• • •

Some months earlier in Madrid, in the Villanueva building of the *Museo del Prado*, he had gone to view Brueghel the Elder's painting *The Triumph of Death,* and even now was unsure how long he had stood before it. It was as if time had stilled around him. As if his innermost visions had been projected onto the wall of the gallery.

He had not known where to rest his eye. On the molten orange landscape with its pools of fire, its spewing clouds of black, volcanic smoke? Or the medieval village besieged by an exterminating army of skeletons, banners of war hoisted above their skull heads, the hollow sockets of their eyes showing only a pitiless adherence to their single objective? Here they hacked at the living with broadswords. Here they impaled them on the points of spears. There a cadaverous looter knelt over his prostrate victim, holding knife to throat to deliver the finishing stroke. In the right foreground, a peasant woman who had fallen atop a pile of twisted corpses raised her arms in a futile plea for mercy as a bone soldier stood with one conquering foot planted on her body, his battle-ax swinging inexorably downward. Where to rest the eye? On which scene of fabulous annihilation? The death barge advancing over a mire of crushed bodies and blood, its skeletal crew wrapped in the white cerements of the grave? The townsman hanging, limp, from the single forking limb of a shattered tree? The emaciated dog, all skin and protruding ribs, sniffing hungrily at the child in its fallen mother's embrace? Or the revelers in peacock finery scattering from their dinner table in helpless panic as a swarm of cadaverous marauders closed ranks around them?

Where, indeed, to rest the eye?

The painting had been remarkable. Absorbed in its sweeping infernal beauty, Siegfried Kuhl might have believed its creator had reached a hand across the centuries and tapped deep into his mind for inspiration. His umbilical connection to it had been overwhelming. It had at once seemed to draw its energy from him and infuse him with its own.

Until that unforgettable experience, Kuhl had never been moved by a work of art. He had gone to the museum out of curiosity and nothing more, compelled by Harlan DeVane's remark that he might find it of interest. Six months ago, it had been. After the debacle in Kazakhstan, where only a chance diversion had allowed him to break away from the Sword operative with whom he'd grappled in the launch center's cargo-processing facility.

The man's features were framed in his mind in photographic detail. Whenever he pictured the sharply angular jut of his cheekbones, the set of his mouth, he would feel the restless desire for vengeance slide coldly through his intestines. As he felt it now, six months later and a continent away, sitting at a window table in a brasserie called *La Pistou*, opposite the Champs de Bataille Parc, in Quebec City. Watching the entrance to the park, waiting for his lovely courier to arrive.

Kuhl's failure at the Cosmodrome had been a severe blow. Driven underground, wishing to get far ahead of his pursuers, he had altered his appearance, obtaining colored contact lenses, darkening his hair, filling out his lips with collagen injections, even growing a short beard. Then, in his global migrations, he had found himself in

Spain for a time, and he realized it was no accident that brought him there.

DeVane had understood how it would be for him to see Brueghel's masterpiece, reflecting, as it did, the grim sensibility of an age when the Black Death had raged across continents, an indiscriminate scourge exempting no man or authority, no civilized institution, from being laid to waste. An age when none knew whether to blame Heaven or Hell for their miseries.

What power a man who let neither hold sway over his conscience, a man of iron and will, could have seized amid such upheaval. In violent action Kuhl was calm. In chaos he was whole. In the storm amid cries of turmoil he was strongest. And in strength he achieved fulfillment.

DeVane had understood, yes. And it seemed in retrospect that his comments had been as revealing as they were insightful—most probably by design. He found it amusing to lay out enigmatic, far-winding paths for others to untangle.

At any rate, his Sleeper Project must have been well along at that point. Kuhl was not a scientist, but he had sufficient knowledge of the basics of genetic engineering to be certain it would have taken years to produce a pathogenic agent of the type generated at the Ontario facility. The procurement of recombinant DNA technology and raw biological materials would have been a difficult, expensive undertaking. As would the search for top experts in the field from around the world. And preliminary challenges of that sort would have paled to insignificance before those that emerged in the later developmental stages.

The complexities of manipulating a viral organism's

genetic blueprint were manifold. Given the additional requirement that its infectiousness be keyed to a particular genetic trait—blue eyes, left-handedness, familial diabetes, ethnic and racial characteristics, the possibilities were endless—the difficulty of the task became even more considerable. Still, the techniques needed to create such a microbe had been the focus of widespread experimentation in both private and government laboratories in the most advanced nations. And DeVane had gone several steps beyond. His criteria had been that the Sleeper pathogen respond to an unlimited range of inherited human characteristics *on demand,* laying dormant until activated by a chemical trigger or set of triggers. That it could, therefore, bring about symptoms in targets ranging from specific individuals to entire populations, depending entirely on which trigger was selected for dispersal.

In effect, he had overseen the successful creation of a microscopic time bomb. It could be customized to order, residing harmlessly in one host, hatching explosive malignancy in another. It could be as precise as an assassin's bullet or as widespread in its capacity for devastation as the Plague itself.

It was, Kuhl thought now, nothing less than the ultimate biological weapon.

He looked out the window and saw her emerge from the park, his lovely pale rider, punctual as always, crossing the Grande Allée to the brasserie, her blonde hair tossing in the wind, the collar of her dark, knee-length coat pulled up around her neck against the inclement weather. Though still a month off by the calendar, winter had made an early intrusion into the region, and spits of snow were blowing from a dark gray sky over the bare, rolling fields and ragged trees west of the Citadel.

Kuhl was glad of this. In the long spread of park fringing the cliffs above the Saint Lawrence River, the armies of France and Britain had fought their climactic battle for domination of the region. Yet in the warm seasons, flowers bedecked the soil where the blood of generals had been spilled, and strollers sniffed the perfumed air in the smothering tameness of landscaped gardens.

Those floral blankets scattered to the wind now, the harsh contours of nature were uncovered, appealing to something in the stony fastness of Kuhl's heart.

She spotted him from outside on the sidewalk, their eyes making contact through the window, a smile tracing at her lips. She entered the restaurant and strode directly toward his table, walking ahead of the punctilious maitre d' who approached her at the door, motioning to indicate she'd already found her party. Kuhl rose to greet her, touching his lips to the soft white skin below her ear as he came around and helped her out of her coat, she lightly touching the back of his hand with her fingertips, he allowing his kiss to linger on her neck a moment before turning to give the coat to the maitre d'.

They sat. Kuhl had been drinking mineral water, and he waved for the waiter, a quick snap of his hand. She ordered wine, an American Pinot Noir. The waiter hovered beside the table as she tasted it and nodded her approval to him, then hurried off, noticing the impatience in Kuhl's glance, giving them their privacy.

"Did you have a pleasant trip?" he asked.

"Yes."

"And your lodging?" he said.

"It's fine," she said, her English bearing the faint, indeterminate accent characteristic of those who have lived in various parts of the world. "I've missed you."

He nodded silently.

"Will you be joining me at the hotel tonight?" she asked. Turning her wineglass in her hands.

He leaned slightly forward over the table.

"I would like nothing better," he said. "But we have other dictates."

"Which can't be postponed, even for a short while?"

"I leave Quebec before sundown," he said. "And your flight to the States is scheduled for early tomorrow morning."

"There have been so many flights lately." She hesitated. "I'm tired."

He met her gaze. She was a receptive sexual partner, and he enjoyed her more than any of his other women. Exploring and penetrating her body was like opening a series of catches, one after another after another, unlocking progressively greater measures of her passion until she was his fully and without inhibition. There was exquisite power in reaching to the core of such lust. In being able to control its tornadic outpouring. And power was ever a temptation.

"We will be together. Very soon," he said. "But . . ."

"Dictates." She fell silent, lowering her eyes to her glass. After a few seconds she looked back up at him. "I understand."

Kuhl nodded and reached into the inside pocket of his sport coat, producing a black enameled gift box of the sort that might hold a bracelet, along with a small card envelope. He held both out to her across the table.

"I've gotten you something very unique," he said. "The rarest of items."

Anyone happening by the table would have seen her smile as she took them from him, their fingers making the briefest contact.

"Thank you," she said.

He leaned his face closer to hers, dropped his voice to a near whisper.

"In San Diego you will be meeting with someone named Enrique Quiros," he said, his lips scarcely moving at all. "The note I've written in the card will tell you the rest."

She nodded with understanding and carefully placed the box and envelope into her purse.

"I'll be sure to read it back in my room." She was looking into his eyes again, her own eyes shining, the smile on her lips no longer contrived for the benefit of idle viewers. "I wish you could be with me."

Kuhl acknowledged a stirring inside him.

"Soon," he said.

"Tell me when—"

"After this is done, I promise," Kuhl said. "We can go to Madrid, if you'd like." He paused a moment. "It is special to me."

She looked at him.

"Madrid," she said, raising the wineglass again, touching its rim to her bottom lip, letting it rest there a moment before taking a sip. "Yes, I would like that very much. Would like it to become special to both of us."

Kuhl watched her and nodded.

"Surely," he said, "it will."

● ● ● ●

"How long you been sitting on this?" Lucio Salazar said, the fingers of his right hand digging into the arm of his fleecy burgundy sofa, his other hand holding the last of the digital prints Lathrop had given him to scrutinize, the rest of the infrared photos on the coffee table in front of him.

"What do you mean?" Lathrop said, answering Salazar's question with one of his own, knowing damn well what he meant. This asshole had the balls to think he was going to interrogate *him*. It was pretty funny. "Your load was grabbed last night, I'm here today."

Salazar looked at him. He was a large man in his late fifties wearing a cream-colored tropical suit, a pale blue shirt open at the collar, and tan Gucci loafers. There was a Rolex with an enormous diamond-crusted gold band on his right hand, a diamond ring on his left pinkie, a diamond stud in his right earlobe. A gold figure of some saint or other hung from a chain around his thick neck.

"I was asking when you found out these fucking *maricónes* were going to make a move on me," he said. "If I had known sooner, I'd have been able to do something about it."

Lathrop's expression was calmly businesslike.

"You can get furnished with bad information from any weasel on the street and wind up chasing your own tail." He leaned forward and tapped one of the snapshots on the coffee table with his finger. It showed Felix Quiros and his men cutting the knapsacks off the backs of Salazar's massacred Indian couriers outside the smoking ruin of the tunnel entrance. "I get a tip, I check it out before coming to you with it. That's *quality,* Lucio. And it's what I provide."

"Value for the dollar, eh?"

Lathrop grinned.

"Believe it," he said.

Salazar fell silent again. His gold and jewels twinkled in the sunlight pouring through the glass wall that faced the beachfront below and behind him. These days, Lathrop thought, the base price of a Del Mar home with an ocean view was maybe six, seven hundred grand, and that was if you were talking about something the size of Monopoly board real estate, where you had to stand tiptoe on the roof with a set of binoculars just to catch a glimpse of the water. A place like Salazar's sin citadel here—built to his specs on a bluff, sprawling enough to contain the entire population of whatever burro shit Mexican village had spawned his proud ancestral line of cutthroat thieves, highwaymen, and pimps—a place like this had to have cost him in excess of three mil.

After perhaps twenty seconds, Salazar leaned forward over the table and studied another of the pictures, his eyebrows knitted in brooding thought, slowly shaking his head from side to side as he recognized the body of the coyote Guillermo.

"El muerto nada se lleva y todo se acaba," he said in an undertone.

The dead take nothing with them and everything comes to an end.

He glanced back up at Lathrop. "You know if Felix was being stupid on his own, or does the stupidity go up the line?" he asked.

"Felix? Come on," Lathrop said, preparing to stir in the lie. "He might have his boys glom car computers, shake down bodega owners, nickel-dime stuff, on his own string. Might even get away with laying an extra cut on a key before he delivers it, skimming a few ounces for himself. But his big cousins are just letting him run off the leash so he feels a player instead of a punk, and even Felix isn't brainless enough not to realize how far to take it before he smacks into a brick wall. What happened at the tunnel—he'd never in his miserable *life* try it without their endorsement."

Lathrop watched the thought lines on Salazar's forehead deepen. He was seething, and with very good reason. In tight with the old-line South American growers and processors from the days when his father headed the clan, Lucio's organization had been smuggling contraband across the U.S.-Mexico border for over half a century, starting with hot cars back in the fifties, and here in California was the principal polydrug distribution outfit along the Pacific coast, carrying cocaine, dope, pot, methamphetamine, name your favorite poison, from Chula Vista clear on up to Los Angeles and Frisco. The Quiroses were way down the hierarchy, with transit routes inland from northern Sonora into south Texas and sections of New Mexico, and until recently hadn't done anything to challenge the Salazar empire, sticking to a relatively insignificant share of the coke market. New drug money, you might call them. But since they'd gotten tied in with El Tío's network a year or so back—it was hard for Lathrop to believe he'd still been with the El Paso special field division at the time, my oh my how things had changed—there had been signs they were looking to make inroads into Salazar's territory. What was now causing Lucio such profound and well-warranted distress was the sheer nerviness of the act— not only stealing some heavy dope, but intentionally humiliating him in the process, smearing his couriers all over the arroyo, killing his drivers, and leaving them with their mouths chock-full of their own privates.

You go dissing someone like Lucio Salazar with that kind of impunity, you're sending a big, bold-faced message that there's major juice behind you.

Salazar was still shaking his head with combined anger and dismay.

"I can't accept this," he said.

Which, Lathrop thought, was absolutely right on, assuming he wanted to stay in business.

"It's got to be fixed," Salazar said.

Which, Lathrop thought, equaled taking serious retaliation.

Salazar looked at him.

"You find out how the Quiroses knew when my shipment was coming, anything else about their setup, I give you my word of honor it'll be worth a jackpot," he said.

Lathrop nodded, making an effort not to smile. He often wondered if guys like Salazar copped their dialogue from television and the movies or vice versa. Or whether it was some weird kind of self-perpetuating loop. Reality mimicking fiction mimicking reality.

"I'll see what I can do," he said and rose from his chair feeling mightily satisfied with his performance . . . and just as strongly convinced it would lead to the results he desired.

Next stop on the road, Enrique Quiros.

"I'm leaning in favor of Ricci's idea," Gordian said to Nimec from behind his desk.

He reached for the container of rolled wafers in front of him, opened it, slipped a wafer out of the container, and stirred it in his coffee so the drink would pick up the flavor of its hazelnut praline filling. This new morning ritual was in observance of his wife's latest dietary commandment: *Thou shalt not drink hazelnut coffee.* Her prohibition of his favorite blend rose from her theory that its hidden calories and fatty oils were responsible for the five-pound weight gain and slightly elevated cholesterol level revealed by his latest routine checkup.

The flavored coffee of which he'd been drinking three to five cups a day for the past year, therefore, was gone and out, per spouse's orders, replaced on her shopping list by the cream-filled wafers he was allowed to dip, stir, and consume twice a day to satisfy his hazelnut craving, the equivalent of nicotine chewing gum to a smoker trying to quit the habit.

Admittedly, though, the sweet sticks were tasty, if not to say addictive, in their own right.

"My primary reservations concern the delicacy of placing our RDTs in host countries that might feel threatened by their activities, perhaps with some justification," he said, letting the wafer steep in his coffee. "Or, trickier still, inserting them into hostile countries where we know in advance that their presence would be unwelcome."

Across the immense desk from him, Nimec was trying not to betray his delight at now having gotten his second "yes" of the day—albeit another qualified one—with a fair and highly unexpected degree of ease.

"I can relay your concerns to Tom, see that he addresses them in a formal written proposal," he said.

Gordian pulled the wafer stick out of his coffee and took a bite.

"That would be a reasonable start," he said, looking happy as he chewed.

Nimec started to lift himself off his seat, eager to make his exit while the going was good.

Gordian raised a hand.

"One last thing before you go," he said.

Nimec settled back down, waited.

"I'm with Megan that Rollie Thibodeau has to accept the plan, at least in theory, before we take it any further."

Nimec considered that a moment, then nodded.

"I'll ask her to talk to him," he said.

"No," Gordian said.

Nimec looked at him.

"No?"

Gordian shook his head.

"You do it," he said.

Nimec kept looking at him.

"She's better with Rollie than I am, two of them go way back," he said. "They've got a rapport."

"And that's precisely why it's going to be you and he who have the conversation," Gordian said. He took a gulp of coffee, the wafer back in his cup like a swizzle stick. "The fractiousness I saw aboard the yacht last week troubles me. If it continues, our organization is going to split into separate camps, and once that happens, we'll cease to be a functional team. Think about it, Pete. It has to stop."

Nimec ballooned his cheeks, slowly released a breath.

"Ought to be an interesting chat," he said.

Gordian smiled.

"Ought to be," he said and munched down the rest of his treat.

SIX

EVERY DAY IT WAS THE SAME, FOR THE WHOLE DAY.
Trying to work through the deepening bog of paperwork
in front of him. Trying to decide which decisions needed
to be made first and which could be deferred until later.
All across his desktop half-finished fiscal reports and
operational plans silently screamed for his attention. Employment applications, personnel evaluations, and equipment requisitions were spilling from his overloaded in
box like tenants from a collapsing high-rise. Only the
adjoining out box was uncluttered, and that sure as hell
wasn't much encouragement. It seemed sadly neglected,
waiting for something to drop into it.

Six months after his elevation to the post of global
field supervisor, Rollie Thibodeau had still to feel any
balance between the continuous supervisory and administrative demands of an organization as large as Sword
and his personal capacity to fulfill them.

It wasn't that he'd been ignorant of the job's responsibilities when Megan Breen offered it to him, nor had he failed to recognize it would mean spending many more hours in an office chair than he ever did heading up night security at UpLink's Brazilian manufacturing compound. Except . . .

A desolate frown creased Thibodeau's face.

Too much sit-down break trousers, he thought. It was a Louisiana bayou adage that went back forever, and he could remember his mother chastening him with it time and again when she'd caught him shirking his chores around the house. Too much sit-down break trousers. You wore out the back of your pants as quickly sitting on your rump as doing honest work. Though maybe his rump *was* the most functional part of him these days, being one of the few spots on his body that hadn't been drilled by a slug in Brazil.

Not that anyone had expressed the tiniest smidgen of unhappiness with his performance to date. On the contrary, Gordian, Nimec, and Megan all seemed to approve of the way he was handling things. The dissatisfaction, the discontent, came entirely from inside him.

"Watcha gonna say, boy?" he asked himself aloud. "Watcha gonna goddamn say, huh?"

Shrugging, Thibodeau reached into his breast pocket—as was his often-noticed preference, he had on the official indigo blue Sword uniform blouse usually reserved for members of active security details rather than executives at the San Jose office tower, where business suits were the norm—and pulled a satiny Montecristo No. 2 from a two-finger leather cigar case. It was one of the few remaining torpedoes he'd brought from Cuiabá, *beaucoup* hard to find, and he'd planned to savor it over some drinks at his favorite local tavern tonight. But he felt ready for some uplifting, damn ready, and wasn't about to stand on occasion.

He had been appointed to one of the top posts in Sword, a post that had, in fact, been created especially for him, with a commensurate raise that boosted him into an income bracket he'd never even considered within reach. Yet he felt a total lack of achievement or gratification, a gnawing absence of confidence that he was suited to the role. Making him, what, some kind of pretender?

Because he knew how much faith was being placed in him by people he respected and cared for, how much rested on his shoulders, Thibodeau was ashamed of himself for feeling as he did.

And then there was Tom Ricci, one of the most galling, cocksure bastards he'd ever met, always pushing fire. Thibodeau hated sharing the job with him, and to compound matters, was angered over the position he'd just been put in because of him. Of being forced to either nix or okay a move to which he'd vehemently objected when it was proposed and that he still maintained was wrongheaded, but that everyone else involved in the decision-making process had been convinced was worthy of a go.

"On a trial basis," Pete Nimec had qualified when soliciting his approval. *"With constant oversight."*

As he'd listened to him, Thibodeau had felt increasingly boxed in despite the repeated attempts to allay his concerns. *Sometimes,* he'd thought, *one bad move could cost you the whole game.*

Now he clipped the end of the cigar with his Swiss army knife, forgoing the expensive double-blade guillotine cutter he'd received as a fare-thee-well from his crew in Brazil. Having been relegated to the back corner of a desk drawer, it was a gift that was much appreciated for the sentiments it represented but was also much too fancy for his liking.

Thibodeau struck a match and lit up, carefully holding the tip of the cigar at the edge of the flame, turning it in his hand until it caught all the way around. Then he raised the cigar to his mouth and smoked.

Looking across his desk at the empty chair where Nimec had sat only minutes before, Thibodeau again recalled his limber pitching style, so reminiscent of Megan's approach that he'd wondered if she had been offering pointers.

"We proceed either unanimously or not at all," Nimec had said, after first relaying the news that Gordian and the others had come down in favor of establishing an RDT section. "Decision this important, it's got to have your support."

Thibodeau's reply was blunt.

"My opinion's what it is," he said. "Don't expect me to change it to suit the boss."

"Nobody wants that, Rollie. I'm here to see whether I can convince you to agree to this, not accede under duress."

"An' Gordian?"

"Gord shares some of your qualms, and he's especially concerned about stretching the hospitality of countries where we might have to send in teams. You spent over a year in Brazil dealing with their government and law enforcement agencies—"

"An' way before that, a couple back-to-back tours of duty with the Air Cav commandin' a long range recon patrol in Vietnam," Thibodeau interrupted. "Choppers would drop us into enemy territory, we'd search and destroy. My units knew our mission an' were the best at what we did. But the bigger mission, one sunk us into the war, that wasn't so clear, an' we both know how it ended." He'd snorted with disgust. "Lesson learned, least by me."

Nimec was undeterred. "What I was about to say, Rollie, is we were hoping you could draw on your experience. Help to define the circumstances that would warrant launching an RDT into the field, stipulate the rules and constraints it would operate under to avert political incidents, and so forth. Give us a total strategic framework."

Thibodeau shook his head.

"Say I ain't willin'," he said. "What then?"

Nimec had looked him straight in the eye.

"Then I walk out of here and into Gord's office and report that the plan's DOA," he replied. "I said 'unanimous,' and I meant it."

Thibodeau was quiet. Nimec's embracing reasonability was hard to argue with, but he couldn't stop himself from trying.

"An' where's Tom Ricci fit into the plan?" he asked. "What's he supposed to do while I'm cookin' up strategy?"

Nimec had seemed prepared for the question. "My idea is for Ricci to concentrate on tactical issues," he said.

"Tactical."

"And on training," Nimec added.

Thibodeau wondered why that stung him. And tried not to show it did.

"You discuss that with him yet?"

"No, but—"

"So how you know he gonna take to it?"

"I don't think he'll object. The field's where his talents would be best applied and where he's most at home," Nimec said. "It'd be a kind of dual-path approach, with Megan and yours truly coordinating." He paused. "I recognize that you two have had trouble meshing, and for the present it seems like the most balanced, workable arrangement."

More silence from Thibodeau. Again he'd felt that he was groping for a reason not to cooperate.

Nimec had moved forward in the chair opposite him, his hands on the edge of the desk, his gaze unwavering.

"Come on, Rollie," he'd pressed. "Give it a try."

Thibodeau waited another few seconds to answer, then expelled a relenting sigh.

"Go ahead an' count me in," he said. "But I got my doubts. Mighty ones."

"Understood," Nimec said.

Thibodeau shook his head. "Maybe, maybe not," he said. "This ain't nothin' between me an' you, but I want my feelings on record."

Nimec responded with a quick nod.

"It'll be easy enough for me to note them in my memo to Gord and carbon copy it to you," he said. "Settled?"

After a moment's further hesitation, Thibodeau had told him it was, more or less concluding their parley on a note of accord. Although that had done nothing to resolve the inner conflict he was experiencing—and still didn't fully understand.

He snapped back to the present, puffing on his Montecristo. As always, he enjoyed the rich flavor of its tobaccos, the mild tingle it left on his tongue. But why wasn't it having its usual calming effect on him? Lifting away his cares in puffs of aromatic smoke?

He pushed himself out of his chair, feeling a sudden need to get out from behind the desk. Fragments of his conversation with Nimec refused to leave his mind— one in particular—and he wanted desperately to shake it. To quiet the mingled resentments swirling around inside him like some sort of nebulous cloud, now swelling in his gut, now sending flares of heat into his chest.

"My idea is for Ricci to concentrate on tactical issues. The field's where his talents would be best applied . . . where he's most at home."

Thibodeau strode around the desk and paced the office with his hands behind his back, the cigar thrust straight out between his lips, smoke pouring upward from the corners of his mouth.

Then, abruptly, he ceased to pace. He realized he was standing in front of his desk, staring at his heaping in box.

Staring at it with eyes that burned fiercely with anger and frustration.

Ricci. Tactical issues. Field's where he's most at home.

His hand shot out with sudden violence, sweeping the in box off his desktop. It struck the wall with a crash, papers spilling from it, littering the floor. Thibodeau felt the vicious urge to take a giant rushing step over to the box and kick it across the room like a soccer ball, to stamp it to pieces before getting down on his knees and tearing up its scattered contents as he came upon them, flinging the tiny shreds of paper into the air, watching them drift down on his office furniture like tiny bits of confetti. . . .

And then he got hold of himself. All at once, got hold. The red haze of anger peeled from his vision to leave him looking at the strew of forms and documents that had flown from the overturned in box, his expression marveling and horrified, hardly able to believe his eyes.

What had he done?

What in God's name was *wrong* with him?

Thibodeau stood there as if waiting for an answer.

When it didn't come after a long while, he knelt and slowly began gathering the papers off the floor.

In his navy blue blazer, olive golf shirt, and dark khaki slacks, Enrique Quiros might have been a particular brand of contemporary executive: Ivy League, thirtyish, perhaps the founder of some Internet-based corporation. The cut of his wavy black hair was short, neat, and unfussy. The glasses through which his intelligent brown eyes peered out at the world were lightweight tortoiseshell with wire stems. His slender build was that of a careful eater and dedicated exerciser.

He was, indeed, an alumnus of Cornell Business School. The prismatic lettering on the door of his thirdfloor office suite in downtown San Diego read Golden Triangle Services, a corporate name apparently referring to the area northeast of La Jolla, where it was clustered in among many of the city's upstart, high-tech businesses.

The office decor was bright and open, with smooth plexiglass surfaces, beige carpeting, some muted abstract prints on the walls, and a spacious conference corner where a pair of his bodyguards now sat on a raw-sienna leather sofa, looking respectable and respectful, eyeing

Quiros's visitor indirectly, as feral wolves might to signal cautious nonaggression.

The slight bulges of the firearms hidden under their sport jackets would have been unnoticeable to the average observer, but Lathrop had discerned them immediately as he arrived for his appointment. He wasn't at all bothered. The guns were solely for their employer's protection, and Lathrop intended no threat. Also, he himself was carrying and had confidence he'd be able to take both men out before their hands got anywhere near their weapons, in the unlikely event of a problem.

"Nice new office, Enrique," Lathrop said, approaching his desk. "You're moving up."

Quiros smiled and indicated the chair opposite him.

"The economy chugs along, whistle blowing," he replied. "Like everyone else, I try my best to ride the curve and, if possible, stay a little ahead of it."

Lathrop sat. He could remember when Enrique's speech had been thickly accented with what they called Spanglish on the peninsula. This was before he had gone off to school, when his father was still alive and running the operation. Now he sounded like a TV news announcer, having acquired the flavorless pronunciation and intonation that was known as General American Dialect in college diction courses, absent any trace of ethnicity or regionalism. The benefits of a higher education.

Quiros shrugged his wristwatch from under the sleeve of his jacket and checked the time.

"You called just at the right moment, Lathrop," he said. "A half hour later, and I'd have already left for an appointment."

"I won't be long."

"Frankly, I was surprised to hear from you at all.

You've been doing a lot of work for the Salazars, and it made me wonder if you'd chosen to give up your independence for steady employment."

Lathrop shook his head.

"Freelance is more enjoyable," he said. "Make your own rules, don't have to ration your sick days."

Quiros was smiling again. "I'd have thought Lucio and his brothers would run a looser ship than your former taskmasters."

Lathrop shrugged.

"Life gets confusing when people think they know things that they don't," he said.

Quiros looked at him. "What do you have for me?" he said, dropping the banter.

"Information more valuable than any dollar amount I can lay on it."

Quiros's eyes came alive with interest behind his lenses.

"If I can depend on its accuracy," he said, "you can depend on being satisfied with my money."

Lathrop took a moment to review the latest modification of his story line. It was becoming a little complicated, and he needed to stay on his toes.

"Four nights ago, your nephew Felix and his friends grabbed a shipment the Salazars were bringing up from Mexico," he said, getting right to it. "I'm talking sixty kilos, maybe more, a major load. Took out a bunch of Salazar's people and cut up a few of them to send him a message."

Quiros had immediately begun shaking his head in denial.

"You've got to be mistaken," he said. "Felix has been

troublesome in the past, but doing something like that isn't in him."

Lathrop shrugged mildly.

"I'm telling you what happened. You don't want the rest, fine."

Quiros studied him a moment, then gave out a long exhalation.

"Let's hear it," he said.

Lathrop hadn't expected any other answer.

"Since you started running with the top dog in South America, word from my sources is Felix has been acting like he's untouchable," he resumed. "When he got tipped off about the product that was being muled over, it hyped him up to where he couldn't resist pissing in the Salazars' front yard to mark territory."

"What are you saying? That knowing I'd be opposed to an action that rash, Felix went ahead and moved without my consent?"

Lathrop nodded. "So you wouldn't interfere."

Quiros was still trying to push off acceptance. "Felix is impulsive and sometimes acts in ways that aren't very smart, but he has enough sense to realize I'd find out about the theft. And I won't question his loyalty. If you're suggesting he didn't tell me because he means to keep the profits to himself—"

"You didn't hear me say that, Enrique. Maybe he figures to make a quick turnover on the product, impress you with a surprise jackpot. All I know is, he did this thing. I don't know why he did it. And I'm not here to speculate on his motives or put myself in the middle of your family business."

Quiros was frowning unhappily.

"Okay." He produced a sigh that was even longer than the first. "What else can you give me?"

Lathrop prepared to cinch his knot of deception.

"Like I said before, Felix made a mess at the scene of the rip-off, but from what I hear, one of the Salazars' men lived long enough afterward to tell who was responsible," he said. The lie sounded good as it left his mouth. "Lucio holds you personally to blame. He can't see Felix having the *cajones* to go ahead with something this heavy without you ordering it or at least giving it your blessing."

Visibly agitated, Quiros didn't say a word for perhaps a full minute. The fingers of both his hands were outspread on the desk in front of him, arched as if he were pounding chords on a piano, pressing down hard enough to make them white around the nails.

Lathrop waited. He was sure now that Enrique had bought his story, and could practically visualize the question forming in his mind. The trick was not to show he saw it coming.

"I'd like to find out how Felix learned about the shipment," Enrique said at length. Clearly, he understood that there would be dire repercussions if Salazar was truly convinced the hijack had been done with his authorization and if he didn't move quickly to correct that impression. "Do you have anything on that?"

Lathrop shook his head no. Convincingly. And thought about the meet he'd set with Felix to ensure Enrique *never* found out.

"You want me to do the research?" he said.

"It would be helpful." Quiros abruptly checked his watch again and straightened. "We'd better put a wrap on this. I have to be going."

Lathrop's head tilted back a little, the hinges of his jaw relaxing, his lips parting as if to taste the air. Upset as Enrique had been a second ago, he'd managed to compose himself—outwardly anyway—and Lathrop gave him credit for that. But the way he'd almost jumped from his seat when he looked at his watch seemed very peculiar. If the appointment he'd remembered was pressing enough to cut their business short, given the significance of what they'd been talking about . . . well, it would have to be pretty important itself, wouldn't it?

Damn important, in fact.

Careful not to appear the least bit curious, Lathrop stood, told Quiros he'd be in touch, then turned and walked past the two bodyguards in the conference area and left the office.

He was eager to find out what was in the wind.

SEVEN

FOR BETTER OR WORSE, LATHROP SUPPOSED IT AL-
ways had been his nature to look at the dark side of
things. Probably, he'd been born with that disposition
... an "insufferable gloom," wasn't that the phrase in
the Poe story? Always, always, he'd been compelled to
poke around under the rug or lift up the rock and see
whether some secret nastiness might be exposed underneath.

As he moved between the joggers and strollers on the
path leading around the carousel in Balboa Park, Lathrop
remembered reading somewhere—in his downtime he
would go through stacks of books, gobbling them the
way some people did potato chips—that in French, *car-
rousel* meant "tournament," while the Italian word *ca-
rosello* translated to "little war," giving origin to the
English *carousel* when one of the later crusading armies,
composed of knights and mercenaries from throughout
Europe, went marching off to relieve their boredom
through a healthy dose of bloodshed and noticed that

Ottoman Turk and Arab cavalrymen would practice their lancemanship by charging toward a tree on horseback and trying to jab the weapon's tip through a ring hung from a branch. When the industrious European warriors brought the idea back home—those who hadn't been slaughtered because they were too wasted from drinking and debauchery to put up any kind of fight—the tree became a rotating pole, and the real horses became wooden mounts that got cranked around by a chain-and-mule contraption, but the purpose of the whole rigmarole was still a martial exercise.

So the merry-go-round had started out as a drill for impaling your enemy with lethal accuracy, and Lathrop had known it since he was writing book reports in grade school. Other kids would reach for the brass ring to win a free ride; he'd imagined somebody sticking it to his tender young gut if he didn't make the grab. It was the same with everything. When other kids saw their pet kitties flip their rubber squeak toys up and over their heads with their paws, they thought Puss, Tabby, or Spooky was just the smartest and the cutest, a regular cat-baseball major leaguer. Lathrop, meanwhile, went and got a book from the library and discovered that the up-and-over move was an aspect of the hunter-killer instinct, how felines in the wild tossed fish out of a stream prior to making them a dinner course.

The lesson in this for Lathrop was that whenever you played, you had to know you were playing for keeps . . . which, on second thought, had *definitely* been learned for the better, since minus that invaluable insight, he would not have come away from Operations META and Impunity with all his vital organs in their proper relative positions.

Ah, the glory days of a hot-shit deep-cover op.

Now Lathrop slowed to a halt at the edge of the path. He had a good view of the carousel from where he stood and didn't need to get any closer. It was old-fashioned, dating back maybe a century, with a band organ, several rows of antique carved animals, and gondolas on the outside of the platform. Though this was a weekday, the warm, sunny weather had brought visitors to the park in droves, and the ride was filled.

Lathrop bent as if to tie his shoelaces and gazed covertly at the spinning platform through the lightweight, black-framed eyeglasses he'd donned in his car. An instant later, he pushed a tiny knob at the hinge of their left stem with his fingertip, and a rectangular augmented reality panel appeared on that side. Seeming to hover about two feet in front of him, the AR display was in fact being projected onto the upper half of the plain plastic lens by the microelectromechanical, or MEMS, optical systems embedded in the frame of the glasses.

A twist of the control knob focused the image reflector/magnifiers in the lens and smoothed the display's borders.

"Profiler," Lathrop whispered into the pickup mike clipped to his collar.

On his vocal command, an audio link through a slender cable running down under his windbreaker to his hidden wearable computer—the same device he'd had on his belt the night of the tunnel ambush—launched a bootleg version of the UpLink International face-finding application sold to him by Enrique Quiros. Talk about an intriguing turn of the wheel.

Lathrop waited as the software loaded. To conserve memory, he'd installed a minimized version that contained a search index of ten thousand terrorists, criminals, and their known associates and would show the twenty closest matches in the AR panel. The program's full-option setup on his desktop computer would have let him scan many times that number, and Lathrop knew he could have accessed its database resources over his wireless network connection. But that was a time-consuming distraction in the field, and the pinhole digicam in the bridge of his glasses would capture an image of his subject that he could review at his convenience.

He continued to watch the carousel's jumpers slide up and down on their poles as it went around to the cycling pipe music. Most of the younger kids were belted onto the menagerie animals that made up the inner rows: spotted pigs, smiling fairy tale frogs, and brightly colored birds with long, arched necks that might have been fanciful cranes or ostriches. On the tall king's horses behind the gondolas were their older brothers and sisters, some with their parents standing alongside the saddles to steady them. A group of whooping, overly giddy teens that Lathrop nailed as stoned on pot occupied the remaining painted ponies.

None of them was his concern.

Estimating he had about a minute to fiddle with his sneakers without attracting attention, Lathrop concentrated on the twosome sitting like sweethearts in a gondola at the perimeter. Except, he thought, this was no such snuggly interlude.

The man was Enrique Quiros. Lathrop didn't recognize the blonde looker riding with him, but he'd been on enough tails in his day to read their body language and was positive that whatever was going on here was strictly business.

This afternoon was proving to be much more interesting than he could have anticipated.

After leaving Quiros's Golden Triangle front in La Jolla, Lathrop had pulled his Volvo out of the hourly garage around the corner, swung back toward the office building, and double-parked about halfway down the street, where he'd gotten a good view of its front entrance. That was the only way in or out besides the loading and emergency doors, and Enrique wouldn't have seen any reason to leave through them.

Five minutes later, Quiros emerged alone onto the busy sidewalk, turned in the opposite direction from Lathrop, and walked a block to yet another of the neighborhood's ubiquitous indoor garages.

Lathrop followed, stopped near the garage, and watched some more. It wasn't long before Quiros came driving out in a custom Porsche Carrera 911, the vehicle of choice for ostentatious, drug-dealing slime crawlers. Probably he'd called ahead for the attendant to have it ready.

Lathrop allowed Quiros to get about two car lengths ahead of him and then angled his Volvo into the flow of traffic. The 911 made a left onto A Street and headed north on Twelfth Avenue, following the road to where it became Park Boulevard, moving along toward Balboa Park at a moderate speed. At the intersection beyond the overpass, Quiros waited at a red light, took a left on the green, drove a short distance, and then turned right into the macadam parking lot back of the Spanish Village Art Center.

There were plenty of available spaces, and Lathrop swung in five or six slots down the aisle from Quiros, between a Ford Excursion that could have carted around the entire Osmond clan and an only slightly less house-y minivan. As he'd watched Quiros step out of the 911 and walk north, away from the art center toward the carousel and zoo entrance, he got his jogging clothes out of the gym bag on the passenger seat and changed into them, stuffing the sport jacket, dress slacks, and cordovans he'd shed into the bag.

The concealment offered by his tinted windows and the large, unoccupied vehicles on either side convinced Lathrop nobody would be able to peek in on him, but he doubted it would have raised an eyebrow even if that were the case. Guys did stranger things in their cars. And all he'd have looked like to some busybody who might notice was a working stiff who'd sneaked away from his desk to play hooky in the springlike weather.

Keeping Quiros in sight, Lathrop brushed back his hair and put on the Nike baseball cap resting on his dash. His first law of disguise, a baseball cap was the perfect standby, as long you didn't wear one with a team logo that might stick in anyone's memory. Costume beards, wigs, facial prosthetics, and other materials of that sort were great tricks of the trade, but preparation was needed to use them effectively, and Lathrop had been working on the hoof.

He added the AR glasses last, plugging them into the hidden microcomputer belted around his waist.

Within minutes after Quiros left his car, Lathrop made his own exit and trailed behind him to the carousel, where the slinky blonde had been waiting for Enrique near the ticket line.

Now he watched them circle around and around, talking rapidly, as if trying to cram in whatever had to be said before the five-minute ride came to a finish. Lathrop was hoping he'd be able to piece together their conversation on playback using the speech-reading component of his desktop software, which employed context-sensitive logic to fill in sequential blank spots when their faces spun away from his digicam lens or the carousel's movement blurred the video input, also compensating to some extent for the cross talk that occurred during ordinary verbal exchanges.

As the carousel whirled on, the Profiler floated a dozen possible hits, overlaying the bottom of the mug shots with their known or assumed names, ages, nationalities, and a requisite listing of offenses.

Lathrop was mildly disappointed. He'd have liked to ID the blonde on-site, but it was clear she wasn't any of the criminal candidates that had popped into his display. Still, he was charmed to have stumbled onto this little tryst and had plenty of recorded conversation to study later.

He straightened, figuring he'd bent over his shoelace long enough. Also, the ride was grinding to a halt, and he was concerned Enrique would start in his direction after getting off. The guy might not suspect he was being shadowed, but neither was he an oblivious fool.

Lathrop was about to move on down the path when he noticed something that caused him to risk staying put another few seconds. As the gondola spun past on one of its final slow revolutions, Blondie abruptly opened her purse, brought out a smallish object, and gave it to Enrique. A box, dark and shiny, the kind Lathrop imagined they'd carry in those exclusive Rodeo Drive jewelry stores.

He watched with sharp curiosity. The quick handoff squelched any second thoughts that might have occurred to him about this being a lovers' outing. It didn't even seem especially amicable. There were no smiles. No meeting of the lips, chaste pecks on the cheeks, or air kisses. Moreover, Enrique looked reluctant to accept the box, almost nervous, stuffing it into the pocket of his sport jacket like it was red hot to the touch.

Lathrop's chin tilted upward. His lips parted and curled. He drew in a breath. That transaction was it. Right there. The reason for the meet. And he'd captured the cherished moment on his wearable's flash memory card.

Or had he?

Excited, Lathrop indulged his urge to confirm it.

"Exit Profiler, run video," he said into his mike, watching the gondola pull away from him.

Another two voice commands, and the scene was replayed on his eyeglass display.

A thrill shot from his spine into his arms and fingertips. Beautiful. And to think a few seconds ago, he'd felt let down.

He supposed he could have hung around some more, drifted among the crowd until he'd observed where Quiros and his lady companion headed once they left the ride. But experience told him it was time to fold. And he was sure they'd be going their separate ways, at any rate.

Enrique had gotten what he came for. As had Lathrop himself.

Thinking he couldn't be happier with his afternoon's work, Lathrop turned from the carousel and took the walkway back toward the parking lot.

● ● ●

"Three Dog Night. Jefferson Airplane. The Troggs," Ricci read aloud, leaning over the selection tabs on the big vintage jukebox in Nimec's poolroom. "Got to admit, Pete, you're—"

"A wild thing?" Nimec snapped his fingers.

"Groovy," Ricci said.

Nimec grinned.

"That's the same model juke that was in the hall where I spent the whole summer of '68 with my father. A Wurlitzer 2600." He patted the machine's fake wood-grain side panel. "Same songs, too. Three selections for a quarter, ten for fifty cents."

Ricci looked at him.

"Must've been some year."

"We were on a streak, and flush for a change. Couldn't miss the sweet spot on a cue ball for anything," he said. "I don't think it would've mattered if we'd been trussed and blindfolded, which is how I bet some of the mugs considered dealing with us before they paid up. These were some hard, tough sons of bitches, let me tell you."

"How come they behaved?"

"My old man was harder and tougher."

Ricci nodded.

Nimec went around the soda bar. It was white with a red Coca-Cola bottle-cap design on the base, chrome trim along the counter's edge, and a half-dozen white stools. Everything looked a little grubby. The chrome finish was scratched and dulled in places. There were cigarette burns on the countertop. Some crumbled and yellowed padding was pushing through a tear in the leatherette cushion of one of the stools.

"How about something to drink?" Nimec said from

behind the pump. "The cola's got the right proportions of syrup and fizz. And I have frosty mugs. Or there's beer, if you want."

Ricci sat on one of the stools, inhaled air thick with the odor of stale cigarettes and cheap cologne.

"Better make it soda," he said. "I start out hugging a drink, three hours later I wind up wrestling with one. Like that Bible story, when Christ wrestles with Satan in the desert."

Nimec looked at him.

"Except," he said, "Jesus, you're not."

Ricci gave a vague impression of amusement.

"The truth shall set you free," he said.

Nimec poured two colas from the fountain, puffs of condensation dispersing from the ice-cold mugs as he filled them and then handed one to Ricci across the countertop.

They drank in silence. Then Ricci lowered the mug from his lips with an *ahhh* of appreciation.

"Good," he said. "Not too fizzy, not too syrupy."

Nimec smiled.

Still holding the mug by the handle, Ricci made a scratch in the thin rime of ice on its outer curvature with his thumbnail.

"You going to tell me why I was invited here?"

Nimec gave him a nod. "Your RDT proposal's been rubber-stamped on a trial basis," he said. "I figured you'd be pleased. And I wanted to give you my congratulations in person rather than over the phone."

Ricci sat there looking at him for a long moment.

"Thanks, Pete," he said. "And not just for the well wishes."

Nimec shook his head. "I don't deserve any credit for

this. The idea was yours. You're the one who sold Gord on it. Sold everybody on it. Some of us just took longer than others to realize they'd been persuaded."

"And maybe wouldn't have at all if you didn't push."

Nimec shrugged and said nothing.

"The ragin' Cajun among the enlightened?" Ricci asked after a moment.

"To be honest, he's not gung ho. But he's willing to suspend his opposition and give things a fair chance."

"Didn't think fairness was one of his capacities."

Nimec put down his mug and leaned slightly forward over the counter.

"About Thibodeau," he said. "He's a little headstrong, maybe going through some difficult personal times, I don't know. But he's also a good man, stand up to the bone."

"And?"

"Your comment on the *Pomona* about the circumstances that got him shot was a low blow. He may have deserved it from you at the time, and I'm not going to be critical. But between us, his actions in Brazil weren't careless or foolhardy. They were heroic, expedient, and they saved a lot of lives, very nearly at the cost of his own. I would hope you could acknowledge it."

Ricci was briefly quiet.

"Say I do," he said. "Say I even respect him for it. You asking me to admit that to anyone but you?"

Nimec shook his head.

"I know when I'm already running ahead," he said.

They sat drinking their Cokes in the deliberate shabbiness of a pool parlor generated from thirty-five-year-old memories and impressions

"So when can I start putting together the new section?" Ricci said after a while. "Soliciting volunteers for tryouts, that sort of thing?"

Nimec glanced at his watch.

"It's three o'clock on the button," he said. "You okay with about five after?"

Ricci gave him the barest smile and lifted his soda to his lips. The frost on the mug had now melted to leave behind glistening beads of moisture.

"Bottoms up," he said.

On the books, Felix Quiros earned his bread from the family-owned automobile salvage business he managed on the outskirts of San Diego. But his veal was in the money he made shipping various hot American vehicles to countries throughout the world via Mexico.

Sometimes in broad daylight, mostly at night, these were driven into the fourteen-acre yard directly from the streets and garages where they were stolen. The spiffiest models would be rolled into long aluminum vans that would cart them across the border at illegal transit points. The less-desired vehicles were dismantled for parts in Felix's chop shop.

As he gazed down between stacks of crushed automobile bodies in the dark of this chill, moonless November night, Lathrop could see a shadowy line of maybe five or six cars pass through the chicken-wire fence across the yard toward where the metal vans waited with their extended ramps. A couple of others were moving along a different gravel path toward the lifters, conveyers, and compactors in the recycling and demolition area.

It was almost like watching them roll into an automatic car wash, he thought. Neat.

"So, when I gonna find out why you got me here rattling my stones, instead of us meeting inside where it be nice and warm?" Felix said, standing there with Lathrop amid the rows of gutted and flattened vehicles. He hugged himself for warmth, rubbing his hands briskly over his shoulders. "What the fuck's this about?"

"Privacy," Lathrop said.

Felix tipped his head toward the trailer at the far end of the scrapyard.

"That right over there *is* my private office, *comprende?*"

Lathrop looked at him.

"You have a fresh mouth, sonny. Ought to consider finishing school," he said. "It did wonders for Enrique. Who's the reason I'm here."

Felix made an unsatisfactory attempt at minimizing how much that piqued his interest.

"Ain't got to be disrespectful. All I'm saying, we both gentlemen, ought to give ourselves our props," he said. "And what's up with my uncle, anyway?"

"Main thing far as you're concerned is I met with him today, and he happened to mention that he's upset about you moving on Salazar without his nod."

Felix struck a posture of bluff rejection lifted straight from some MTV hip-hop video, head pulled back, chest thrust forward.

"How'd he find out I got anything to do with that?" he asked. "And why he want to talk to *you* about it?"

Lathrop released a deep breath.

"Okay, time to cut the wiseass bullshit," he said. "You didn't hear me say our meeting was about you. Enrique made a comment, and I figured you might want to know what it was. Far as who clued him it's you did the hijack,

I don't have the foggiest idea. Maybe you opened that big show-off's mouth of yours to somebody with an even bigger one."

Felix shook his head rapidly.

"No way, no way," he said. "Besides, if Enrique's in a burn about this, how come you didn't put in a good word? You the man told me when Salazar's shipment was coming. You the man told me Enrique wouldn't have faith I could do the job. Told me to keep it under the fucking table till after the product's turned over, split the earnings with him afterward, finally get him to *recognize* me. You the man, Lathrop."

"Doesn't mean I'm your guru. Or your lawyer. It's not my place to jump into the middle of a family tiff. I gave you my best advice before, figured I'd give it now. No extra charge. Go talk to Enrique. Tell him the truth, be clear you weren't intending to hold out on him. Just omit the fact it was me who put you onto the shipment."

Felix tossed his head and did a kind of petulant shuffle, kicking the toe of his shoe into the dirt.

"Omit, right," he muttered. "How I know it wasn't *you* gave me up to my uncle?"

Lathrop expelled another long breath, glanced quickly around to be sure nobody was lurking amid the walls of the junk-metal canyon into which he'd lured Enrique, wanting to avoid making a mess of the punk's trailer. A mess that would have to be scrubbed and sanitized before he could be on his way.

"I warned you about talking nasty," he said. "You should have listened."

Felix suddenly became still. Swallowed. His expression showing an awareness that he really had opened his mouth too wide this time.

"What's that supposed to mean, man?" he said.

The silenced Glock nine appeared in Lathrop's hand as if he'd snatched it out of nowhere.

"Means you're gone, Felix," Lathrop said. "Gonzo alonzo."

He brought up the pistol and squeezed the trigger twice, putting two slugs into the precise center of Felix's forehead before he knew what hit him.

Cleanup here was easy. Lathrop put on his gloves and disposed of the body in one of the junked cars down the aisle with a rusty but undamaged trunk lid, stuffing it inside the trunk, pushing the lid shut, even getting it to latch.

Then he went back to toss some dirt over the blood and skull fragments.

Lathrop wasn't looking to be overly thorough concealing the kid's remains. It really didn't matter whether Felix was discovered by some Quiros stooge or eaten by foraging rodents. Just as long as nobody could pin anything on him.

Ten minutes later, he slipped out of the salvage yard unnoticed, anxious to get back home. Tired as he was, he meant to take a closer look at the videos he'd taken of Uncle Enrique and Blondie on the carousel.

Not to mention that his cats needed feeding and a little tender loving care before he fell into bed, the three of them having been left alone since very early that morning.

EIGHT

MARGARET RENÉ DOUCETTE LIVED ALONE IN A three-story ancestral townhouse in the heart of New Orleans, attended by her servant of long years, an aging Creole woman named Elissa, who occupied the detached slave quarters out back. Engaged by Margaret René's parents when she, their only child, was just nine or ten, Elissa had stayed on as caretaker of the house after it was willed to Margaret René as part of a large inheritance upon their sudden, untimely deaths.

At the time of the automobile collision that killed them in 1990, Margaret René was thirty-two years old, recently married to a financial consultant with a carriage trade brokerage firm, and three months expectant. Though she and her husband had purchased a new riverside home in Jefferson Parish, they decided to put that property up for sale and move into the Vieus Carré residence.

Despite her grief, Margaret René had found solace knowing the family she planned to raise would be embosomed in a place so full of sentimental attachments for her, where the spirits of her forebears seemed still to inhabit the high-ceilinged bedrooms and parlors, the graceful interior courtyard with its terra-cotta tiling and bowers of lush, tropical greenery, imbuing them with a healing and supportive warmth.

Since those days, a decade gone now, the hope of renewal that eased Margaret René's sorrow had been peeled away from her like bloody strips of skin under a torturer's flaying knife.

Her son—christened Jean David, after her father— had seemed a normal, if colicky, infant for the first six months of his life. But ominous signs of problems far worse than simple cramping had soon manifested. He'd had difficulty swallowing, and his food often would not stay down. There would be unpredictable spikes and dips of body temperature that could not be associated with common pediatric illnesses. When he was ten months old, Margaret René noticed an odd jerkiness to his movements and a gradual loss of previously acquired physical skills. His balance would fail even when he was holding the bars of his crib, and he would be unable to sit straight in a high chair. Playthings would drop from his straining grasp, his fingers sometimes clenching around his thumb as in a newborn—a fist that would lock tightly shut, the fingernails digging into his palm until it bruised, and on one occasion bled profusely.

In precautionary tones, the child's doctors had recommended a blood sample be taken and sent to a laboratory specializing in the detection of lysosomal disorders, a term unfamiliar to Margaret René and her husband until then, broadly explained to characterize a range of defects in a type of cellular membrane. When clinicians at the lab noticed an almost total deficiency of galactosylceramide B, a bodily enzyme vital to the development of the brain and nervous system, they hastily forwarded the specimen to yet another medical facility in Philadelphia for further testing. More frightening, alien terms such as *leukodystrophy* and *DNA mutation* and *myelin sheath* were mentioned to the parents during this tensely waitful period. As Margaret René struggled to understand them, she had often felt as if she were listening to the indecipherable chants of the voodoo priests who had been said to wander the narrow streets of the Quarter in her girlhood.

The final diagnosis was devastating. Jean David was found to have globoid cell leukodystrophy, or Krabbe's disease, a rare genetic disorder transmitted by a pair of carrier parents. The enzymic compound surrounding his nerve fibers was decayed, like insulation that had been eaten away from electrical wiring, causing the nerves themselves to degenerate and die. While the disease's symptoms could be managed and possibly slowed, there was no cure, no stopping or reversing its progression. It was terminal in virtually all infantile cases. Only the length of its course was uncertain.

For Jean David, the slippage was rapid. As his first birthday approached—a joyous occasion for the parents of healthy children—the breakdown of his motor system led to paralysis and near blindness. There were bed sores that went to the bone. He would burn with fevers for days, growing weaker with each prolonged episode. He soon lost the ability to take solid foods and had to be nourished through entubation.

As the pressures of coping with Jean David's steady decline had escalated in her, Margaret René had tried reaching out to her husband for support, but his private suffering had plunged him into his own downhill slide. He became uncommunicative and began drinking heavily. Problems at the office led to his having to accept a forced sabbatical. He would rise from bed in the middle of the night, leaving the house without notice, his mysterious departures lasting from a few minutes to several hours. At times he was gone until well after daybreak. When he arrived home after the first such absence, he'd claimed to have taken a long drive to clear his head. Later on, he would not bother with explanations.

Margaret René supposed his affairs should have been obvious to her, but all her thoughts had been turned toward her waning son. Everything else had seemed peripheral to giving him whatever comfort she could.

Finally Jean David developed a severe case of pneumonia from which he was not expected to recover. By then, Margaret René's anguished prayers at his crib side were no longer for a miracle to spare him but for God to put an end to his ordeal, to grant him a compassionate surcease.

Her pleas went unanswered. Jean David lingered for weeks.

He was just sixteen months old when he passed away.

Margaret René's marriage survived him by less than a year.

Was it possible to feel guilt over a flaw in one's own biology? For that guilt to be transferred to the person with whom you, by chance combination, produced a doomed, tormented offspring? Margaret René did not know how else to explain the resentment and seeming aversion her husband developed toward her. In bed his back would be turned. He had refused to seek marital counseling, and in the heat of an argument confessed to having met another woman. He was in love with her, he said. He wanted a fresh start, he said. A divorce, he said.

And then he had left her.

This was ten years ago.

A decade, gone, since Margaret René had retreated into solitude. Still vigorous at seventy, Elissa maintained an atmosphere of old-world elegance, seeing that the expensive silk upholstery and antimacassars on the chairs and sofa were neatened and mended, the antique rosewood furniture polished to a rich gloss, the crystal chandeliers, ivory statuettes, and antique china bric-a-brac regularly dusted. When required, professional help was called for servicing and repairs. But for Margaret René, the townhouse had become a cold, somber fortress. After returning from her son's funeral ceremony, she had placed the urn containing his cremated remains on the fireplace mantle in the grand salon, then draped the gilt framed mirror above it with a heavy cloth, not wishing to see her pain reflected; there at her insistence it hung to the present. And these days, the oil portraits of ancestors that had once given her consolation seemed to gaze severely down from their places on the walls as she wandered the silent rooms and hallways, thinking of poisoned hope, of love turned to ashes.

On rare occasion, Margaret René would step onto the balcony overlooking Royal Street and lean over the wrought-iron rail to watch the residents of the city pass below, imagining their conversations, trying to guess which ones had been seared by life's bitter lessons and which had yet to learn them. But otherwise she rarely went outside, leaving Elissa to order the groceries and take care of her various needs.

Margaret René did not, however, consider herself to be uninvolved with the world. Her parents had entrusted her with guardianship of their financial wealth, amassed over generations, and the inheritance had to be monitored and protected. She remained in intermittent contact with lawyers, estate managers, investment counselors, and a select handful of others. Old money came with old secrets, some quite dark. Margaret René had always understood this, as had her parents and their parents. Throughout the years, she had met men who could arrange certain things, perform certain services, discharge certain requests that people of common extraction might deem illicit or forbidden. *Facilitators,* her father had called them. Their names were neither spoken in public nor ever forgotten, and Margaret René had been mindful of keeping her ties with them . . . one such individual in particular.

Shunning direct personal interaction, ill at ease on the telephone, she had purchased a desktop computer and, quickly becoming proficient with it, would routinely attend to her correspondences over the Internet. Late at night, she would sit at her desk reading and responding to E-mail. And when she had finished with this, Margaret René would remain on-line to engage in another increasingly consuming pursuit.

With her browser she had located and assembled an extensive directory of Web sites relating to human genetic diseases, most of them with hyperlinks to associated resources, many providing message boards and E-mail addresses through which the families of the afflicted could network to share information and advice based on their personal experiences.

A curious, unrevealed visitor prowling the boards,

Margaret René would crawl down the lists of postings about care options and treatments, about experimental therapies, about advances in genome research that might someday lead to cures. And as she pored over them, reading one message after another, deluged with their preponderant optimism, a bitter juice would rise into her mouth.

And she would think of her own poisoned hope.

Of her love turned to ashes.

And with what she told herself was sympathy and goodwill, Margaret René decided to break her silence and send E-mails of her own to those she felt had been betrayed by false encouragements.

Realizing her motives might be misinterpreted, might even elicit feelings of enmity, she established an account with an encryption remailer that would deliver her messages anonymously, stripped of any data their recipients could use to respond to them or trace her identity.

To the mother of an infant daughter with GCL about to begin treatment with an experimental drug, she wrote, *Kill the child now. She will never improve.*

To the parents of a young adult with a related neurological disorder seeking donors for a bone marrow transplant purported to stay the progress of his disease: *The surgery will be futile. Spare yourself unnecessary pain and be resigned to your inevitable fate.*

To the parents of a child in the advanced stages of still another leukodystrophy: *Prepare for what comes after the end. You have seen the awful fruit of your passion, and it will drive a wedge of revulsion between you. Dissolve your marriage amicably before the faith is breached.*

To a doctor offering palliative advice: *Your lies are*

transparent. You are a filthy vampire who seeks to capitalize on the suffering of others.

At first the E-mailings had been a periodic activity, reserved for those unsettled nights when memories would churn inside her and rest would not come. But in recent months Margaret René had grown increasingly preoccupied with them. Heedless of the clock, she would write her notes into the emergent dawn with an absorption that was nearly trancelike. It was not until the light of full morning came streaming through her lace curtains and over the *èvantails lataniers* near the window behind her, the palmetto leaves stenciling fan-shaped patterns of shadow across the room, that she would at last go to bed. Having found she needed less and less sleep as time passed, she would awaken shortly before noon and eat the light breakfast Elissa prepared, anticipation building in her breast as she began thinking about her next session at the computer.

When darkness arrived, Margaret René's consistent practice was to first check her unfiltered E-mail application for messages relating to financial affairs, hastily reply if necessary, then switch to her anonymous account and type out the dispatches of compassion she had mentally composed during the day.

Until tonight.

What happened tonight had changed everything.

Margaret René sat staring at her computer display now, openmouthed. Just minutes ago she had completed her usual log-on to the proxy server and noticed that a ciphertext E-mail had arrived. Instantly her eyes had widened. She had provided only a single person with the digital key code that would allow him to send a message to her via the anonymous account. A facilitator of matchless capabilities, with whom both her father and her former husband had dealings.

Her hands shaking with excitement, she'd typed in her decryption key.

The E-mail simply read:

AWAKEN THE SLEEPER.
FEE: 50 MILLION
INSTRUCTIONS TO FOLLOW WITHIN ONE
WEEK

Margaret René's pulse quickened. Perhaps a year before, in a private chat room over an encrypted link, the originator of the current message had posed a question to which she'd replied with complete straightforwardness, although interpreting it as a mere hypothetical.

She could recall their exchange verbatim.

"What would you give to terminate all children with leukodystrophies while they were still in the womb?"

"I would give anything."

"And if it meant the death of the carrier parents?"

"That would be for the best."

"And if it meant your own death as well?"

"Better still."

And that was the end of it. He had cut the virtual link, and Margaret René had heard absolutely nothing more from him for a considerable while. But his probing inquiry had kept drifting in and out of her mind. What had been the reason for it? As much as she'd wished for an explanation, she had known better than to ask for one, known he would inform her in his own time.

Months passed before stunning notification of the Sleeper Project had arrived in the form of an E-mail attachment. Reading it with a mixture of eagerness and incredulity, Margaret René had at last understood what he had been leading toward in his prior communication.

What he claimed to have achieved had seemed beyond imagining. Beyond yearning.

Margaret René was advised to await future word of the specific date and terms of the offering and refrain from any interim contact lest it become void. Somehow, she found the will to comply. And as days turned to weeks without another announcement, she had nearly convinced herself that his assertion of success had been premature. While he had never before failed to deliver to her family, she had wondered if perhaps this time he had overreached.

And then tonight . . .

Tonight . . .

Her thin face bathed in the ghostly radiance of the computer screen, her heart thumping in her chest, Margaret René felt as if she were poised on the threshold of a dream.

Yes, tonight, everything had finally changed.

• • •

AWAKEN THE SLEEPER
FEE: 50 MILLION
INSTRUCTIONS TO FOLLOW WITHIN ONE
WEEK

The Arab mind is prone to express itself in a pragmatic and concrete way, and as Arif al-Ashar, the Sudanese minister of the interior, sat reading the E-mail attachment on his computer screen, his thoughts immediately took the shape of an unambiguous proverb: "In any vital activity, it is the path that matters."

His dilemma was that each of the paths before him gleamed with fabulous inducements, as if paved with sterling silver.

Where, then, to place his forward foot?

For decades his government in Khartoum had been engaged in civil war with rebels in the nation's south, their opposition fanned by Dinka tribesmen of black African origin who had resisted acceptance of *shari'a,* the strict Islamic code of law and conduct imposed after the revolution. Instead, the infidels clung to the barbaric spirit worship of their ancestors or the Christianity spread by missionaries in centuries past, calling for partial autonomy or complete separation, it all depended on which of their many factional groups one chose to heed, and when a particular group made its demands—for they seemed to change as often as the rebel leadership.

The situation had been a morass as far back as al-Ashar could remember. There was a period when the Dinkas had formed an alliance with the Nuer, a bordering tribe with whom they shared—and often feuded over—livestock grazing areas and water resources in the riverine plains around the White Nile. Taking strict measures to suppress the guerilla activities, Khartoum had deployed military land and air elements to the region, sealing it off to UN observers and representatives of the so-called humanitarian aid organizations that were plainly tools of the American CIA—Westerners who in their ignorance, presumptuousness, and mongrel weakness would have been quick to condemn a nation for exercising its right to preserve internal security and engage in a cultural cleansing that would bring about a politically unified and devoutly virtuous society.

Indeed, al-Ashar felt his government had shown the

southerners greater leniency than was warranted by their anarchic conduct. Upon eradication of the villages that gave support to rebel garrisons, women, children, and the elderly were spared execution. Mercifully gathered from their crude thatch huts in what their people chose to term *kashas,* or roundups, they were sent to relocation camps in which ample attention was given to their welfare. Boys certain to be indoctrinated into rebel bands if left to hear the lies and distortions of family members sympathetic to their cause were transferred to separate facilities—the southern refugees who had fled to Ethiopia, Kenya, and Eritrea chose to call these *abductions* or *kidnaps*—where they were given suitable Arabic names, taught the holy ways of Islam, and trained to be loyal members of the national militia upon reaching the age of conscription. Was this not generous? Did it not show commendable restraint?

In spite of Khartoum's efforts to impose order, the rebels persisted in their defiance, but a political dispute had flared between the Dinka and Nuer commanders and left their Sudan People's Liberation Army divided and weakened. Old tribal conflicts over land and water rights were revived, and soon the former confederates were firing Kalashnikovs at one another. Government forces capitalized upon this by moving into the breach and seizing enemy base towns where the opposition troops were in disarray. With drought and famine spreading across the countryside to further devitalize the rebellion, Sudan's lawful ruling establishment—the National Congress Party to which Arif al-Ashar belonged—had been encouraged that it might finally be subdued. Partly to silence international cries of outrage that had resulted from the propagandizing of Dinka refugees to gullible representatives of the American and European media, airdrops of water, grain, and medicine had been allowed into the southern part of the country.

There was a second, tactically advantageous reason for the admission of relief shipments, however.

Also struck by drought, the Nuba Mountains in the north had presented a distinct problem for the government. Infiltrating their high notches and passes, SPLA bands had become entrenched in pocket strongholds near remote villages inhabited by Nubians, an indigenous people that had by and large refrained from participation in the civil war, sharing neither the southern tribes' desire for independence nor the Arabic population's devotion to Islam. In allowing food and other supplies to reach the plains, the government had gambled that the rebels in the Nuba range, who were low on provisions, would be lured from their hideaways in attempts to replenish their stockpiles. And while the Nubians presented no armed threat in themselves, their refusal to accept *shari'a,* and their racial kinship with the SPLA, made them an undesirable and potentially destabilizing presence. Khartoum's hope had been that they, too, would be coaxed from their villages into the relocation camps and government-held towns.

With attack helicopters and army raiding parties lending it impetus, the initiative had produced estimable results.

Then, as Allah would have it, another set of complications arose.

Over the past three years, a series of intertribal councils initiated by Dinka and Nuer elders had led the squabbling rebel factions toward reconciliation. Simultaneously, America and its UN allies had exerted increasing diplomatic pressure on Khartoum—directly as well as through Arab-African intermediaries—to allow relief drops into the Nubas and arbitrate a peace agreement with the southerners, backing their demands with the ever-present threat of trade sanctions. Sharing a long border with Sudan to the north, its commercial shipping and agricultural health dependent on the Nile waters flowing through both nations, Egypt in particular had no great wish to see the southern Sudan split off into a non-Arab, potentially antagonistic sovereign state—but neither could it risk losing American economic and military support. Thus, it had encouraged a compromise settlement to the extended civil war.

Weary from decades of struggle and natural disaster, facing a resolidified insurgent movement that was liable to keep the fighting at an impasse, torn by rifts between religious conservatives and secular reformers in its own parliament, Khartoum had capitulated to mounting demands and entered into a peace dialogue with the rebels, the stated agenda of which was to grant the southern provinces an as-yet-unspecified level of self-determination.

Displeased with the government's acquiescence, Arif al-Ashar and a small group of his fellow conservatives had at that juncture committed to secretly hunting for a more palatable alternative. Arif al-Ashar himself had contacted a one-stop provider of black market arms, technology, and mission personnel with whom he'd had a long-standing affiliation—and the upshot was the message that had just appeared, then dissolved, on his computer display.

Now the question for al-Ashar remained: Which shining path to take?

Without official government approval, funds for his venture would have to be secured through clandestine means, and there were limitations to what could be funneled from existing budgetary appropriations before the drain became noticeable. The wealthier members of al-Ashar's parliamentary cabal were certain to pledge additional monies, but the product's high price tag was still restrictive, and hard choices needed to be made.

He clucked his tongue against his front teeth, watching the file attachment devour itself on his screen. A single disease trigger capable of leveling the Dinka and Nuer without causing a pandemic that would affect all the peoples of sub-Saharan Africa had to be keyed to a gene or gene string unique to those tribes, did it not? Yet even assuming an exchange of such genetic markers had occurred through racial ancestry and generations of living in close proximity to one another, intermarriage between tribal members was traditionally discouraged, and the number of individuals who shared a unique hereditary trait—and were likely to be susceptible—would be fewer than al-Ashar wished. A minimum of two triggers, obtained at a cost of a hundred million dollars, would therefore be necessary to ensure satisfactory results.

But what if only one of the tribes—say, the Dinka—were targeted? Arif al-Ashar's brow creased in thought. That could prove to the best advantage. The infection would still be sweeping in scale, decimating their population, while claiming significant casualties among Nuer of mingled bloodlines. In the short term, this would mitigate the impact of a brokered treaty granting the south full or partial independence, leaving the survivors too ravaged by their losses to pose a foreseeable threat to the north. At the same time, Khartoum would have presented a moderate face to the world by having shown a willingness to reach a negotiated solution to the civil conflict. And as long as the triggers were available, dealing separately with the Nuer remained an option.

The third path al-Ashar saw before him seemed less appealing initially, but he would not dismiss it out of hand. Were the outbreak to occur among the Nubians, the Sudanese north would be purged of ethnic and cultural impurity to a highly acceptable degree. Foreign aid to the stricken mountain dwellers might be allowed to demonstrate the government's new charitability and to blunt criticisms of its supposed indifference to human rights. As talks with the south commenced, international mediators would be tacitly made to understand that a hard-line prosouthern stance could once again lead to a cutoff of access to relief providers. The humanitarian issue that the Westerners had been using as a political lever against Khartoum would become a mallet poised to swing down from above them.

His brow creased in thought under the white wrappings of his *emma,* al-Ashar reached for the cup of spiced tea called *shai-saada* that had been steeping beside his computer. Eyes closed, he inhaled the steam curling up from it before taking his first sip, savoring the feel of its moist warmth on his cheeks, the aroma of cloves and mint, the pleasurable tingle it left in his sinuses.

Safety was in caution, regret in haste, he mused. Time remained for him to confer with his brothers in the ministry and arrive at a decision.

For the moment, al-Ashar would relish his sense of wide-open possibility, of roads that glowed with their own bright silvery light stretching out to even brighter crossings yet unglimpsed.

Wherever it led him, the journey was going to be memorable.

NINE

HE HAD CHECKED INTO THE HOTEL FIVE DAYS AGO
and would need to stay perhaps another two before the
diamonds-for-weapons deal was concluded. In this part
of the world, haggling was a recreational activity, and
ordinarily simple arrangements took on needless and in-
finite complications. But there was a wealth of precious
stones to be derived, and he always fulfilled an assignment to which he'd committed.

And he could not claim that he hadn't known what to
expect.

Antoine Obeng was a thug, a rebel warlord who had
secured an official government post through guileful ma-
nipulation after the fractures of civil war were weakly
repaired. Now he was chief of police in the nation's
capital, a title that validated his ego and legitimized the
power he relished above all else. But he continued his
behind-the-scenes leadership of the outlaw militias that
roamed the city at will and held the inestimably produc-
tive mines in the countryside by force of arms.

Much could be said for his endurance in a nation where political control changed hands often and violently, and death by assassination was the fate of most competing warlords.

Nonetheless, it was only the convenient location of the top-end hotel and its exceptional services catering to diplomatic and business travelers from abroad that had curbed the visitor's annoyance over the inexhaustible convolutions of the bargaining.

A man of rigorous discipline, he preferred sticking to a tight routine. Every morning since his arrival he had taken a swim in the indoor pool at six o'clock, a time when few others were outside their rooms and he stood the best chance of having it to himself. It was also the one time each day he felt at ease moving about without his personal guard, wanting an interval of solitude.

After taking the elevator up from his room to the twelfth-floor recreational area, he would put on his bathing trunks in the locker room between the gym and solarium, rinse off in the shower, then walk through the short connecting corridor to the glass-enclosed pool and do his laps for precisely an hour.

On the first day, a garrulous Dutch banker had intruded on his privacy and asked whether he cared to have breakfast in the hotel restaurant after finishing his "dip." Shunning interaction with strangers, he had tersely declined and ignored the man until he'd backed off.

In the three days since, he had found the pool empty and gone about his laps without disturbance.

Then, today, he had reached the locker room and again encountered undesired company.

Habitually alert, he whisked his eyes over the men inside. Both were fit and in their midthirties. One had blond hair, the other brown. They were wearing workout clothes and speaking American English to each other with the easy familiarity of close friends or associates. The blond-haired man had a somewhat tousled appearance and a light growth of beard. He was neatly hanging his street apparel in a locker. His companion sat removing items from his gym bag. A folded towel and sports bottle were on the bench next to him.

Superficially, they seemed of a type. Professionals on an overseas junket. Of no particular interest to him besides being trespassers upon what he had come to regard as his proprietary domain.

But he trusted the unconscious perception of environmental cues we call instinct. And something in the air told him to be careful.

As he stood inside the entryway, the men gave him mannerly nods. He noted them without response and went to the nearest free locker to the door, an ear attuned to their conversation.

"The taxis around here, Jesus, that ride from the airport gave me bruises where I sit. Plus he must have just missed getting us crunched at least twice," said the man with the twenty-four-hour stubble. He yawned. "Thought I'd never make it to the conference."

The one on the bench looked amused. "You should've listened to my advice, taken a *metered* cab. Their drivers have to be licensed. And they carry identity cards."

"Like that's going to do you any good. Or you really think the insurance companies pay off around here? Assuming they *have* insurance companies."

"Maybe not, but you'd know who to curse out for putting you in a body cast."

The bristle-cheeked man grinned and reached inside

the locker to adjust his trousers on the hook. The other's hand was returning to his bag.

Without letting another instant pass, the morning swimmer abruptly abandoned his locker and strode back out the door.

The pair in the room exchanged glances.

His hand coming out of the gym bag with a .22 N.A.A. Black Widow, the man on the bench sprang to his feet and slipped the five-shot minirevolver into the belly band under his sweatshirt.

The stubbled man simultaneously turned from his open locker, leaving its door flung wide. From his trouser pocket he'd removed a holstered Beretta 950 BS semiautomatic, his own choice of a peekaboo gun. He stuffed the deep-concealment holster into the pocket of his loosely fitting workout pants.

Both trotted to the doorway, then slowed as they went into the hall and looked up and down its length.

Neither saw any sign of the swimmer.

They split off in opposite directions, each using restraint to keep from moving too quickly. If the swimmer had about-faced for a reason unconnected to their presence—as they hoped was the case—it would do no good to raise his suspicions now.

Reaching the bank of three elevators, the brown-haired man glanced at the floor indicators above their doors. The numbers over the first and last cars were dark. The second elevator in line was descending, the number eleven and Down arrow lit up. He pressed the call button to be certain that the stationary cars weren't sitting on his floor, the swimmer perhaps having ducked inside to wait out his pursuers, trick them into thinking he'd taken the other car. Send them chasing it via the stairwell while he stayed put.

No such luck.

Both cars began to rise from the ground-floor entrance lobby, obviously unoccupied.

He returned his eyes to the indicator panel above the middle car.

The eight had flashed on.

Seven, six, five . . .

The elevator stopped at the fourth floor and its indicator light blinked off.

He frowned, looked down the hall at his partner, shook his head.

"*Shit,*" he muttered to himself.

The Wildcat had retreated to his den.

"I can't figure where we slipped up," the blond man was explaining over his handheld radio. "One minute he's walking through the door, heading toward a locker, then he just takes off. In and out . . ."

"Never mind," Tom Ricci said into his communications headset. He'd heard the locker room banter through installed surveillance mikes and thought the slipup was evident. *You went incognito, you stuck with what you knew, kept your act simple. Instead, they'd gotten too clever for their own good.*

There was an impermeable tunnel of silence over the radio. Then, "How do you want us to proceed?"

Ricci took a breath. Along with a couple of snoop techs named Gallagher and Thompson, he was across the street from the hotel, in an office hastily rented through a cutout and used as a spy post for the past several days.

"Stay at the hotel," he said. "You'll hear from me."

More silence. The blond man at the other end of the trunked connection understood what Ricci's order meant. He and his buddy were finished. Removed from the action, and soon to be cut loose from the fledgling RDT. *Good night, take care, see you again sometime.*

"Okay," he said, his regret and disappointment evident despite the digital scrambling process that robbed so much tonality from the human voice.

Ricci aborted contact and passed Thompson's headset back to him. He wasn't unsympathetic to the snatch team but neither were their hurt feelings of paramount concern to him. The bungled opportunity at the hotel meant things were about to get a lot more difficult for him and the rest of his task force.

They had maintained a constant watch on *Le Chaut Sauvage*—the Wildcat—almost from the moment the terrorist arrived in the country, acting on reliable word from a plant among Antoine Obeng's inner circle. In essence, their operational model was the Mossad's abduction of Adolf Eichmann from his safe haven in Argentina a half century ago: success achieved through simplicity of planning and execution. A small team watches the target's patterns of movement, subdues him when a clean opening is presented, rustles him out of the country.

No witnesses, no fuss, no muss.

There were, however, some major differences between the past and present scenarios. The Israeli agents had shadowed their target for months without interference from Argentinian officials, who had a decent political relationship with their government, were aware of their activities in the country, and had lent them a sort of passive endorsement. By contrast, Ricci's team had no such temperate climate in which to carry out a mission that had necessarily been planned on short notice. They were undermanned and underresourced. They were in a nation that was on the shakiest diplomatic terms with America and just recently had been taken off the State Department's list of designated terrorist sponsors. The capital's top cop was a crooked, venal son of a bitch who exercised his power in shameless cahoots with bands of khat-chewing thieves and looters. And, most significantly, the Wildcat was in the city at his direct invitation, enjoying the protective graces of the police and criminal militias that Obeng commanded with equal impunity.

It was a difficult and potentially ugly situation for Ricci and his men. If they got into a pinch, there would be no U.S. liaison—no one at all—to provide a bailout. They were entirely on their own string.

You asked for it, he thought, *you got it.*

Thompson had turned to him from the multiplex transmitter.

"What's next?" he said.

Ricci leaned back in his chair. The answer to that question depended on his assessment of what the Wildcat had or had not come to suspect and, moreover, what his degree of suspicion might be—which meant Ricci needed to slip into the skin of a mercenary killer and international fugitive. The scary part was that it came easily to him. So easily it had made him close to dysfunctional when he was working undercover with the Boston P.D. So easily he'd eventually requested a transfer out of the Special Investigations Unit on psychological grounds.

And here he was again. Back where he didn't want

to be. He could know his enemy, see the world through his eyes, walk in his shoes. Sure he could. It was a natural inclination that he distrusted for the lines it blurred, an effortless reach into the darkness within him.

If he were the Wildcat, what would he do?

Had the topic of conversation in the locker room been the weather or hotel food, had the two men inside been exchanging war stories about fatherhood, home repairs, deadlines, *simple* stuff, chances were that the Wildcat would have hardly paid attention to them, and they'd have been able to make their intended move on him as he got ready for his swim. But instead, they chose to gripe about the local taxi service, and that had seemed unconvincing even to Ricci. An American traveling to this country for a business conference, staying at an expensive, first-class hotel, was no small potato with whatever firm he represented. It was far more likely than not that a courtesy car would be waiting for him at the airline terminal. And that the driver engaged by his corporate hosts would treat him like royalty.

Okay, then. The two men's small talk had struck a false note, and their quarry had been sensitive to it. But not all hosts were equally hospitable. It wasn't inconceivable that they'd have taken cabs from the airport, and it wasn't as if they'd done anything that was a tangible and conclusive tip-off—revealing their firearms too soon, for instance. Would their clumsiness have been enough to make the Wildcat drop out of sight, abandon an immensely profitable deal that was well on the way toward finalization? Or would he instead opt to take extra precautions and accelerate the pace of his talks, clinch things before leaving the country?

Ricci stared at the ceiling and thought in silence a

while longer. He imagined the tactile sensation of holding the illicit diamonds in hand, their weight and smoothness, his fingers clenched tightly around the forbidden gems.

Then he sat forward, looked at Thompson and Gallagher.

"We're shifting to our fallback options," he said. "Let's have the intercept teams keep close tabs on the airport and other departure routes just in case. But five gets you ten our guy isn't going anywhere before he pays Obeng another visit."

Ricci's bet was on the money.

It was late afternoon when *Le Chaut Sauvage* appeared. Two of his bodyguards had preceded him out of the hotel, looking up and down the street, scouting for any indication of a threat. Then one of them made a discreet all-clear gesture with his hand, and the Wildcat emerged onto the sidewalk, another couple of guards trailing a few steps behind.

Minutes earlier, a line of five police vehicles had arrived at the entrance, two standard patrol cars followed by a diesel-fueled South African Lion 1, reinforced from frame to engine block with ballistic-and-blast-resistant carbon fiber monocoque. After pulling the big, armored four-by-four up to the curb, several of its uniformed occupants had exited and leaned against its heavy flank with their arms folded imposingly across their chests.

The group from the hotel moved straight toward the Lion 1. One of the uniforms standing beside it opened the rear door, and the Wildcat climbed in back between the original pair of bodyguards to have left the hotel. The second two hovered beside the vehicle until his door shut and then went to the lead police car and got into it.

Behind drawn shades in the office across the street, Ricci and his techs watched on an LCD panel as the motorcade pulled into the two-way avenue bisecting the downtown area and then rolled eastward, the pictures feeding from 180-degree trackable spy eyes suctioned to the windowpane.

Ricci glanced at the city map on the wall above the monitoring station. East was toward police headquarters, Obeng's official seat of corruption, its location circled on the map with a red highlighter. His unofficial cradle lay west of the downtown area. Ricci had penned the words "Gang Central Station" above the blue circle that marked its coordinates.

A vertical crease etched itself in the middle of his forehead. Something wasn't kosher about what he'd just observed. A few somethings. If the Wildcat believed he might be under surveillance, why stroll out the front of the hotel, head so openly to the cop station, make the trip there surrounded by a goddamned cortege?

"Alert the strike team at Gang Central that company's on its way," he abruptly said to Thompson.

Thompson spun around in his chair and looked at him.

"Will do," he said, sounding confused. His eyes went to the wall map. "But—"

"I can read that as well as you," Ricci said. "The whole scene in front of the hotel was a dupe. Like a game of three-card monte. Soon as Wildcat reaches police HQ, he's out the back door and into a different vehicle." He paused, his mind racing. "We'll keep one of the tail cars on him. Let's have the others sit outside the cop station, make themselves just conspicuous

137

enough so our man feels comfortable he's outsmarted us," he said.

Comprehension dawned on Thompson's face. He nodded briskly and turned to the multiplexer.

Ricci chewed the inside of his mouth, still thinking hard, making sure he'd covered all his bases. Then he rose from his chair and grabbed the shoulder-holstered FN Five-Seven pistol that was hung over the backrest.

"Have Simmons and Grillo bring around the tac van," he said, and strapped on the holster. Basics first; he would finish gearing up en route. "I'm heading out to meet them."

Since before the civil war, Antoine Obeng had presided over his rackets from a five-story commercial frame building set back from the street on a low hill in one of the city's quieter outlying neighborhoods. A paved blacktop turnaround gave motor access to the main doors and led to the entrance and exit ramps of its sunken parking garage. Descending behind it were three or four yards of terraced slope and manicured shrubbery, below which the neat plants yielded to a snarl of wild, thorny growth that went down another thirty feet to the bottom of the hillside and then extended outward into a small, flat, muddy barrens.

On the ground floor were two businesses that Obeng owned and controlled through tamely obedient surrogates: the main offices of a shipping/mailing company and a travel agency. These afforded the warlord with useful fronts for laundering a portion of his criminal earnings, distributing forged documents, and orchestrating a multiplicity of smuggling operations, a partial index of which included the transport of stolen luxury cars and antiquities, bootlegged music and video recordings, illegal weapons and narcotics, and the meat, hides, horns, and hooves of exotic animals killed by poachers in wilderness preserves all across central and western Africa.

Like everyone else in the city, the thirty or so employees of Obeng's front businesses were aware of his command of the militias and indeed could not have possibly failed to notice the regular comings and goings of his hoodlum lackeys. But only a few knowingly participated in his lawless undertakings or profited from them in any way. The majority of these men and women showed up each morning for an honest day's work, went home to their families at quitting time, and brought home modest paychecks at the end of the week.

They were what Tom Ricci had called "solid citizens" back when he'd carried a detective's tin.

They were also convenient human shields for Obeng.

From Ricci's standpoint, this was not good.

As he sloshed through a foul-smelling drainage culvert in a near squat, his boots awash in brown sludge, his arms, legs, and ballistic helmet soiled with wet clots of grime that had peeled like fresh scabs off the curved, close-pressing top and sides of the channel, Ricci knew the worst things that could go wrong with his maneuver would be having innocent civilians taken hostage, injured, or, even more unthinkable to him, killed during its execution.

Morally wrong, operationally wrong, politically wrong. Rollie Thibodeau had correctly pointed out aboard the *Pomona* that the mere presence of his RDT on foreign soil shredded several chapters of international law. Without question, the course of action on which they were now embarked would trash the rest of the rule book.

But Ricci had come a long way to collar the Wildcat, stalked him with all the resources at his disposal, and he was not going to succeed by knocking on Obeng's front door and politely asking that his guest step into the waiting arms of justice.

Neither would he do so by shrinking from a calculated risk.

Given the best opportunity for a nab that was liable to present itself, Ricci damn well intended to exploit it. If he screwed up, he was ready to take the heat. And his darling admirer Megan Breen could flash her razzle-dazzle smile as she watched him swing in the wind like a gallows bird.

Ricci dismissed that unpleasant image from his mind.

He'd been twice on the money today, after all.

As expected, the Wildcat's ride to the police station had been a classic casino shuffle. Soon after arriving there, he left in different clothes than he'd worn out of the hotel—taking a side exit rather than the back door, the only detail not to meet Ricci's prediction to the letter—and was then chauffeured off in the passenger seat of an unmarked sedan that pulled into the crosstown avenue's westbound lanes and clanked along seemingly on two cylinders, an authentic touch that allowed it to blend nicely with the crumpled matchboxes driven by the average motorist in this land of plenty.

Thirty minutes later, that car swung into the parking garage at Gang Central.

Ricci and his strike team had been ready and waiting in the swampy, weed-clogged field out back.

Now he crawled toward the building by way of the subterranean overflow channel beneath the hill, his helmet-mounted torch beam lancing sharply into the dimness. Like the men slogging along at his rear, he was clad in a mottled woodland camouflage stealth suit with protective knee and elbow pads and an ultrathin Zylon bullet-resistant lining. Besides the Five-Seven in his side holster, he was toting a compact version of UpLink's variable velocity rifle system—or VVRS—submachine gun, a second-generation variant that was half the size and weight of the original, that was manufactured with an integrated silencer, and that fired subsonic ammunition. The rotating hand guard, which manually adjusted the earlier model's barrel pressure from lethal to less-than-lethal, had been replaced by MEMS circuitry that did the job at the fast and easy touch of a button.

A snap-on attachment under the barrel resembled and was technologically related to a laser targeter, though it served a very different function. While Ricci disliked the way the device threw off his weapon's balance, its use by the entire team was crucial to their objective.

They had brought other equipment from the tac van as well, some of it defensive in nature.

Because he had taken point, Ricci held in his left hand a portable vapor detector that looked oddly similar to the super-eight movie cameras he remembered from distant childhood, and was presently scanning for environmental hazards that ranged from the toxic methane, nitrogen, and sulfurous gases of decaying sewage to chemical and biological weapons agents to the minutest airborne traces of the explosive ingredients of booby traps. In the event its beeper alarm sounded, a backlit LCD readout would specifically identify the threat, with the beep tones increasing in rapidity as the instrument was brought closer to it. Should that threat prove to be chem/bio or the products of organic decomposition, each member of the strike team was ready to convert the carry bag strapped over his shoulder into an air-powered, filtered-breathing system at the pull of a zipper, worn as if it were a masked and hooded vest. Should a bomb be detected, they would hopefully steer clear of its triggering mechanism.

And there was still more equipment, some of it suppressive, referred to as public order weapons by law enforcement personnel with a penchant for cooking up new euphemisms every fifteen seconds.

Call them what you wished, their fundamental purpose was to incapacitate their targets without causing serious injury.

Ricci's absolute intent, second only to bagging the Wildcat, was that no harm come to the innocent civilian workers in the building. This was foremost out of bounds. But he was also determined to avoid using deadly force on any of Obeng's rotten cops, and for that matter against Obeng himself, all of whom held nominal claim to being upstanding members of the population. Even the militiamen would not be permanently damaged, if possible, though Ricci was giving his ops some leeway in dealing with them, as it was unlikely their country's heads of state, eager to improve relations with America, would raise a commotion over the loss of a few known malcontents whose looting and violent behavior threatened their own government's stability, and who they were consequently better off living without.

Cramped from kneeling, Ricci led the way through the narrow drainage duct for another ten minutes. Then his torch disclosed its circular mouth a few yards up ahead. He moved forward and saw that it opened out some three or four feet above the bottom of a cement-walled tunnel with room enough for him and the others to stand upright.

He raised a clenched fist to signal a pause, then glanced over his shoulder at Grillo.

"Drop's maybe a yard," Ricci told him in a hushed voice. "Everybody be careful. Looks to me like the tunnel's ankle deep in water. Not much of a flow, but it's bound to be slippery."

Grillo nodded and passed the word to Lou Rosander, the man behind him, who in turn relayed it to the next in line.

Ricci inched over to the opening and sprang down.

He landed with a splash. A layer of slime coated the floor under the stagnant water, but he had a good sense of balance and was aided by the corrugated rubber soles of his boots.

The rest of the team hopped from the pipe one at a time, all of them joining him in short order. They immediately formed up in single file.

Ricci looked around. The passage was almost chamberlike measured against the constricted tube from which he'd jumped. Other tunnels of nearly equal width and height branched off from it in various directions.

They had reached a major juncture of the system.

Ricci did not need to consult his underground street plan to know which of the diverging passages to take. He had committed the system layout to memory before proceeding with his mission, just as he'd memorized the location of the drainage pipe's outflow opening from the high-res GIS data provided by Sword's satellite mapping unit.

With another crisp hand signal, Ricci turned toward the dark hole of the tunnel entrance to his immediate left and stepped into it, his feet squishing in the muck.

His men followed without hesitation.

"Okay," Rosander whispered. "I see a single attendant. I don't think he's one of Obeng's goons. Or that he's gonna be a problem."

"He in a booth?" Ricci asked.

Rosander kept peering through a thin fiber-optic periscope that he'd coiled upward through the metal drain cover above him. With maybe four feet of clearance between the floor of the sunken garage and the bottom of the sluice in which they were hunched, a six-year-old would have had difficulty standing erect, let alone the ten grown men of Ricci's team.

"No," he said. "The guy's nodding off in a chair against the wall."

Ricci nodded.

"There anybody else around we have to worry about?" he said.

"Give me a sec."

Rosander rotated the fiberscope between the thumb and forefinger of his left hand, his other hand making adjustments to the eyepiece barrel to focus its color video image.

"Not a soul," he said.

"Number of vehicles?"

"I'd say about a dozen, including the rattletrap that brought the Wildcat."

Ricci nodded again.

He reached into a gear pouch for a breaching charge, peeled the plastic strip from its adhesive backing, and pressed the thin patch of C2 explosive—a compound as powerful as C4, but more stable—against the ceiling surface until it was firmly secured. Then he took the "lipstick" detonator caps out of a separate pouch and inserted them. Before blowing their mouse hole into the sunken garage, his team would back through the runoff duct to keep a safe distance from the blast and falling masonry.

After a moment, Ricci turned to Simmons and handed him the vapor detector.

"I'll go in first, take down the attendant," he whispered. "Stay close, and don't forget the regs."

"Right."

Ricci got his radio out of its case on his belt.

While the explosion he was setting off would be small and contained, any explosion was by definition noisy, and therefore would be heard by those in the building unless masked.

Ricci had arranged for something even noisier to do just that.

A few blocks east on the crosstown avenue, two men in the white uniforms of emergency medical responders had been waiting patiently in the cab of a double-parked ambulance.

After receiving Ricci's cue, the driver cut the radio and turned to his partner.

"We're on," he said.

They raced into traffic toward Gang Central, the ambulance's light bars flashing, its siren cranked to peak volume and howling like a thousand tortured wolves.

• • •

Seated across a desk from Obeng in the warlord's second-floor office, *Le Chaut Sauvage* heard the ululant wail of the rapidly approaching medical vehicle and tilted his head toward the window.

"Is that one of yours?" he asked, his voice raised over the deafening clamor.

Obeng shook his head no.

"An ambulance," he said.

The Wildcat gave him a questioning look.

"You're certain?"

"Yes," Obeng assured him. He was almost shouting to be heard. "Even here people get sick."

As he leaped up through the small crater in the garage floor, Ricci didn't know whether it was the detonating C2 or the eardrum-piercing shrillness of the ambulance siren that shocked the attendant from his dozy position on the chair.

Not that it made a jot of difference to him.

The attendant shot to his feet now, his chair crashing onto its back, his features agape at the sight of men in visored helmets and tactical camo outfits pouring out of a rubbled, dust- and smoke-spewing hole that hadn't existed a split second before.

Ricci swiftly bound over to him and pressed the squirter of the dimethyl sulfoxide cannister clenched in his gloved fist.

The attendant raised his hands over his face on reflex, but the stream of odorless, colorless DMSO . . .

A chemical with myriad properties that was originally an incidental by-product of the wood pulping process, used as a commercial solvent for fifty years, a medical organ and tissue preservative for about forty years, and a pain reliever and anti-inflammatory with limited FDA approval for slightly less than thirty years . . .

A chemical that in the past decade or so had attracted the close attention of nonlethal weapons researchers because of its instant penetration of human skin and its capacity to completely sedate a person on contact and without side effects if administered in sufficient concentration . . .

The DMSO running down over the attendant's outthrust palms and fingers made him crumple like one of the foam training dummies Ricci sometimes used in hand-to-hand combat practice.

Ricci caught the attendant in his arms to ease his fall, lowering him gently onto the floor. Then he quickly rose and scanned the garage for ways to reach the building's aboveground levels.

There was a single elevator about ten yards to the right. Not a chance his men were going to box themselves into that death trap.

His gaze found the door leading to the stairwell to his far left, on the opposite side of the garage.

He turned toward the rest of the men, now standing back-to-back in a loose circle, their individual weapons pointed outward, covering all points of the garage while they peripherally watched for his gestured command.

Ricci was about to wave them toward the stairs when he heard the distinct sound of the elevator kicking in. He glanced in its direction, his eyes fixing on the indicator lights over its door.

It was coming down the shaft from the ground floor.

Coming down fast.

• • •

Grillo had likewise turned to face the elevator, his eyes narrowed behind his helmet visor.

He watched its door slide open seconds after its hoisting motor activated, appraised its passengers at a glance.

Don't forget the regs, he thought, needing no real incentive. The man and woman inside were a couple of honest Injuns if there'd ever been any, probably customers leaving one of the quasi-legit businesses right upstairs.

They took maybe a step out of the car and then froze at the scene that met their eyes, both simultaneously noticing the assault team, the unconscious garage attendant, and the debris-strewn hole in the floor.

Grillo didn't give them a chance to recover from their initial confusion.

He whipped his hand down to his belt, unholstered his stingball pistol, and pulled the trigger twice.

The mini–flash bangs it discharged hit the floor directly in front of their feet, the fragile rounds shattering like eggshells against the hard cement to produce startlingly loud reports and blindingly bright bursts of light.

The couple staggered dazedly, the woman covering her eyes with both hands, the man tripping backward to sprawl with the upper part of his body inside the elevator and his legs stretched out. Its door tried to close, struck his hip with its foam rubber safety edging, automatically retracted, tried to close again, hit him again, the whole sequence repeating itself over and over as he writhed there on the floor of the garage.

Grillo put the stingball gun away, satisfied with how the weapon had delivered. Poor guy was going to have some bruises to show for his unexpected adventure, but what could you do?

He looked at Ricci.

Ricci completed his interrupted hand signal, waving at the stairwell door.

His team dashed across the garage in its direction.

The men climbed the stairs as one, as trained, a single composite organism armored in synthetic materials, their guns bristling like deadly spines.

A few steps below the first-floor landing they paused for Rosander to peer around the corner with his telescopic search mirror, a low-tech, reliable, simple tool. Ricci's cardinal rule was in play here: Use the fiber-optic scope when you wanted maximum stealth, but when the actual insertion began, when speed was of the essence, you didn't want to screw with finicky shit like flexible electronic coils and video apertures.

Nobody in sight, they hustled up onto the landing. Ricci motioned for two of them, Seybold and Beatty, to split off from the others and cover the first floor. This was an organism that could divide and reassemble itself as required.

Up the next flight of stairs, ten now having become eight; Ricci and Rosander were in the lead.

Midway to the second floor, on the next landing, Rosander again stuck the pole around the corner and saw the reflections of three men on the mirror's convex surface.

He signaled quickly. Two fingers pointed at his eyes: *Enemy in sight.* Then three fingers in the air, revealing the number of opponents on the way down.

"Militia," he mouthed soundlessly to Ricci, who was squatted beside him.

Ricci nodded.

His men readied themselves in the short moments available. This time they wouldn't be facing a bleary-eyed garage worker or a couple petrified with astonishment, literally struck blind on the way back to their car after booking a trip to paradise at the ground-floor travel agency.

They held their guns at the ready.

The militiamen continued downstairs toward the landing.

Ricci's hand was raised, motionless, slightly above shoulder height: *Hold your fire.*

It was his show. His and Rosander's. They could not worry about taking accidental hits from their own teammates behind them.

The militiamen were carrying assault rifles, Russian AKs. One of them glimpsed the assault team below.

His gun muzzle came up as he grunted out a warning to his companions.

Ricci squeezed the trigger of his baby VVRS, its electronic touch control set for maximum blowback. Lethal as lethal could be. And quiet.

The militiaman fell to the landing, spots of crimson on his chest. Then a quick burst of gunfire from above, bullets swarming down the stairwell.

The still body of the guy he'd hit pressing against his shins, weighty against his shins, Ricci stayed put and swung his weapon toward the remaining two. The mirror in one hand, Rosander had lifted his gun with the other and was already spraying them with ammunition. A second man collapsed, rolled downward, olive fatigues stained red. The third kept standing, got off some more counterfire, and Ricci heard a grunt from Rosander as the pole of his inspection mirror flew from his fingers and went clattering against the metal risers below.

Edging back against the handrail, out of the shooter's direct line of fire, Ricci triggered his gun again, aiming for the legs, and when he saw the legs give out, finished the militiaman with a sustained burst to the chest.

Silence. A pale gray haze of smoke.

Ricci looked around at Rosander.

The visor of his helmet was splashed red. Dripping red where he'd been hit. Ricci could not see his face through it.

He glanced at the others behind him, shook his head.

They couldn't linger here in the enclosed stairwell. They had to keep moving. The exchange of gunfire had been brief and probably wouldn't have been heard too far beyond the concrete walls of the fire stairs. But it might have drawn the attention of someone nearby.

Keeping his eye on the mission, Ricci ordered his unit to resume its hurried advance.

As they passed over the bodies lying across the stairs, Grillo snatched the search mirror from where it had dropped.

They would need it later on.

The strike team pushed through the door to the second-floor hallway, each of its members familiar with the floor plan, knowing the exact location of Obeng's office at the rear of the building.

The thing none of them knew was what sort of obstacles to expect along the way.

The corridor was empty as far as they could see.

Closed office doors on either side. Then, perhaps ten yards up, an elbow bend. They would need to turn it, head down another short, straight length of hallway, round another corner. And then they'd be there.

Easily said.

They ran forward, guns at hip level, eyes sweeping the sides of the hall.

Ricci saw a door open a little. Third ahead on the right. He signaled a halt, pointed to it. His men fanned out, sticking close to the walls for cover.

Watching.

Waiting with their guns angled toward the door.

The crack widened, widened, and then a muzzle poked through.

The wait extended. An eternity of seconds. More of the weapon appeared. A semiautomatic pistol. Its barrel slipped tentatively outward into the hall.

That kind of firearm, that kind of cautiousness, Ricci was betting they were dealing with a cop here.

He looked into the eye peering out at him through the crack.

"Toss it!" he said.

The hand ceased to move but held onto the pistol.

Ricci kept looking into that eye. The man behind the door could see how his team was equipped, the serious ordnance they were carrying. Maybe he'd have the brainpower to realize he was outclassed.

"We're not interested in you. Or any other officers with you," Ricci said. "Lose that gun, come out with your hands up, you'll be fine."

There was another hanging pause.

Ricci couldn't afford to delay any longer with this small fry.

"Last chance," he said. "Give it up."

The opening between the door and its frame widened. Ricci lifted his weapon, prepared to fire.

The pistol dropped from the man's hand onto the corridor floor. Then he stepped out of the office, arms raised above his head.

A uniform, sure enough.

Ricci moved forward, kicked the relinquished gun aside, then grabbed the cop by his shoulder and pushed him face against the wall for a frisk.

He patted him down hurriedly, found a revolver in an ankle holster, and handed it back to one of his men, a young recruit named Newton. The cop wasn't packing anything else.

Ricci hauled his captive away from the wall and stayed behind him, his gun pressed into the base of his spine, his free arm locked around his throat. Using him for cover in case anyone in the office decided to do something stupid.

At his nod, Grillo and Simmons moved to either side of the half-open door, flanking it, their weapons steady in their hands.

Ricci slammed it the rest of the way open with his booted foot.

The office was nearly bare. A couple of chairs, a metal desk with a push-button telephone on it, a trash can beside the desk.

Two more uniforms were inside, both with their hands high in the air.

Ricci glanced at Newton.

"Dump whatever weapons they've got in there," he said, indicating the trash can with a jerk of his chin. "The phone, too. Then pull the can out into the hallway."

Newton did as he was ordered.

Ricci thought a moment, then shifted his eyes back to the now-empty phone socket on the wall. He still had the first cop in a choke hold.

"You already ring your boss to tell him we're here?" he said into his ear.

The cop didn't respond.

"I can hit the redial button, see who answers, find out what I need to know myself," Ricci said. "Be better for everybody if you save me the time."

The cop still didn't answer.

Ricci pushed the snout of his gun deeper into his back.

"I mean it," he said.

The cop hesitated another second, then finally nodded his head.

Thirty seconds later, Ricci and Newton had backed into the corridor, leaving the disarmed cops in the office.

"Stay put for half an hour, then you're free to leave," he said from the doorway. "You get the urge to do something different, you might want to keep in mind we don't mean your boss any harm. And that no outsider's worth getting killed over."

He pushed the door shut, turned to his men.

"Obeng and his guest of honor know about us," he said. "But we're between them and the elevators and stairs, the only routes out of the building unless they want to start jumping out windows, and it's a long drop down the hill from Obeng's office. So they either go through us or they're stuck where they are."

He looked from one man to the other. Their eyes were upon him.

"Cornered animals fight hard," he said. *"Capice?"*

Nods all around.

Ricci inhaled.

"Okay," he said. "Let's move."

They continued up the hall toward Obeng's roost.

At the final bend in the corridor, Grillo held out the search mirror's curved pole, glanced into it for barely a second, pulled it back, and turned to the others behind him.

"Four of Obeng's goons, headed straight toward us with AKs," he whispered to Ricci. "Not a dozen feet away in the middle of the corridor."

"Take them out," Ricci said. "I want it done yesterday."

The strike team launched around the corner in a controlled rush, firing short, accurate bursts with their guns.

Two of the militiamen dropped before they could return fire, their weapons flying out of their hands like hurled batons. The remaining pair split up, one breaking to the left, the other to the right.

Ricci heard the whiffle of subsonic ammo from a baby VVRS, saw the man on the left fall to the floor, arms and legs wishboned.

One to go.

The militiaman who'd run to the opposite side of the corridor was bent low against a closed door, practically flattened against it, seeking a modicum of cover in the shallow recess as he poured wild volleys into the hallway.

Ricci hugged the wall, aimed, fired his weapon, unable to get a clean shot at his target. His sabot rounds whanged against the door frame, missing the gunnie, but causing him to duck back and momentarily lay off the trigger.

Ricci knelt against the wall. Out of the corner of his eye, he saw Grillo and the others take advantage of the distraction and dash up the hall toward Obeng's office.

He held his weapon absolutely still. Let the gunnie lean out of that space one inch. Just a single goddamned inch . . .

Up ahead, Simmons was sweeping the entrance to Obeng's office with the ionic vapor detector, checking for explosives that might be rigged to a tripwire or similar gimmick. Good. The rest were in their entry-preparation positions. Grillo and the newbie Harpswell on one side of the door. On the opposite side, another green recruit named Nichols held the rammer, while the more experienced hands, Barnes and Newton, stood behind him.

Suddenly, movement from where the militiaman was huddled. His back still pressed to the door, he lifted his hands. The tip of his AK tilting outward. His knees unfolding slightly.

Ricci inhaled through gritted teeth.

This was going to be it.

As the gunnie scuttled into the hall, his weapon spitting bullets, Ricci caught him with a single shot to the center of the chest. He went down hard, his green fatigue shirt turning brilliant red.

Ricci pushed from the wall, racing around the fallen bodies in the corridor to join his team. He could see Simmons complete his scan, move himself out of the doorway—

His eyes widened. Nichols had suddenly moved *toward* the door with the rammer, was swinging it back for momentum, about to drive it against the jamb, unaware of Barnes reaching out to stop him.

"Hold it!" Ricci shouted. *"Fucking hold it!"*

He could see Nichols try to check himself, but the warning registered an instant too late. His entire upper body was already into the forward swing.

The rammer hit the door and it flew inward with a crash, and that was when the attack dogs came lunging out. Pit bulls, five of them, silent and vicious, their voice boxes surgically removed. Called *hush puppies* by the SWAT personnel Ricci had known in his police years, too often encountered in crack-house raids, they were usually maddened from drugs, torture, and starvation, reduced to a core of frenzied, bestial aggression by their keepers.

Their muscles humped and rippling under their pelts, jaws snapping, lips peeled away from their carnivorous white fangs, they sprang into the corridor and were on his men in a heartbeat—

"Stop!" A voice from Obeng's office. "Sit!"

The pit bulls stopped in their tracks and got onto their haunches, immediately heeding the firm command.

"That's it, that's it, nice doggies," the voice said. This time coming from just inside the doorway.

A hand reached from the entrance, rows of shiny gold and silver bracelets clattering around the wrist. Then an arm in a colorful, hand-beaded shirtsleeve.

The man who stepped into the corridor a moment later had performed his role to the hilt, even dressing the part of a warlord.

He bent over the dog nearest the door, scratched behind its ear, then reached into his trouser pocket for some biscuits and began passing them out to the obedient animals.

They crunched them happily, tails wagging, crumbs flying from their jowls.

"Hate to be the one to say this," he told Ricci, looking up at him. "But—"

The Sword op who'd been the Wildcat for the week-long training exercise strode from the office to finish the sentence for him.

"But your guys just got their balls chewed off," he said. "And probably some other chunks of their anatomy, too."

Expelling a long breath, Ricci turned from the office door in disgust. Down the hall, the militiaman he'd nailed with his practice round rose from the floor and pulled his dye-soaked shirt away from his chest.

"Shit's sticky," he muttered. "And *cold.*"

Ricci glared over at Nichols.

In that kid's case, getting his balls chewed off was exactly what he could look forward to.

No playacting.

TEN

AWAKEN THE SLEEPER
FEE: 50 MILLION
INSTRUCTIONS TO FOLLOW WITHIN ONE
WEEK

IN SUBURBAN ILLINOIS, A MAN NAMED LANCE JEF-
ferson Freeman, formerly known as Ronald Mumphy . . .

An identity he'd shed once he emerged from federal
prison upon getting his investment fraud conviction
overturned on a so-called legal technicality, the appellate
judge reluctantly citing an error in the submission of
prosecutorial discovery filings . . .

In his home office in the affluent town of Hanscom,
Illinois, the reborn and redubbed Lance Jefferson Freeman, or simply L. J. as his devoted Internet radio show
listeners affectionately called the founder and crown
minister of the White Freedom Church, was having
thoughts that were in many respects identical to those
of Arif al-Ashar in East Sudan, which was quite extraor-

dinary, given the vast gulf of miles, culture, ideology, and personal background separating them. Even more remarkable in terms of their congruence, L. J.'s thoughts had also framed themselves as a familiar saying, albeit one that took its context and meaning from a classically (though by no means uniquely) American experience.

"A kid in a candy store," he muttered to himself. "That's what I am, yes, mister . . ."

Meaning, in other words, that L. J., too, was coming to understand he would have to prioritize between the many ethnic groups he wished to see deleted from existence, like the terse three-line solicitation about to be electronically wiped from his computer screen.

L. J. lifted a pencil off his desk and started nibbling at its eraser with his large, white, perfectly even front teeth. Then he checked himself, recalling that his dentist had warned him the nervous habit could damage the cosmetic bonding he'd recently gotten done. When you were in the public arena, a media personality of sorts, a smile was your calling card. So scratch the pencil. You did not need to constantly chew on something when you were trying to plan things out.

L. J. lowered the pencil from his mouth but instead of putting it aside found himself tapping it against the top of his desk. *Well, no harm in that*, he supposed. Whenever he got chugging along on full horsepower, he'd work up a potent head of steam and had to find a way of blowing a little of it off somehow.

L. J. tapped. Where was he? Oh yes, the Jews. The Jews. They would be high on his list. Probably foremost. It was through books given to him by a cellmate during his prison stint (the most influential had been titled *The Wisdom and Prophesies of Adolf Hitler, The Protocols of the Learned Elders of Zion*, and *Satan's Seedline: The Evil Race*) that L. J. had learned the truth behind the Zionist Occupied Government, or ZOG, that had secretly wrested control of America from its God-chosen founders through its institutions of high finance, absorbing it into their multinational New Imperium and using fiat money . . .

In other words, the legal tender minted by the Federal Reserve Bank, from penny coins to printed notes of every denomination . . .

Fiat money to replace gold and/or silver weights and measures as an honest system of exchange, thereby allowing usurious Jewish moneylenders to manipulate interest rates and leech away the assets of the Anglo Saxon, Teutonic, and kindred white races, who, in their natural superiority, were the only blessed and rightful inheritors of the kingdom of God—the United States, in other words—just as they had craftily fleeced the people of Germany before the heroic martyrs of the National Socialist Party had stood up in brave resistance.

L. J.'s pencil-tapping quickened. The Jews, absolutely, it had to be them. Pulling together fifty million to rid the land of their domination wouldn't be difficult, considering the resources of his more well-off supporters, a core group of patriots and true believers who'd pledged to open their wallets for the cause. In fact, right now he was projecting a surplus of funds, enough to simultaneously purge another corrupting racial element from society. The tough thing was deciding which one.

Well, truth be known, maybe not. L. J. supposed it got back to his readings about the preservation of racial rights when he was behind cell bars, a whole lot of material written by some high-gigahertz thinkers and supported by the work of people like the world's leading phrenologist, an eighty-two-year-old pioneer who'd run an institute of his own in Austria since before World War II. Anyway, L. J.'s early research had made it clear that the black race presented the second greatest threat to the children of Adam, these being people of ruddy complexion, in other words *whites,* according to a biblical code that yet another of L. J.'s favorite authors had unraveled.

The blacks were number two because they, along with other non-Caucasian minorities, had entered into a Satanic conspiracy with ZOG to commit genocide . . .

A word that meant the destruction of a group through race-mixing rather than mass extermination, as the Jewish-run reference book companies had tried to redefine it by perpetuating the myth of the Holocaust, of which there was no evidence except a bunch of lies and doctored photographs produced by the Secret Disinformation Bureau of Eisenhower's treacherous Allied Expeditionary Force, but that was another can of worms right there.

The blacks. Threat number two. Because their goal was to commit genocide upon the children of Adam by intermarrying and procreating with them in violation of divine will.

"Meaning they have to go," L. J. concluded aloud. "Go straightaway into the bottomless pit, yes, mister."

He tapped away at the desk with his pencil. A plan of action, that was what he'd come up with here, and he was feeling pretty good about it. The Jews and blacks first. And then, well, he would have to evaluate his progress. See where his finances stood, and measure the rest of the social contaminants against each other to determine which presented the greatest immediate dangers. Right off the bat, he figured the Asians were prime candidates; you never knew what insidious machinations they were up to. And the Hispanics, of course, with their plot to annex the southwestern portion of the United States to Mexico . . .

And so it went for L. J. Freeman, crown minister of the White Freedom Church, in his Hanscom, Illinois, home office, his thoughts rotating around their fixed axis of hatred like the rings of some dark and hostile planet, twisting on and on and on into the outer extremities of the night.

The headquarters of the Black Exclusivist Movement was located on the first and second floors of an uptown Manhattan tenement that the group's leader, the Reverend Nate Grover, had paid for in cash by adding a dozen calendar stops to the busy lecture circuit that netted him several million dollars in yearly honorariums, which he guessed maybe sounded like a lot when Whitey got to attacking him on the tube, always talking about his extravagant lifestyle, using that phrase to jab at his integrity every time his name got mentioned. *Reverend Nate Grover, whose extravagant lifestyle includes a multimillion dollar home in East Hampton, Long Island, a collection of thirty antique cars, a large personal staff, and art and antiques estimated to be valued at this or that or the other amount and so on and so extravagantly forth.* As if a man of African descent in this twenty-first-century America wasn't supposed to earn the same or more than some retired white political flack or no-selling white writer who couldn't pack half as many people into a room, hell, a *third* as many people, talking shit to

163

spoiled white college students who looked like pale, cloned pigs.

A few months back, when Grover was organizing his annual Liberty Uprising March on Washington, a woman reporter from one of those TV news magazine shows had one of her own personal staffers—which you damn well better believe *she* never got criticized for having at her beck and call—had her flunky staffer phone to arrange an interview with him, he figured, why not, get some free media access, told her to come on down . . .

Or *up*, as the case happened to be. No blonde white woman reporter with no major white-controlled news organization Grover ever heard of had to travel *down* from anywhere in the city to get to Harlem, 50 Rockefeller Center being about as far uptown as they ever got without being flanked by a camera crew and probably notifying the goddamn NYPD where they were going in case it wanted to provide an armored escort.

He'd told her to come on down, figuratively speaking, and two days later, she was swishing through the door in her Barbie doll outfit with stiletto heels and a full set of accessories, all sugar and spice, you know, even commenting that she was impressed by his office space. Said she wished she had something as nice and roomy down at 50 Rock or wherever, which should have clued him in about what was coming next.

Then the videotape starts to roll, and what do you know, what *do* you know, Barbie doll changes into the She Creature before his eyes, goes into a jam about how when he bought the building "for a song," he'd hired contractors to "totally gut and renovate the lower stories that would house your offices, putting off repairs and

improvements to the thirty or so crumbling rental apartments on the third, fourth, and fifth floors—in large occupied by working poor black families—for some
unspecified future date."

All the while she's saying this, she's smiling at him
like a shark.

"Do you see," she asks, moving in for the kill, "how
it is that charges of opportunism and hypocrisy have
been leveled against you from various quarters?"

For a minute Grover was tempted to ask what she
expected to find here, somebody in a Huggy Bear pimp
suit sitting around some kind of piss-and-shit stinking
junkie shooting gallery, and you want to please explain
who you're referring to with that phrase "various quarters"? But even though she'd got an irritation going in
him, Grover reminded himself that this was what you
called a media opportunity, a chance to mainstream himself, and took a deep breath. The plan here was to give
her Reverend Nate Grover *Lite,* formulated for popular
consumption so the Great White American Unwashed
didn't develop a mass case of acid reflux.

"Try doing too much at once, no way anything gets
accomplished," he replied. "The improvements to the
rest of the building have been temporarily delayed, I
underscore the word *temporarily,* because as a civic
leader representing the black community, I've been
forced time and time again to react to various acts of
unprovoked brutality by the authoritarian powers that be,
whose agenda is the continued oppression of my people."

Grover figured he'd done okay, given her an earful
while staying cool for the camera, but She Creature was
determined to stay on the attack.

"Speaking of agendas," she said, "I'd like to give you the chance to explain some of your own recent statements, which polls indicate the vast majority of white people *and* African-Americans find incendiary and frankly disturbing. You have in numerous speeches accused the federal government of flooding urban neighborhoods with narcotics and automatic firearms, specifically targeting high-school-age children in—this is a direct quote—'a covert program to instigate their mass suicide-murder through the evils of violence and addiction.' You also called for African-Americans to refrain from all transactions with white-owned businesses, withdraw from the democratic election process until a political party open only to black candidates and voters is established, and, I'm quoting you again now, 'assume the license to make war upon our enemies and achieve a noncapitalist economic system,' referring to the police as 'a demonic army of persecution that must be brought to its knees by any means necessary,' which seems to espouse the very violence that you acknowledge is devastating inner-city black youth. What's still more controversial, you're said to have begun echoing the separatist policies of the Black Panther movement in its earliest days, explicitly advocating . . ."

The partition of several states into an independent black territory, possibly in the South, that was *absolutely* what he'd been talking about at his campus engagements, though he'd known it to be about as achievable as an exodus of the people to Shangri-la on a giant magic carpet. But every so often, when he was in front of a crowd, something would kind of pop out of his mouth that caught their attention, just shook the room, you know, and when that happened, he'd take off improvising, get them more fired up, reasoning that part of his job as an orator and motivator was to keep his listeners from falling asleep in their seats, and moreover that it didn't actually matter if some his declared goals were way, way in the outfield, as long as he stuck to his general message. In his mind, he was like a kid making a wish list, asking for twenty, fifty, a hundred different presents for Christmas, figuring he'd be lucky to see even one or two of them . . . but also figuring it couldn't hurt to ask, because you never knew what might turn up under the tree, all gift-wrapped and shiny. That was the thing in life, you really never did know.

Still, as Grover had sat in his office with the television cameras from the big-time, number-one-rated network news magazine rolling away, conscious that his interview would be seen in millions of homes across the country, it had occurred to him that maybe he ought to ease off some of his positions, soften his earlier comments, take another deep breath and remember that he was supposed to be Reverend Nate Grover Lite.

And then, just as he was about to respond, he'd seen this out-for-blood look in She Creature's eyes, seen that she was ready to get in his face again no matter what he said, and all at once he flashed red hot with anger. And he'd thought, *What the fuck, give her what she wants.*

"I have come to believe that coexistence between blacks and whites within a single society is impossible," he'd abruptly found himself answering. "I have come to believe that until the day all my brothers of color remove themselves from this wicked nation and form a North American state governed by and for themselves, they will continue to wear the chains of enslavement that brought them to its cursed shores. I have come to believe anything *short* of complete separation of the races is futile and will bring on their mutual destruction. And as to the comments you've mentioned, I emphatically and unapologetically stand by them."

Grover's single modification, which had jumped right off the top of his head, was that he would be willing to consider the state of New Jersey and sections of Pennsylvania and Ohio as components of an exclusivist black territory, should the southern states prove somehow unobtainable.

It went without saying that Grover's interview had made a huge splash in the ratings. It also went without saying that he'd for sure kissed his ticket to mainstream U.S.A. good-bye, along with any frequent flyer offers that might have come along down the line if he'd held his temper. But he had refused to worry about what might've been if he'd done this or if he'd said that, because he'd done what he'd done, said what he'd said, and none of it could be taken back.

And besides, look what it had led to.

Just *look*.

The day after the program aired—the very next morning, in fact—was when the E-mail arrived. Who it came from was a surprise; Grover hadn't done business with him for ages, since he'd agreed to wash some dirty money through the movement's tax-free charitable accounts in exchange for a percentage, which had gone toward subsidizing his first Liberty Uprising March. And before that, it had been the ecstasy distribution deal in Los Angeles . . . but the e thing was years ago, a *lifetime* ago far as Grover was concerned, when he was just a few shaky steps out of Rampart and needed the green to make sure he didn't fall flat on his face. These days, he practiced what he preached, damn well did, and would never again under any circumstances help put poison into the bodies of black youth.

No way he was going to do that again.

Out of curiosity, though, he'd opened the E-mail before any of the others on his queue.

That was when Reverend Nate Grover learned about the Sleeper bug.

If the message had been from anyone besides the man who'd sent it, Grover would have dismissed it right off as a weird prank. But he'd known *that* man didn't play games. That his bulletin about the super germ he'd developed, customer satisfaction guaranteed, was something that could be taken dead seriously, wild as it seemed.

Grover had awaited the actual offering ever since. Hoped it would appear each time he switched on his computer. And today, now, at last, it had:

AWAKEN THE SLEEPER
FEE: 50 MILLION
INSTRUCTIONS TO FOLLOW WITHIN ONE
WEEK

Suddenly, items one through one hundred on Grover's wish list could be his for the asking.

Wild as it seemed, for the asking.

The North, the South, the Midwest . . . to hell with grabbing *slices* of the American pie when he could have the whole thing laid before him in shiny gift wrapping, like the best and biggest present under the tree on Christmas morning.

• • • •

At fifty million dollars, Murdock Williams considered it a bargain. A first grader could calculate the profit-versus-loss margins easily enough; he wasn't talking quantum physics here but simple checkbook arithmetic.

Williams's lawyers had already offered that elderly couple on the Upper East Side, what, two, three million dollars to relinquish the lease to their rental apartment and vacate, guaranteeing them a two-bedroom elsewhere in the city. This was far more than the building's other occupants had gotten—Williams believed the highest any of them had been paid was 1.5 mil—and *they'd* all jumped at the offer. You were talking about handing over a pot of gold, giving them the chance to strike it rich by ordinary standards, how many people wouldn't?

Well, those two fossils Mr. and Mrs. Bognar, obviously. Husband something like eighty, wife only a few years younger, living in the same York Avenue apartment for half a century, you'd think they might appreciate a change of scenery before God lowered the boom. Instead, they were sticking like old wallpaper.

It wasn't that Williams harbored any personal animosity toward them—would he have upped the buyout offer if he did? In fact, there was some sympathy in him. Some understanding. His own great-grandparents had been from Russia, fled the pogroms, arrived in America with next to nothing. He was sure he still had a photograph, or daguerreotype, whatever, of Fred and Erna Waskow, bearers of his pre–Ellis Island family name, hanging on a wall somewhere in one of his homes. The Bognars, they'd come over as refugees when the Russkies pushed into Budapest in '56, so there was a definite feeling of kinship in Williams's heart. But no real estate developer ever reached his level of success by shying away from the bottom line, sympathy and understanding aside.

The Mews was what they called those East Side apartment houses, erected around wide, gated courts and areaways in the late 1800s. Williams could see how historic-minded types found them appealing, although history didn't cut it for him personally. Occupying big hunks of river frontage, they had started out as sanatoriums where moneyed tuberculosis patients could come for the then fresh air, and thirty or forty years later were converted into dwellings for the city's growing middle class—predominantly Hungarian and German immigrants displaced by one overseas conflict or another. In the 1980s, the addresses became fashionable, attracting droves of yuppies from hither and yon, but a sizable number of Europeans from yesteryear had clung to their rent-stabilized apartments throughout the neighborhood transition.

When Williams acquired the properties from their former owner, he'd paid top dollar, knowing full well that the purchase price would represent only a fraction of his eventual expenses. But his bean counters estimated his long-range profits to be in the hundreds of millions, possibly over a billion dollars, way off the board like that, the real value being in the airspace above the existing structures.

Just six stories tall, they were a colossal waste of prime living space as they stood. Because the row of four contiguous buildings included a corner lot, Manhattan zoning regulations allowed them to be torn down and replaced with a single high-rise skyscraper that would dominate almost an entire square block and soar at least ninety-five stories above the city, surpassing in height the residential tower that Williams's famous rival was raising opposite the United Nations . . . the very same competitor-slash-mogul who was always getting his picture on the front pages, and who had presold penthouse units in his building for upwards of ten million dollars apiece before so much as a single drop of concrete was mixed for its foundation.

At stake, therefore, was a staggering bundle and also the posterity Williams would finally achieve by owning the largest residential structure in New York City, ergo the country, ergo the *world*.

With the *t*'s crossed and the *i*'s dotted on his ownership papers, Williams had lost no time making lavish buyout offers to the residents of the buildings, about 75 percent of whom had happily taken the deal. A smaller group of tenants had waited for him to sweeten the pot, which he'd done by somewhat upping the dollar amount and in some cases tossing in the free relocation proviso.

It wasn't long before the remaining holdouts cleared the premises—except for the Bognars, who refused to budge from the Mews to which they were sentimentally attached. The Bognars, who would not change their minds regardless of how much cash was shoved at them, be it over, under, or around the table. The Bognars, who, despite their advanced age, appeared to be in sufficiently good health to stay put in their apartment for years to come before finally giving up the ghost.

And *years* was longer than Williams intended to wait.

After having his last buyout offer snubbed, he'd instructed his attorneys to start eviction procedures against the Bognars, but even the Legal Aid interns they got to represent them had possessed the savvy to call his bluff. The rent-control laws were ironclad when it came to validating their current lease and giving them a renewal option once it lapsed. Moreover, as sitting tenants, they were by the same legislation entitled to renew indefinitely.

Blown out of the courtroom, catching heat from senior-citizen advocacy groups that had salivated over the chance to make the Bognars a cause célèbre, Williams in desperation got in touch with certain admittedly shady operators about providing what might be called *extra*legal recourse. He was thinking that these operators—who had their hands in the construction industry among many others around town, controlling the unions, drywall suppliers, plumbing and electrical companies, you name it, from behind the scenes—might be able to throw a scare into the couple, something of that nature. But when he'd made his request to one such acquaintance over dinner in Little Italy, Williams was told that the fuss made by the various senior-rights organizations on local media outlets had created an awkward hitch.

"Think about it," his acquaintance had explained. "All the bad publicity you've gotten on this, a wasp stings one of those decrepit old farts, and he or she cries *ouch*, somebody's going to claim the fucking thing was trained and sent on its mission by Murdock Williams."

Williams had looked at him pointedly across the table.

"You people are supposed to be experts at persuasion, and I can't see how this is a tall order," he'd insisted. "Besides, I'm not the only one losing out while the old farts sit on a fortune. Or don't you understand how much of this wealth your organization could be sharing?"

The other man had stared at him a moment, then slowly lowered his fork onto his plate.

"Isn't me who's misunderstanding," he'd replied. "I said there were problems, not that we couldn't get past them. You sit tight, I need to approach somebody I know of. He's on another level from everyone else, so I'll have to go through the Commission. If he thinks he can help, he'll reach you."

And reach Williams he did. The original notification had been E-mailed to him within a week, and it struck him as the craziest damned thing. A designer virus, that was what the sender had declared he could provide. There might have been a hundred other proposals Williams wouldn't have questioned for an instant, recognizing that his acquaintance moved in a realm that was beyond his experience. But it had seemed absolutely far out. He'd had trouble giving credence to it.

Little by little, though, a belief in the claim's legitimacy had begun to emerge in his mind. Something about the way his unidentified contact had been spoken about at the Little Italy meeting had impressed Williams. This cyberspace phantom commanded deference from a man who was almost nobody's lesser.

Nor was it just that. Under the advisement of his broker, Williams had bought heavily into the genomic futures market, but not before doing his homework. Projects that involved the mapping of human and nonhuman DNA were on the verge of leading to a scientific revolution on a scale with the coming of the industrial age, the harnessing of atomic energy, and the advent of the microchip in its ramifications for society. Genomic research promised rapid breakthroughs in the prevention and diagnosis of disease, drug treatments, the farming of lab-cloned body parts for transplantation . . . there was no telling what advances to expect, no keeping pace with those that had already been made. Nearly every day some new application of biotechnology was announced, so why be skeptical that a customizable virus had been hatched? The longer Williams contemplated it, the more the idea that one *hadn't* was what started to look far-fetched.

In fact, he'd thought, it would be selling short his own biotech investment folder to doubt the probability—and Murdock Williams never bet against himself.

He replied to the E-mail with a note requesting that he be advised when the product was ready for issue and then tried his best to focus on other business. Still, in his idle moments, Williams would visualize his building soaring above the riverfront, a lasting, commanding monument to his mastery of the developer's art. And as far as it went for that old couple, how much time could they have left before they reached their expiration dates, anyway? Cancer, heart attack, stroke, everybody got hammered sooner or later. Williams honestly felt he'd just be hastening along the inevitable.

As his appreciation for the beauty of the solution increased, his craving to gratify his drive and ambition became unbearable. Had the "cyber-phantom" taken any longer to respond, the impatience would have eaten him up alive.

Thank heaven the wait was finally over. He'd have paid ten times the asking price to end it.

Awaken the Sleeper, fee fifty million, instructions to follow within one week, he thought now, the message that had finally showed up in his on-line mailbox ticking in his mind like a NASDAQ readout.

A week, one more week—seven days until he could get things rolling.

Williams knew he'd be counting down the hours.

ELEVEN

SAN DIEGO, CALIFORNIA
NOVEMBER 8, 2001

"I CAN'T DO WHAT YOU'RE ASKING. IT ISN'T AN OP-
tion."

"I'm sorry you feel that way, Palardy," Enrique Quiros said. "Because, as a matter of fact, it's your *only*
option."

"Don't use my name. It isn't safe—"

Quiros shook his head and indicated the portable bug
detector on the seat between them.

"There's where you're mistaken again," he said. "Because this is my *Safe Car*. Honestly, that's what I call
it, just as some people might give their cars endearing
little names like Bessie, Marie, or whatever."

Palardy let out a sigh. The Safe Car in which they sat
was a Fiat Coupé that Quiros had driven into the parking
lot outside the cruise ship terminal on Harbor Drive. It
was six P.M., the upper rim of the sun sinking into San
Diego Bay, the area outside the terminal crosshatched
with dusky shadows. Palardy had left his own Dodge

Caravan several aisles away when he'd reluctantly arrived in answer to Quiros's summons.

"Those pocket units aren't reliable," he said. "Their bandwidth sensitivity's limited. And certain kinds of listening devices operate in modes that won't scan. It's my job to know this sort of thing, my goddamned *job,* or did you forget—"

"Settle down. I haven't forgotten anything," Quiros interrupted. "This vehicle is garaged on my property, and the grounds are under constant video surveillance. There are alarms. Canine patrols. Unless I happen to be inside it, as now, it's never parked anywhere else."

They looked at each other, Palardy seeing his own features reflected in Quiros's dark green Brooks Brothers sunglasses. He'd always found it offensive when a man wore tinted lenses during a talk with somebody who wasn't wearing them, in this instance himself, the concealment of the eyes a blatant means of gaining distance and position. State troopers, paranoiacs, egotistical movie stars—so many personality types, and yet that desire to set themselves apart was an attribute they all shared.

"Open areas are hard to secure; even the military has problems with them, I don't care how many watchdogs or alarms you've got." Palardy sighed heavily again. "Listen, I'm not trying to argue. My point's just that it doesn't hurt to be careful."

Plainly tired of the subject, Quiros reached into the inner pocket of his sport jacket and produced a zippered leather case.

"Let's make this short so we can both move on," he said, holding the case out to Palardy. "Everything you'll need is in here."

"I told you I can't do this. It's too dangerous. It's too *much* for me."

Quiros looked at him in silence for several moments. Then he nodded to himself, turned toward the front of the car, and leaned back against his headrest.

"Okay," he said, staring straight ahead with the case still in his hand. "Okay, here's how it is. I'm not interested in what you have to tell me. When you wanted money to pay off your gambling debts in Cuiabá, you were glad to sell off confidential information about the layout and security of an installation that it was your job to protect. When you were rotated back to the States and found yourself in hock again, loan sharks riding all over you, you became more than eager to slink into your employer's office and collect material for a genetic blueprint that you knew would be—"

"Please, I don't feel comfortable talking about—"

Quiros raised his hand. The gesture was slow and without anger, but something about it instantly quieted Palardy.

"If I were you, I wouldn't feel comfortable, either. Because you've done worse than break bonds with every professional trust that's been placed in you. You've been an accessory to acts of murder and sabotage. And if that information were to surface, it could put you away in prison for the rest of your life."

There was a brief silence. Palardy swallowed spitlessly. It made a clicking sound in his throat.

"A decision's been made for you," Quiros said. "It's too late for objections or disavowals. And my advice is to drop them right now. Or I promise you'll regret it."

Palardy swallowed again. *Click.*

"I didn't want to get involved in anything like this," he said hoarsely.

Quiros stared out at the terminal in the deepening pool of shadows near the harbor's edge.

"It could be we have that in common," he said, his voice quiet. And paused a beat. "You'll do what you have to do."

He extended the case across the seat without turning from the windshield.

This time, Palardy took it.

In a rental van on the opposite side of the parking aisle, Lathrop began to pack his remote laser voice monitoring system into its black hardshell camera case. From the rear window panel of the van, the invisible beam of the device's near-infrared semiconductor laser diode had been aimed at a ninety-degree angle through the back windshield at the Fiat's rearview mirror.

It is a basic rule of optics that the angle of incidence is equal to the angle of reflection. What this means in practical application is that a beam of coherent light—that is, a beam in which all light waves are in phase, the defining and essential quality of a laser transmission—will bounce back to its source at the same angle at which it strikes a reflecting surface, unless that surface creates some sort of modulation, or interference, to throw the waves out of phase, causing some to bounce back at different angles than others. Vibrating infinitesimally from the conversation inside the Fiat—perhaps a thousandth of an inch or less with each utterance—the window glass had caused corresponding fluctuations in the optical beam reflecting off it, which were then converted into electronic pulses by the eavesdropping unit's receiver, filtered from background noise, enhanced, and digitally recorded.

Lathrop had gotten every word spoken inside the car. And though he wasn't yet certain what they all meant, one thing was eminently clear to him.

After days of following Enrique Quiros in a succession of rentals and disguises, days of following his instincts, his patience finally had been rewarded with a deeper and richer load of pay dirt than he could have imagined.

TWELVE

THE INSTANT PALARDY ENTERED ROGER GORDIAN'S office, a strange feeling came over him. Everything seemed the same yet different, like in one of those dreams that was so close to real life you awoke confused about whether its events had actually occurred. The setting of the dream might be the place you grew up, the home you lived in, the park across the street, it didn't matter. You knew you were somewhere familiar, but things weren't quite the way they should be. Both inside and outside yourself.

It was like that for him this morning. The same yet different.

He tried to shake that floaty, disoriented sensation as he strode across the carpet toward Gordian's desk.

"You'll do what you have to do," Quiros had insisted. And Palardy thought now that he could.

He could do it.

Because this was only a day after his regular countersurveillance sweep, Palardy was not carrying the Big

Sniffer or any of its accompanying equipment, which made him a bit more conspicuous than he otherwise might be. But once Enrique Quiros had forced this thing upon him, he'd known he would want to get it done right away. That zippered case he took from Quiros, it had felt so heavy in his hand, so heavy in his pocket. Like some superdense piece of lead being drawn toward the earth's magnetic core, pulling him down with it. Every minute he held onto it, that downward pull grew harder to resist. Palardy needed to get the thing over with before he sank into the ground.

He'd arrived at work a little before seven o'clock, the usual time for countersurveillance personnel—their sweeps were always conducted before the corporate workday began so as not to interfere with business—and then had gone straight up to Gordian's office suite, prepared with an excuse, should anybody be around. And it had turned out someone was. Though the boss almost never came in before seven-thirty, a quarter of eight, Palardy knew his administrative assistant, Norma, would often arrive much earlier to get a jump on her filing, scheduling, whatever other duties admins performed. And sure enough, she'd been at her desk in the outer office today when Palardy stepped out of the elevator.

Damn good thing he'd had that story ready.

"Morning, Norma," he said, amazed that he could stand there and smile while feeling like he was about to plunge through a hole in the ground. "How goes?"

She'd looked up at him from her computer screen with mild surprise.

"Hi, Don," she said. "Don't tell me it was your twin brother I saw here yesterday with that fancy bag of tricks?"

"Nope, sorry to report there's just one of me to go around," he said.

"I'm crushed on behalf of all womankind," she said with a mock frown. "So what brings you back to us?"

"Actually, I think I must've misplaced one of the fancy little gizmos that *go* in my bag when I made the rounds." Palardy's words seemed to reach his ears from a far corner of the room. "Maintenance tells me it isn't in the lost and found, so I'm retracing my steps."

Part of his mind had expected Norma to be suspicious. To sit there with her eyes boring into him, discerning something was amiss. Though the rest of him had known that was irrational. Known the reason he'd given for his encore appearance would sound perfectly ordinary and believable.

And, of course, it did. She had waved him toward the door to the inner office.

"Be my guest," she said.

Now Palardy stood over Gordian's big mahogany desk, his back to the door, and hurriedly put on the white cotton gloves he'd brought in his pocket. Just to the right of the blotter was a can of rolled wafers. A month or so before, Palardy had been running behind schedule with his sweep, and the boss had come in and waited at the desk as it was completed. Swirling a wafer in the cup of coffee he'd poured for himself, Gordian had complained in a kind of lighthearted way about having to swear off flavored coffee, and the two-per-day wafer stick allowance his wife had insisted upon instead.

Palardy had clearly remembered that instance in Quiros's car the other night. And was remembering it again as he reached for the can of wafers, pulled off its plastic lid, and set it down on the desktop. The can was more than three-quarters empty. Maybe ten wafers left inside. He got the flat leather case out of his coverall pocket, unzipped it, produced the disposable syringe, and laid it beside the can lid. He'd already drawn the solution from the ampule and tossed it. This should take him sixty seconds, ninety max.

Get it over with, he thought. *Get it done.*

With his right hand, he fished one of the wafers out of the can. With his left he inserted the syringe's needle deep into the opening at one end of the rolled wafer and depressed the plunger about a millimeter. Colorless, odorless, tasteless, the contents of the ampule would indiscernibly permeate the wafer's cream-filled center.

Removing the needle, Palardy put the wafer back in the can, and injected a second, a third, and a fourth wafer.

That would be enough. Would have to be. There was more of the suspension in the hypo, but he couldn't bear staying in the office any longer. His stomach felt like a brick of ice.

Palardy closed the can, returned the syringe to the case, and slipped the case back into his pocket.

He was taking off his gloves when he heard the doorknob turning behind him.

His heart tripped.

"Any luck?"

Norma's voice. From the doorway.

It was the worst moment of his life to that point. Worse, even, than his last terrible meeting with Quiros. Balanced equally between guilt and terror, he went numb everywhere, the blood seeming to flush from his veins.

Somehow Palardy managed to stand perfectly still,

185

managed to keep his body between his hands and the doorway until he'd finished peeling the gloves from his fingers and stuffed them into a patch pocket on his thigh.

He turned toward Norma. She was leaning into the room through the open door.

"No," he said. Realizing nervously that he hadn't looked himself over, hadn't made sure the gloves weren't sticking out of his pocket. Wondering if she could see them. "Not a bit."

The receptionist studied his face a second, shrugged.

"Sorry, my dear," she said. "But in the meantime, don't look so worried, I'm sure your thingamajig will turn up."

She didn't notice, Palardy thought. *Merciful God, she didn't notice.*

He nodded.

"Yeah," he said. "Suppose I can manage without it, meanwhile."

Then the phone on her desk chirruped.

"Better answer that, hope you don't mind letting yourself out," she said and ducked her head back into the outer office area. "I'll remind the cleanup crews to stay on the lookout."

Palardy took a gulp of air, smoothed his coveralls over his body with sweaty palms. The gloves weren't showing. She hadn't seen anything. He was going to be okay.

A moment later, he followed Norma into the anteroom, exchanging a smile and a wave as he went past her desk, got into the elevator, and rode it downstairs.

Moving on legs he could hardly feel through a world that would never again seem to be the one he'd always known.

• • •

"Hi, Ash," Gordian said into his office phone. "Your wheels down at LAX yet?"

"On the ground, safe and sound," she said. "I'm calling on my cellular from the arrivals terminal, so you can stop biting your nails."

Gordian smiled. Nearly four decades of flying planes ranging from Air Force bombers to his private Learjet had made him a well nigh unbearable backseat pilot, and he became even more fretful whenever his wife or kids took to the air with someone else's hand at the controls.

Grown kids, he reminded himself.

"Trip okay?"

"Couldn't have been smoother," Ashley said. "How are things at the office?"

"Not without pockets of turbulence," he said. "I just retreated to my desk after running into one, matter of fact. You know Mark Debarre? The Marketing veep?"

"Sure. Nice guy."

"Usually," Gordian said. "You should've seen him sprout fangs at today's sales conference. Almost sank them into one of the guys from Promotions when they got into a flap about whether to call those information download kiosks we've developed *Infopods* or *Datapods*."

She laughed.

Even from hundreds of miles away, the sound warmed him. It was like being able to hear a sunbeam.

"Which was Mark's preference?"

"The first."

"And yours?"

"I'm back and forth."

"Hmmm," she said. "I'll think about it over the weekend, give you my opinion, if you'd like."

"I'd like."

"Then consider me on it," she said. "Meanwhile, Laurie, Anne, and yours truly are about to hold a marketing conference of our own at the luggage claim. We wish to become the most enthusiastically vulnerable, suggestible consumers we can be."

Gordian smiled, reached into his tall can of rolled wafers, fished one out of the can, and let it steep in the cup of coffee on his desk. Ashley's pre-Thanksgiving shopping weekend with her sisters in L.A. was a lollapalooza that had grown in size, scope, and budget each year, seemingly by conscious design.

"Did I hear you say *luggage claim?*" he said. "Since you're only going to be away from home for two days, my impression was you'd be okay with carry on."

As always, Ashley knew a setup line when it was pitched to her.

"The suitcases, my love, are for bringing home the bounty," she said.

"Guess I'd better wait till you're done with the charge cards before filing for Chapter Eight, then."

"That would be considerate." She laughed again.

A sunbeam touching the wings of a butterfly, Gordian thought. *On the brightest and bluest day of summer.*

"I really should get cracking," Ashley said after a moment. "Meet you at Julia's house Sunday afternoon, okay?"

"Why don't I pick you up at the airport," he said. "We could drive there together afterward."

"Really, Gord, you don't need to bother. It's easier for me to arrange for a car."

"Well . . ."

"Besides, some father-daughter alone time might be

good for the two of you. And I know you'd like to finish that doggie corral you're building for Jack and Jill."

"That I would . . ."

"Then knock yourself out," she said. "*I* certainly will."

Gordian pulled his wafer out of his coffee, examined it idly, dunked it back into the cup.

"You win," he said. "Have fun. And give my regards to your partners-in-buying."

"Will do on both counts," she said. "Love you."

"Love you, too, Ash."

Gordian hung up the phone, reached for his cup, sipped, and decided the wafer stick had imparted all the hazelnut flavor it was going to. The result wasn't quite as satisfying as the high-sat-fat coffee blend he'd relinquished at Ashley's insistence, but having the wafer to snack on with his hot beverage offered something of a consolation.

He took a bite of the end that had been soaking in the coffee, like a man playing Russian roulette without even an inkling that he holds a cocked and loaded revolver in his hand.

This, his second rolled wafer of the day, was not among those Palardy had injected.

Three hours later, Gordian would sneak a third into his daily allotment as a perk to himself after hearing more cries and lamentations from his fueding execs.

That was the bullet that got him.

"You have any thoughts about why I asked to see you here this late on a Friday afternoon?"

"Well, sir—"

"Tom's fine for now," Ricci said. After seven months

189

on the job, he guessed he was past due making up his mind how he wanted to be addressed by his subordinates.

"Yes, sir," Nichols cleared his throat nervously. "Tom."

Ricci looked across his desk at the kid.

"And what might they be?"

The kid's face was confused.

"Your thoughts," Ricci said.

"Oh." Nichols cleared his throat again. "Well, it's late Friday afternoon . . ."

"Which I already established," Ricci said.

"Yes, you did, sorry, Tom . . ."

Ricci wound his hand in the air.

"My assumption was that you'd waited till the end of this week to complete your evaluation of my actions during last week's training exercise. And, uh, that you wish to discharge me from the RDT before next week gets under way."

Ricci looked at him.

"That had occurred to me," he said.

The room was quiet a moment. In fact, it was dead still. Late Friday afternoon, almost everybody had gone home for the weekend. Even the corridor outside was deserted.

Ricci glanced at the wire-basket penholder on the desk near his left elbow, decided it was situated too close to him, pushed it farther away, decided he liked its original position better, and returned it there.

"We know what went wrong with the office penetration," he said. "Looking back, you want to tell me how it *should've* been executed?"

Nichols took a few seconds to think and seemed to

get steadier and less antsy as he did. The kid had close-cropped blond hair and cheeks that Ricci doubted would have any fuzz on them if he were to miss shaving for a week. But there was a toughness underneath the schoolboy looks, a focus. And he had the build of someone who exercised with intelligence, shooting for overall fitness and stamina rather than bulk. Ricci had observed these qualities while working briefly with him in Kazakhstan, and then again during the first-round tryout drills for his RDT.

"Our targets were confined to the room. Without any known means of exit but the door, according to our floor-plan schematics. That was to their disadvantage," he said at last. "To their advantage, they knew we were outside, and the doorway gave them a narrow, direct, and easily covered zone of observation and fire." He paused again. "We could have created multiple diversions before and during our entry. A breaching charge could have been placed on the wall adjacent the door. A profusion of chemical incapacitants and distractive tools were available to us. There may have been time for our outside support teams to launch gas projectiles through the outside window. Primarily, though, I should have waited for your specific orders, directions, and countdown before attempting to break through the door."

The kid sat rigidly in his chair. He seemed to be making a tremendous effort to contain his embarrassment. And somehow that made Ricci feel embarrassed for him.

"You were crackerjack until you swung that rammer," he said. "Didn't miss a beat when we were surprised by those guys coming down the stairs. Or when we got into that firefight in the hall. Both of 'em were tough situations. What happened at the last? Adrenaline take over?"

Nichols' smooth cheeks flushed a little.

"Not exactly, sir . . . *Tom,* sir . . ."

He shook his head.

"Go on," Ricci said. "Let's hear it."

The kid inhaled, exhaled.

"When you ordered us to neutralize the men in the corridor, your words . . . what I heard you say . . . was that you wanted it done yesterday." He breathed again, looked at Ricci. "At the time, I took it to mean you wanted us to directly move on to the next stage and complete the seizure of our target. In hindsight, I think . . . that is, I *know* . . . I was too eager to please you and make the grade."

Ricci was quiet a moment.

"I've got this theory about mistakes," he said. "That they're always waiting for us, sort of like hidden mines or trapdoors. Every step along, we've got choices to make. The better ones are usually just enough to get us a little further ahead. The worse ones have this crummy way of being more final. Of doing us in. Which doesn't make for joyous odds."

Ricci eyed his penholder, transferred it to his right side, then his left, then more toward the middle of the desk.

"I've been a soldier, and I've been a cop," he said, looking up at the kid. "Met guys on both jobs who got into trouble not knowing the difference between obedience and blind obedience. Maybe it ought to be emphasized more. Showing men how to see the line, I mean. It can be thin. Razor sharp. Slippery. But if that's where you choose to live, you better be wise to the terrain."

He paused. "I'm your commander. My orders are supposed to be clear. You tell me the words I used had a part in your screwup, I'll take it into consideration, give you a second chance. But there won't be a third. Because we're talking life and death. For you and your teammates. And because, on *my* team, just following orders won't cut as an excuse. You've got to use your head. All your judgment, everything you've learned, your understanding of what the mission's about. Of what we're about. And keep the line in sight."

Nichols sat quietly in his chair.

"Thank you," he said after a few seconds, looking awkward. "I appreciate what you've done for me. And I'm sorry—"

Ricci interrupted him with a motion of his hand, looked at his wall clock.

"Go home," he said. "It's late on a Friday afternoon. Weekend's calling."

"Yes, sir," the kid said.

Ricci looked at him. Opened his mouth, closed it. Then looked back at his penholder and resumed shifting it around his desktop.

Nichols rose from his chair and left the office.

THIRTEEN

ROGER GORDIAN AWOKE SUNDAY MORNING CON-
vinced he was fending off a bad cold.

To be sure, he'd felt more than a little out of sorts the
day before but had attributed that to being wearied from
a busier-than-average week at the office, the predictable
stresses of running an enterprise that spanned five continents—and, at last count, twenty-seven nations—compounded by Friday's difficult sales conference. And he'd
been keeping a close eye on Tom Ricci's war games at
the New Mexico training camp. Although Ricci had
been frustrated with their ultimate resolution, his team's
performance had struck Gordian as mostly exceptional.
That they'd stumbled at the end wasn't as important to
him as how they'd performed overall and what lessons
they'd learned from their errors. Why hold operational
maneuvers but to work out the kinks?

Still, a long, draining week. And with Ashley gone
off to storm the checkout counters of Los Angeles, it
felt incomplete, as though a seam had been left out of

its cuff. The house was less of a home when she was away, too quiet, its rooms emptier and larger. Gordian sometimes couldn't believe how much time they'd spent apart before he'd drifted from the matrimonial through lanes onto those eye-opening rumble strips a few years back.

Also, he'd admittedly gotten used to having Julia around, despite their frequent tense moments. She seemed delighted with her new place, and he was delighted for her. But a part of him selfishly missed fathering her and being trailed at his heels by her lovably annoying greyhounds.

After turning in early Friday night, Gordian spent most of Saturday with a mystery novel on his lap, unable to muster the energy for much of anything else. When he'd warmed the homemade chili Ashley had left in the fridge and its smell failed to charge his appetite, he'd conclusively diagnosed himself as an exhausted and lonesome bird separated from his flock. Nobody to pay attention to him. No eternally ravenous dogs nosing at his plate. Not even his daughter to give him one of those zinging looks that said he couldn't do anything right.

Gordian had listlessly eaten half a bowl of the chili and picked up his crime novel again, figuring he'd read the last few chapters, discover who murdered whom and why, shower, and go to bed. But after about ten or fifteen minutes, his eyes had felt tired and grainy, and he decided to cut straight to the shower and bed phases of his second wild night of bacheloring. He'd wanted to start out for Julia's first thing, anyway, eager to attach the spacers and siding strips to the posts of her dog corral. Though he'd already set the posts, and the strips had been cut to size at the lumber yard, it would be a demanding affair to complete just one side of the basket-weave fence. And he was secretly hoping to start on a second section that afternoon.

Then, as he'd risen from the chair in his study, Gordian had experienced a wave of mild lightheadedness. It was over in seconds, and again all he could think was that he was blown out from a rough week, though perhaps more so than he'd guessed. A few extra hours of shut-eye would do him a world of good.

But his sleep was shallow and fitful. Each time he stirred uneasily to glance at the illuminated face of his bedside clock, he'd find only a short time had passed since he'd last closed his eyes. Twenty minutes, forty, no longer than an hour.

At about two A.M. Gordian roused, chilled and sweating. His throat hurt when he swallowed. There was a dull pain behind his eyes. His arms and back were stiff. Whatever was wrong with him, it didn't feel like a case of simple exhaustion anymore. He felt damn unwell.

He sat up against his pillow and drew his knees to his chest, trembling in the darkness. His mouth was parched, the stiffness in his muscles had become a throbbing ache, and his stomach was unsettled. After a while, he went into the adjoining bathroom for a drink of water. The sudden brightness of the bathroom light sharpened the pain at the back of his eyeballs, and he had to turn the dimmer control down low before going to fill his glass.

As he stood over the sink, it occurred to Gordian that a couple of aspirins might help him. He reached for the bottle in the medicine chest, shook a couple of tablets into his hand, and gulped them down with his water. Then his eye fell on the thermometer inside the chest.

He should take his temperature. If Ashley were home, she would insist on it. But a fever would mean he'd probably have to can his visit to Julia's, and he had looked forward to seeing her and making progress on that dog pen. Besides, Ash would be meeting him there with her purchase-laden suitcases, each doubtless weighing a ton. She was counting on him to help load them into the trunk of the car and drive her home. All he needed was to be sick and useless to everyone.

Gordian made up his mind to take his temperature if his condition didn't improve by morning. Well, *later* in the morning, he thought, remembering the hour.

In fact, he'd slowly begun to feel better on his return to bed. The chills abated, and he found that his muscle cramps were likewise easing. Maybe he'd caught some kind of twenty-four-hour bug, and it had peaked overnight. Or maybe the aspirin had done the trick.

At around three-thirty, Gordian again fell asleep and did not reawaken until the alarm buzzed four hours later.

Sunday came on warm and radiantly clear. With his face turned into the golden sunlight flooding his bedroom window, Gordian started to think he might not need that thermometer after all. His lower back was still aching, and his throat hurt a little when he swallowed, but there were no signs of feverishness or nausea.

He got up, went into the kitchen to fill the coffeemaker, then decided tea might be a smarter pick. He carried it to his screened-in veranda and sat looking out at Ashley's hillside arbor gardens, sipping from his cup, a gentle, rose-scented breeze wafting over him. Perfect weather for working outdoors. He'd finish the tea and then see how he was doing before reaching a conclusion about whether to go on with his plans.

By eight, Gordian felt considerably recuperated from whatever had hit him the previous night. No sense treating himself as nonfunctional. He would push forward on the corral, take it slow and easy, maybe get a bit less of it done than he might like. He'd always believed moderate physical exertion was a better remedy for a cold than lying around the house. Better for him, at any rate.

Gordian went back into the kitchen and rinsed his cup and saucer in the sink, thinking he should have a bite to eat before leaving for Pescadero. Food didn't tempt him, though. As he turned toward the bathroom for another quick hop under the showerhead, he heard an inner voice argue that skipping breakfast was far from advisable for a person who'd been as sick as he was a few hours ago, and who was looking ahead to a long, active day. But he was sure he'd regain his appetite once he reached Julia's. He could fix himself some toast, an English muffin, risk incurring her wrath and sneak a morsel or two to Jack and Jill. Like old times.

What he wanted right now was to wash up and hurry into his clothes. He was anxious to get moving with things, and the worst of his illness really did seem to be behind him.

"Megan, I'm wondering if it's appropriate for us to discuss a matter of Bureau policy under these circumstances."

"Is my nearness bothering you? Because I can slide over the other way. No offense taken."

"It isn't how close you are per se—"

"Then what is it you find questionable? That we're in a hot tub together? The whole idea of conducting business exclusively in sterile office settings is fossilized, and that isn't just my opinion. There are a million and one studies that show—empirically *prove*—relaxed and stimulating environments are the places to confer—"

"Come on, help me out here—"

"I'm trying, Bob. What do you think Bohemian Grove is about except the intersection of government and private af—?"

"Forget Bohemian Grove. We're both *naked,* or haven't you noticed? And I won't get into the subject of our intersecting the past couple of days."

That brought a smile to Megan's face.

"Get into it all you want," she said.

Her emerald eyes met his gray ones.

Lang looked back at her in speechless silence.

They were sitting shoulder-to-shoulder on the curved bench of the hot tub, neck deep in 180-degree water, steam rising into the 45-degree Shenandoah Valley air around them in vaporous ribbons and curlicues. Over and beyond the lattice rail screening their room's rear deck, the redwood hot tub upon the deck, and their nude, soaking bodies in the tub from the eyes of their hosts and fellow weekenders at the Virginia B and B, over and beyond on the forested Allegheny mountainsides across the valley, the hardwoods in autumn foliage were watercolor dashes of cinnamon brown against the sweeping dark green brush strokes of the predominant pine cover.

"Bob?"

"Yes?"

"You seem to have blanked out."

Lang sighed.

"My problem," he said, and then paused. "That is, what I believe may be unseemly is that you are making

199

a substantial professional request of me while we're very busily engaged in an extraprofessional relationship. Asking that, in my capacity as Washington Bureau chief, I seek to waive or broaden existing security classifications to give UpLink International access to privileged investigative files."

She shrugged. "We were entirely clothed when I made the request. Neither of us had yet seen the other unclothed at the time. Truthfully, I hadn't begun to entertain the notion that we would, though the fantasy did arise one dark and lonely night."

He shook his head in consternation.

"Be straight," he said. "You can see how there might be at least an appearance of impropriety."

"Sure I can," she said. "But do *you* believe I've been sleeping with you to cloud your objectivity, compromise your integrity, entice you to violate national security, whichever perception concerns you—?"

"That's ridiculous—"

"And do you think I'd *stop* sleeping with you as a consequence of your denying us access, if that proves to be your determination?"

"No, of course not—"

"So why don't you help *me* get things straight," she said. "Give me a rational explanation why the farther along we've come in our friendship, the farther away you've tilted from opening the databases. Since I know who I am, and you seem to know who you are, I can't see either one of us violating our principles for a tumble in the sack."

"Or a splash in the tub, I suppose," Lang said. "I don't know. Maybe I don't have a clear and sensible answer for you. But I've always kept my personal life separate from my responsibilities to the Bureau. Mixing them is something new to me. It throws the formula out of whack."

"Would you rather limit your mating prospects to women you meet in bars and nightclubs?"

He looked at her.

"I think you're being a little unfair."

Megan was shaking her head now, her face dead serious.

"What isn't fair is putting boundaries on what we've got going because you're jittery about messing with some artificial formula," she said. "The workplace is where adults meet. Where they get to know one other, sans hackneyed pickup lines. I don't see anything wrong with that. Or how our having grown close suddenly makes us Mata Hari and Benedict Arnold."

He was quiet. They sat there alongside each other, steam billowing around them into the chill air, shimmering in the sunlight.

Megan craned her head back, looking up into the open sky.

"One last time," she said after a moment, still staring upward. "My feelings for you aren't predicated on whether UpLink obtains the clearances. But I've got my job obligations, too. Gord isn't about to take no for an answer, and he's got heavyweight contacts from the president on down. I'd prefer we not have to make an end run around you. And I hope that if we must, you'll understand and won't let it pull us apart." Her voice caught. "That would be a waste. And make me sadder than I can begin to express."

Silence.

Lang gazed out at the brown-and-green-splashed mountains in the distance.

"Tell Gordian he'll have my decision by the end of the week," he said.

Megan nodded without looking down.

He turned to her, studied her upturned face for several seconds.

"It must be hard sometimes being a woman and strong," he said.

Her eyes lowered. Met his again.

"Sometimes," she said.

He leaned close and touched his lips to her shoulder. Brushed them along her neck, the line of her chin, the soft flesh below her ear, caressing her face, stroking back her hair with his fingertips, leaving behind traces of white gooseflesh.

"I'm not going anywhere," he whispered and slid his arm around the bareness of her waist to draw her closer, kissing her on the cheek, on the corner of the mouth. "I'm in for whatever happens."

She made a low sound in her throat, her lips parting against his.

"Let's make something happen right now," she husked, and kissed him, smiling as their mouths and tongues joined. She put her hand on him under the water, closed it around him under the water, moved it with quickening intensity under the water. Lang's hand slid down over her hip, down over her thigh, lower, finding her, touching her, matching her rhythm, their eyes locked, their bodies pressing together, moving together, swaying, locked . . .

The two of them losing themselves in each other,

making something happen there in the water on the deck beneath the wide and borderless blue sky.

In a sense, Gordian was right about his building of the corral having a therapeutic effect on him. He knew a doctor would not have condoned it. Might have strictly disallowed it. But he felt the warmth of the sun on his back, the smells of mown grass and freshly dug earth, and the robust physical workout helped carry him through most of the day.

Standing in his daughter's backyard now, Gordian inspected his workmanship and nodded to himself with approval. He'd developed and patented scores of breakthrough technologies, pioneered advances in communications that had transformed governments and economies, but his justifiable pride in those achievements had never topped his pleasure in building something with only wooden boards, a box full of nails or screws, and a handy set of tools.

It was a feeling that was no less keen today than it had been when Gordian was a thirteen-year-old boy pounding together a tree house in Racine, Wisconsin. The ordered routine of readying his tools and construction materials relaxed him and gave him a chance to organize his thoughts. He enjoyed the way a number of careful and methodical steps that followed a proven design would yield visible results within a relatively short time frame. And he enjoyed the direct connection between hands-on effort and outcome, especially when they were for the benefit of someone he loved.

While it was a bit of a damper to realize he was inexplicably getting on that particular someone's nerves, he'd almost come to accept that as status quo.

Gordian removed his safety goggles, slipped them into his tool belt, and flapped his T-shirt to dry the perspiration on his chest and armpits. Certainly he'd been functioning at well below 100 percent. He was breathing hard, his sore throat bothered him, and a nagging, raspy cough had developed over the last few hours. Every so often he would get a pang between his shoulder blades and down at the base of his spine as a reminder not to push too far. But that sun felt great, and there hadn't been a recurrence of the vague dizziness and shakes he'd experienced the night before, and he hadn't looked for trouble by mentioning any of it to Julia. She would surely overreact and push him into a lawn chair, where he'd spend the rest of the afternoon shooing away flies and mosquitos.

No thanks, he thought. He could decide for himself when he'd had enough. Parental privilege.

Gordian blotted the sweat from his eyes and forehead with his sleeve, put his cordless power drill into its belt holster, folded his arms across his chest, and continued to look over his handiwork. The fencing's interwoven board construction required more fuss than, say, an ordinary stockade, but the wider spaces between its boards allowed enough wind filtration to keep it upright during the worst imaginable coastal blow. And gave the greyhounds convenient openings to peep through.

Each side of the square corral was to measure twelve feet by six feet, its horizontal plywood strips sized at a little over four feet long—any longer and they would tend to weaken. Gordian had needed to start off the first side by installing four posts at four-foot intervals. After he'd plotted the corral's measurements with a tape ruler, twine, and temporary stakes on his last visit, he had dug the first row of postholes, filled their bottoms with gravel for drainage, and then driven the posts into the ground with a heavy mallet, repeatedly checking their vertical line with a carpenter's level, packing soil into the holes as he went along. It had been vigorous work that left him streaked with dirt and sweat and with a blistered finger or two in spite of the gloves he'd worn. But it wasn't supposed to be easy, and he hadn't minded.

This morning, Gordian had resumed where he'd left off, using his power tool to fasten the horizontal strips to alternating sides of the posts, moving from bottom to top and right to left. What he was presently looking at was the open space between the last two posts. Once he got the horizontals up to close that gap, he'd be done with an entire side of the corral, his modified goal for the afternoon. Well, almost done with it, since that would still leave him having to thread the vertical spacers through the strips. But it was a relatively quick and undemanding task, and he could ask Julia to help him with it before leaving for home.

Gordian had another brief spate of coughing and cleared his throat but didn't bring up any fluid, and he was left a bit winded afterward. It was odd, that dry shortness of breath. He didn't seem to have any of the accompanying mucus and watery congestion that was usually symptomatic of a cold. Not even a runny nose. It was as if he'd sucked in a handful of plaster dust and couldn't expel it from his lungs.

He cast a guarded look over at Julia's back porch, afraid she might have heard his latest hack attack. Fortunately, though, she was busy with the tuna and swordfish steaks on her gas grill. When Ashley had called to report that she'd been met by her pickup car at the airport, Julia had gotten into an instant rush to prepare dinner. Maybe too great a rush. The drive from San Jose International would take about an hour in light traffic, and on Sundays, Highway 1 ordinarily became crammed with bumper-to-bumper mall-goers. This close to Thanksgiving, you could count on it. Much as he was anxious to see his wife, Gordian estimated they had a good forty minutes before she arrived, and Julia knew the Bay Area traffic situation as well as anyone. Besides, Ashley would want to relax for a while before eating dinner.

Gordian sighed. Call him oversensitive, but he thought Julia's glued attention to the barbecue seemed an excuse for her utter and deliberate *in*attention to him. Whatever was bothering his daughter, her emotional state was always best revealed by her attempts to conceal it, to appear calmly preoccupied with her chores and projects, to veer off on her own and peripheralize everything and everyone around her. It was an exasperating quality Gordian found easy to recognize, given that the river from whence it flowed happened to bear his name, first and last.

Unfortunately, recognizing it didn't mean he had the vaguest idea how to deal with it. On the one hand, he didn't like being ignored during what he'd hoped would be a chance for some father-daughter bonding, to paraphrase Ashley. On the other, he didn't want Julia regarding him so closely that she'd detect he was less than the picture of health. Was there no happy medium?

He stood there looking across the yard at the house, and after a few moments became aware that Jack and Jill seemed to be compensating for their mother's cold-shoulder routine. *Nice doggies.* Leashed to the porch rail a cautious distance from any edibles, they had fixated on him in their high-strung and illimitably questioning way, their ears cocked in his direction like swivel antennas, their eyes penny brown circles of curiosity. Gordian had once heard somebody refer to the breed as "pushbutton dogs" because of their habit of lying perfectly still and silent for hours on end, comically anxious as they watched their owners tend to their business, only to snap onto all fours with a spring-loaded, running bound when it was time to be fed or walked. And while the term had been used with affection, he'd been distressed to learn this peculiar behavior came from years of being cooped in racetrack kennels that barely allowed them the room to stand or turn, let alone interact with other dogs. As a consequence, they became social miscasts, insecure about their status, never quite able to tell what was expected of them or how to behave. And so they kept their constant watch, waiting for reassurance, all bottled energy.

Sad, Gordian thought. But thanks to the greyhound rescue people and Julia, things had vastly changed for them. And would change even more for those particular greyhounds when their corral was built and they could gallop around outdoors to their hearts' content.

He turned, ready for his next go at the fence. The pile of forty boards he'd set out for himself this morning had dwindled to a mere ten spread neatly across the grass. Now that today's section had started to take definite shape, he could scarcely wait to get the rest of them up.

Gordian was stooping to lift an armload of boards when the lightheadedness washed over him again. He flashed hot and cold. His heart fluttered irregularly, then began to pound.

He took several deep breaths. The gritty rattle in his throat wasn't any comfort, but he soon grew steadier and felt the pounding in his chest subside.

Within seconds, the spell was over. Gordian knelt on the lawn, his head clear again. Still, he couldn't keep on like this. He would have to get himself checked out. He'd call the doctor tomorrow morning, try to squeeze in an appointment for the same day. He was confident as ever that he wasn't suffering from anything more serious than a nasty cold. Maybe a touch of the flu. But it couldn't just be disregarded ad infinitum.

He glanced over at the porch. Julia remained involved with her cuts of fish, shifting and flipping them over the flame with her spatula. She hadn't noticed his little episode. Good. He'd pretty much recovered and was thinking he could mount the rest of the boards in twenty minutes, tops. Close that space. Then he'd quit. Grab one of those lawn chairs, relax in the sunshine. And wait for Ash.

He gathered half the siding boards on the ground, carried them to the fence posts where he'd be working, and squatted to get the lowermost board in place. Then he took the drill from his holster, checked to see that the screwdriver bit was firmly in the chuck, pulled his goggles over his eyes, and reached into his pouch for a screw.

His power tool slugged the screw into the wood easily, its fat motor startling the birds out of a nearby tree with its racket.

The board went on without a snag. Gordian reached for the next one, positioned it, and was about to squeeze the drill's trigger switch when he heard Julia calling him: "Dad!"

He looked over his shoulder and saw her approaching across the lawn. She was outfitted in black capri pants, espadrilles, and a sleeveless blue midriff blouse that precisely matched the color of her eyes. And Gordian's eyes as well, though it was not something he noticed at that moment.

What he was noticing was the tight, controlled expression on her face. The overdone casualness of her stride.

He braced himself as she reached him.

"Time for a break. We'll be eating soon," she said in a flat, clipped tone.

"Hey Dad, you're doing a fantastic job!" Gordian thought. *"I couldn't have expected better from a professional carpenter!"*

He raised his goggles and regarded her from his crouch.

"I'm almost finished with this side of the corral," he said. "Your mother hasn't even arrived yet . . ."

She shrugged. "I thought maybe you'd want to wash up before she gets here."

"You're the greatest, Dad! I love you! Jack and Jill love you! We all love you like mad! I honestly don't know what we'd do without you being around!"

Gordian tried not to look set upon. He felt a burr in his throat and cleared it to stave off a cough.

"Her car just left the airport half an hour ago, and you can imagine what the roads are like today," he said, wondering if his voice sounded as weak and croaky as it seemed. "We should have plenty of time . . ."

Her gaze flogged him.

"Okay," she said. "Whatever."

Baffled, Gordian watched her turn away and walk

back toward the house. It struck him to call after her, ask her to help him understand the nature of his current transgression, but he thought it might just provoke an argument. He decided the wisest thing to do was concentrate on his undertaking, keep his distance, and maintain a frail peace until Ashley arrived.

Gordian managed that with considerable success. He attached the rest of the boards he'd carried from the shrinking pile and then brought over the five that were left, all without getting into knots about Julia's inexplicable attitude.

Then he was on his last board. He aligned it between the posts with a swell of anticipation and squeezed the trigger of the drill. It whined to life in his hand—

And then the dizziness overtook him in a surge that almost spilled Gordian off his feet. He staggered drunkenly, his gorge heaving into his throat, rancid and scalding. His vision went gray around the edges, and then the grayness spread over everything, and he felt his body go loose, the drill jolting in his right hand. He experienced a hot, piercing pain in his opposite hand an instant before releasing his grip on the power tool's trigger. Just as the gray turned to black, he saw a bright splash of redness gush from the burning spot from the wandering drill bit.

"Dad!"

Julia. Calling him from somewhere at a distance. Her tone of voice so different than it had been only minutes before.

"Dad, Daddy, oh no, *oh my God, DADDY—*"

Lost in darkness, spinning in a whirlpool of darkness, he felt every part of himself melting away, turning to liquid, rushing into the ground.

It's all right, hon, please don't sound so scared, Gordian thought he heard himself say.

In fact, the words never had a chance to leave his mouth.

FOURTEEN

SAN DIEGO, CALIFORNIA
NOVEMBER 14, 2001

THE BODY OF FELIX QUIROS DID NOT QUITE GO TO
the rodents. Nor was it exactly found by other members
of the Quiros clan.

His executioner would later be amused to hear that
they split the difference.

First cousins to one another, third cousins to Felix on
opposite sides of his lineage, foremen at his auto salvage
yard, and low-level functionaries in the criminal family
business, Cesar and Jorge were far from quick to attach
his three-day absence from the yard to the notion that
any harm had come to him, and even slower to associate
it with the scuttling, scratching noise they heard down
the aisle of junkers.

Every so often, Felix would shoot down across the
border to those Tijuana bars where the young *putas*
came three for the price of one, bring them to a hotel
room, turn them on to some dope or ecstasy, get fucked
up, and drop out of sight for days on end. Cesar and
Jorge were well aware of his bad habits and guessed they

had been the guys taking care of the scrapyard's daily operations ever since Enrique handed it to Felix in an attempt to give him a firm set of responsibilities and keep him from running into trouble, but he'd kept on doing it anyway. Just let him get his hands on a little cash, and you could count on him going no-show until he'd blown every cent of it looking for degenerate kicks.

Felix was here, he wasn't here, Cesar and Jorge didn't think it was of much consequence either way. They knew about their own obligations. They had the keys and entry combinations to every part of the scrapyard and usually found that it was less trouble to manage things without his high-hat bullshit. When he'd asked them to participate in that score connected with the Salazars' goods from Mexico, they'd told him he was a maniac and refused. Because Felix was the illegitimate son of Enrique's sister, Cesar and Jorge kept from voicing their opinions of him except between themselves, though the pair had a strong feeling that whatever they thought about the twit was hardly anything that wouldn't have occurred to his uncle a hundred times, and that nobody would have faulted them too much for anything they said. Still, you had to observe certain proprieties.

When Cesar finally noticed the sounds at around noon, it barely aroused his interest. A dumping ground like this, acre upon acre littered with decaying vehicles filled with half-eaten hot dogs, burritos, candy bars, Twinkies, ice cream cones, soft drink containers, and other rotting trash people left inside them, a place like this was home to every sort of creature you could name. And then some. After a while, you didn't actually have to see them to know which ones were nearby. You could identify them just by the sounds they made.

That scratchy rustle, Cesar immediately knew it was a sign of rats. Some people, ones who didn't have the same experience with them as Cesar, who didn't spend as much of their goddamn lives around them as Cesar, thought they mainly came out at night, but here in the yard you could expect them to appear at any hour of the day. You got used to them being nuisances, used to seeing them dart between the cars, used to hearing them scavenge for food. They'd crawl in through broken windows or holes in the undercarriages, even climb into the trunks and chew through the upholstery of the backseats to enter the junkers. Bring an egg sandwich from the luncheonette for breakfast, a gray, ugly fucker that was bigger and meaner than a Chihuahua was liable to catch a whiff, come right out into the open, right into your trailer or shed if there was a space wide enough for it to crawl through. Sit there staring at you with the shiny beads of its eyes like it expected you to hand over the food. At a certain point, Cesar and Jorge had got to chucking empty beer and soda cans at the rats to scare them away, but some were so bold they'd stay right where they were unless you caught them smack in the head, rearing up on their hind legs, baring their white needle teeth like they were daring you to take another pitch, give it your goddamn best. Finally, Jorge started shooting them on sight when they got too close . . . and not with a BB gun, either. Jorge, he'd hit them with rounds from his nine mil, *bam, bam, bam.* Said that someday he would come in with an Uzi and chop away at the bastards until every last one was blown to pieces.

So it didn't seem exceptional at first, that sound. This was a little after twelve noon, maybe eighty degrees out, a warm day for November, the sun baking straight down on the wrecks to recook the spoiled food and crap inside them, raising a stink into the air that got the rats salivating. You could spend the rest of the day trying to scatter them, banging new dents into the already battered auto bodies with bats and crowbars, risk getting bitten if you weren't careful. And for what good reason?

Bearing this in mind, Cesar was initially inclined to overlook the *skritch-scratch* of their claws and the gnawing of their teeth, having been headed toward the office trailer for the phone number of this guy who repaired the heavy equipment, wanting to call him down to look at a forklift that had gone kaput.

But then he'd hesitated and found himself turning toward the noise. No question, a lot of rats were making it. Very definitely a whole lot. It gave him the creeps, thinking about them teeming somewhere just out of sight behind the wall of cars. Maybe some other kind of animal had wandered into the yard and dropped dead. A bird, a cat, a fucking coyote, Christ only knew. It had happened in the past, and what you wanted to do in that case was clean things out, torch the car if need be, or before you knew it, a whole section of the yard would be swarming with all kinds of vermin. Worms, flies, maggots, a disgusting situation.

So what Cesar had done was reach into his pocket for his flip phone, buzz Jorge over at the recycling plant, and tell him to haul ass over with his niner.

It took him maybe ten minutes to show, a crowbar in his hand, his pistol in a belt holster under his hanging shirttails. And when he did, Jorge agreed Cesar's feelings were merited.

"Sounds to me like there's a *lot* of goddamn rats back there," he'd said, and passed the crowbar to Cesar. "Better clean it out or we gonna have some kind of infestation."

Which was, of course, almost word for word what Cesar himself had been thinking.

The noise leading them forward, they inched their way between twisted front panels, jutting bumpers, partially unhinged doors, and fallen wheel covers. It was like being inside an oven here, heat shimmers above the stacked auto bodies. The scratching was very loud, and you could hear the rats squealing excitedly. And the *stink,* Jesus, that odor of broiling garbage was enough to make Cesar's stomach clench.

Suddenly Jorge grabbed his shoulder and steered him to the right. He had his gun in his free hand and was pointing it at the back of an old Buick sedan.

But Cesar had already seen the rats. There had to be dozens of them. Fat ones with pale, slopping bellies that dragged underneath them. Smaller ones not much larger than mice. They were squirming over, under, and around the trunk. Crowding on its closed lid, climbing on each other's backs, a frenzied jumble. They did not seem to notice the two men. Or maybe they were too worked up to care about them.

A sound of horror and disgust wringing from his throat, Jorge swung his pistol downward and pumped three rounds into the carpet of rats on the ground. Cesar saw a rat explode as it flopped into the air. The rest that had been clustered near the rear wheels and bumper went scrambling away, but a few of them still clung to the trunk lid, pawing at its flaked, peeling finish.

Jorge raised the gun and fired. Another burst of fur, blood, and guts. Something warm splashed Cesar's cheek, and he winced with aversion. And then the rats were springing from the trunk, tumbling from it, scattering in every direction.

"We gotta see what's inside!" Jorge yelled, his face sweaty, gesticulating at the trunk with his niner.

The crowbar against his thigh, Cesar stepped reluctantly toward the Buick. He glimpsed a hairless tail slip out of sight under its chassis, shuddered, and stopped.

"Yo, c'mon, open the fuckin' thing!"

Cesar nodded without saying anything. He worked the flat end of the steel bar under the trunk lid between the latch and corroded rubber weatherstripping. Then he pushed down on the crowbar with both hands, using his full weight for leverage.

It took very little prying to disengage the trunk's rusted latch. The lid popped creakily.

The stench that rose with the moist, warm air that had been trapped inside was sickening. Cesar gagged and clapped his palm over his nose and mouth. Then Jorge reached across his chest and pushed the lid open the rest of the way.

They stared into the compartment as another blast of foulness gusted over them.

The corpse was saturated in a reddish stew of blood and other juices. Its clothes were gummy, and the fluids had seeped into the trunk's lining. Cesar and Jorge saw a pale hand, a bloated stomach under the scrunched-up shirt and jacket.

Two large rats had managed to burrow through to the compartment. They withdrew their smeared, gummy snouts from inside what was left of the skull and squinted out into the bright daylight.

The dead man might not have been recognizable except for his clothes. The same familiar clothes he'd been wearing when they'd last seen him.

Their eyes wide, Cesar and Jorge exchanged a glance of shared incredulity.

Felix Quiros's whereabouts had been discovered, and Tijuana this sure as hell wasn't.

Blood for blood. That was how he felt it had to be.

Enrique Quiros sat alone in the San Diego office with the words Golden Triangle Services fronting the outer hallway, his designer glasses folded in his shirt pocket, elbows propped on his desk. He was leaning forward into his hands, eyes closed, the balls of his palms pressed against their lids.

Never in his life had he felt so tired.

It had been an hour since he'd returned from the salvage yard and seen the ghastly remains of his nephew. Dumped inside that trunk. Packed into that trunk with his own blood. And the smell. It seemed to linger in Enrique's nostrils even now, so strong it was almost a taste at the back of his tongue. In his car driving back downtown, he had found an unopened roll of breath mints and popped one after another into his mouth, chewing each in seconds, crushing them between his teeth. That hadn't helped. He'd stood by the car just briefly. A minute or less. But he thought the stench of Felix's decomposing flesh would stay with him for a very long time to come.

Head in hands, he massaged his eyes. On the desktop near his right arm was a small leather case that he had withdrawn from a concealed safe elsewhere in the office suite. Inside it was a plastic ampule and a wrapped, sterile syringe. His reward from *El Tío* for having relayed a matching kit to Palardy, and a sure means for revenge against the man culpable for his nephew's death.

Although Enrique was not a scientist, he had a solid layman's understanding of the incredible biological weapon he'd been given. The clear liquid sealed inside the ampule was a neutral, harmless medium for transport and administration of the microscopic capsules suspended within. But a single drop held a concentration of hundreds, perhaps thousands of microcapsules. And since each of those capsules was a tiny bomblet packed with trigger proteins that would allow the Sleeper virus infecting every human being to "awaken," that drop would be sufficiently potent to kill the target of an attack many times over. All that was required for the virus to mutate into its lethal form, attach itself to a specific genetic feature, and amplify, was its victim having a sip of water that had been implanted with the trigger, a bite of food, . . . or, Enrique thought darkly, a mint of the sort he'd been crunching down in the car.

And the fluid medium was only one among many methods of getting a trigger into the human body. If your desire was to take out a single individual, you could introduce it to whatever he was having for lunch. If you wanted to be rid of his family as well, you might inject their Thanksgiving turkey before the holiday dinner. Widen the bull's-eye to include a larger group of people, and you'd distribute the trigger across a sweeping number of routes. Instead of the food on the table you could saturate an entire population's food supply—and beyond. Spread it over their farm soil, dump it into their reservoirs, float it through the air they breathed. Turn their environment into an extension of your weapon.

Enrique supposed the release of a powdered or aerosol

medium would give the best shot at effecting a mass exposure. In fact, he had heard El Tío had done exactly that with the Sleeper virus itself. Just as whispers had reached him that Alberto Colón, who had died from mysterious causes last month, was El Tío's first pigeon to die from a precision bio-strike.

Enrique had little doubt that the rumors concerning the virus's dissemination were true. Whether those about Colón were accurate, he didn't know. But it seemed a novel coincidence that the Bolivian president-elect had been poised to threaten the South American coca growers and suppliers from whom El Tío's distribution network—of which the Quiros family was a part—obtained the majority of its product.

Right now, however, Enrique had something else to occupy his thoughts. A very personal affair had to be settled. And though he was inclined to stick with his initial feelings about how to do it, he wanted to deliberate on them further, confirm that he wasn't allowing himself to make a dangerous blunder.

The difficulty now was that he was used to making calculated, rational decisions when it came to business. But in his business, things weren't always that clear. Actions might be rational and emotional without contradiction. Violence could send simultaneous, definitive messages to both the heart and brain. And there were traditions that must not be violated. Matters of honor and loyalty.

He pictured Felix in the trunk of that car. His head blown to pieces and gnawed by rats. His flesh cooking in a soup of his own blood.

An effective message right there.

Enrique lifted his head from his hands, straightened,

slipped his glasses back on, and sat quietly staring at the wall. The poor, brainless kid had overstepped. His stunt had hit the Salazars where it hurt. What choice did Lucio have except to retaliate? Enrique and his people had been aggressively cutting into his market, and because Lucio knew they were backed by El Tío's international organization, he'd had to accept it, become resigned to shrinking profits. Success brought competition; it was a basic law of trade. However, he would not let himself be muscled aside, could not allow everything he'd built up to be usurped. He had to protect his interests. And if Lucio believed Enrique had condoned Felix's move, as Lathrop said he did, he would be especially pressed to show it was a big miscalculation. Show where he drew his limits. Show a steep price had to be paid by the transgressor of those limits.

Enrique understood this. He appreciated that Felix had brought about his own fate with his deeds. And in a way, he'd also dictated the steps Enrique now must take, irrevocably linked him to a chain of action and consequence whose end could not be foreseen. Even in his sorrow over what had happened to Felix, Enrique resented him for that. And he suspected he always would. Were it not for him, this whole thing would never have gotten started.

But Felix had been his nephew. He could not let Lucio Salazar get away with his murder. Because it would make the Quiros family look vulnerable and invite further trouble, despite their powerful affiliations. And family was supposed to look after each other.

Enrique glanced down at the leather case on his desk, remembering the night he'd met Palardy at the harbor. To be involved in the assassination of somebody with

Roger Gordian's fame and stature, even if his connection couldn't be verifiably established . . . it was insane. There again, his hand had been forced. He'd had to play along with El Tío, knowing very well that his almighty friend might otherwise become his most formidable enemy.

He scowled. To a greater or lesser extent, maybe all actions you took were predetermined. He didn't know. He wasn't a philosopher. But what he did know was that Felix's killing demanded retribution, and that the contents of the ampule would ensure it was achieved. A drop of it, one drop administered to the food or drink Lucio Salazar was renowned for consuming with boundless passion, and the Sleeper inside him would begin its ferocious process of incubation. Disease would rage through his body, eating away his cells and tissues like the hungry little creatures in that old Pac-Man game. His suffering would make death a craved relief. And Enrique would have full deniability. Moreover, only the merest few would even suspect Lucio had been murdered.

But how would it send a message? How would it demonstrate that Enrique Quiros—college-educated, soft-spoken Enrique—had the qualities to control and build upon the empire he'd inherited from his father? That he was a man who stood on his honor and loyalty? A man who could conduct himself with strength?

Blood for blood. In his world, that was how it had to be. It was a principle that was understood from the brothers and sons who would be Lucio Salazar's successors, down the line to his street-level dealers and enforcers.

Lucio could not die in bed of some untraceable sickness.

If Enrique was to be respected, his hands would have to drip red.

Taking a deep breath, he turned his eyes from the leather case and reached across his desk for the telephone.

Lucio Salazar's wristwatch read ten minutes past two in the afternoon when he received an unexpected and somewhat puzzling telephone call from Enrique Quiros.

Their conversation, such as it was, lasted just over sixty seconds.

A pensive frown on his face, Salazar replaced the receiver on the end table beside him. Then he sat back in his couch, turning his head to look out at the rippling blue surf far below, his hand moving from the cradled receiver to the large gold charm around his neck.

He was thinking that this was maybe the third time they had exchanged words since Enrique had taken over the family operation from his father, their last direct contact having occurred the year before, when they had gotten together to smooth over a territorial dispute between a couple of their lieutenants. At the time, he'd expected Enrique to assume airs, him having gone to that top college and all, but it turned out he'd been reasonable and respectful. Well, okay, sort of lacy, too, but he hadn't come up the hard way like his old man, dodging lawmen on both sides of the border with carloads of bootleg whiskey and cigarettes. Most important to Lucio, he'd conducted himself okay, showed integrity, before and after. They had reached a compromise agreement that satisfied everyone involved, cemented it with a handshake, and Enrique had observed it to the letter. Since then—this was *over* a year ago now, you wanted to be accurate—there hadn't been any problems between them, except for a few minor bumps and bounces they'd settled through intermediaries. Not until his prick nephew Felix had jacked Lucio's shipment of black tar and slaughtered his people outside that fucking tunnel.

Lucio fingered his charm, a representation of Saint Joseph, patron of workingmen and heads of families— categories he very much fancied encompassed his position in the great order of things.

On the phone, Enrique had said he wanted to go man-to-man, resolve their problems before they got any further out of hand, turned into a crisis that damaged their relations beyond repair. Meet at Balboa Park over by that reflecting pond in the Spanish City two nights from now, neutral ground, a public place where they'd be free to talk without worrying about bugs or taps. He'd suggested they bring their guards to keep lookout, not bothering to elaborate, which would have been tactless. Obviously, guards would be a precaution against any surveillance the law enforcement community might have going on one or both of them, but the foremost reason for his suggestion was to dispel any concerns Salazar might harbor about the meet being a setup of some kind.

And that had been it. No mention of why Enrique was suddenly anxious to reverse the course toward war that he himself had set or how he planned to compensate the Salazars for their losses. This had raised Lucio's eyebrows. Even if Enrique assumed the reason for the meet was clear and preferred getting into details about it in person at the sit-down, some stated acknowledgment that a grievous wrong had been committed had been due. And although the omission had not elicited any comment from Lucio, he'd tucked it away in a mental back pocket as he'd accepted Enrique's proposition.

Night after next, Balboa Park, eleven o'clock sharp. You got it.

And they'd hung up.

His face lined with thought now, Lucio continued to gaze out at the satiny water beyond the strand edging the Del Mar cliffs, his hand tugging away at his Saint Joseph pendant.

He would keep his appointment at the park. Absolutely. He'd given his word that he would attend, and it would be to the mutual benefit of their families to reach a settlement and resume their activities without battling around. But that did not mean he was about to make a mark of himself. If Enrique had a razor blade in the casserole, he intended be prepared, bring along a few surprises of his own. There were still two days until the meet, two days for him to conduct some research, do whatever possible to gain some insights into what was happening inside Enrique's camp, get the lowdown on whether he might have a hidden agenda. And it only made sense that the first step in his investigation should be to contact Mr. Lowdown himself.

Grabbing the phone off the table again, he set it on his lap, lifted the receiver, and hit the speed dial button that would put him in touch with Lathrop.

FIFTEEN

LATE MONDAY AFTERNOON, ROGER GORDIAN LAY asleep in his room at San Jose Mercy Hospital, having been given a series of physical examinations, blood tests, and chest X rays throughout the earlier part of the day. At four P.M. on Sunday, he had been transported to the hospital aboard an ambulance, accompanied by his daughter, Julia Gordian Ellis, after losing consciousness in the backyard of her Pescadero residence. When the emergency vehicle appeared in response to her frantic 911, Gordian had a fever of 102.7°, was suffering from dehydration, and had lost several ounces of blood from a superficial wound to his left hand inflicted by the power tool he had been using at the time of his blackout.

The medical technicians aboard the ambulance were able to control the bleeding and dress his injury on scene, and they administered oxygen and an electrolyte IV, which revived him during his transport to the hospital. Gordian was fully awake and alert upon reaching the ER, where he was joined by his wife, who had been contacted via her mobile phone by Julia while en route to Pescadero from San Jose International Airport.

At that time, Gordian's temperature remained elevated, and he was experiencing respiratory difficulties, a painful sore throat, abdominal pains, nausea, muscle aches, and chills. An initial examination by interns on rotation led them to a preliminary diagnosis of influenza and stress due to overexertion. In spite of his repeated insistence that he was fit enough to be discharged and recover at home, the severity of his symptoms led doctors to suggest that he be admitted for routine monitoring and testing, a recommendation to which he eventually acquiesced at the strong urging of his family members.

Within an hour of his arrival at the ER, Gordian was moved to a private room on the hospital's fifth floor. As was standard procedure for high-profile individuals, hospital security offered him the option of registering under an alias to deflect attention by ambulance- and celebrity-chasing reporters. Though he was disinclined to accept this preferential treatment, his wife and daughter prevailed upon him to reconsider and finally got him to capitulate with reminders of his past unhappiness with the media, striking a particular nerve by mentioning the outrageous factual distortions of Reynold Armitage, the financial columnist and television commentator with an unknown ax to grind who had been unduly eager to pronounce UpLink International DOA in the middle of a shareholder's crisis the year before, and who might be expected to jump at the chance to write Roger Gordian's premature obituary if word of his illness leaked to the press.

On Ashley's recommendation, the door sign beside room 5C would read: *Hardy, Frank*.

By Monday morning, Gordian's fever had lowered to 101° and he was feeling stronger, though his breathing continued to be strained and he showed little desire for food. His standardized physician's treatment sheet—known by the memory key ABC/DAVID to every fourth-year medical student, physician's aid, and registered nurse—listed his condition as stable on its third line, between the *Admit to:* and *Diet* information. The next line (*A* for *Activity*) had a check mark in front of the words *Bed Rest*. Blood and sputum samples were ordered in the space that read *Studies* and *Lab* on this particular hospital's form (synonymous with *Intake and Output* in the next-to-last line of the trainee's mnemonic). The final line, listed as *Medications* (i.e., *D* for *Drugs*), called for a moderate dosage of acetaminophen every four hours pending the lab results, which were not expected to return positive for anything more severe than the flu.

At 8:30 A.M. sharp, Ashley and Julia arrived to visit, Julia leaving at 10 o'clock to attend a meeting at the fashion design firm where she'd recently been hired as a public relations consultant, Ashley staying on until Gordian shooed her home at noon with reassurances that he was doing fine—though she made a point of reassuring him that, fine or not, he could count on seeing her again by dinnertime.

Around three in the afternoon, Gordian's attending nurse came to take his temperature, pulse, and blood pressure readings, give him his prescribed Tylenol capsules, and scribble something on his chart. A few minutes afterward, he became groggy and let himself doze off for a while.

At four P.M., as Gordian slept on the fifth floor, a

nurse on station duty two floors below briefly left her desk for the ladies' room. The moment she did, a man in the crisp white uniform of an orderly entered the station from where he had been drifting near a supply closet, treading quietly in crepe-soled shoes.

Keeping an eye out for the nurse, he pointed-and-clicked through several menus on her computer and retrieved the bed assignment information on all patients admitted in the past twenty-four hours. He could have chosen to use any of the networked unit computers at any station in any ward in the building. This was simply a convenient opening; amid the constant movement of a busy hospital, he would have had no trouble finding others.

Seconds later, the data on the patient in room 5C appeared on the computer, minus his falsified name.

Returning to the opening screen, the man left the nurse's station and strode along the hall until he found a small, unoccupied patients' lounge and entered it. There he slipped a wireless phone from his pocket and placed a call on a digitally encoded line.

"He's here," he said into the mouthpiece.

The bottleneck elevator rose from the upper sublevel and opened to release him with a pneumatic sigh. Emerging into the corridor, he turned to the right and walked past high-security doors marked with signs for the laboratories in the connecting hallways behind them. Some displayed the universal biohazard symbol at eye level, their red-and-black trefoil pattern conspicuous against the surrounding grayness.

He carried himself lightly for a man of his muscular proportions, and this partially went to explain the dead silence of his progress down the hall. But as the fluorescent panels overhead neutralized shading and shadow with their suffused radiance, so did the thick concrete walls seem to dampen sound, flatten color, deduct from between them all except the essential and functional.

While the drab work environment required varying degrees of acclimatization from most of the personnel who spent their days and nights physically isolated even from the outlying northern wilderness, Siegfried Kuhl found it to his decided liking. There was a sense of impregnable weight and austerity that suited him. But he felt something beyond that, an unseen force. On occasion, he would put his two hands against a wall and feel the strong vibrational pulse of machinery behind it, the pumping of compressed-air streams to microencapsulation chambers and "space suits" in the Level 4 laminar flow enclosures underground. At such times Kuhl imagined himself to be touching a hard womb of stone, the life forms within seething and twisting in furious gestation.

Kuhl advanced through the hall, men and women in surgical scrubs moving singly and in groups toward the laboratory entrances on either side of him. Comparable in his mind to Los Alamos at its inception, this was the only facility of its type on earth, at the frontier of the development and mass production of biological weapons—of which the Sleeper virus was the current acme. Its operations covered every stage of the pathogen's creation from genomic analysis and DNA splicing to its cultivation, stabilization, and chemical encoating. The microbe's trigger mechanism additionally required the concurrent and coordinated applications of protein and molecular engineering processes. And experimentation to refine the virus continued with the goals of accelerating its lethal progression within the target host or hosts, increasing its resistance to potential cures and inoculations, and addressing the need for variant strains that would provide buyers with widened options, allowing them to select from among diverse packages of symptoms.

There was still work, much work, to be done before perfection was achieved.

Now Kuhl reached a reinforced steel door that divided the corridor beyond from the rest of the building. No signs marked the entry. He put his hand against its intelligent push plate and paused for his subcutaneous vascular patterns to be IR scanned and matched against a binary file image in an allied database.

A millisecond later, a green indicator light flashed on. Then the vaultlike door swung inward without a sound as the flow of current to the armature of its electromagnetic lock was briefly interrupted.

Kuhl entered a short passage. He was alone here. The walls to his left and right were featureless, the door to the single office at the passage's opposite end made of dark, heavy wood. Its knob was of gleaming brass.

He went to the door and waited. There was no need to announce himself. The biometric scanner that had allowed him into the hallway would have identified him to the office's occupant, and his approach would have been monitored with hidden cameras.

A moment later, the door opened, Harlan DeVane standing on the other side, his hand on the polished brass handle, wearing a white shirt, white tie, and custom-tailored black suit of perfect outline that might have been stenciled onto his bony frame.

"Siegfried, come in," he said, and motioned him inside with a flick of his pale, thin hand. "You'll be pleased to hear the news I've received about Roger Gordian."

Back at Salazar's palatial house by the sea, Lathrop was enjoying himself tremendously.

Facing Lucio across the room, watching his expression go in stages from astonishment to acceptance to resentful anger, he couldn't have said whether the greater kick came from a regard for his own expert connivance or the reaction it had instigated.

Six of one, he thought.

He sat looking out at the breathtaking view of the sea and waited for Lucio to digest what he'd been told.

"Okay," Lucio said at length. "Help me be sure I've got this right. A step at a time. Because you threw me for a loop here, and a whole lot depends on me not misunderstanding you."

Lathrop nodded.

"First off, you're saying absolutely Felix is dead. You're sure there's no mixup it's him they found in that car trunk."

"Couldn't be surer," Lathrop said, poker-faced.

"Now, second, you can confirm it was Enrique who killed him—"

"Ordered him killed," Lathrop corrected.

"Ordered his own nephew killed. Because Felix was holding out on the profits from the load he swiped from me."

"It's a little more involved," Lathrop said. "Everybody tolerates some skimming. But Felix was greedy. Claimed he was the one who did the tunnel boost, took all the risks, and deserved to keep every cent of the earnings. Bragging about it to anybody who could warm a barstool next to him. And that was only the last straw. He was running hustles left and right, and it was common knowledge he was on the pipe. Getting crazier and crazier. Becoming a major embarrassment."

Lucio shrugged. "Was me looking to burn the competition, steal their goods, I wouldn't have trusted the kid with the job. But say I'm Enrique, and I do, and then hear he's spending my percentage. Being family, I talk to him direct. Let him know he's making a big mistake and better get on track."

"Enrique did that plenty of times. He called Felix in last week to give him one more chance. And instead of apologizing to Enrique, offering him a percentage of the take from the hijack, Felix told him to shove his grievances where the sun doesn't shine."

"Stupid," Lucio said and shook his head.

"Yeah."

"Took *cajones,* though."

"Yeah. But dumb and ballsy can be a bad combination."

Lucio was thoughtful.

"Let's get to the next step," he said, shifting his large frame on his wine-colored sofa cushions. "Enrique decides enough is enough. Sees the kid isn't afraid of him. Sees he can't be disciplined. So he's gotta go. That on the mark?"

Lathrop nodded.

"Lousy position," Salazar said. "Felix being his nephew."

"Which is the reason he's been claiming it was *your* family that had Felix scrubbed," Lathrop said. "Like I

233

told you before, Enrique's story to his sister is that the Magi of Tijuana held a conference across the border about how to handle the problem of the tunnel boost. According to him, you'd already planned the hit to make an example of Felix but wanted a vote of confidence from your brothers before moving ahead."

Lucio seemed affronted.

"That don't even make sense," he said. "I want the kid taken out, I'm gonna be damn sure his body disappears permanent. The way Felix was living, it could've been weeks before anybody figured he wasn't off on some fucking jag."

Lathrop looked out the window, appreciating the expansive view of the sea without end.

"Enrique's head of the family," he said. "His sister admires him. She believes what he tells her."

"But I'd have to be *tonto,* an idiot, to order a dump job that leaves Felix in a car in his own place of business."

"She's not in the life. She probably doesn't know how things work. Or if she does, she could be too overcome with grief to think that clearly about it. All I can say is he convinced her you're responsible, and now she's demanding that he retaliate."

Lucio was shaking his head again.

"This would be funny, if it wasn't so incredible," he said. "Enrique has Felix steal my shit. Kill my people. Then they have a falling out over revenue from the hijack. Enrique does Felix, fingers me to his sister as a scapegoat. She tells him I have to die for whacking her son. Next, I get a phone call from Enrique, who says he wants to meet. Work out our problems. And I agree to it. Figuring maybe he's realized he made a mistake and wants to offer reparations. But his real purpose is to do *me* now." He thumbed his chest. "I'm going about my thing, not stepping on anybody's toes, and Enrique's trying to make me a victim twice over."

Lathrop looked at him. The yarn *was* quite a nifty little twister.

"This isn't just about Enrique satisfying his sister," he said as a finishing touch. "You have to remember where and how this started. The tunnel job was a message. He absolutely means to shove you out of California and knows he has El Tío's fist behind him. Felix was a marionette when he was alive, and now that he's dead, Enrique's still using him as a prop for his act."

Lucio scowled with contempt.

"El Tío," he said. "Everything's disorder since he's come into the picture. Fucking *disorder*."

Lathrop said nothing.

Lucio sat there sucking his front teeth for a while. When he leaned forward on the couch, Lathrop was amused to notice the back of the cushion underneath him lift high off the springs from his ample weight.

"You got anything else?"

"That's it."

Lucio sucked his teeth some more.

"All right, Lathrop. You're the best. And you can count on this tip being worth a nice bonus," he said. "As far as how it goes between me and Enrique, we'll see which of us is the fucking idiot two nights from now at the park."

Lathrop nodded.

It did indeed promise to be an interesting showdown, and he fully looked forward to being ringside.

• • •

"It is interesting how we measure our accomplishments," DeVane said. "I have many successes behind me, and envision more to come. Widespread ventures that yield abundant rewards. Yet the satisfaction I feel at this moment cannot be reckoned. A single person downed. A problem resolved. I hadn't realized Roger Gordian had gotten quite that deeply under my skin."

Kuhl sat across the desk from him in silence. Behind DeVane, slightly to the left of his chair, was one of the few windows in the entire building, a fixed pane of one-way multilaminate glass able to absorb the impact of a bomb blast or high-powered sniper fire. Perfectly square and soundproof, it somehow imparted a greater sense of separateness from the outlying woodlands than would have been presented by a solid wall. Kuhl saw deer tracks in the snow running toward the white-frocked forest spruces and understood the wild longing of the confined predator to lunge against the glass wall of a zoo or aquarium exhibit, a pull older than anything that could be devised to suppress it. And DeVane didn't fool him. His mannered behavior was embroidery. A wrap he wore as neatly as his expensive suits, and to deliberate effect. But he, too, knew the impulse to strike and taste blood.

"Gordian's condition," Kuhl said. "Were you told of it?"

"He remains among the hospital's general population, which means we can infer that he's still in the early stage," DeVane said. "But the symptoms will progress quickly enough."

Kuhl was without expression.

"I propose that our backups be put in full readiness," he said.

DeVane smiled, his lips flitting back from his small, white teeth.

"Your exactitude is always appreciated," he said. "Yes, I agree, let's surely be prepared for anything."

There was a brief pause. Then DeVane gestured toward the computer station against the wall to his right, its glowing display filled with rows of unopened E-mail messages.

"Along come the trigger orders, even as we sit here," he said. "Multiples in some cases. To no surprise, our Sudanese friend has informed me that he's found a deep well of capital. As have many of his neighbors in the desert. It's enthralling, the eagerness of my clients. Those in the noisy public arenas. Those in solitude. Those who fear differences of ethnicity and morphology. They want greater prestige, greater wealth, a world refashioned under their influence. Or they seek to inflict their internal damage upon mankind, spread the stains of dead loves and passions. Hardly a person to whom I've made my offer isn't groping. And three days from now, they'll all have the opportunity to chop away at each other." Another flit of a smile. "We're in the money, Siegfried. And I have faith that humanity will keep us in it to stay."

Kuhl peered through the thick synthetic glass at a large bird swooping from the conifers.

"Among the buyers are interests in mortal conflict. They represent titanic polarizing forces," he said. "The Sleeper triggers will give them a power of mutual destruction that has been unprecedented in history."

"This concerns you?"

"I don't fear the prospect of harsh change."

DeVane looked at him.

"Ah," he said. "You've wondered about me."

Kuhl nodded. Outside the sealed room, he could see the shadow of the bird's outspread wings create shifting patterns of light and darkness on the rippled carpet of snow.

DeVane formed a cage with his fingers.

"There is a story, a very ancient one, about a child of the god who rode the chariot of the sun across the sky," he said. "It illustrates my way of seeing things."

Kuhl waited. DeVane stared at his finger cage intently, as if to capture his thoughts within it.

"As the tale goes, the son was abandoned by his great and celestial father to struggle on the hard earth with his mother, and did not learn of his paternal heritage until he was on the verge of manhood," he said. "And then his claims were ridiculed. The rejection and denial of all that he was, all the potential within him, caused him unbearable humiliation. So he went to his father's manor. Traveled to the Palace of the Sun to ask the chance to prove his birthright, ride the chariot for a single day." DeVane paused, his face taut around his cheekbones, his gaze fixed on his interlocked fingers. "The father's first reaction was to scorn him. Deny his request. We can imagine he disputed his paternity, refused to acknowledge the youth was of his blood. But the son possessed an inbred strength of will and prevailed. Perhaps he used coercion, blackmail, the threat to reveal an affair his father had long kept hidden from his highborn peers. Who knows? The young man did what was necessary to get what he wanted. A chance. And he climbed aboard the chariot with a thousand warnings. Fly too high and the earth will freeze, drop too low and it will burn. Steer too far to the left or right and the monsters of the void will snatch you with their claws, suck you into the great darkness. These attempts to dissuade the youth only made him more eager to seize the reins and take to the heavens." DeVane returned his eyes to Kuhl, the cold shine of steel in them. "Unfortunately, control of the horses did prove beyond him in the end. They were primal forces, you understand, and he was raised on the soil, dirt under his fingernails. Wherever he passed thundering through the sky, chaos was left in his wake. The countryside was seared with fire. Crops blazed. Ice caps melted to flood great cities. Oceans turned to columns of steam. His whipping, runaway ride shook the world. Chaos. But when, at last, the most powerful of the gods struck him down with a lightning bolt, sent him plunging to the ground in flames, the son went to his death without regret. Because in pursuing his ambition, he'd soared above and beyond the limitations of his origins. Beyond what anyone foresaw for him. Beyond those who'd tried to humble him. He had been audacious, and audacity often has consequences. He'd known it from the beginning. Yet what a run it was, Siegfried. *What a hell of a run.*"

DeVane fell silent. He took a deep breath, unlocked his fingers, leaned slowly backward in his chair. When he next spoke, his voice was calm and quiet.

"Is your curiosity satisfied?" he said.

"Yes."

"Then back to business." DeVane's hands were open on the desk. "Is there anything else we should discuss?"

Kuhl nodded.

"Our recruit in UpLink. The one who administered the trigger to Gordian," he said. "He is weak and faithless."

DeVane shrugged his shoulders. "A small fry swimming out of his depth and poisoned along with the big fish."

"As he must realize by now," Kuhl said. "I ask myself, what if he tries to bite us in his final thrashings?"

DeVane's eyebrows lifted.

"I see," he said. "And you suggest . . ."

"That El Tío have Enrique Quiros put the little creature out of its misery. The sooner the better."

DeVane regarded him with his coldly metallic eyes.

"Your advice is well taken," he said. "I'll contact Enrique."

Kuhl nodded again and rose from his seat. The large, dark bird had flown off, and there was nothing to be seen past the window panel but the hoofprints in the empty whiteness between the building and the great masts of the trees.

He turned, strode toward the door.

"Siegfried."

Kuhl looked over his shoulder. DeVane's eyes were still steady on him.

"You now know much about me," he said.

"Yes."

"As much as anyone living ever will."

"Yes."

DeVane looked at him another moment, then nodded.

Kuhl reached for the doorknob and let himself out of the office.

Sick.

He felt so sick.

Palardy crouched with his head over the john, the bathroom tiles hard against his knees. The taste of acid and nails filled his mouth, and his stomach felt twisted inside out from the repeated vomiting. He'd been at it since Sunday night, losing his half-digested dinner in painful wracking fits. And it had only gotten worse when his stomach was emptied of its solid contents, his spasms going on through the morning, the digestive juices spurting sour and rancid into his throat. And worse still when there was no more bile left in him, when he'd started to dry heave.

Maybe three o'clock in the morning he'd thrown on some clothes, gone down to the twenty-four-hour convenience store for some ginger ale, hoping that might settle him. Twice, three times during the short walk over he'd had to stop, reel toward the curb, and hug a lamppost to keep from losing his feet. But his stomach cramps had been unbearable. And there was the dizziness, the sidewalk seeming to lurch underneath him with every step. It had taken a big piece of forever to get to the store, find the soda, and pay for it, the clerk looking at him like he was a drunkard or a drug addict come to rob the place. Palardy was certain he'd had his hand on something under the counter—an alarm button, a gun, who could tell?—as he'd rung up the sale.

And then the agonizing return to his apartment building. Another small eternity. He'd sat back on his sofa and drunk the soda warm. Taking small sips, figuring his system could tolerate a little at a time.

Palardy supposed that was when he'd first noticed his sore throat. Could be it had been developing gradually throughout the night. Maybe he'd have felt it sooner if his stomach hadn't been in constant throes. But it was pretty inflamed, and he doubted it could have gotten that bad all at once. His tonsils felt as big as thumbs, and he had trouble swallowing. And he'd felt these lumps on either side of his neck; he guessed they were swollen glands.

Drinking that soda had itself been an ordeal. And ultimately, it was for nothing. The trip to the deli, his slow, careful sipping, for nothing. The ginger ale had jetted from him in a fountain before he could make it to the bathroom, spilling over his hands, onto the upholstery, onto the carpet. Bubbles of soda mixed with spit and phlegm.

After that, Palardy hadn't tried to swallow anything, liquid or solid.

Sick, he was so god-awful sick. A few minutes ago, he'd thought his guts would tear themselves apart, come squeezing out of him in bloody nuggets. Those dry, ratcheting heaves, his whole body hurt from them. His back and sides as much as his stomach. Jesus. And the way his heart was beating right now, slamming against his ribs, rapid and erratic. Jesus Christ, it was horrible.

Palardy hung over the toilet, gasping, clutching his middle. Waiting to see if his latest attack had really passed or if another round of spasms would sneak up on him.

After a while, he decided he'd gotten a temporary reprieve and rose to his feet, holding the sink to steady himself. He reached for the tap, splashed cold water on his face, swished some in his mouth, and spat into the basin. The horrid taste didn't leave him. He hadn't expected it would.

Palardy staggered out the bathroom door, his head heavy. He was cold and trembling. In the hallway he got a flannel blanket from the closet and tossed it over his shoulders. Then he made his way back to the living room and dropped onto the couch.

What was happening? What was the matter with him?

He sat there wrapped in the blanket, trying to get warm. Wishing he could relax. But a terrible thought kept asserting itself in his mind. If not from the onset of the sickness, then soon after, he'd started to wonder whether it could be connected to what was in that hypodermic case Enrique Quiros had given him, to what had been in the ampule. Only a gullible fool could have neglected to consider the possibility. It had occurred to him the night he'd met Quiros at the harbor that anybody who would risk ordering someone as important as Roger Gordian to be hurt or killed would be capable of doing whatever it took to cover his tracks. Of doing away with anybody who might increase his chances of being tied to the act. In the car, Quiros had seemed uneasy about his own involvement. Eager to be through with it. Palardy couldn't remember the exact words he'd used, but they had hinted that he had no personal interest in harming Gordian and was having his strings pulled by someone higher up the line. That he was looking out for himself the same as Palardy.

It had been a jarring revelation. Palardy never thought of himself as a criminal, couldn't have felt more different from Quiros. And to realize they had that in common, realize they would go to equal lengths to protect themselves . . .

Jarring as hell.

Palardy was aware he was the only link between Enrique Quiros and Roger Gordian. Eliminate him, and the trail would be cut. This had come to him right there in the cruise ship terminal parking lot. Before parting ways with Quiros, he'd raised his fears indirectly and asked how he was supposed to know that exposure to the contents of the ampule wouldn't have some terrible effect on him. And Quiros had spent several minutes explaining that the liquid was harmless in itself, the final ingredient of a biological recipe unique to the individual being dosed. Without every one of the other precise ingredients in your makeup, there was nothing to fear. You could consume a gallon of the stuff, and it wouldn't have any effect.

Palardy had no trouble grasping the general concept. He'd followed developments in genetic research in the news, read plenty of magazine articles. Moreover, UpLink International had owned one of the major genetech firms until its downsizing maybe a year ago, still retaining a stake in the company, and Palardy had been chummy with some of the people who worked there. So he was knowledgeable enough about their research to understand that Quiros's reassurances had been worthless. Because the recipe was only as unique as the person brewing it up chose for it to be. Imagine he wanted to get rid of everybody with brown hair, or some other feature shared by an untold number of people. What would that do to the mortality rate of those exposed to his "final ingredient"? Wouldn't that make it more of a final solution?

And there was another part of Quiros's explanation that Palardy had sensed was intentionally misleading. If he wanted to talk about the agent being tailored to a person's inherited traits, fine. But how was Palardy to be sure Quiros hadn't had somebody get hold of *his* genetic diagram for that very purpose? Pluck a few hairs from *his* comb, some dead skin from *his* shower floor?

Sneak into *his* apartment and contaminate his orange juice, bottled water, or cold cuts with a few millimeters of a trigger formulated especially for the genetic cake mix called Don Palardy? How was he to be sure?

Palardy sank back against the sofa cushions and listened to the sound of his own labored breathing. This morning, when he'd phoned in sick to work, his intention had been to call the doctor next. But the thoughts swirling around his brain had made him decide against it. Made him petrified of doing it, in fact. If he'd caught an ordinary bug, it would eventually run its course. Yet if his symptoms were being caused by a virus or bacteria invented in a laboratory, some microbe the doctors couldn't identify, his sole hope of staying alive would be to reveal what he knew about it. And even assuming he could figure out some way to withhold how he knew what he did, when his disease was found to be the same one Roger Gordian had contracted, it would inevitably lead to questions he'd be unable to slip. Then he'd be implicated in a murder, the first of its kind, his name up there somewhere in infamy with Lee Harvey Oswald. And he'd be as dead as Oswald, too.

His face pale and sweaty, his body aching, Palardy closed his eyes. There had to be something he could arrange. Something he could do to get back at Quiros in case he'd been duped. Used and discarded. Maybe he was getting carried away with himself, and everything would turn out okay. But just in case, just in case, there had to be *something* . . .

And then, suddenly, it crossed his mind that there was.

SIXTEEN

WHEN ROGER GORDIAN'S PERSONAL PHYSICIAN, DR.
Elliot Lieberman, reviewed his case report Tuesday
morning, he was left puzzled and dismayed.

Gordian was undoubtedly a sick man, but the cause
of his illness was a mystery. The flulike symptoms that
hospitalized him Sunday afternoon had shown an appreciable improvement soon after his admission, continued
along that positive trend throughout Monday, and then
had taken a sharp, unexpected downturn over the past
several hours. At around midnight he'd called the duty
nurse to his room because of renewed difficulty
breathing, chills, and a stabbing headache severe enough
to have awakened him from sleep. His temperature had
spiked to 103°, its highest since his arrival in the ER,
and at last reading hadn't dropped from that elevated
mark. And although his respiratory distress was relieved
by oxygen given through a face mask, Lieberman had
heard a threadiness in his exhalations during a stetho-
scopic exam he'd performed a couple of hours ago, and

he immediately ordered an X-ray series, which showed pulmonary shadows that hadn't been evident in radiographic images taken the previous day—a typical sign of fluid buildup in the lungs. Lieberman asked for additional pictures at twice-daily intervals and regular updates on Gordian's condition, thinking that any further decline would likely require his patient be transferred to the intensive care unit. Then he had retreated to his office to examine the charts and laboratory results.

The bewildering thing was that the early suspicion of influenza had been ruled out, as had its most serious complication, viral pneumonia. A rapid-culture nasal swatch test to detect A and B type flu antigens—molecular components of the viral strains that stimulated defensive reactions by the body—had shown the specimens to be negative. A second type of quick diagnostic on a mucus sample from Gordian's throat produced identical results within twenty minutes. Both methods were considered 99 percent reliable, an analytical certainty for all intents and purposes.

Sighing with frustration, Lieberman sat leafing through the papers on his desk for the third time, seeking any clues he might have missed. His grandmother, rest her soul, could have catalogued Gordian's symptoms with a touch to his forehead and a look down his inflamed, blistered throat with a flashlight, instructing him to open wide in Yiddish. And despite the framed sheepskins and certificates on his office wall, Lieberman's present insight into his condition went little deeper than that. Examination of Gordian's blood under a microscope had eliminated the common bacterial pneumonias—primarily pneumococcal, but also staphylococcal, and the even rarer Legionella strains responsible for Legionnaires' disease. There was no sign of related chlamydial and mycoplasmal organisms. The serological workup had shown a raised level of lymphocytes, the white helper cells in the bloodstream that responded to an attack by foreign microbes. This was basically confirmation of Grandma's home diagnostic method—clinical evidence that infection was present and the immune system was sending out scent hounds to scout for antigens, just as the swab tests had done. But while the lymphocytes were evidence that a virus was breeding inside Gordian, they would do nothing to establish its identity.

Lieberman had checked San Jose Mercy's databases for similar undiagnosed cases reported within the last forty-eight hours and found none. An expansion of his computer search to include the past week, then the past month, also drew blanks. He had next contacted associates at nearby hospitals by phone to see whether they might have recently encountered anything that resembled Gordian's illness. Again, nothing. However, something had to be done to find out what Gordian was up against. His body was at war with a stealth invader and clearly flagging in its battle. Unless and until its identity was specified, an effective course of medical treatment to aid him would be impossible.

Lieberman inhaled, exhaled. He ought to know what he was confronting here, and he did not. That alarmed him tremendously. He needed to consult with someone who could provide some guidance and specialized expertise.

Lieberman lifted the receiver off his phone to get the chair of the virology department on the line but then decided that call could wait a bit and hung up without punching in his extension. There was another person he wanted to speak to first. One of his oldest friends and colleagues, Eric Oh was an epidemiologist with the California health department who had performed some of the principal research on molecular methods for the identification of unrecognized and emerging pathogens and been a celebrated virus hunter for the Centers for Disease Control in Atlanta before marrying a hometown girl who'd insisted he stop fiddling with BL4 pathogens, and move back West to settle down. It was a downright breach of protocol to involve Eric before consulting with a senior departmental head in this hospital. And the criteria that would normally warrant contacting government officials—a cluster of reported cases distinguished by symptoms akin to Gordian's or data suggesting a full-scale outbreak of an infectious disease in the community—were absent. A single patient with an ailment that had stumped his humble general practitioner for less than forty-eight hours did not constitute a public health hazard, even if that patient was somebody of Roger Gordian's prominence.

But Lieberman was getting gut radar signals. The kind you grew to credit more and more with age and experience. And insofar as he was concerned, an informal meeting of the minds with Eric could hardly be considered reproachful professional conduct.

His lips compressed to a barely visible stitch on his long, careworn face, Lieberman retrieved Eric's phone number from his pocket organizer and once again reached for the telephone.

". . . can't believe I was so thoughtless . . . so *stupid* . . . spent three Sundays in a row building a pen for my dogs . . . all I did . . . give Dad a hard time . . ."

Julia's voice penetrating his sleep, Gordian stirred, opened his eyes. She was sitting with Ashley near the foot of his hospital bed, back out of the way of the tubes and electronic monitors connected to him.

He lifted his arm from his side and weakly pulled the loose-fitting oxygen mask down below his chin. The women noticed he'd awakened and turned to face him, starting to their feet.

"Get me a drink of water, everything's forgiven," he managed. The inside of his mouth felt dry and clotted. "Deal?"

Julia was at his bedside in a snap, her mother behind her. "Dad, I don't know if you should be taking off the mask—"

He moved his hand.

"Breathing's fine right now." The words scraped out of him. "Just thirsty."

Ashley was already lifting the pitcher from his rolling tray. She filled a paper cup halfway, passed it to Julia, and then pressed the button to raise the upper part of the bed.

Gordian reached for the water as Ash straightened the pillows underneath him, but Julia shook her head.

"Let me hold it for you," she said. "Better take it slow. Little sips, okay?"

Gordian nodded. He wet his lips, rinsed the water over the sticky film on his tongue. Then swallowed. The coolness going down the hot, reddened lining of his throat was indescribably welcome.

"Thought you two were going out to grab a bite," he said.

"We did," Ashley said. She stepped closer and

touched his cheek. "You were asleep when we got back."

He looked at her.

"How long was I out?"

"A while . . . I'm not sure . . ."

Gordian shifted, checked his beside clock. Almost two in the afternoon. He'd been sure he had drifted off for fifteen, twenty minutes at the longest. Make that a couple of hours.

He shifted his gaze back to his wife. Ash had put on her face, as she liked to say. Not that she needed to wear much makeup. So many years of marriage, she looked like the photos taken of her when they were newlyweds. But he could see dark crescents under her eyes. Small lines at their corners that hadn't been there before.

"Do you feel like having lunch?" she said, gesturing toward his tray. "The nurse left some lunch. There's a turkey sandwich. Jell-O, naturally—"

He shook his head.

"A little later, maybe," he said. "My legs are cold. Air-conditioning's turned up kind of high, don't you think?"

He saw Ashley give Julia the briefest of glances. *Maybe not so high,* he thought.

"I'll go ask for another blanket at the nurse's station," she said.

"Count on me waiting right here."

She gave him a wan smile and went out into the hallway.

Gordian took down some more water, thanked Julia, then eased back against his pillows. The window shades were drawn, but the daylight seeping in around them seemed too bright. He let his eyes close for a second.

When he opened them, Julia was watching him on the bed.

"You aren't at work," he said.

"No kidding."

"It's a new job," he said. "I'd hate for you to have any trouble."

She sat gently on the edge of the mattress.

"It's okay," she said. "I used the old parent-in-the-hospital scam."

"Good one," he said. "Let's play it to the hilt."

She took hold of his hand, still watching him intently.

"You hear anything new from Dr. Lieberman?" he asked.

"Not since early this morning," she said. "He was supposed to look over your information and meet us here, but got called off on an emergency."

Gordian nodded, felt the tender swellings under his jaw. It reminded him of when he'd had the mumps as a kid.

"Dad . . ."

He looked at Julia, noticed that her eyes had suddenly moistened.

"Honey?" he said. "Something the matter?"

She was shaking her head, but at some unspoken thought rather than in answer to his question.

"What you heard me saying when you woke up . . . I'm sorry. About how I've been treating you. About the way I acted the other day when you were over at the house." She squeezed his fingers more tightly, swiped away a tear with her free hand. "I've been such a self-absorbed jerk since the divorce. . . . God, Daddy . . . I don't know *why* I keep taking things out on you. . . ."

"Might be because we're two of a kind," he said.

"Good at not being good with our emotions."

Julia tightened her grip on his hand, her eyes glistening.

"It's like I keep my feelings inside until they fill me up, you know?"

"I know."

"Like they're all mixed together, and I don't have a clue how to deal with them, and instead try to push them somewhere *deeper* inside. Convince myself they'll go away. And then the pressure only gets worse—"

"I know," he said. He smiled at her. "Doesn't make it easy on the people we love. Just ask your mother."

They were quiet for a moment, hands joined at Gordian's side.

"You'll sort things out," he said finally. His throat was on fire, the temporary relief from the water he'd sipped long gone. "It takes time. You've been through changes, difficult ones—"

He was interrupted by a soft knock on the open door.

They both turned their heads toward Dr. Lieberman just outside in the corridor.

"Julia, Gord," he said. His face was drawn. "I hope you'll excuse my lateness; it's been one of those days."

"Tell me about it," Gordian said in a ragged voice. "Hello, Elliot."

Lieberman's eyes made a quick tour of the room as he entered. "I was hoping to find Ashley—"

"I'm right behind you."

He glanced over his shoulder, saw her standing in the hall with a folded blanket draped over her arm, and stepped aside to let her move past him.

"Good," he said. "I'm glad the three of you are here."

They looked at him. It went through all their minds

at once that neither Lieberman's tone nor his expression remotely approached gladness, his chosen figure of speech aside.

He reached back and closed the door, then stood silently for what seemed a very long time.

"We have to talk about my findings," he said. "Talk very seriously."

"Here's what little I know," Megan said. "The boss's condition hasn't improved since this morning, and the tests aren't showing what's wrong with him. His doctor, I think his name is Lieberman, has put in a call to an epidemiologist at the Department of Health in Sacramento."

She was looking at Pete Nimec and Vince Scull, the three of them seated in Nimec's office at UpLink headquarters, their meeting hastily convened minutes after Ashley Gordian phoned to update her from the hospital.

Nimec's eyes held steady on her face. "That's it?"

She nodded.

"Doesn't make sense," Scull said. "A case gets kicked up to state level, it means there's either gotta be a rash of ones like it or a suspicion that whatever's hit Gord is contagious . . . and a threat to the public welfare."

Megan shook her head.

"That's what I assumed, too," she said. "But Ashley explained the contact's strictly unofficial. Lieberman has a personal relationship with the government man, and he's reaching out."

They were silent for a while.

"What the hell are we supposed to do?" Nimec said. "And don't tell me to wait and pray for the best."

Megan regarded him gravely.

"Pete," she said, "sometimes you can't charge to the rescue."

He expelled a breath.

"Goddamn," he said. "God*damn*."

More silence.

Scull frowned, rubbing a hand back and forth over his smooth, hairless expanse of scalp. Then he looked at Megan.

"I'm thinking maybe we ought to investigate," he said.

"Investigate what?" she said.

"Same things as the white coats," he said. "You look at a whole bunch of dots and try to draw in the lines that connect them. I mean, if you get right down to it, this wouldn't be any different than what's SOP at my job."

"I don't follow."

Scull rubbed his head again.

"Listen," he said. "I'm in another country conducting a risk analysis from a corporate perspective, I first pretend I'm from Mars, throw every preconception I have from my mind. Make like a sponge and soak up everything I can. You with me so far?"

She nodded.

"Now I've been there long enough to get a sense of what the place is about, and I notice a potential problem. Some political, economic, or social instabilities that could threaten our company interests," he went on. "I examine the cause or causes, trace their origins. It can be complicated. There are always buried issues and agendas. But I focus on the ones that are exposed. Follow their threads. Most often, they'll lead to others that aren't so visible. And then I follow them. And when I know everything I can within whatever time frame's imposed on me, I spin the threads into a regional profile and scenario plans. Then make my recommendations on what our investment strategy should be."

"Okay, I've still got you," Megan said. "Now help my chronically prosaic mind with the rest."

Scull thought for a moment.

"Say you're a medical sherlock. There's a disease you don't recognize, you want to trace *its* origin, same's I'd do with some radical political movement in Frickfrackistan," he said. "So you start looking at how the person you're treating might've acquired it. Where's he been lately? Who were his contacts? You maybe hit on another case that can be linked to him, you can pretty much surmise the sickness is communicable. The next step is to figure out its vectors. How it's spreading. Whether it jumps from rodents to people. Or rodents to insects to people like bubonic plague. Or gets passed directly from person to person. Name your route. The main thing is that once the information's in your pocket, you're on the way to finding your germ. And then you can maybe come to terms with it. Figure out how to deal with the thing." He looked from Megan to Pete. "You see where I'm coming from?"

The other two were nodding, Megan with her eyebrows raised.

They sat in pensive silence again.

Then, from Nimec: "Where do we start?"

Scull turned sideways in his chair and rapped his fist on the wall.

"Right here, Petey. UpLink HQ," he said. "Where the hell *else* but the boss's home away from home?"

• • •

Palardy was dreaming he was in the hospital. Or at least he thought it was a dream. It was hard to tell sometimes what was real and what wasn't. Like the day he'd gone into Gordian's office with the syringe. That had seemed as if it was a dream, too. He remembered how he'd seemed to be floating in space as he walked through the door, his sense of unreality. Of being inside and outside himself at once. And that was how he felt now. So maybe it was all in his mind. Not just the bad things that had happened to him lately, the things he'd done, but everything since Brazil. The gambling, his selling those blueprints to the space station facility to make his vig, his wife leaving him . . . and then back to the U.S.A. and more bets, more shylocks, more betrayals demanded of him and carried out. All a dream, every minute of it. Every hour, day, week, and month, right up to and including his coming down with the sickness. Merrily, merrily, merrily, merrily, life was . . .

Life . . .

Was life. Or something like that.

In the dream he'd been slipping into and out of tonight, these latest installments of his dream of life, or life of dream, whatever, he was in a hospital bed, tucked between clean sheets, feeling loads better. The fever was gone. Gone, the glands in his throat swollen to the size of golf balls. And the heaves and coughs and the blood that had started coming out of him with the coughing, red streaks in his phlegm, then clots, streaking the sink when he spat into it, darkening the water of his toilet, staining the bowl even after he'd flush and flush and flush . . .

Gone, all gone. Pain and trouble down the drain. The doctors had treated him, the nurses were tender and attentive, and he was comfortable, on the way to being cured. And whenever he opened his eyes and found himself back in his apartment, lying alone in his bed, twisted up in his soiled, wet, stinking sheets, his head on a pillow soaked with bloody discharges from his nose and mouth, whenever he'd opened his eyes and seemed to wake alone, so alone, Palardy would force himself back into that other place, that place of comfort, where the physicians were skilled and the nurses were kind, and he was getting better, so much better, in a warm, clean bed. And then the only thoughts to disturb him would be about the message in a bottle, the riddle sent to himself and not to himself, so people would be able to figure out what happened to him in case anything bad did happen.

That message, that payback, that whopping fuck-you to his betrayers . . . the problem was that it could come right back at him, be a disaster for him if things turned out okay and he recovered, if it was found before he got released from the hospital to intercept it.

Definitely a thought to intrude on his peace of mind, intrude on his dream, jolt him back to the lonely reality of the apartment where he lay wretched and shivering and very possibly dying in his own bodily filth.

In fact, it was pulling him back there right now, and the timing couldn't have been worse. Because in the present snippet of his dream of sweet mercy and healing, a nurse had been about to care for him, quietly entering his room, softly coming around his bedside, and oh, and oh, and oh, although he couldn't quite see her features, Palardy was sure she was beautiful, like his wife on their honeymoon, when they'd made their first baby, beautiful like his wife, and he didn't want to leave her, he didn't want to . . .

Palardy opened his eyes. Unsure of his bearings, his sense of place confused. He seemed to be back in his apartment, in his moist and jumbled bed. Sometimes it was hard to be positive on awakening. The shades were drawn to keep the sun from lancing into his eyes. The lights were out for the same reason, that terrible pain in his eyes. The room was so dim, it was hard to know. But he thought he was in his apartment. Awake now. And yet he still had the feeling somebody was with him, near his bed.

He blinked rapidly. If this was his own place, if he was no longer in the dream, then nobody belonged inside it except him.

Who could be . . . ?

Suddenly afraid, Palardy struggled to lift himself on his elbows, craning his head from side to side.

Initially, he thought the man standing to his left was disfigured. His face smashed and flattened. Then he thought his eyes still might be blurry with sleep, and blinked some more to clear them.

And then he realized the man was wearing a mask.

A stocking mask.

His fear mounting exponentially, Palardy summoned what little strength remained in his body and raised it higher off the mattress.

And was shoved back down by a black-gloved hand on his chest.

The hand held him.

Pressed hard against his ribs.

Kept him from moving at all.

He tried to speak but could only groan through his

scaled, blue lips. Then tried again as the man's free hand reached into a pouch or a bag on his belt . . . reappeared with something that finally unlocked his vocal cords . . .

"Who?" he managed. "Why . . . ?"

Palardy would die without an answer to the first question.

As for the second, his conscience had already answered it for him.

SEVENTEEN

FROM REUTERS ONLINE:

Spokesperson insists Roger Gordian has not suffered stroke

Web Posted at 1:14 p.m. PST (2114 GMT) *SAN JOSE*—Reports that UpLink International CEO Roger Gordian was hospitalized for a massive stroke last weekend were denied this afternoon by a corporate spokeswoman. "There has been a rash of false speculation that I would like to dispel. Mr. Gordian is undergoing thorough tests after experiencing some dizziness and physical discomfort while doing yard work at a family member's house Sunday," longtime UpLink executive Megan Breen told Reuters, reading from a prepared statement. "He's a

very active man and may have
overexerted himself, but I can
positively assure you that a stroke is
not suspected by his doctors."

Ms. Breen offered no specifics
about Gordian's condition and
present location but added that he
was fully alert and had expressed his
eagerness to return to work.

The billionaire defense contractor
and communications entrepreneur
became the subject of ill-health
rumors when information surfaced
yesterday that he had unexpectedly
canceled several meetings with key
Senate and business leaders . . .

After hearing Lieberman summarize Roger Gordian's
symptoms and lab results over the phone, Eric Oh, his
colleague at public health, became concerned enough to
ask him to fax over the case report the instant they hung
up.

Oh waited at his machine, plucking each page out of
the tray as it was transmitted. His hurried reading
prompted him to make an equally fast callback.

His impressions corresponded to Lieberman's—Oh's
version of gut radar, which he'd dubbed his "Spidey
sense" in homage to his favorite childhood comic book
character, was giving him physical tingles. He urged that
a fresh specimen of Gordian's blood be transported to
the renowned virology lab at Stanford Medical School
in nearby Palo Alto for examination and recommended
that Lieberman follow the usual guidelines for a potential biohazardous threat and ship a second viable sample,
dry-iced, to the Centers for Disease Control in Atlanta.

"I'd also appreciate you getting another tube of sera to the research facility at Berkeley," he said. "I consult with researchers there pretty often, and we have a good working relationship."

"I'll need to make matters official," Lieberman said. "Advise the departmental chairs, obtain their authorizations."

"Think you can rustle them together this afternoon?"

"I'll give it my best."

"One more thing before I forget—Gordian's X-rays. The reports note you've had series taken every twelve hours. Can I see your originals? From the initial images to the most recent. I'll send them right back to you tomorrow morning."

"No problem."

"Great, they should give me a better sense of how this has evolved," Oh said. "The material's out to Stanford within the hour, I'll drive down to personally sign for it and get cracking."

"I thought you mentioned you were taking Cindy out for an Italian dinner tonight."

"She got used to losing me to an electron microscope and assay plates the day our honeymoon ended, Eli."

It was late afternoon when Pete Nimec stepped out of the elevator to find Gordian's admin staring at his office door from behind her desk.

"Norma," he said. "How you holding up?"

She turned to him slowly as he approached.

"As best I can, Pete," she said. "Has Mrs. Gordian gotten in touch with you again?"

He shook his head. "We assume she will after that government epidemiologist has a look at things."

Norma was quiet.

"I don't want to think about him not being in there." She indicated Gordian's office with her cheerless eyes. "And somehow I can't think about anything else."

Nimec looked at her.

"I know," he said.

"Nothing seems right," she said. "It's so strange. He's one of those people I've taken for granted will always be with us. I can't imagine him being seriously ill. He's so much *larger* than most . . ." She paused. "I'm sorry. Of course it doesn't make sense."

He reached across the desk and touched her shoulder.

"Maybe not," he said. "But you aren't alone. Everybody who cares about him feels that way a little."

She put her hand on his and let it rest there a moment. "Thank you."

He nodded in silence.

"It's incredible how much Mr. Gordian is able to manage," she said then. "I've spent the past two afternoons canceling his appointments. That luncheon with senators Richard and Bruford from the Armed Services Committee. Meetings with senior executive board members. With a representative from the Silicon Valley Business Alliance. I can't tell you how many others."

"You have to field a lot of questions from the press since that stroke story appeared?"

"Enough," she said. "I've stayed with Megan's official explanation to the letter. Dizziness, maybe too much yard work, routine tests."

"That'll hold a while," he said.

"And hopefully we won't have any reason to go beyond it."

"Hopefully." He paused. "Norma, while we're on the

subject of Gord's schedule, I need a favor. Something Vince Scull thinks might be important to the doctors. Would you be able to provide a list of his verifiable contacts over the past couple, three weeks? The ones with whom he physically connected, that is."

She looked at him.

"Yes, I log all his engagements into an electronic scheduler," she said. "The calendar automatically appears when I turn on my computer every morning. I input whether the date is kept, missed, or reshuffled. Occasionally, Mr. Gordian will have me enter a list of talking points beforehand. Or his handwritten impressions of how the meeting went."

"I won't ask for Gord's private notes. Just the names of people he met and who they work for. Maybe where their meetings took place. Can you swing that for me right now?"

"Pete, I'll do anything to help. Now, later, don't hesitate to check with me for whatever information you want," Norma said. The thought that she could be of use had given her a kind of animation. "Would you like a printout or disk?"

"A copy of each sounds good to me."

"You've got them," she said, then slipped a rewritable CD into her drive and began tapping on her keyboard.

"I'm sorry, truly sorry, but I can't help you with that information," said Carl VanDerwerf from behind his desk. His job title at UpLink was Managing Director of Human Resources.

"An' I'm tellin' you I got to have it," said Rollie Thibodeau from the seat opposite him.

The two men stared at one another, clearly at an impasse.

"We have to be sensitive to the privacy of our employees," VanDerwerf persisted. "Moreover, there are state and federal laws. You may not be aware of the penalties we could incur. The liabilities were someone to press a suit about your prying into their personnel records for confidential details—"

Thibodeau held a hand in the air to interrupt him.

"Never mind these people's ages, work experience, or whether they like to pole vault or pole dance in their rec time. Doesn't matter to me if somebody's a kleptomaniac, nymphomaniac, single, married, divorced, a bigamist, or takin' care of his or her shut-in Aunt Emma," he said. "Just give me the names of employees in this building who took sick days the past couple weeks, and the departments where they work. You got to have that on file."

VanDerwerf produced an exasperated sigh. "Certainly we do. For payroll and insurance purposes. But if you'd allowed me to finish my sentence a moment ago, you would know the law requires that we keep an individual's medical background confidential."

"Nobody's talkin' *background.*" Thibodeau said. "What you got your neck poked out for? Just let me know who's called in sick lately. An employee does or doesn't choose to get into the reason why, it be up to him."

VanDerwerf sighed again.

"Sir, just as you are responsible for our corporate security operations, I supervise all phases of personnel function. At all levels from senior executive to mail room clerk. My decisions must be guided by UpLink's established policies and procedures and by applicable government regulations." He pursed his lips, ran a finger across his neatly trimmed salt-and-pepper mustache. "Now, I'm not denying that unanticipated situations will sometimes arise that demand judgment calls. Should you care to explain the basis of your request . . . address my own need to know if it is associated with rumors circulating about Mr. Gordian's condition . . . I'm sure we can reconcile our differences in a mutually amenable, commonsense manner."

Thibodeau glowered. "You sayin' it ain't okay for me to ask a fella straight on whether he had a cold or a sprained ankle last week, but it's fine for you to stick your bill into the boss's affairs through a third party?"

"That is an oversimplification rendered in insulting terms. My capacities include oversight of UpLink's health-care costs, and Mr. Gordian is covered by our corporate policy. The wall of silence surrounding his absence stands to put me in a difficult position with our provider. I merely suggest we trade off—"

"I heard enough, you officious little prick." Thibodeau pushed off his chair and stood over the desk. "Talk about insults, what do you call wastin' my time, pretendin' to be grieved up over employees' rights when you only lookin' to talk trash—?"

"That was not my intention—"

"Come see!" Thibodeau boomed, thrusting a finger at him. "You don't commence to turn over what I gotta have, you'll know how a bug feels when it's been stepped on with a hikin' boot."

VanDerwerf blinked, rapidly stroking his mustache, spots of color on his cheeks and forehead.

Then he released his third and longest sigh yet.

"Okay," he said in ruffled capitulation. "My staff's ready to leave for the day. I'll have them get the names to your office first thing tomorrow morning."

Thibodeau shook his head and sat.

"Best make that *your* office in fifteen minutes," he said and glanced at his wristwatch. "Meanwhile, I'll just make myself comfortable an' wait for them right here."

True to his promise, Eric Oh was at the Stanford lab in time to receive the radiographs and diagnostic specimen from Lieberman.

They arrived via special courier a little after five o'clock, the serum packed separately in accordance with international requirements for transport of fluid, tissue, cultures, and other substances believed to contain etiologic agents—live microbial organisms that were potential causes of infectious disease in human beings.

Or, as they were broadly categorized in the rule books: Dangerous Goods.

Its seal wrapped in waterproof tape, the labeled vial had been placed in a tubular plastic container, the spaces around it filled with sufficient wadding to absorb every drop of sera within should an accidental leak or breakage occur in handling. The secondary receptacle was then capped, taped for watertightness, labeled with the name, address, and phone number of the sender at San Jose Mercy, and encased in an outer shipping canister. Besides a duplicate of the sender's identification and contact information label, this third canister bore the standard tag for biomedical etiologic materials prescribed by the federal Department of Health, Education, and Welfare, highlighted by a bright red biohazard trefoil against a white background and bearing the appropriate phone number for notification of the CDC should the package become damaged.

These same procedures had been followed for the transport of the sample to Berkeley, as well as for the air shipment of the sample to Atlanta, with additional black-and-white stickers mandated by the International Air Transport Association for containers of dry ice and infectious substances.

Before putting on his protective attire and bringing the package into the virology lab's biosafety cabinet, where he planned to spend perhaps an hour or two studying its contents, Eric rang Lieberman to let him know it had reached him safe and sound. He then went out to a nearby fast-food restaurant, ordered a couple of cheeseburgers to go, and ate them drowned in ketchup, trying to imagine it was the tomato sauce he'd so looked forward to enjoying at his canceled dinner.

He knew he was kidding himself, of course.

There wasn't the slightest chance in the world that the burgers would relieve his unfulfilled longing for calamari.

And given his suspicions about Gordian's case, there was also virtually no chance he'd be leaving the laboratory for many long hours to come.

"From what I can see here, we got thirty-four employees in the building called in sick over the last three weeks," Thibodeau said.

"Seven . . . no, sorry, make that *eight*, are currently out," Megan said.

"None of them for longer than three days," said Ricci.

"The rest of the absences average two days," Nimec said. "I do notice one person, a Michael Ireland in Legal, who's been down five and counting. . . ."

"Mike fractured his leg rock climbing," Megan said. "He and his fiancée are friends of mine."

"Scratch his name off the list," Scull said and did so on the copy in front of him, drawing a line through it with his pen.

It was a quarter to seven in the evening, regular work hours long past, Nimec's office once again having become a strategy room for Sword's core leadership group . . . plus one, since Vince Scull was, technically speaking, not a member of the organizational security division. They had pulled up chairs to whatever flat surfaces were available—or reasonably clearable—and were poring over photocopies of the separate computer printouts obtained by Nimec and Thibodeau, verifying, cross-checking, and generally hoping for a lead that might steer them toward a carrier from whom Roger Gordian could have received his infection.

"Anyone think it's worth talking to the people on Rollie's list who took off sick and are already back to work?" Nimec said.

"My opinion's that it isn't, with one possible exception," said Ricci. "This bug has the boss flat-out kayoed. Somebody's on his feet after a couple days, he's not likely to be our contact."

"That's if it hits everyone the same, a big assumption to make," Scull said. "Certain people could have a natural resistance and be mildly affected. Or not be susceptible at all. Or they could be what are called asymptomatic hosts, intermediaries for the bug to hitch a ride on. Our germ bag might be unaffected but have an acquaintance or relative who's deathly sick—"

"Point taken, Vince," Nimec said. "But I think our

hunt has to stay narrow for now, or we'll find ourselves lost in the woods."

Thibodeau nodded. "The direct route gets us nowhere pickin' up tracks, we widen our range."

Megan looked at Ricci. "You mentioned an exception . . ."

"Yeah. A James Meisten. His name's the only one that's on both lists." He looked down at the printouts spread side-by-side in front of him. "He was out sick yesterday, back today. Also met with the boss last Friday."

"I know him a little," Megan said. "He was at the Marketing and Promotions conference about the info kiosks."

"So we phone him at home tonight even though he's returned?"

"I suppose it couldn't hurt." She frowned. "Candidates aren't exactly leaping out at us, are they? And when I weigh what Vince said . . . it gets so tangled. I can think of so many possibilities off the top of my head. Assuming the carrier is even a human being as opposed to something that flies, creeps, or crawls, he doesn't have to be a person who actually had a scheduled meeting with Roger. It could be somebody who chatted with him in the hallway or elevator. Or whose office he popped into on the spur of the moment. Or who shook his hand during a thirty-second introduction. And that's before we even consider people on his appointment schedule from *outside* the company. Businessmen. Politicians. Social interactions we don't have the vaguest idea about. He has friends, family members . . ."

She let the sentence trail.

"Thought we were sticking to the straight and narrow," Ricci said to her. "We've got Meisten, which is better than nothing. And, far as it goes for the boss's unplanned contacts, we should look at Thibodeau's list, try to pinpoint employees most likely to have crossed his path without an appointment over the course of a normal workday. See if that takes us anywhere."

"I've already been doing that," Nimec said. "Only name that stands out as a possible is Donald Palardy."

"Palardy heads one of the sweep teams," Thibodeau said. "Rotated out of Brazil 'round the same time I did."

Nimec was nodding. "He called in sick Monday."

Ricci looked at him.

"A day after the boss collapsed."

"Yeah. And he's still on the absentee list."

Everyone in the room was momentarily quiet.

"Don't see how we can read too much into this," Scull said. "Sweeps are conducted early, right? Before most of us get to work. We've no reason to believe he and Gord have ever been in the same room together."

"No reason to think they haven't, either," Ricci said.

"I know for sure Palardy's been inside the boss's office," Thibodeau said. "We got four teams in the building. All of them be assigned permanent sections. An' his section includes the top executive suites."

Ricci exchanged glances with him.

"No shit," he said.

"Non," Thibodeau said.

There was more silence in the room.

"I think we ought to give him a call," Ricci said.

Lathrop exited the CNN Web site after finding no updated headlines about Roger Gordian's condition and then restored the Profiler application to his computer screen.

Blondie's luscious face reappeared in front of him, enlarged and enhanced from the digital video he'd taken near the carousel in Balboa Park. None to his surprise, the program still hadn't made her. The only reason he'd bothered running her image through it again was that he'd procured a handful of new investigative files from one of his infoworms—although for some reason this particular worm wasn't penetrating very deep inside the apple lately and soon would be worthless as an informant. It was part of the natural order of things, Lathrop thought. The ebb and flow. They rose to grace, they fell. They gained access, they lost it. But he had other sources at his disposal in a lot of different places. And there were always prospects to be cultivated among the greedy and disenchanted.

Leaving his desktop on, he swiveled around in his comfortable leather office chair and reclined to watch his coon cat toy with a favorite ball of yarn. She prodded it with her front paws to set it rolling and then crouched in readiness to pounce, her tail flicking back and forth on the floor.

"Okay, Missus Frakes," he said in a fond tone. "Let's see you go for it."

The cat cooed at the sound of his voice. Then she sprang upon the wound-up yarn and twisted onto her back, holding the ball against her middle with her forelegs, kicking and raking at it with her sharp rear claws.

Lathrop smiled a little. She would work the thing till it became unraveled and spread loosely across the carpet. Just as he was working his own ball of yarn. The biggest he'd ever chanced upon.

He sat thinking about what he actually knew, what further information he'd been able to surmise from it, and what choices and opportunities the sum total presented to him.

His surveillances at Balboa and the harbor parking lot combined to tell a pretty amazing story. Whatever her identity might be, it was certain Blondie was a courier for El Tío. And her purpose in meeting Enrique Quiros had been to deliver the jewelry box for the obscure narco distributer and instruct Enrique to pass it along to the guy he'd then arranged to meet harborside. His name was Palardy. A member of the security or countersnoop team at UpLink International whose gambling jones had gotten him in over his head with some serious operators, and who'd paid off a piece of his debt by turning over classified information about the defense systems of UpLink's manufacturing compound in Brazil. El Tío's involvement in the terrorist raid on that base was unclear to Lathrop, but it probably didn't have much importance at this stage, and he hadn't concerned himself with it.

The main thing for him was to keep on top of what was happening now. Because events were already moving fast, and he had the sense they were about to kick up to a breathless pace.

It was interesting how sellout dupes like Palardy could be so utterly blind to the traps being set for them. How they never realized that the type of men who were using them would keep their hooks in until every bit of usefulness was exhausted. At the harbor, Palardy and his current user had talked about genetic blueprints, disease triggers, stuff Lathrop had needed to research afterward. And there was enough he still had to check out. But despite a lingering question mark or two, he'd gotten the gist of their encounter . . . and stripped to the bone, it all came down to blackmail and murder. Palardy had been given some kind of biological agent, something new under the sun, and been ordered to take out Roger Gordian with it.

Lathrop tilted a little farther back in his chair, continuing to watch Missus Frakes relentlessly pull apart the yarn with her teeth and claws.

That's the way, all right, he thought. *Work the bastard.*

In the Safe Car—ha-ha—Palardy had understandably squawked with resistance. Quiros's errand would bounce him from the role of informant to killer, and he'd never planned for things to escalate that far. But Quiros pushed, bringing up what dirt he had on him, and that made him shut his mouth and agree to cooperate. It was a variation of a theme Lathrop had seen repeated time and again in the territory he chose to prowl, though one notable distinction about the enactment featuring Quiros and Palardy was that neither had been inclined to get mixed up in Gordian's assassination. That Quiros was himself muscled into it. This had become apparent from his protestations to Blondie and a couple of indirect comments he'd made to Palardy—the latter being moments of commiseration and empathy that hadn't exactly caused Lathrop's eyes to mist. But he supposed he was a cynical audience, having maybe seen the basic plot unfold once too often.

After that night at the harbor, Lathrop had concentrated on the script he'd drafted for Quiros and Lucio Salazar without their knowledge. It had netted him a sweet take, and the blowout climax promised to be refreshing fun. But in another twenty-four hours, it would be time to move beyond it. Turn a bend, head on out toward virgin soil.

If he'd needed any incentive to urge him along, nothing could have been better than the news reports about Gordian's hospitalization.

Lathrop glanced around at the pretty lady on his computer screen and remembered the afternoon he'd followed Enrique to his rendezvous with her. Remembered watching the carousel make its slow rotations with the "Blue Danube" piping in the background, the rowdy, stoned-out teenagers on the lead horses rising from their saddles, stretching their arms to reach for the silver and brass rings above them, only the gleaming brass worth a prize.

A smile ghosted at the corners of Lathrop's mouth again.

The brass ring.

He'd gotten hold of it. Without ever climbing aboard the platform, stalking the periphery on his ceaseless, solitary hunt, he'd been the one who caught hold. And that left him having to make two major decisions.

Namely when to claim his prize and how best to trade on its indescribable value.

"Third time I've called, and still no answer except from his machine," Ricci said. "Where the hell is Palardy?"

"Who knows? Maybe he went out for some groceries."

"He's supposed to be sick."

"Doesn't have to mean he's bedridden. A person has to eat, no matter how lousy he feels. If there's no food in the house, you live alone, you go buy some."

"Third time in an *hour,* Pete. If I'm under the weather

and need orange juice or something, I might run over to the corner deli. But I wouldn't make a whole shopping excursion out of—"

"Whoa," Megan said, putting up her hand. "I think you two are getting way ahead of yourselves."

They looked at her from their chairs in Nimec's office.

"How so?" Nimec said.

"It could be that he's turned off the ringer on his phone to get some sleep, or doesn't hear it, or just doesn't want to answer."

"Or maybe he was feeling better and went out for fresh air," Scull said. "For all we know, the guy had a stomach bug and is already back to normal."

"If that's the case, why wasn't he at work today?"

Scull shrugged. "He might not have felt normal till earlier tonight. I'm only agreeing with Meg that—"

"You see me phone his section chief ten minutes ago? You remember our conversation?"

"Sure I do—"

"What he told me, this section chief, was that the last time anybody heard from Palardy was when he phoned in yesterday, and that the guy sounded sick as a dog, and he was supposed to call back today to report how he was doing. And never did."

"I said I remembered—"

"The section chief, his name's Hernandez, also said he thought it was very odd that Palardy didn't call. In fact, I'm pretty sure he started to use the word irresponsible, too, but checked himself."

"Probably didn't want to get him in hot water with us," Thibodeau said.

"I agree. But that doesn't change anything," Nimec said. "The sweeps aren't a haphazard affair. If they become disorganized, we start to have countersurveillance lapses."

"Exactly," Ricci said. "Guys on these teams show up for duty at five-thirty, six o'clock in the morning. And unless it happens that one of them wakes up feeling too sick to come in, like Palardy did Monday—"

"Or a last-minute emergency comes up . . . car breaks down on the highway, kid's got a fever—"

"Which wasn't the case—"

"Then Hernandez has *got* to have his people give him notice the day before," Thibodeau said, finishing Ricci's sentence. "Arrange to pull a replacement off another team. Be sure every area in the building due for a sweep is covered."

Ricci nodded.

"Especially when it's a team *leader* who's going to be out," he said. "Hernandez is sticking with his man until he learns the score, and I'd do the same. But Palardy being MIA is a bigger deal than he wanted us to think."

Megan shook her head. "I'm still not sure I understand what the three of you are saying—"

"What *I'm* saying is Palardy might be too sick to call. Might've passed out same as the boss." He snapped his fingers. "Just like that."

"You've made quite a huge leap," she said. "It's possible we've hit on a disciplinary problem rather than anything having to do with Gord."

"Meg's right," Scull said. "Don Palardy appears for work tomorrow morning, fit as a fiddle, your whole discussion's moot. Like I said before, I can't see reading a whole lot into his absence. Not at this stage."

Ricci looked at him.

"Maybe not," he said. "But I tell you something, Scull. He doesn't show bright and early, I want to know his home address. Because wherever he lives, I'm heading over there to see what's up."

Dr. Eric Oh thought they resembled water lilies.

Clusters of beautiful, perfectly formed lilies floating on the surface of a quiet pond.

This quality of simple structural perfection was the essence of the virus's enduring success as a life form. It was also what made them ideally suited for comparison study with an electron microscope. Every virion of a type was identical. An intact specimen of a virus from the blood of a patient in Mozambique would be the mirror image of a specimen of the same family, genus, and strain grown in culture at a California research laboratory, assuming it was likewise undamaged. To an experienced researcher it would look as though they had been manufactured at a single factory, on a single, orderly assembly line. You saw one, you'd seen them all.

At three o'clock in the morning, Eric was still at the Stanford lab, examining the photographs he'd snapped with its state-of-the-art Hitachi instrument beside those he'd called up on his computer from the vast database of EM pictures compiled and shared by medical and biological research facilities around the globe.

As with any sort of photography, setting up the shot was the difficult part of the process; once you got to the shutter click, you were home free. From the moment he'd scanned Gordian's case report, Eric's mind had been whispering *virus*. After he'd inspected the first-generation X rays sent by Lieberman, that whisper became an urgent shout. But the problem in taking pictures of viruses was that they tended to be camera shy. The tiniest were dwarfed even by common bacteria. Scientists measured their size in nanometers—*billionths* of a meter. On this infinitesimal scale, a single droplet of blood became a vast, unmapped sea of crests and troughs where they could remain undetected unless present in great numbers. And the greater their numbers, the worse the infection. It was therefore easier when investigating deadly viral illnesses to find colonies in samples from autopsies of the dead or patients in late-stage disease than in samples taken from less advanced cases.

Eric had hoped from the start that Roger Gordian wasn't going to make life easy for him. When his viewing of an unconcentrated drop of serum failed to reveal any viruses after nearly two hours, he considered it a break. Better he'd needed to take the extra step of placing a sample in a centrifuge to pack as many organisms as possible into a concentrate than have an abounding population instantly jump out at his eyes. Viruses were unsparing, mechanistic parasites that used up the living cells of their hosts as they bred. Given Eric's fears about the nature of Gordian's infection, a sample that teemed with virus particles might have suggested a bleak prognosis indeed.

After centrifugation, Eric had used filter paper to drain the circular grid bearing his concentrated sample, then stained it with a solution of 2 percent phosphotungstate that was conductive to electrons. He had known that his processing would damage whatever viruses might be displayed, and that further deterioration could be expected from the ionizing effect of the microscope's electron beam. But while there were methods of cryogenic preparation that could have substantially reduced, if not altogether eliminated, the loss of a specimen's structural integrity, these techniques were finicky and took time. And Eric's goal was to aid in Gordian's diagnosis and treatment, not his postmortem, which meant he had to be expedient. He had weighed the two options against each other and decided to go ahead with conventional EM, reasoning that an adequate amount of the sample remained for the lab's regular staff to perform cryo EM later on, should his own examination indicate it was advisable.

Now Eric removed his glasses and sat rubbing his eyes, strained from too many long, sleepless hours fixed on the visual panel of the EM. The only reminder that his stomach wasn't completely empty was an occasional repeating of the ketchup-sopped burgers he'd picked up for dinner. He knew he ought to go home, pop some antacid tablets, and climb into bed. But the pictures wouldn't let him budge.

He put the glasses back on and looked at his micrographs. Then at the electronic library shots on his computer screen. His gaze moving between them again and again.

Lilies. On a quiet pond.

As an epidemiologist with the CDC in the midnineties, Eric had been one of the primary investigators who had worked to identify the mystery illness that scourged the Four Corners Navajo tribal reservation in the Southwest and then gradually made its way eastward, killing better than half its victims—many of them young, otherwise healthy individuals—within days of their first symptoms. The infections began with mild flulike respiratory problems and rapidly progressed toward systemic crash, the walls of the capillaries in the lungs breaking down, developing tiny leaks that bled out into the surrounding tissues until they became inundated with fluid and sometimes swelled to double their normal size. In many of the fatal cases there was a similar breakdown of stomach membranes. The external signs of terminal-stage disease were especially horrible as the blood vessels in the body's mucous membranes and subcutaneous tissues deteriorated, causing petechiae, pinpoint hemorrhages of the eyes, mouth, and skin.

In the early days of the contagion's spread, the inhabitants of Four Corners came to refer to the epidemic simply—and for Eric chillingly—as *sin nombre*. Without a name. That designation stuck with it after intensive scientific detective work eventually determined the disease was a new strain of hantavirus, a lethal hemorrhagic fever whose occurrence was never previously recorded in North America.

The tingles Eric had felt on first perusal of Gordian's case report had stemmed from the combination of his respiratory problems and the abnormal lymphocytes and diving platelet count in his bloodstream. Platelets were essential to the body's healing factor, minuscule patches that gathered to stop bleeding and release clotting agents. A normal platelet count averaged 150,000 to 350,000 per microliter of blood. Gordian's count had been 120,000 per microliter when he was admitted to San Jose Mercy—borderline low. It had then fallen to 90,000 Monday morning. On the most recent workup, it declined even more pronouncedly to 50,000 per microliter.

Eric had seen nearly the same profile in *sin nombre* patients entering the pulmonary edema phase of the disease. And changes in Gordian's chest X rays had also been discomfortingly familiar. The vague skeins of shadow across his lungs evident on Sunday's pictures had become linear opacities of the airspaces within twenty-four hours, visible as short perpendicular white streaks at their bases. By Tuesday afternoon, there were longer lines developing from the hilum, the crowded interchange where the blood vessels, nerves, and bronchi emerged into the lungs.

Sin nombre, he thought.

Without a name.

The liliform viruses now on Eric's computer screen were micrographs that he and his colleagues on the CDC investigative team had taken eight years ago . . . and the shots he'd gotten out of the EM's photographic chamber tonight bore an undeniably striking similarity to them.

As in the original series, the organisms were circular in shape. As in the originals, their envelopes were ringed with binding proteins that enabled them to attach to the outer membranes of host cells. But the architecture of their nucleocapsids—the core material within the viral envelopes that held the genomic code for their replication and entry into the cell—showed a subtle variance.

Studying the set of images he'd isolated from Roger Gordian's bloodstream, Eric could see none of the roundedness typical of the nucleocapsids on the database specimens of *sin nombre,* or for that matter in any of the related old-world hantavirus strains he'd encountered in his scientific career. Instead, they appeared long and straight, almost filamentous, even when computer-enhanced.

Eric couldn't go beyond guessing whether this anomaly represented a difference in the genetic makeup of the separate specimens until a polymerase chain reaction, or PCR, probe was conducted on Gordian's samples, and the actual RNA sequences could be compared against the codes of all other known hantaviruses. But his immunogobulin capture assays—fluorescent dye screening tests developed in the late 1980s that produced results within three or four hours—had shown weak positives for several catalogued strains of the disease, with the brightest green glow on his lab slide appearing for *sin nombre*. While that, too, had been relatively pale, it had made Eric nervous as hell once added to the rest of the evidence before him.

His eyes hurting, his stomach hollow, he sat there tensely in the lab, frozen behind his computer as dawn crept its slow way into the sky outside. He could say very little absolutely except that Roger Gordian was in serious trouble. But he believed in his bones that if Gordian didn't have *sin nombre,* he'd contracted something very much like it.

That a close relative to the disease without a name, one nobody had known about, had just shown up on the doorstep.

The doe strode softly into the thick stand of trees, her tracks like broken hearts in the fallen snow. Food was plentiful here, the low-hanging pine boughs bunched with cones, the needle buds on the saplings still succulent, only beginning to brown in their cold-weather dormancy.

Scanning a moment for predators, she saw nothing disturb the vegetation, heard nothing except the hushed whisper of the breeze. Then she lowered her head and tore at the young trees with her flat, blunt teeth, lacking incisors to bite into them.

The knife slashed up from beneath the dark shelf of a branch, plunged hilt-deep into the softness of her throat, then slashed crosswise once and again. Arterial and venous blood gushed over the animal's white down and stained the snow under her front hooves mingled shades of red. She collapsed heavily, the brightness of life frozen in eyes already dead.

Kuhl knelt to pull his knife from the wound, traces of vapor steaming from its wet blade.

For the first time in weeks, he felt released.

Gordian awoke, gasping for air.

Feverish and disoriented, unable at first to remember where he was, he felt certain a hand was clapped over his nose and mouth. Then he got his bearings. He was in his hospital room. His bed light off in the dimness of early morning. A thin crack of illumination spilling under his door from the outer corridor.

Air.

He needed air.

Gordian struggled to pull down a breath, his body arched off his mattress from the effort. But his lungs didn't respond. They felt heavy and clogged. A muffled gurgling noise escaped him. *Air*. He fumbled under his chin for the oxygen mask. Couldn't find it. He reached down to his chest and still couldn't locate it. Groped about on his right side, where he sometimes clipped it to the safety rail. Not there.

The oxygen mask. He needed the mask. Where was it?

His mouth opened wide, he swung his arm up over his head, found the feed hose running from the wall, and with a surge of relief slid his fingers down along its length. Feeling for the mask at the end of it—

His newborn relief suddenly plummeted away into confusion.

The mask . . .

He was already wearing it.

He cupped his hand over its curved plastic surface, pressed it against his face, drew hard. Air hissed through the tube. He could hear it over the strangled shreds of sound coming out of him. Hear it flowing into his mask . . . but that was where it seemed to stop. His throat, his chest, were blocked.

Desperate, choking, feeling as if his chest were about to explode, he clawed for the emergency button at his side to summon a nurse, hoping to God one was very nearby.

EIGHTEEN

THE CONDOMINIUM SUBLEASED BY DONALD PALARDY
belonged to a large block of units UpLink International
had acquired to house its midlevel employees in one of
the newer planned developments in Sunnydale—a suburban community with the conceit of a major city, about
fifteen miles south of San Jose.

By the time he got into his car to drive down Wednesday morning, Ricci had started wondering if Megan and
Scull could have been right about him making too much
of Palardy's absence. Maybe Palardy had put on a well-
rehearsed sick voice when he'd phoned Hernandez to
say he wouldn't be at work the previous Monday.
Maybe he'd met a hot number in a bar and spontane-
ously decided to take her on a cruise to nowhere. Maybe
he would be in bed with his phone unplugged, munching
on potato chips and watching game shows or reruns of
sixties sitcoms on cable television. In hindsight, Ricci's
all-fall-down comment about Palardy and Gordian
seemed a bit silly, even to him. And his finger-snapping

had made it sound sillier. Of course, everyone had agreed that something wasn't kosher about Palardy's continued dereliction after three days, and felt it was at least worth checking out.

His thoughts had gone on in that mode until he finally located Palardy's condo after several wrong turns leading onto streets named for different native flowers that all sounded alike to him, past rows of two-family stucco buildings that all looked alike.

Then Ricci stopped questioning himself and started noticing things. It was a mental shift to a scrupulous objectivity that grounded every good cop the moment he arrived at the scene of an investigation. And Ricci doubted even the Boston Police Department officials who'd once thrown him into the political winds would have disputed that he'd been among their best.

As he rolled his Jetta into the driveway, his first observation was that Palardy's van was in his carport. His second was that Palardy hadn't brought in his newspapers for a few days—there were three lying on his walk in their plastic delivery bags. That could mean he was home and too sick to bother picking them up or that he'd gone off somewhere without his vehicle, although he might own more than a single set of wheels.

He strode to the door, rang the bell, and waited. No one answered. He fingered the buzzer again, keeping it depressed a little longer. Still nobody. Then he knocked without getting a response. After a few minutes, he leaned over to peek through the glass panels on either side of the door, but they were covered with louvered screens. The shade was likewise fully drawn over the front window.

Ricci buzzed again, let another minute pass. He heard a sound from inside, listened, realized it was the racket of a cuckoo clock. Palardy didn't come to the door.

Ricci tried the doorknob. Locked. He bent to examine it out of old habit. A typical key-in cylinder lock. He could retract the bolt with a credit card in ten seconds flat. In fact, the door had been opened that way before, judging by the scratches on the rim and doorframe. That prompted another observation. The scratches looked as if they might be fresh.

He considered this a moment. The marks might not have the slightest significance. Ricci would have been hard pressed to count how often he had accidentally gotten locked out of his own home and used a charge card to work his way inside. It was easy once you got the knack. Anybody could do it. Every cop he'd known. And Palardy, being a trained countersnoop, it seemed reasonable to assume he wouldn't need to hire a locksmith if he forgot his house keys somewhere. Not with a Minnie Mouse job like this. On the other hand, Palardy had unexplainedly dropped from sight, and Ricci's probing mind couldn't rule out the chance that someone else might have gained entry.

He thought about using the card trick to admit himself right now but then dismissed the notion. That very sort of tactic had once helped his detractors pin the rogue-detective label on him. And he was just getting comfortable at UpLink.

He stood there at the door, attempting to remember the street where he passed the management office. Fuchsia, was it? Or Manzanita? Unable to decide, he returned to his car and drove around a while, looking for the place.

A quarter hour and multiple wrong turns later, he found it on Lupine. The building manager was a man named Perez whose reservations about admitting a stranger to Palardy's apartment unit began to dissipate the instant Ricci flashed his UpLink Security ID card. And no wonder, since the company owned half the complex.

"We're pretty concerned," Ricci said. He kept his card displayed. "Nobody's heard from him in days."

Perez seemed fascinated with the Sword insignia.

"I do this, got to stick around while you're inside," he said with a heavy Mexican accent.

"Okay by me."

Perez nodded. "Lemme grab the key ring, I meet you over there."

Ricci offered to give him a lift instead, dreading another wrong turn. With Perez beside him to furnish directions, it took under five minutes to get back to the condo.

In the walkway Perez fumbled with his keys for a second, found the right one, and pushed open the door.

They found the living room unoccupied. Utterly still except for the ticking of the cuckoo clock.

"Palardy?" Ricci stood in the entry. "You here?"

Silence. Stillness.

Ricci stepped past the building manager to another door, slightly ajar. He glanced over his shoulder. "This the bedroom?"

Perez nodded.

Ricci rapped the wood. Again no answer. He grabbed the doorknob and entered.

In the doorway behind him, Perez inhaled sharply at the sight of the body.

Ricci's memory of the photo he'd pulled from the security files confirmed it was Palardy. He was lying in bed on his back, his eyes wide open. A blanket covered him to the chest. His face was gray, with dark purple blemishes on the cheeks and forehead. His mouth was twisted into what appeared to be a grimace of pain. The hand sticking out from under the blanket was hooked into a claw, the visible portion of his bare arm also lesioned.

"You should stay back," Ricci said to the building manager.

He didn't need encouragement.

"*Sí,*" he said shakily. "I got to call the cops—"

"Have a cellular on you?"

Perez nodded.

"Good." Ricci inclined his head toward the telephone on the bedside stand. "I don't think you want that one anywhere near your mouth."

Perez nodded again and crossed himself, staring inside from the entrance.

Ricci produced a business card and pen from inside his sport jacket, wrote hastily on the back of the card, and handed it to him. "Do me a favor; contact the guy whose name and number I jotted down. That's Pete Nimec, at UpLink. Let him know what we found here. If you don't mind, I think it might be better if he's the one who gets in touch with the police."

Perez nodded a third time and took the portable phone out of his pocket.

Ricci turned back into the room, reached into his own pocket for the scrub mask and latex gloves he'd brought with him, and put them on. Then he went over to the bed for a closer look at the dead man.

The skin at the back of his neck pebbled.

Palardy's stomach had tossed up whatever was inside it. His gaping, cyanotic lips were crusted with vomit. His face, too. It had overflowed onto his pillows, sheet, and blanket, leaving them splashed with yellowish stains.

Ricci examined the nightstand. Besides the phone, it held a small reading lamp and a half-filled glass of something that might have been apple juice or a soft drink. The glass was on a coaster between the bed and phone. Ricci frowned, thinking. Or rather, letting a thought that had already occurred deep in his mind rise to a conscious level. Had he felt an attack or seizure coming on, Palardy surely would have attempted to call for help. Very likely overturned the glass when he was groping for the phone. Dropped the receiver, if he'd managed to get his hand around it. But they were neatly in place. And the way Palardy's blanket was pulled up to his chest, he almost could have been tucked in. Passed away without stirring from his sleep.

But his contorted features and hand signified that his death had been neither peaceful nor painless.

Ricci's frown grew. So far, the picture wasn't coming together for him.

He looked around the room. The two windows to the left of the bed were closed. On the right wall was what looked like a vintage baseball-dugout clock, the Brooklyn Dodgers logo on it. Quite a collector's item. The rest of the sparse furnishings were contrastingly unremarkable. A television on the small dresser opposite the foot of the bed. A desk with one of those inexpensive fabric office chairs pushed underneath it. Next to the desk, a computer printer on a wheeled stand. All he could see on the desktop was a small stack of billing statements clipped to their payment envelopes, a few pens and pencils in a souvenir coffee cup, and a box of facial tissues. Its surface was otherwise bare.

Ricci stepped over to the desk and rolled back the chair, then crouched to look into the kneehole.

The two bidirectional data cables on the floor weren't attached to anything at his end. One had a parallel port connector, the other a phone-style plug-in jack. Ricci's eyes traced the first cable to the back of the printer. The other cable went to a LAN modem on the carpet about four feet away. The network modem's power light was glowing green to indicate it was turned on. From there another cable ran along the edge of the carpet toward the bed and then behind the headboard to a small metal plate below the windowsill. Yet another led from the same plate to the television set.

Palardy had a high-speed cable Internet connection. Made sense. It was probably on the corporate tab.

Ricci rose and turned toward the entrance. Perez was already putting away his phone.

"I talk to your friend," the building manager told him. "Says he gonna call police right away. Says you should stay and meet them."

Ricci nodded.

"I want to look around some more, anyway," he said through his mask. "You still feel like keeping an eye on me, that's fine. But I figure you might rather wait outside."

Perez glanced over at the corpse, then back at Ricci.

"Yes," he said. "Maybe outside."

Ricci nodded again.

"One question," he said. "Do you know if Palardy owned a computer? Ever notice a machine on his desk when you were doing repairs, or anything like that?"

Perez shrugged.

"Can't remember. I come inside here maybe two, three times before today, that's it," he said. "Why you ask?"

Ricci grunted and shook his head.

"Just curious," he said.

Ashley Gordian was alone with her husband. Such a basic thing. So fundamental. A woman and the man she loved, the man with whom she'd shared a thousand intimacies, together. But she'd had to battle a small army of doctors, plow through their unanimous objections, to make it happen. She understood their reasons, of course. Their fiduciary responsibilities, their obligation to prevent the transference of his infection, their genuine concern for her welfare. And she'd agreed to abide by their restrictions when they finally relented and allowed her into the room into which Roger had been moved, a room in isolation from the rest of the hospital . . . what she'd overheard one of them refer to as a "warm zone." She had put on protective attire. Let herself be wrapped from head to toe. A cap, mask, and gloves. A smock over her outer clothes. Booties over her shoes. There could be no part of her that was left exposed. No direct contact with him for the fifteen minutes they'd reluctantly given her. Her flesh could not touch his flesh.

Married three decades, and their flesh could not touch.

She looked down at his unconscious form, a large, fit

man rendered so fragile in so incredibly short a time, tubes running into his nose from a mechanical ventilator, the pressurized air flowing into his lungs to keep them open, to force oxygen into them, prevent them from drowning in this body's own fluids as he lay there, unable to breathe for himself.

She looked down at him now, looked down at him and wanted more than anything to remove the gloves from her hands, tear them off and soothe his brow, and knew she couldn't, couldn't peel away the layers of plastic and rubber and synthetic fabric separating them.

But their hearts . . .

She inhaled through her mask and stepped closer to the bed.

Their hearts, she thought, would not be unjoined.

"Gord," she said. "It's me . . . Ashley . . ."

She heard the tremor in her voice and paused to control it. *Come on, you can do better. Be strong. For him.*

"I know I look like a wrapped piece of fish, but trust me, I dressed up for you," she said. "I'm wearing that blouse you always compliment, the blue silk one, underneath this miserable smock."

His eyes remained closed. He did not move. The ventilator pumped breath into him.

"Hannah's flying in from Connecticut today. I think she's tired of Julia being the daughter who gets all your attention. Brian, he's going to stay home from work to take care of the kids while she's here. You should have trusted me all those years ago when I said he'd make good husband material. . . ."

She brushed her gloved fingertips lightly over his cheek, a sterile contact that was the closest she could come to feeling him.

The ventilator pumped.

"The doctors, they're really hustling to make you well, and trying to be nice to me in their doctorly way," she said. "This morning I was introduced to a specialist . . . Eric Oh. He's looking into your case, running tests, and thinks he might have an idea what's wrong with you. He was asking me whether you might have come into contact with *rodents* lately, of all things. And you know, there I am, worried sick about you, listening to his questions, wanting to do anything I can to help, and all of a sudden I get this crazy urge to lay into him for insinuating we don't keep a clean house."

Another pause.

"Well, I managed to calm myself without saying anything I'd live to regret, and decided it's possible some field mice could have nested in our basement . . . or even been in Julia's yard when you were working on the dog corral. So now they're sending teams out to look around both our properties for droppings, I think they said." She shrugged. "Mouse shit, honey, in my kitchen. Can you believe it? Maybe I *should* have cracked that doctor one, huh?"

He did not move.

Not a flicker under his eyelids.

She listened to the ventilator pump.

"Oh, some good news," she said. *Strong, strong.* "Everybody's starting to talk Super Bowl for the Packers. I've been hearing it all week on the news. They're playing at home Sunday, I think it's that team from Florida you always gripe about. The weather's been so cold in Wisconsin, they already have snow on the ground, and I know you say that gives your boys the advantage over the competition, that they can *take* a little nip in the air...."

She felt a sob well suddenly into her throat and clenched her teeth against it. Pushing it back down inside her. Banishing it.

"Anyway, back at the ranch, Megan and Pete and the crew are doing some sleuthing of their own. Trying to see if they can find somebody who might have passed you the bug. You know how they are, wanting to make everything right. I swear, they'd go to war with the universe for you. And I know Pete would turn red in the face if he ever heard me say this ... Vince, too, ... oh God, *especially* Vince ... but I think they love you almost as much as I do. Really love you, Gord."

She became aware of movement behind her, turned to look over her shoulder.

A nurse. Signaling her from just inside the door.

Ashley nodded, held up a finger.

The nurse returned the nod and withdrew.

Ashley leaned forward over the bed.

"I'm getting the hook," she said in a quiet voice. "They only give me a few minutes at a time. The doctors, that is. You know how they are. So before I forget to give you the *best* news ... aside from the football predictions, naturally ... before I forget, I want to announce that I've decided to lift the ban on flavored coffee. It's over. Finished. As of today. When you get out of here, it's hazelnut, French vanilla, mocha java ... whatever you want. So you hang in there, okay? *You hang in.*"

Ashley wiped her eyes with the back of her arm, breathed, heard the ventilator breathe for her husband.

Then she became aware of the nurse at the door again.

In silence, she touched a rubber glove to her heart, gently touched it to his heart, and straightened.

They can't be unjoined, she thought.

And slowly pulled herself away from him and turned to leave the room.

NINETEEN

PHIL HERNANDEZ, THE CHIEF COUNTERSNOOP, WAS snagged to lead Nimec and Ricci into Palardy's office minutes after Ricci returned from Sunnydale. Ashley Gordian had called with word of her husband's rapid downturn and isolation, and the two Sword ops couldn't afford to lose any time.

"You know anybody who fraternized with Palardy?" Nimec asked Hernandez. "Buddies from work, outside contacts, girlfriends . . . ?"

Hernandez shook his head. He was a tautly built man in his late forties with graying hair, skin the color of sun-baked ocher, and intelligent brown eyes.

"Don kept to himself," he said. "Didn't even mention he used to be married till I noticed that snapshot over there and asked him about it." He tipped his head toward a small picture frame on Palardy's desk. The photo showed a plump woman with a nice face and lively smile crouched on a beach blanket with two small children. A boy and girl who might have been twins and were certainly very close in age. "Don told me he was divorced a few years ago. Wife took custody of the kids. I think she lives somewhere back East." Another shake of his head, this time accompanied by a sigh. "Jesus, I suppose I'd better see if I can get her address from personnel, somebody's got to notify his family."

Ricci nodded. "If an asshole named VanDerwort gives you any flak—"

"VanDer*werf*," Nimec corrected.

"You let us handle him," Ricci said.

Ricci glanced around the room. It was a tiny, windowless cubicle as unremarkable as Palardy's condominium had been. A computer workstation stood against one wall. On a credenza opposite it were a pair of headphones and some other sweep equipment, mostly minor accessories. Heavy-duty apparatus like the Big Sniffer were kept under electronic lock and key in a secure storage locker elsewhere on the floor.

Nimec was looking at Hernandez. "Did Palardy's behavior seem at all unusual lately?"

"Far as his health?"

"That, or anything else. In your opinion."

Hernandez thought a moment, then shrugged.

"Nothing stands out in my mind," he said. "The last time I saw Don must've been Friday. Maybe nine o'clock in the morning, after his sweep. He seemed a little quiet, but that's how it was with him. I won't say he got moody. You could ordinarily expect him to be pleasant. He just wasn't the type to talk about his personal life."

"So you've told us," Nimec said.

Hernandez shrugged again.

"The job's repetitive. You come in, make your

rounds, do your paperwork. Most of the guys walk through the door in the morning, pour their coffees, can't wait to tell each other whether they had a good night, a lousy one, saw a movie, won at poker, got drunk, got laid, you know. And I encourage that."

"Relieves the tedium," Nimec said.

A nod. "I'd rather have my people happy than unhappy. The priorities, though, are that they're reliable and thorough. And Don is. *Was*. Kept his men on their tiptoes."

"In what way?" Ricci said.

"Every way you'd want from a team leader. Don was tight about his records. A stickler for equipment maintenance. And nobody was more up on the latest antibug technologies. He knew his stuff, was always requisitioning upgrades."

"The first time we talked, you acted like it wasn't anything to set off air-raid sirens about when he stopped calling after Monday. Somebody's that diligent, how come you didn't think it was a bigger deal?"

Hernandez looked abashed.

"Honestly, I was damn concerned," he said. "But I figured that whatever could make him act so out of character had to be pretty serious, and I wanted to give him a little slack. In case it was something personal, know what I mean?"

Ricci regarded him steadily. "He's one of your own, you look out for him."

Hernandez nodded.

"Listen, if you hadn't beat me to it, I would have headed down to his place tonight myself," he said. "Been the one to find the poor guy."

"Lucky me," Ricci said. He expelled a sigh. "Palardy's records . . . where'd he keep them?"

Hernandez waved at the computer against the wall.

"In there. He entered his reports every day, sent copies directly to my terminal at the end of each week. Once a month I'd get his assessment of our surveillance countermeasure protection level, which is standard practice for all team leaders."

"Sounds like a lot of typing," Nimec said.

"That's true," Hernandez said. "But it's how we plug holes. And avoid new ones."

Ricci was rubbing his chin. "The reports get written up in the building? During business hours?"

"Depends," Hernandez said. "Sometimes when they're making their monthly assessments, the team leaders would rather take the work home with them than park it here."

"Palardy, too?"

"Sure," Hernandez said. "Detailed as his were, he'd never have left this office otherwise."

"He must have had a desktop PC at his condo, then."

Hernandez gestured vaguely with both hands.

"You're the only person I know who's seen the inside of the place," he said. "I *can* tell you that he brought in a notebook computer every so often."

"He ever leave it behind?"

"I really have no idea. Suppose it's possible."

Ricci glanced around the little room. There was no sign of the notebook and not many spots where it could be. He went over to the workstation, pulled open its drawer. It was filled front to back with carefully labeled file folders. Nothing else. Questions picking at his mind, he recalled the two disconnected cables under Palardy's bedroom desk.

He turned to Hernandez.

"I need to sit down at his computer and check out what's on Palardy's hard drive," he said. "Might take me a while."

Hernandez's expression showed reluctant acceptance.

"You call the shots," he said. "If I asked you why, would you tell me?"

Ricci looked at Nimec, got his nod, looked back at Hernandez.

"The boss is in bad shape," he said. "Nobody's sure what has him down, but we're afraid it might be the same thing that took out Palardy. And we want to trace Palardy's contacts. Try to connect the dots before this situation gets any worse."

Hernandez stood without saying anything for a moment. Then he stepped over to the computer and turned it on.

"It's all yours," he said. "You need any help, call me in my office. If I'm not there, page me."

Ricci nodded. He was thinking Hernandez was okay.

"Appreciate it," he said, and sat behind the monitor to see what he could see.

Lucio Salazar met them in Tecate, a small border town and smuggler's gateway on the Baja Peninsula, about a half hour's drive east of Tijuana.

Despite the necessity of the trip, Lucio supposed it was only as his driver pulled over to the drab motel on *Avenida Benito Juarez* that he altogether believed he was about to arrange for the death of Enrique Quiros, son of his old friend Tomás, with whom he'd pilfered fruit and bread from the outdoor market stands of Tijuana when both were ragged strays without a whole pair of shoes between them. The prepubescent Lucio already looking after his younger brothers, looking to survive on the street, long years from becoming the clan leader of *Los Magos*. Just another cast-off son of a whore and some unremembered clench in the night, insignificant as a stain on a dirty sheet. And maybe it wasn't until he was in the room with the men he'd hired for the job, looking at one of the guns that would be used for the takedown, that his purpose in coming there really sank into his heart.

He had cause enough to believe things were well beyond any other solution. For openers, Lathrop's information was always solid, and he had been definite that Quiros meant to put him in the grave. Then, by pure coincidence, the scouts he'd sent to Balboa the night before had spotted a group of Quiros's men outside the park, skulking around for twenty minutes before they took off. While they could have been there for the same reason as Lucio's own men, wanting to familiarize themselves with the grounds in case of a double cross, he doubted it, considering what he'd learned of Enrique's recent maneuvers. And he could not overlook the tunnel raid.

Even so, Lucio guessed some part of him was still holding onto a shred of hope that violence would be avoided in this instance. That their differences could be reconciled out of respect for Tomás's memory. But again it came down to a matter of survival. At any cost.

Now he studied the weapon being exhibited for him like some enticing rarity, a Walther 2000 sniper rifle with a special optical attachment on the scope. After a couple of minutes, he glanced up at the slight, dark-eyed man who'd laid it across the bedspread.

"Let's talk money," he said.

The little man nodded. "We each take twenty thousand. Half up front. The balance when it's done."

"Eighty large is high—"

"Not for us, it isn't. And the total is a *hundred* thousand. Nonnegotiable. There's a fifth member of the team at the control station."

Salazar gave him a look of hard appraisal.

"Nonnegotiable," he echoed.

"Yes."

"I don't like your position, I can take this contract elsewhere."

The little man's eyes glittered.

"You can," he said. "But you won't get the same thing we deliver."

Salazar kept looking at him. He motioned toward the Walther.

"Your tricked-up piece doesn't impress me," he said. "I'm not concerned with anything but results."

"I understand that. This isn't about flash. We just like people to know some of what's behind our asking price."

Salazar was quiet. Then he released a long sigh.

"Okay," he said. "We have a deal."

The little man nodded.

"We'd better go over tonight's timetable," he said.

The first application Ricci accessed on Palardy's computer was his E-mail reader, thinking it would be the logical place to search for contacts. Before checking his address book, Ricci scanned the unopened messages on his queue. Most were from subscriber lists related to countersurveillance issues. A few were obvious junk mails. One was an order confirmation from an E-bookseller.

Only the third description caught Ricci's interest. It said:

FROM SUBJECT RECEIVED
DPALARDY@UPLINK.COM NONE 11/14/2000
4:36 AM

Ricci turned to Nimec in the chair beside him, pointing toward the mailer's address.

"Look at that," he said. "Palardy sent it to himself."

"Early Tuesday morning," Nimec said.

"Very early."

And almost a full day after anybody at UpLink last heard from him, both men thought.

Nimec leaned forward. "Well, open it already. What are we waiting for?"

Ricci highlighted the description on the screen, double-clicked his mouse, and read the contents of the email:

RHJAJA00BHJM00WHRH!JM00WHBHJA00
TJAJ00?!CAJBJTRH
GWRHMVGCRHUGBHAJ00RHJBAJ00.
RHBHCAJBJTRHGCBHGWJA00TJ:CARHJA00
CATJJA00UG?!BHJBJAMVGCRHJA00
RHJBJA00RHGW!!
RHJA""ALRHMFTJJAUGRHBH
:MVGCRHJA00TJJGWH!
AJ00JPGCTJTJJA00UGRH!?
JA00RHUGBHMVBHJARHJTRH
JA00GWRHJB.JAMVJGTJJA
00""MVGCBHAJMV,TJGCJBJMJMRHJA
JGTJJA00!CA!BHJTRHGWRH.

He looked at Nimec again.

"What the hell's this?" he said.

In their full-faceplate biohazard ensembles they might have been astronauts exploring another world. But this was no alien landscape. This was the Gordians's home and hillside, and the team of state and CDC virus hunters called in by Eric Oh had to comb every inch of their property for the dried rodent excreta known to transmit hantavirus to humans.

The white space suits with their protective apparatus were burdensome and tiring to wear. Communication between team members was enabled only through two-way radio. Their air packs weighed forty pounds. Their thick, multilayered gloves made it difficult to get hold of things. Their heavy, steel-toed boots made walking itself a rigor.

The suits could be hard on their surroundings as well. Preservation of Ashley's lovingly maintained gardens was impossible in the scrupulous probe for contaminants. It was imperative to inspect any area that might be visited or inhabited by field mice and similar creatures. Her herb patch was dug up, delicate rosebushes were sheared, the mulch around her shrubs was shoveled and bagged. Climbing plants that had flourished on her arbors for a decade were lopped off near the ground, where the little mammals might forage among the root beds. In some instances, the bowers and trellises themselves had to be taken down for the biologists to get at likely sites for established nests or burrows. Dozens of traps were set for live specimens that would be tested for the presence of virus.

Nor was the interior of the house spared these disruptive but necessary intrusions. Mice and voles common to the region used the smallest openings to enter and exit from the outdoors, and these were often found in places normally screened from sight. Furniture was moved, rugs lifted, carpets unstapled. Library shelves were cleared of books, wainscoting panels detached from the wall. Gordian's cluttered basement workshop was virtually taken apart piece by piece. In the kitchen, cooking cupboards were emptied, and utensils and appliances were swept from their shelves. The built-in stainless steel refrigerator, freezer, dishwasher, ice maker, and wine captain had to be removed from their cabinets, their outer insulation pulled away. As outside the residence, many traps were laid.

Miles to the south at Julia Gordian Ellis's new home in Pescadero, a second group of investigators in moon suits conducted a procedurally identical hunt for the source of contagion. Forced to abandon the premises, Julia went to stay with a friend, bringing only her dogs and a suitcase full of clothing. Intense focus was put on the section of backyard where her father had been building his greyhound corral, the theory being he might have disturbed an underground rodent den while excavating soil for its posts. The standing section of fence was disassembled, its laboriously installed posts extracted from the ground.

These painstaking efforts of course proved fruitless, for in the end, not a trace of virus was uncovered.

"Hello. Eric Oh, please."

"Speaking . . ."

"Eric, it's Steve Karonis over at Sobel Genetics. I know you asked me to call on your direct office line, but I must've misplaced the number. Had to go through the switchboard . . ."

"No problem. What've you got on Gordian's virus specimens?"

"Everything is strictly unofficial, okay? Even with our whole staff on this, we need twenty-four hours minimum to make a reliable determination, and it hasn't even been—"

"It's unofficial."

"All right, hold on to your seat. The PCR screening shows your isolate doesn't match any known strain of hantavirus. Which from what you've already told me, shouldn't come as a surprise—"

"Then why am I still supposed to be worried about falling down?"

"Because . . . and again, this is only based on initial results . . . but there appear to be RNA sequences that don't occur naturally in the species. Or in the family. They're at the regulation sites on the genome, right where you'd expect to find them if, well, components had been inserted—"

"Are you telling me the virus was artificially *modified*?"

"I'm telling you there are signs of genetic modification, yes."

The phone cradled between his neck and shoulder, Eric looked down at his hand.

He was indeed holding on to his seat, literally holding on, his knuckles white as bleached bone.

"You want to say the words, or have I got to be the one who jumps first?" Ricci said from behind Palardy's computer.

Nimec's eyes were still on the E-mail they had opened.

"It looks like code," he said. "Some kind of code."

"And we're off into space."

"What do you make of it?"

Ricci shrugged, staring at the screen in contemplative silence.

"Be straight with me," Nimec said. "When Hernandez was in here with us, I heard you question him about Palardy maybe leaving a notebook computer around here. I saw you look for it in the drawer. And that made me pretty sure you noticed more at Palardy's house than you've let on."

Ricci turned to him. "How come you didn't say anything to me?"

"Figured you had your reasons for being quiet, and you would talk when you were ready."

Ricci nodded.

"I wasn't trying to keep secrets," he said. "I just like to have my thoughts in order before I lay them out. And I'm not sure that I do. That any of what's on my mind makes sense."

"You asked me to jump, and I did," Nimec said. "Your turn."

Ricci regarded Nimec another moment, then nodded again. He told him about the marks he'd seen on the door to Palardy's condo, about the odd positioning of his body given the presumed cause of death, about the cables he'd noticed under Palardy's desk.

"I looked everywhere for a computer before the cops showed, Pete. And I can tell you there wasn't one in the place," Ricci said. "No computer, not a single diskette, either. And that bothered me. Bothers me even more now that we know Palardy sent an E-mail from *some* machine at a time we can assume he was at home." He paused. "Another peculiar thing caught my eye before I left. Palardy'd installed one of those floor bolts behind the front door. Lets you open the door to see who's outside when there's a knock, and not have to worry about a robber pushing his way through. You trigger it with your foot from inside. Know the kind I mean?"

"Sure."

"Well, it wasn't locked. You figure somebody goes to the trouble and expense of having something like that installed, he's going to shoot the bolt while he's home at night."

"So you think somebody opened the door with a credit card, reached inside to disengage it, let himself in. That it?"

"Wouldn't take a master thief," Ricci said.

Nimec looked curious. "Okay, say it happened. What's next? The intruder lifts Palardy's computer and data storage media for some reason?"

"Yeah," Ricci said. "Or maybe he kills Palardy first, then takes off with it—"

"Hold on. You've told me yourself that Palardy was obviously sick."

"Sick isn't dead, Pete. Sick can still talk." He nodded at the screen. "Or send coded messages to his office."

Nimec didn't comment for a while. Then he said, "Give me your theory."

"There are poisons that aren't easy to detect or might be overlooked by a coroner if the vic's already on his way out and somebody wants to speed along his exit. You used to be on the job same as me. How many times you respond to a sudden death call, take one look around, another at the DOA, and know on account of what you saw that it was a murder disguised as something else? An accident. A routine suicide. A heart attack. I'm telling you, Palardy's body was arranged for viewing."

"You got that from the appearance of the scene, okay. I'm not doubting your eye. But where's the connection to Gord in this? They've found virus in his blood specimens, so we know *he* wasn't poisoned."

Ricci shot him a look. "We're in thin air together, right? So just between us, Pete, what if the boss and Palardy were both infected with the virus? On purpose. If that's the case, we don't know what Palardy could have told us about it or who'd want to stop him from talking."

Nimec took a deep breath.

"The cops and public health investigators are rushing Palardy's autopsy. I'll stay close to them. Make sure they conduct a toxicological exam for anything that could mimic or speed up the symptoms of the disease."

"Sounds good."

Nimec thought a minute. "Okay, then what? Let's suppose they find Palardy and Gord were exposed to the same germ. Or turn up some forensics that would bear out your suspicions about the circumstances of Palardy's death—"

Ricci interrupted him. "There's no reason we should wait for them to get that far. Wait for any of their results to gain ourselves a head start. And we goddamn well *know* there's something funny about Palardy's message. Why not have the people in our crypto unit put on their decoder rings?"

"That's already occurred to me," Nimec said. "I can have them on it right aw—"

He noticed the computer display unexpectedly go blank, and out of habit checked the power light to see whether it had lost current or gone into a sleep mode. Then cartoonish winged clocks and watches began floating across it in random patterns, satisfying his interest.

"Screen saver," he said, voicing his minor realization aloud. "Time flies."

Ricci glanced at the display.

"Fits," he muttered.

TWENTY

"SOMETHING LIKE THIS, ONE LOOK AT IT TELLS YOU almost as much as it doesn't," James Carmichael said without elaboration. He was seated behind Palardy's computer, studying the enigmatic series of letters and punctuation marks in his E-mail.

Nimec and Ricci exchanged glances from where they stood, bookending him. His statement itself struck them as a bit mysterious, but that was almost expected. Before Roger Gordian lured him into his employ, Carmichael had been a third-generation National Security Agency analyst, his grandfather having worked for the cryptologic intelligence organization from the time of its Cold War inception by secret presidential memorandum—back when the government was still mum about its existence, and Washington insiders cheekily referred to the NSA acronym as standing for No Such Agency.

"How about you walk us through," Nimec said. "Starting with whether we're all on the same page about it actually being a code, and not what happens when somebody's out of his skull with fever and doesn't know what he's typing."

A thirtyish man in shirtsleeves with sharp blue eyes and a bumper crop of wavy black hair, Carmichael looked over his shoulder at Nimec.

"Sorry," he said. "The minute I start to sound condescending, permission's granted to whump me across the back of the head."

Nimec smiled a little. "We'll allow you one free pass."

"Deal." Carmichael turned back to the screen. "Okay, first, I think we can rule out that it's the product of an incoherent mind. It's too systematic in its construction. I also think what we've got in front of us isn't strictly speaking a code but a cipher. People use the terms as if they're interchangeable, but there's a distinction, and it's important for more than semantic reasons. Codes substitute whole words with letters, numbers, symbols, phrases, or other words. Ciphers create substitutions for independent letters or syllables, and they allow for more complex communications. They're the basis of modern electronic encryption. A good way to keep them straight might be to compare codes to ancient hieroglyphics or pictographs, ciphers to the alphabet. Imagine Shakespeare trying to write Hamlet using pictures on the wall, and it'll be apparent why ciphertext is more refined and efficient."

"You can tell the difference right off?" Ricci said.

"Usually, yeah." Carmichael said. He indicated several spots on the lines of characters. "Frequent recurrences of letter groups are a fair giveaway that they're replacing small linguistic units. See the letter pair, or bigram, 'BH'? It appears ten, eleven times. You wouldn't expect the same word to be repeated that often within a relatively short message . . . but a letter or syllable, sure. And then there's the back-to-back use of the polygram 'JM00'. That probably equals a double-letter combination in plaintext—"

"Plaintext being . . ."

"The words you're trying to conceal," Carmichael said. "As opposed to ciphertext, which would be the characters you're using to conceal them."

Ricci was nodding his head. "That's all there is to this nut, it should be easy to crack," he said. "The regular . . . the *plaintext* . . . alphabet has twenty-six letters. Which means you'd have an equal amount of ciphertext groups, right? One group for each letter, A through Z. Run all the possible matches through a computer, how long would it take to kick out the one that lets you form real words that add up to real sentences instead of nonsense? Simple math, there are only so many possibilities."

Carmichael looked at him. "Your logic makes sense as far as it goes, but leaves us with a couple of big problems," he said. "One, let's assume Palardy's ciphertext groups correlate to letters in the English alphabet, and not some other with a greater or lesser number of characters. Figuring out that part might just be the first step toward getting to the clear—the hidden message—since we don't know that there aren't added levels of encryption. And two, any cipher worth the thought and effort needed to create it incorporates nulls. These could be letters, digits, symbols, maybe punctuation marks that don't fit the system and can complicate things."

"Wouldn't your computers be able identify them for that very reason?" Nimec asked. "Exclude them because they *don't* fall into the pattern?"

"With time," Carmichael replied tersely, looking at him in a way that conveyed he was all too aware of its desperate shortage.

Silence hung a minute. Then, from Nimec: "It's crazy. Palardy composes a secret message before he dies, E-mails it here. He must want us to be able to get at it. I can't see why else he goes to the trouble."

Carmichael nodded. "Agreed. Even if his purpose was to frustrate us, put us through our paces . . . and we don't know it was . . . I still bet he'd provide a key. Either separately or hidden within the cryptogram."

"You think you can do it?" Nimec asked Carmichael. "Find the key, whatever Palardy's intentions might've been?"

"I'll have my people go over every bit of data on this terminal's hard drive. And any removable storage media he might have left behind. See what we learn from them." A sigh. "I know we can do a successful crypta-nalysis. Break the system without a key. But truthfully, I can't estimate how long it would take. Could be hours, days, even weeks."

"Goddamn it." Ricci frowned. "If Palardy wasn't playing games with us . . . wanted to tell us something . . . what the hell was he thinking? Why bother encrypt-ing his message?"

"The only reason I can figure would be to keep it from whoever got into his apartment and carried away his notebook," Nimec said.

"If that's it, he could have sent the message in plain language and then wiped it from his notebook's mem-ory," Ricci said. "Reformatted his hard drive to be pos-itive it couldn't be recovered."

"Unless he was worried about somebody being able to pull it from our mainframe."

"If our security's been compromised to that extent, Pete, we'd both better turn in our resignations."

Carmichael had been listening quietly, his eyes narrowed in contemplation as they spoke.

"Any objections if I toss a hypothesis of my own into the pot?" he said.

"None," Nimec said.

Carmichael looked from one man to the other.

"Maybe Palardy wanted the person who got hold of the computer to know he'd sent us a message but have to sweat about what information it contained," he said. "In other words, maybe he wasn't playing with our heads, but *his*."

By Wednesday afternoon, Enrique Quiros's eyes were so familiar with the message in the Sent column of Palardy's E-mail program that it might have been burned into their retinas. He had spent hours trying to make sense of it. Long, futile hours.

Quiros switched off the notebook computer that had been brought to him from Palardy's condominium, closed its lid, and reached for the tumbler of scotch on his desk. It was not his usual habit to drink before sundown, but his nerves badly needed steadying. One by one, his recent problems had compounded. Felix's idiotic stunt, Felix's murder, his forced hand in setting up tonight's appointment with Salazar. And now everything he'd feared from the moment he had climbed aboard the carousel with that blonde had come about. She had sucked him into the conspiracy to kill Roger Gordian, made him an instrumental participant, and he had known that he would live to regret it.

Palardy had been cringing and manipulable, but Enrique had never thought he was stupid. He had felt all along that Palardy might be prepared for treachery, that once he realized he was a doomed man, he would want to expose the people he knew had used and discarded him. And he would find a way to do it before he could be stopped.

Quiros lifted the glass to his mouth and took a good, deep swallow. He didn't know how to decode the message. Didn't have the slightest clue. Perhaps the great and inviolable El Tío would possess the means, but Enrique was not anxious to commit suicide by sending it up the line to him. If its purpose was what Enrique believed it to be, no good could come of that. Not for him. Although El Tío's whereabouts and identity were protected by blind upon blind, Palardy would have surely implicated Enrique, pointed the way to his door . . . and that was where El Tío would quickly cut the trail to his own.

Quiros tossed back the rest of his whiskey. It was out of his hands now. Completely out of his hands. The fucking heavens were about to rock.

He could only go about his plans for tonight, deal with Salazar, and wait to see whether there would be someplace to take cover when the sky came tumbling down in a million pieces.

Her hair golden in the California sunlight, she strode toward the airline ticket office with a shopping bag on her arm, drawing glances of uniform appreciation from the males she passed on the street. She was aware of each look—the discreet, the boorish, the passively speculative, the aggressively gaming. As a runway model in Paris and Milan not many years ago, she had learned that some women could trade upon beauty and sex as some men did on wealth and power. The terms of exchange, the boundaries, were what one chose to make them.

In Europe, at the parties in the clubs and aboard the yachts where she was invited after the shows, she had found it was often the truly dangerous men who had been able to provide the things she most desired. It was the oldest of understandings: Take of me, and I will take of you. She had accepted it without hesitation from a succession of lovers and been introduced to circles of hidden influence and inestimable fortune. The lifestyle attracted her, fascinated her, thrilled her.

Eventually she had come to do favors that went beyond the physical, although that was a constant part of the bargain. Sometimes enjoyable, sometimes less so. But no man had ever forced anything upon her. Made her do anything against her will. The assignments she ran across borders, moving from one country to the next under a variety of identities, gave her a wonderful feeling of value and importance, and it only heightened her excitement to know the international laws she had broken while using any one of those assumed names could have put her in prison forever. She had passed under the eyes of authorities, hiding in full view, and it exhilarated her.

Having lived among the dangerous, enjoyed the spoils of their illicit traffic, she in due time acquired a taste for the danger itself.

Siegfried Kuhl was by far the most dangerous man

she had ever met. Once she had been with him, none of the rest had interested her, and she knew no other would again. He had satisfied her with a fullness she had never dreamed might be experienced. What sensual delights could be greater than those he lavished on her? What crimes more damnable than those she'd committed for him?

Now he had finally sent word. Although his affairs in Canada had not yet concluded, he would have the opportunity to leave for a few days and had made plans for them to be together. Where he had promised. In the place that was special to him and would become special to her.

She turned into the ticket office, waited on a short line, then walked over to an available clerk.

"Hello," he said, smiling at her from behind the counter. He looked like a sheep, soft and penned. "How may I help you?"

"I would like a reservation for a flight to Madrid," she said and gave him the date she wished to leave.

He nodded, tapped his keyboard with one finger.

"How many passengers will there be?"

"Just myself," she said.

He glanced up at her.

"A lovely city, one of my favorites," he said amiably. "Have you traveled there before?"

"Only for a brief stopover," she said. "But I'll be joining someone who is very well acquainted with it."

"Ahh," he said. "Business or pleasure?"

She looked at the clerk and mused that his entire bleating existence was not worth the most transitory and unremembered of her many disposable aliases.

"Pleasure," she said and smiled back at him. "Strictly pleasure."

"Carmichael." Ricci leaned into the room in the crypto section. "How's it going?"

"The same as it was when you asked fifteen minutes ago," Carmichael said. He turned toward him in his swivel chair. "And when Megan Breen and Vince Scull stopped in ten minutes ago. And when Pete Nimec buzzed me just bef—"

Ricci held up his hand.

"Don't uncork." he said. "I just asked a question."

"Listen, I'm not the one who needs to stay cool," Carmichael said and gestured toward the computer he'd carried out of Palardy's office, now on his gray steel desk. "I've already told you I'd report any progress. I've made multiple copies of the hard drive, and my team's sifting through it all, sector by sector, file by file. That's at the same time we're trying to determine whether the message might precisely conform to some classic model of encipherment. We're hitting the books. Researching the Freemasons, Vigenère, Arthur Conan Doyle for God's sake . . ."

He let the sentence fade, blew air out of his mouth.

Ricci looked at him.

"Okay, I read you," he said. "Anything I can do to help?"

"Keep the distractions away. This came at us damn fast. I know everybody's stressed, but you've got to give us a chance. Let us do our work." He paused, settled. "I've got a few hunches to check out. If they amount to anything, you'll be the first to know about it."

Ricci nodded. He stood quietly looking into the room

a moment. Carmichael had connected Palardy's CPU to a large, wide, flat panel display mounted on the wall above his desk, and clocks were winging across it. With the screen saver's teal blue background, the effect was more than a little surreal, as if they were flocking in the air outside a window.

"There they go again," he said. "Up and away."

Carmichael at first looked as if he hadn't understood Ricci's meaning, then he realized where his eyes had gone and swiveled halfway around in his chair.

"I have to get rid of that," he said, glancing at the panel. "Pops into my face every five minutes.

Ricci remembered the antique dugout clock in Palardy's bedroom, then the eerily musical call of the cuckoo in the death-house silence of his living room.

"A thing for clocks," he snorted.

Carmichael turned to him.

"What did you say?"

Ricci noted the cryptographer's sudden look of interest.

"Clocks," he said. He heard himself take a breath. "Palardy had some kind of goddamned thing for clocks."

At her desk, Megan Breen had been thinking constantly about the boss, and she told everyone that her eyes were red because of allergies. Some visitors to her office even fell for it.

She heard her private line buzz now and picked up, tossing a crumpled Kleenex into the trash.

The caller was Ashley Gordian.

"Ashley, hello. How is—?"

She stopped. Waited for Ashley to say something at the other end of the line. How to balance the need to tackle reality against her fear of what it might be?

"Gord's condition hasn't changed in the past couple of hours," Ashley said. Megan almost sighed with relief; at least he wasn't worse. It was strange how the definition of good news became relative once the ground started to slide. "He did open his eyes for a little while around lunchtime. The nurse couldn't be sure how alert he was, and I wasn't in the room. I can't . . . they won't let me stay with him. But I've already told you that, haven't I?"

"I think so, yes," Megan said. In fact, Ashley had told her, and more than once. She sounded lost. "Are you at the hospital right now? There's nothing pressing at the office, and it would do me some good to get away. We could have coffee—"

"That's why I was calling," Ashley said. "I think you *should* come down here. And that you'd better bring along Pete or one of the others. I've heard from Eric Oh, the epidemiologist. There's been some word about Gord's illness, and I don't know exactly what to make of it. Except that it's important." She paused. "I'm sorry I'm being disjointed . . ."

"Don't worry about that, Ashley. My guidebook's open in front of me, and it says it's allowed under the circumstances."

Megan heard Ashley move the receiver from her mouth and clear her throat.

"Thank you," she said after a moment.

"Thank the writer."

Another brief silence. When Ashley spoke again, her voice was a bit steadier. "Eric's heading over to meet me," she said. "And Elliot Lieberman, Gord's regular doctor. Eli has an office at the hospital . . ."

"Yes."

"Someone from Richard Sobel's genetics lab is also coming. The tests are still inconclusive, and I'm sure they wouldn't be willing to disclose anything if they didn't trust us to be discreet. Not yet. Not until they had more proof. People would jump all over them. Attack their reputations, lump them with flying saucer theorists—"

"Ashley . . . what is it they've found?"

Ashley took an audible breath. The words weren't coming to her lips easily. "They think that the virus was manufactured," she said at last. "That someone may have specifically designed it to kill . . . to *murder* . . . Roger."

Megan held the phone a moment, stunned. "I'll be right over," she said.

Ten minutes after ousting Ricci from his office, Carmichael sat at his desk with the door locked behind him, his telephone unplugged, and his intercom and corporate cellular turned off. Before severing these contacts with the outside world, he had instructed the group of analysts working on Palardy's secret communication to call him on his personal cell phone if they shook anything loose.

He needed to be alone. To think. And puzzle out what appeared to be a simple—even primitive—cryptogram that he was sure Palardy must have known would be decipherable to UpLink's specialists, experienced pros who were used to making and breaking messages generated with the most sophisticated methods of algorithmic encryption.

There was something about the bigrams and polygrams . . . something that kept tickling Carmichael's mind right below the uppermost level of consciousness, trying to burrow up to the surface like an insect through a thin layer of soil. It had been about to emerge before the flurry of interruptions from Ricci and company startled it away. Now, absent distractions, he hoped to coax it back out of its hidey-hole.

To help him focus, Carmichael had added a clip-art icon from his word processor to the string of ciphertext transmitted by Palardy, and the image on his wall panel looked like this:

RHJAJA00BHJM00WHRH!JM00WHBHJA00 TJAJ00?!CAJBJTRH GWRHMVGCRHUGBHAJ00RHJBAJ00.RHBH CAJBJTRHGCBHGWJA00TJ:CARHJA00 CATJJA00UG?!BHJBJAMVGCRHJA00RHJB JA00RHGW!!RHJA""ALRHMFTJJAUGRHBH :MVGCRHJA00TJJGWH!AJ00JPGCTJTJJA 00UGRH!?JA00RHUGBHMVBHJARHJTRH JA00GWRHJB.JAMVJGTJJA00""MVGC BHAJMV,TJGCJBJMJMRHJAJGTJJA00! CA!BHJTRHGWRH.

He sat at his computer console and stared at the cryptogram. It reminded him a lot of the type that might have been incorporated in an old-fashioned potboiler, circa the 1890s, meant to amuse and challenge the astute reader with a basic knowledge of encipherment techniques. And he had a feeling Palardy had wanted it that way. Wanted it to be just difficult enough to buy him time to retract it unbroken, should that become advantageous, and simultaneously rattle whoever might steal his laptop in the event he was harmed *beyond* retracting it.

Carmichael stared at his monitor. It almost was as if he'd stepped into a Holmes novel. Or one of Poe's prototypical mystery stories. And the damnedest thing, the thing he would never have admitted to anyone outside his crypto section, was that getting to the clear might have actually entertained him were the stakes not so terribly high.

"Give it to me, Palardy," he muttered into the silent room. "Give me something."

A thoughtful expression on his face, hands poised over his keyboard, Carmichael decided to remove the punctuation marks from the character string. They had almost jumped out at him as nulls on first impression, and that feeling had only grown stronger as he studied it.

He typed, repeatedly tapping the delete key. The image in front of him was now:

**RHJAJA00BHJM00WHRHJM00WHBHJA00
TJAJ00CAJBJTRH
GWRHMVGCRHUGBHAJ00RHJBAJ00RHBH
CAJBJTRHGCBHGWJA00TJCARHJA00
CATJJA00UGBHJBJAMVGCRHJA00RHJBJA
00RHGWRHJAALRHMFTJJAUGRHBH
MVGCRHJA00TJJGWHAJ00JPGCTJTJJA00
UGRHJA00RHUGBHMVBHJARHJTRH
JA00GWRHJBJAMVJGTJJA00MVGCBH
AJMVTJGCJBJMJMRHJAJGTJJA00
CABHJTRHGWRH**

Carmichael stared at the monitor. Trying to stay mentally loose and limber, slip into what athletes liked to call "the zone," a space where you didn't second-guess yourself, where you let yourself be guided by the automatic cognitive and sensory processes that equaled instinct.

"Come on. Give it up."

He typed again. Letting his thumb give the space bar some action. Splitting up the obvious letter groups to leave him with:

**RH JA JA00 BH JM00 WH RH JM00 WH BH
JA00 TJ
AJ00 CA JB JT RH
GW RH MV GC RH UG BH AJ00 RH JB AJ00
RH BH CA JB JT RH GC BH GW JA00 TJ CA
RH JA00
CA TJ JA00 UG BH JB JA MV GC RH JA00 RH
JB JA00 RH GW RH JA AL RH MF TJ JA UG
RH BH
MV GC RH JA00 TJ JG WH AJ00 JP GC TJ TJ
JA00 UG RH JA00 RH UG BH MV BH JA RH JT
RH
JA00 GW RH JB JA MV JG TJ JA00 MV GC BH
AJ MV TJ GC JB JM JM RH JA JG TJ JA00 CA
BH
JT RH GW RH**

Carmichael stared at the monitor. All right, he thought. Getting somewhere. And here it came again, that tickle of a thought in his brain soil. Some of those discrete letter pairs . . . What was it about them that seemed to bait it out?

Carmichael did a quick cut and paste to put the combinations that kept drawing his eye onto a separate screen:

GW JA TJ JM AJ

He stared at them.

"Come on, come on, let's see you. Come on ou—"

He straightened in his chair and sat very still for about five seconds. Then he abruptly reached into his pocket, activated his cellular, and called one of his section mates.

A woman answered.

"Michelle?" he said.

"Jimmy, hi, what's up?"

"Better head over to my office. I think I've got something figured."

Her tone was crisp. "Be right with you."

"Thanks." Carmichael's finger paused over the disconnect button. In his excitement, he'd almost forgotton to ask for what he wanted her to bring along. "Michelle, still there?"

"Yeah, Jimmy, I was just putting back the phone."

"A favor. It's no big deal, I suppose. We can get the info easily enough on-line or something—"

Impatience: *"Jimmy—"*

"Sorry, Michelle, I'm a little hyped," he said. "Since you're passing the reference library anyway, would you see if you can find that book on the American presidents?"

• • •

The highway's posted speed limit was sixty-five miles per hour. The jet black Beemer's speedometer had ticked up near ninety. This was the Bay Area. Megan Breen was at the wheel. She was in a rush to get to the hospital and hadn't bothered with the radar detector.

Belted into the passenger seat, Rollie Thibodeau gripped his assist handle as she wove in and out of the left lane to pass a Suburban snailing along at a mere seventy-five miles per hour.

She snapped a glance at him through her sunglasses. A deep crease had established itself across his brow. He was very quiet. It occurred to her that six months was not very long ago when someone was recovering from the kind of internal damage he'd suffered in Brazil.

She resisted the urge to sway around the Lincoln now in front of her.

"Rol, everything okay?"

He nodded. "Just thinkin'. Don't slow down on my account."

"Oh. That's not why—"

" 'S'okay, *chere*." He patted her shoulder. "You my favorite gal."

She checked the rearview and passed.

"Those thoughts," she said. "You feel like sharing them?"

He turned to look at her.

"Guess I better." He hesitated. "Came to me what happened to the president-elect in Brazil last month. Colón. I was recollectin' how he took sick, died so sudden. His symptoms . . . ones we know about . . . ones his government didn't cover up . . ."

He didn't have to say any more than that.

His symptoms, Megan thought, had been strikingly similar to Gord's.

She felt her heart clamp in her chest.

"Rollie, UpLink was about to cut a development deal with his administration. Our advance team met with him *weeks* before he died. You remember us talking about it on the *Pomona*?"

He made an affirmative sound.

"There's my thoughts," he said. "All wrapped in a bundle."

Megan nodded and jammed down on the Beemer's gas pedal, shredding over the road like the devil's black stallion.

"Megan phoned," Nimec said. "She's with Ashley and Rollie at the hospital."

Ricci's shoulders tensed almost imperceptibly.

"The boss . . . ?"

"He's hanging on."

"Oh." Ricci breathed. "I didn't know my arch nemesis was heading over there."

Nimec was silent a moment. They were in his office. Just the two of them, by his choice. He'd wanted a chance to toss things around with Ricci before calling Vince Scull.

"Megan grabbed him, hustled off." Nimec paused. "Tom, the docs and lab coats have turned something up. And I've got to tell you, it blew me away."

Ricci looked at him.

"Long and short?" he said.

"Looks like the virus that's affecting Gord was bioengineered. We're not talking about something cultured in some Iraqi or Sudanese 'baby milk factory.' The bug's some kind of mutant created with black bag technology."

"How sure a thing is this?"

"Sure enough for us to run with it," Nimec said. "I asked Meg to give me a dumbed-down explanation of their testing processes. From what I understood, there are confirmed techniques for scanning plant and animal genes for evidence of modification. Before UpLink sold off its biotech division to Richard Sobel, we were doing it for the ag department and other clients. You take a cucumber that has some superficial difference to all the rest at the green grocer, bring it to the lab, and they do a PCR exam, same as they would on a crime suspect's genetic material. The DNA doesn't compare with that variety of cuke, they move on to another level of testing. There are places on the gene string where scientists know to look for . . . I guess they're the equivalent of splices."

Ricci rubbed his neck. "A cucumber isn't a virus," he said.

"But the scientific principles behind the tests are identical. Or close to identical. Meg could give you a fuller rundown. All I can tell you is that these are confirmed procedures," Nimec said. "They've only had, what, a day or two to do the lab work, so I don't know whether the findings meet a standard of proof that would satisfy the scientific establishment. Doesn't matter. Nobody's writing any articles for the *New England Journal of Medicine*. We've been given an inside line, and that's how it stays for now."

Ricci was still and quiet in his chair.

"Ever miss the twentieth century?" he said after a minute.

"More and more."

"But here we are in the future."

"That's right."

"If we have to put up with this bullshit, where are the flying cars? And the robots that pop hot food and drinks out of slots in their chests?"

Nimec managed a half smile. "I always looked forward to the jet packs," he said.

There was a brief silence.

"Where do we go with this, Pete?"

"I was hoping you'd have some ideas. Obviously we've got to learn who developed the virus. And how Gord was exposed."

"The forensics on Palardy might help steer us in the right direction. We've also got to know whether there's anything to his E-mail," Ricci said. He scratched behind his ear. "You hear from our code-breaking whiz?"

Nimec shook his head. "Not for a while. He stopped picking up his phone."

"Booted me right out of his office," Ricci said. "You think we should go knock on his—?"

Nimec's phone broke in with a twitter. He picked up, grunted, nodded, grunted again, replaced the receiver, and abruptly rose from behind his desk. "Timing," he said.

Ricci looked at him. "Carmichael?"

Nimec nodded, tapped Ricci on his shoulder as he hastened around his desk. "Let's move," he said. "He's got something big for us."

"It's quirky but clever, when you take into account that Palardy may have been on his way out when he devised it," Carmichael was explaining virtually as they reached his door. "Sort of a cross between a polyalphabetic and geometric cipher."

What Ricci and Nimec saw on the flat-panel wall monitor facing them was a large graphic:

PRESIDENTS 1-26	PRESIDENTS 1-26 (REORDERED)	CIPHERTEXT/ PLAINTEXT
George Washington	James Buchanan	JB=1=A
John Adams	Abraham Lincoln	AL=2=B
Thomas Jefferson	Andrew Jackson	AJ=3=C
James Madison	Ulysses S. Grant	UG=4=D
James Monroe	Rutherford B. Hayes	RH=5=E
John Quincy Adams	James A. Garfield	JG=6=F
Andrew Jackson	Chester A. Arthur	CA=7=G
Martin Van Buren	Grover Cleveland	GC=8=H
William Henry Harrison	Benjamin Harrison	BH=9=I
John Tyler	William McKinley	WM=10=J
James Knox Polk	Theodore Roosevelt	TR=11=K
Zachary Taylor	William Howard Taft	WT=12=L
Millard Fillmore	George Washington	GW=13=M
Franklin Pierce	John Quincy Adams	JA=14=N
James Buchanan	Thomas Jefferson	TJ=15=O
Abraham Lincoln	John Monroe	JM=16=P
Andrew Johnson	James Madison	JM=17=Q
Ulysses S. Grant	John Adams	JA=18=R
Rutherford B. Hayes	Andrew Johnson	AJ=19=S
James A. Garfield	Martin Van Buren	MV=20=T
Chester A. Arthur	William Henry Harrison	WH=21=U
Grover Cleveland	John Tyler	JT=22=V
Benjamin Harrison	James Knox Polk	JP=23=W
William McKinley	Zachary Taylor	ZT=24=X
Theodore Roosevelt	Millard Fillmore	MF=25=Y
William Howard Taft	Franklin Pierce	FP=26=Z

00=Repeat Initials
Punctuation=Nulls

ROUGH CIRCLE (CLOCK) TABLE

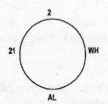

334

"Palardy *did* have a thing for clocks, Ricci, and it's obvious he used one to work out his substitutions," Carmichael went on. "Sooner or later, the computers would have solved this thing mathematically, even without your having made the observation. Just as they would have if some of those letter combinations hadn't jumped out at *my* eye. The GW in particular . . . How many people *don't* immediately think 'George Washington' when they look at that letter pair? Once I let my nose follow that clue, I started noticing other bigrams also corresponded to presidential initials. Jefferson, Jackson, and Teddy Roosevelt's especially popped out at me."

He paused, motioned them into the office. A trim, blonde woman of about thirty-five was standing near the middle of the room.

"Michelle Franks," she said, putting out her hand.

Nimec and Ricci quickly introduced themselves.

She said, "We won't waste precious time with a long explanation . . ."

Good, Ricci and Nimec both thought at once.

". . . but want you to understand how we got this figured, and whipped together the chart in front of you."

"What Palardy did was take a circle and divide it into sixty equal parts by drawing lines across its diameter," Carmichael said.

"Sixty parts, as in sixty minutes on the *clock,*" Michelle said.

Carmichael nodded. "It was obvious to me in Palardy's office that each of his character groups were substitutions. But my first guess was that they stood for letters or syllables, when in fact they stood for numerals."

Right, Ricci thought. *Get on with it.*

"When Jimmy got his hunch about the groups representing the initials of United States presidents—" Michelle began.

"Every one of them *early* presidents," Carmichael cut in. "There were no RRs, as in Ronald Reagan, RN for Nixon, BC for Clinton and so on . . ."

"When he noticed those things, we chose the first twenty-six sets of initials—"

"One for each letter of the alphabet," Carmichael said. "Another thing I might've mentioned in Palardy's office is that the punctuation marks looked like probable nulls. And they wound up being just that. Characters that stand for nothing. Palardy used several: an exclamation point, a period, and a question mark, to name a few."

Which was something both Nimec and Ricci had already discerned for themselves.

"Take the three nulls, add them to the twenty-six initial pairs, and it equals twenty-nine substitution symbols," Michelle said.

"Next you add the double zeros," Carmichael said. "They always follow a set of repeat presidential initials . . . belonging to those who would have served their terms *later* in the chronology of chief executives. Namely Presidents James Monroe, John Quincy Adams, and Andrew Johnson."

"This gives you a grand total of thirty ciphertext characters," Michelle said.

"Half of sixty, and also half of your total number of points on the outside of the circle . . . or circumference of the clock dial," Carmichael said. "After that fell into place, we had to determine which of the letter pairs corresponded to a particular number between one and twenty-six, since that number had to represent a letter in its proper alphabetical sequence. Palardy could have made that part easy by having the numerical order match the order of presidents—"

"Number one being George Washington, two being John Adams, three being Thomas Jefferson, for example . . ."

"But he didn't, probably because it was *too* easy. By randomizing the alphabetical and numerical correspondents . . . leaving them up for grabs . . . he ensured that whoever got to the clear would have to do exactly what you talked about before, Ricci. Run all the possible matches through a computer until it came up with ones that enabled the person to compose intelligible sentences. Either that, or work it out on paper, and that would take forever. And again, this presupposes that the would-be code breaker could recognize the bigrams, the nulls, the pattern in general."

Michelle was nodding. "He must have felt that was unlikely. Felt that *we'd* have the know-how and experience to swing it, but the laptop thief wouldn't."

"So I'm guessing what Palardy did was grab himself a sheet of paper and something like a draftsman's template, draw a circle, and then draw thirty intersecting lines across its diameter. Then he'd write a bigram on one side and pick a number out of his hat to be its diametric opposite, as you can see from the rough table on our graph. And there you are with—"

Nimec checked his watch, exchanged glances with Ricci. Almost five minutes had passed since they'd entered the office. He decided that was long enough.

"Carmichael," he said. "You're coming close to that whump across the head."

Silence. Carmichael looked embarrassed.

"Shit," he said. "I didn't mean to—"

"Don't worry about it," Nimec said. "But we need the clear. Right now."

Carmichael nodded, went over to his computer console, and tapped at the keyboard.

"I've got it in a separate text file, it'll just take a second to open it," he said half to himself. "The lines you'll see on top of the screen show the plaintext as it appears when first deciphered. In the bottom of the panel, I've capitalized letters and inserted spaces and punctuation to make it legible to you. . . ."

Nimec and Ricci looked up at the wall.

The uppermost version of the clear read:

**enriquequirosgavemethediseaseigavehimrogergor-
diantherearemenbeyondeitherofuswhoorderedtinev-
ermeantforthistohappenforgiveme**

The one below it read:

**Enrique Quiros gave me the disease. I gave him
Roger Gordian. There are men beyond either of us
who ordered it. I never meant for this to happen.
Forgive me.**

Nimec and Ricci stared at each other.

"Enrique Quiros," Ricci said. "Pete, that name rings a bell."

"Sure it does," Nimec said. "Quiros heads that drug crew down in San Diego."

"What would he want with the boss? How the hell could he—?"

"I don't know," Nimec said. "But we'd damn well better find out."

TWENTY-ONE

CALIFORNIA
NOVEMBER 16, 2001

"THERE IT IS. ABOUT THREE BLOCKS UP AHEAD OF us. That tall office building, see?" Ricci's contact took a hand off the steering wheel and motioned to his right. "Quiros's front company's on the third floor. Golden Triangle Services."

Ricci glanced out the passenger window.

"Guess it tickles his funny bone," he said.

The driver crawled the car through rush-hour traffic. He was a guy in his early thirties named Derek Glenn with skin the color of roasted chestnuts, a close-cropped nap of black hair, and a toned, broad-shouldered physique.

"His outfit's title, you mean?"

Ricci nodded.

"Golden Triangle. The heroin production and trafficking center of the world," he said. "Thailand, Laos, Burma—"

"Myanmar," Glenn said.

Ricci gave him a look.

"Is what Burma calls itself these days," Glenn said. "Anyway, sure, it's smirky of Quiros. But that's how developers talk about the area north of the city where all the new Web shops have gone up, you know. Including ours."

Ricci made a dismissive sound in his throat. Glenn was with a contingent of Sword personnel assigned to a locally based UpLink division specializing in the development of secure corporate and government intranet sites. He knew the territory and was trying to be helpful. But the lightning run of events that had swept Ricci from Palardy's death room in Sunnydale to this strange city hundreds of miles down the coast within a span of ten hours had left him in an unpleasant and critical mood. He didn't care whether the dope capital's name was Burma, Myanmar, or Brigadoon. He didn't care what sort of pitch the civil boosters were throwing prospective real-estate buyers about the neighborhood. He thought the smoked glass tower where Enrique Quiros was sitting pretty looked like a glassine envelope of heroin blown up to outrageous dimensions.

"Listen," Glenn said. "My point's that Enrique isn't just some slick. Smooth, yeah. But there's a difference. You have to respect him. He's got an Ivy League business degree. He's grounded in his family. And his main thing is to watch out for them. If it wasn't for his old man asking him to take over the rackets before he died, he might have gone legit. But once that happened, he probably felt obliged—"

"I read his make on the flight over," Ricci said.

Glenn was looking straight out the front window.

"The company Learjet doesn't seem like a shoddy way to travel," he said. "One of these days maybe I'll get to check it out firsthand. Fly outside coach on a passenger jet. No screeching infant with diaper rash behind me. No bratty older brother popping chewing gum bubbles in my ear."

"What's that supposed to mean?"

Glenn shrugged.

"I've been in San Diego a long time and figured you'd want to hear what I know," he said. "You don't, no problem. I meet your team at the airport, bring you here, job's done. I can go have a beer someplace nice and quiet. That's the best part of being an enlisted man."

"And the worst?"

"Not anything worth a complaint. But it might be sensible for you to remember I went through the same training program as the San Jose glory boys." He paused. "And maybe some other stuff before it."

Ricci turned to him, then hesitated.

"Sorry I bit," Ricci said. "I'm on the wrong side of lousy. Nothing to do with you."

Glenn kept looking out the windshield.

"There's been talk the skipper's pretty bad off," he said.

"Yeah."

"He going to make it?"

"I don't know. I'm hoping to dig up something that can assist the docs."

Glenn shook his head and inched forward in silence.

"What's Quiros been up to since I called?" Ricci asked after a minute.

"Not much," Glenn said. "He left the building maybe three hours ago. Alone. Took a walk around. Then he went back inside and hasn't gone anywhere since. It's like he was clearing his head."

"Think he smells you've got him covered?"

"Maybe, maybe not. We're pretty good at it. Either way, he hasn't tried to book."

Ricci considered that. After pulling Quiros's file out of the Sword database in San Jose, he'd gotten the phone number of the Golden Triangle front operation and decided to phone him directly. The call had been brief, and Ricci had done most of what little talking there was. It hadn't crossed his mind for an instant to state his reasons or ask any questions. He had identified himself, told Quiros straight out that he was flying down to see him that afternoon, and strongly advised him to be waiting in his office. Though he'd had awful doubts about putting him on alert, it had seemed better than the alternative of making the hour-long trip by air only to miss him and have to hunt for him around town. Ricci had gambled Quiros would understand it was in his interest to know how much he had on him and what he wanted to say. That he would cooperate at least as far as agreeing to meet. And his thinking proved to be right on.

Still, Quiros knew he was in trouble, and he'd had several hours to guess at how much. Even if Palardy's message had exaggerated his involvement in what looked like a deeply spun conspiracy to murder Roger Gordian—one that might be part of a broader plan if Thibodeau's idea about the death of Alberto Colón bore out—it was hard to predict how he would act under pressure. Hard to tell how anyone would act. Ricci had been prepared to hear that he'd dropped from sight, keeper of the family flame or not.

Glenn swung to the right now, provoking aggravated horn honks as he cut across two lanes of heavy traffic to double-park in front of their destination. "Your stop," he said.

Ricci nodded and reached for the door handle.

"Hey, Ricci." From behind him.

He glanced over his shoulder.

"You want backup? I can pull this heap into a garage."

Ricci looked at him a moment.

"No," he said. "Think this might go easier for me solo. But I'd like to buy you that glass of suds later, if you don't mind sitting with a Coke-drinking glory boy."

Glenn grinned a little.

"Company's company," he said.

Ricci exited the car and strode toward the office tower, shouldering through a tumult of homebound office workers. In the lobby, an ornamental rent-a-cop asked his name, called upstairs on the intercom, and then waved him to the elevators. Ricci figured he was with the building's legit security crew. Quiros's personal bodyguards were certain to be waiting upstairs with him.

A few minutes later, he was in the corridor outside Golden Triangle. The door swung inward to admit him before he could buzz, his features running like liquid over the reflective gray-and-blue-toned letters across its front.

The big man who opened the door looked exactly the way Ricci had imagined one of Quiros's people would. As did the other six or seven big, muscular guys planted around his office. Seated at his desk at the far end of the spacious room, only Enrique Quiros didn't altogether conform to expectations, appearing even younger and more spruced than his file photo suggested.

Ricci stepped inside.

"Hold it," the door-opener said. He moved into Ricci's path, his hands outstretched to pat him down.

Ricci shook his head.

"Don't ask, don't tell," he said, and gestured around the room. "My opinion, that might be the best policy for everybody here."

The door-opener looked at him, glanced back at Quiros.

"Jorge's just doing his job," Quiros said in a calm voice.

"Course. I know there are all kinds of classy businesses that make a ritual of frisking people at the door." Ricci was looking at Jorge. "But he touches me, he's going on the disabled list with a groin injury."

Jorge continued to stand there, flat-footed, blocking him. His expression was neutral.

Finally Quiros released a breath.

"You've come to talk," he said. His tone fell midway between questioning and declarative.

Ricci nodded.

"Then I suppose we can make an exception to our usual security procedures if they're bothering you," he said. "Out of deference to your UpLink International credentials."

His face still without expression, Jorge sidestepped to let Ricci pass. Ricci strode across to Quiros's desk and took the seat across from him without waiting to be motioned into it.

Quiros was looking at him through his glasses.

"So," he said. "I've been wondering what this is all about."

"Sure," Ricci said. "Bet my call came as a total surprise."

Quiros said nothing.

Ricci let the silence string out a moment.

"Go ahead," he said. "Say again that you don't have an inkling why I'm here. Say it ten times fast, if that helps get it out of your system. Because I don't intend to mess around."

Quiros stared.

"Tell me what you want," he said.

Ricci tipped his head back a little to indicate the men behind him.

"You rather we talk with or without them?" he said.

Quiros kept staring. "They stay."

Ricci shrugged.

"I know Palardy infected Roger Gordian with a biological agent on your orders," he said. "I know you had him killed to prevent him from ever talking about it if he was nailed or maybe had an attack of conscience. And I know you know he got his message to us anyway."

Quiros's face tightened.

"That's quite a mouthful," he said. "And not a word of it makes sense to me. I've never heard of anybody called Palardy. It's all craziness."

"Right. Crazy as hell. Because the agent isn't anthrax or botulism or ricin or whatever else Saddam Hussein cultured in Muthanna and Al-Salman. It isn't anything the old Soviet *Biopreparat* germ chefs might've auctioned off when they got pink-slipped after the breakup. And it definitely isn't anything you could have whipped together with some kitchen fermenter in the rat holes where you process your crack, smack, and other drugs I'm getting too old to know by their street names. It's a virus engineered with genomic biotechnology, one that isn't supposed to be in the showroom yet. Which makes me wonder how and why you'd get mixed up in this deal."

Quiros looked for a moment as if he was about to say something, then caught himself.

"I told you," he said and shook his head. "I don't have the slightest idea what you're talking about."

Ricci looked at him.

"Think about it another second. Maybe there were rumors in the wind and you dismissed them. Because they were so screwball. Or because they came from pretty far outside your range. Something's reached your ears that can help me and you pass it along, I might force myself to swallow your other denials. Move on from here. But you need to take the offer while it lasts, because it won't be repeated."

Ricci watched Quiros take a slow breath.

"No," he said. "I've got nothing for you."

Ricci was very still.

"Guess I should've counted on you being dumber than you look."

"What's that supposed to mean?"

"It means you're making a mistake. You think you're a player, but you're as much of a stooge as Palardy. And you'll wind up like him. You, your business, your whole precious family. Down the hole. Buried in dirt."

Quiros leaned forward, his hands on his desk, his shoulders very stiff.

"Get out of here," he said. "Who do you think you are? I don't need your insults. Your threats. Don't need you coming to me with some insane story, bringing me problems."

Ricci rose from his chair, got his card out of his wallet, and flipped it toward Quiros. It landed on the floor, close enough to the desk so it almost seemed like he hadn't intended to miss.

"You want to reach me, I should be in town another couple of hours," he said. "Whatever you decide, we'll see each other again. I promise."

He stood there looking at Quiros another second. Then he turned and walked past Jorge and the other guards, pushed through the door, and strode down the corridor to the elevator. He rode it down to the lobby and left the building without once looking back.

"Meg, finally, I thought we'd never connect today except through voice mail," Bob Lang said over the line from Washington.

"Phone tag," she said.

"It gets maddening."

"Yes, it does," she said.

"You calling from home?"

"The office." She checked her watch, saw that it was almost six-thirty. "I was at the hospital most of the afternoon. Thought I'd come in and rake through some of what's been sitting on my desk."

"How's Roger doing?"

"No better." She steadied herself. "They're saying the X-rays show his lungs are near whiteout. Without the ventilator . . . I don't think he'd be able to breathe."

"Hell," he said. "How's Ashley holding together?"

"She's incredible, Bob. If you were there to see her, you'd be impressed. She seems absolutely aware of Gord's condition but won't surrender an inch to discouragement. She puts on a mask and gown, stands at his bedside, and talks to him whenever they allow. He doesn't respond . . . it's doubtful he knows she's there with him . . . and she keeps pushing."

"Does the medical team know anything more about what brought on the sickness?"

She hesitated. What had Ashley told her? *I'm sure they wouldn't be willing to disclose anything if they didn't trust us to be discreet.*

The wall came down.

"No," she lied. "From what I understand, they're still looking at a strain of hantavirus. Or something related."

A pause.

"Meg, I know it's got to be the last thing on your mind right now, but I rushed through your clearances on the NCIC 2000 database. Sword's got full, unrestricted access, all levels of classification. I can send you the entry codes directly via secure E-mail."

"Thanks, Bob, it means a lot." She suddenly wondered what kind of person she was. "Pete Nimec's still here, and he'll be glad."

"I kept thinking about what you said last weekend. About how inverted my reasoning has been. And it suddenly seemed ludicrous. Not trusting myself to make the right decision, when it involves someone I trust more than any other person in the world."

"Bob, you don't have to—"

"I love you, Meg. I probably should have waited to say that over champagne and candlelight. But under the circumstances . . . I don't know how long it will be until we see each other. And I thought maybe it would make everything you're going through a little easier."

She opened her mouth, closed it, couldn't find a meaningful word within reach.

"I—I'd better get those codes to Pete right away," she stumbled.

And abruptly hung up the phone.

Lathrop waited until seven P.M. to transmit his E-mail. He'd calculated that would allow the final members of his cast to hastily make the show's opening call but shave their rehearsal and preparation time to the barest minimum. That was how he liked things: improvisation within a structured framework, the full script in his sole possession, his assembled performers knowing only the bits and pieces relevant to their parts.

Gently lifting Missus Frakes from his lap and setting her onto the floor, he gave the E-mail he'd typed into his computer a quick review, nodded to himself with satisfaction, and sent it off into the wide, crackling electronic yonder with a click.

Shazam, he thought.

When Pete Nimec went to his computer for the NCIC access codes Meg had told him she'd forward, he was sideswiped by the header of an anonymous message in his mailbox. It had been sent to him just minutes before, and said:

SHAZAM! OPEN IMMEDIATELY FOR THE
LIFE OF ROGER GORDIAN.

He opened it.
Immediately.
And read it with astonishment.

• • •

"Well, we're here," Glenn said.

"Here we are," Ricci said.

"Nice and quiet."

"Yeah."

"You uncomfortable being the only white guy in the joint?"

"Not unless you're uncomfortable being the only black guy who's sitting with a white guy."

Glenn took a gulp of his beer. Ricci drank some of his soda. The cheeseburgers and fries they'd ordered had just been carried over from behind the counter.

The bar was on a rundown street in East San Diego, Nat King Cole crooning "Unforgettable" on the jukebox, the owner a black man in his late sixties with silver hair and a bristling handlebar mustache. The small handful of patrons was almost entirely male, and around the same age as the bartender. Behind the booth where Ricci and Glenn were seated, a chunky woman perhaps a year or two shy of the clientele's actuarial mean was swaying to the music alone, her eyes closed, a cocktail glass in her hand.

"So what's next?" Glenn asked.

Ricci shrugged.

"We eat our food, drink our drinks, I head back to my hotel room," he said. "How long you figure our surveillance can stay on Quiros before he gets keen?"

Glenn thought a moment.

"It depends," he said. "Give us some added manpower, and we'll be okay for a while. Use two- and three-car teams. Leapfrog whenever we know his route."

"The team that flew in with me enough support?"

"How many men in it? Ten or so?"

"An even dozen."

"That should be plenty."

"They're yours," Ricci said. He pulled his burger plate closer without enthusiasm. "For all it'll be worth. Even if Quiros doesn't make his tails, he'll still figure we're tracking his movements. And he'll be careful about them."

Glenn looked at him.

"Is Enrique your only lead to whoever did whatever nobody's talking about to Gordian?"

"Yeah."

"Meaning we need to get information out of him fast."

"Yeah."

Glenn picked up his burger.

"It's a predicament. We go too easy on the son of a bitch, he'll keep his mouth shut. We lean on him too hard, he could go underground. I doubt for good, but it's sounding to me like we can't afford to lose any time."

Ricci nodded.

"Between us, Glenn, I figure we've got maybe twenty-four hours before it's too late," he said. "And other than making ourselves feel like we're doing something, I don't know what we've accomplished."

"You have any sort of plan?"

Ricci stared down at his glass a while in silence. Then he looked at Glenn.

"You want to be friends?" he said.

Their eyes had met.

"Sure," he said. "Just make good on your promise to pay the tab."

Ricci was still looking straight into Glenn's eyes.

"There's leaning hard, and there's leaning hard," he said. "Nothing opens up for us by tomorrow morning,

351

I'm on my own with Quiros. And he's going to talk. It might cost me my job. Maybe more than that. A whole lot more. But he'll talk. And he won't have a chance to go anywhere."

Glenn sat with his beer mug suspended below his chin, his fingers clenching the handle. He took in and released a long, tidal breath.

"If it's got to be that way, there's no other choice, I can give you a hand."

"No," Ricci said, his voice firm. "Nobody else involved. I—"

Ricci's cellular bleeped in his jacket pocket. He raised a finger in a hold-on-a-minute gesture, reached for it, and answered.

Glenn waited. He saw Ricci ease upright in his chair, listening without comment, taking in whatever was being said to him with acute interest.

When Ricci returned the phone to his pocket, there was something very close to relief on his features.

"That was Pete Nimec in San Jose," he said. "I think we might've been saved by the bell."

TWENTY-TWO

IT WAS TEN P.M. WHEN ENRIQUE QUIROS DROVE HIS moon-gray Fiat Coupé from the grounds of his Rancho Santa Fe mansion through an electric gate in its eight-foot-high wrought-iron perimeter fence, accompanied by two Lincoln Town Cars that flanked him front and rear.

Much of the short trip from the rarefied North County community to Balboa Park in San Diego proper would be on Interstate 5, alternately known as the San Diego Freeway. Their route to the southbound entry ramp went along a loose braid of quiet, palm-lined streets and county roads and then skirted the cluster of specialty shops and gourmet restaurants in and around the small downtown.

As they passed one of the busier eateries, a dark green Saab 9-5 wagon drew away from the curb a few yards farther up the street, easing in front of Quiros's lead car.

At the same instant, a young man and woman chatting beside a Cherokee parked near the restaurant's outdoor café suspended their conversation and climbed into the

SUV, looking to all eyes like an attractive couple who had gone to dine out on this pleasantly cool November night. The man at the wheel and his companion next to him in the passenger's seat took their place following Quiros's small procession, hanging back a little to remain inconspicuous.

Just before they reached the first of several signs guiding traffic to the freeway entrance, a Toyota Prius gasoline/electric emerged into the intersection from a cross street where it had idled in the shadow of a tall, spray-leafed royal palm and then swung between the Cherokee and the Lincoln immediately behind Quiros.

The Cherokee's driver glanced at the woman to his right. "What's up with the electric razor?" he said.

"Could be its pilot wants to prove you can be fuel-efficient *and* an asshole."

"Or could be that he's trying to queer our tail."

The woman frowned. "We'd better play it safe and inform Glenn," she said.

A moment after the Prius cut in behind the Lincoln, its driver tilted his head unnoticeably upward to speak into the hands-free, trunked-band radio mounted on its roof.

"Very good, we are in position," he said in Castilian Spanish.

On a sleepy residential block southwest of Balboa Park, a customized Town and Country minivan sat in a parking space where it apparently had been left for the night. Its extended cargo area was partitioned from the front section. The bar lock on the steering wheel and blinking burglar alarm light on the dash were meant to convince anyone who might take a close-up look through the glazed front windows that it was unoccupied. Carefully fitted black shades over the rear windows ensured that the radiance of the computer monitors and LED equipment readouts aboard would be hidden from the street.

Should a roaming car thief have chanced upon this particular vehicle and failed to be deterred by the visible security devices, it would have been a supremely luckless blunder. And his last ever.

In the minivan's rear, the little man seated at his control station acknowledged the message from the Prius's driver, told him he would await his further report, and then switched frequencies on his transmitter to notify his marksmen in the park of their target's progress.

"What the hell kind of car is this, anyway?" Ricci said.

"An '88 Buick LeSabre T-type," Glenn said. "Why?"

"Can't belong to the company pool."

"Is that some kind of put-down?"

"No."

"Complaint?"

"No."

"Because you might want to remember that she's gotten you everywhere you've been going all day," Glenn said. "And that not every rolling stakeout's in the chichi North County. You have to blend in with the scenery. Stay unobtrusive."

Ricci looked at him from the passenger seat. "In other words, it's your personal vehicle."

"My personal *sweetheart*." Glenn patted the steering column with affection. "Bought her secondhand from an officer pal in Camp Pendleton who kept her in cherry condition, and she's never let me down."

They rode briefly in silence, moving west on El Cajon Boulevard toward Balboa.

Ricci looked at the dash clock. It was almost a quarter past ten.

"How much longer till we're at the park?"

"Maybe ten minutes or so. I know a few places nearby where we can haul in the car and wait."

Ricci looked thoughtful. "Let's squawk our moving surveillance cars again. See about that Prius."

The Cherokee was now several car lengths ahead of Enrique Quiros's trio in the center lane of I-5. The Saab wagon had dropped back behind them. This tactic of periodically changing lead and follow spots was a textbook example of leapfrog surveillance, calculated to minimize the risk of detection.

The Saab's driver was wearing an earphone mike/lapel transmitter assembly that he'd set to voice-activation mode.

"Roger, the Prius is still keeping pace with us," he said in answer to Ricci's inquiry. His eyes had flicked to his sideview mirror. "It's in the right lane, almost directly abreast of my vehicle."

"You get a look at who's inside?"

"A single male, thirtyish, clean shaven," the driver said. "His windows are tinted too dark for me to give you more than that."

"The way it's switching lanes, staying out of Quiros's line of sight, it doesn't seem like one of his cars," Ricci said over the VHF communications channel.

The driver nodded to himself. "Yeah," he replied. "If I didn't know better, I'd damn well figure it for one of ours."

•   •   •

The snipers had assumed a four-pointed pattern of deployment around the grassy area between the rear of the Natural History Museum and the Spanish Village Art Center to its north, giving them a wide open field of fire. One of them was prone on the roof of the long, three-story museum, his Walther rifle nosed over its baroque ornamental edging. A second was concealed in the 120-foot spread of the exotic Moreton Bay fig tree that had stood behind the museum for almost a century. Opposite the museum, at the northeast corner of the green, a third sharpshooter was atop one of the low stucco-and-tile art galleries of the village. The fourth was posted at the northwest corner, on the roof of another Old Spanish–style cottage.

Each of their high-magnitude night-vision scopes was equipped with an infrared camera head/optical beam splitter attachment. Designed to bend light at a ninety-degree angle as it struck the eyepiece, it would simultaneously relay the shooter's sight image to the rifle-mounted scope and to the control van over a wireless video feed.

Inside the Town and Country, the team commander would have a real-time picture of what his firers saw through their scopes from their separate angles of view. Maintaining radio contact via their tactical headsets, he could coordinate their actions from the moment Enrique Quiros made a move on Salazar until the moment Quiros—and whoever he might have positioned in ambush—fell dead to the ground.

Now the little man waited at his monitoring station and remembered how Lucio Salazar had balked at the cost of his team's services. Their clients often did at first.

But quality was never cheap, and Salazar had gotten the best that money could buy, as he was bound to realize with gratitude before tonight's events ran their ultimate course.

Sitting in his parked Cadillac sedan along with four hand-picked bodyguards, Lucio Salazar shrugged his jacket sleeve back from his wristwatch and read the time.

It was almost half past ten, and he was feeling impatient. Lucio had arrived early to make sure the contract hitters were where they were supposed to be, and once his men had gone out and confirmed their presence, he'd had nothing to do except wait for Quiros to show. Little as he'd wished for this appointment, he was anxious to push the start button and get it under way. He wasn't truly afraid; in his fifty-eight years of living, Lucio had been in far too many tight situations for that. Nor had he acquired any scruples about killing in his late middle age. But for all his preparation, it was his hovering uncertainty, his not knowing what was to come, that was hardest to abide. If he were only convinced of Quiros's intentions, things would be clear to him, and he would know beyond a doubt what to do. He was a man who put a high value on forethought. His operation had thrived as a result of deliberation, planning, and a willingness to compromise—even concede losses, within margins—rather than let himself in for more trouble than seemed worthwhile. When circumstances changed, you had to look at them carefully and know when to make accommodations. Yet here he'd been thrust into a situation where everything hung on split-second decisions and hair triggers. And it didn't feel right to him in the least.

He sighed and glanced out his window, watching for the headlights of Enrique's car to appear in the parking lot entrance.

Feel right or not, what was about to happen would happen anyway.

He just wanted to be finished with it and get back to business as usual.

As Enrique Quiros approached Balboa from the northwest, the third automobile in his entourage separated from the others and took the turnoff to the Cabrillo Bridge. Remaining on the San Diego Freeway, Quiros and his lead car continued to head toward the Pershing Drive exit that provided the easiest and most direct access to the Spanish Village area.

Inside the tail vehicles that had kept pace with Quiros since he'd left the ranch, the members of each surveillance team noted this unexpected development and promptly advised their respective superiors.

"What do you make of it?" Ricci said.

"The bridge hooks up with Laurel Street, and that'll take you over to Balboa," Glenn said. He had pulled the LeSabre into a dark, empty employee lot behind a municipal building on C Street, within view of the park. "It's kind of a long way around. The scenic route, I guess you'd call it. Runs between these two wooded slopes."

"I don't think our guys are interested in admiring the foliage," Ricci said.

"Not that anybody could in the dark," Glenn said and sat thinking quietly. After a moment or two, he turned to Ricci. "What's that E-mail we got again? The exact words?"

Ricci frowned, took his cell phone out of his pocket, and touched a button to illuminate the LCD. Then he pressed a second button on the keypad, retrieved the stored message Nimec had forwarded from San Jose, and opened it. "Here," he said and handed the phone across the seat to Glenn. "Read the damn thing yourself."

Glenn did. It said:

QUIROS. ELEVEN P.M. BALBOA PARK. FINAL CLOSEOUT, EVERYTHING UP FOR GRABS. GET WHAT YOU WANT BEFORE HE'S GONE. FROM ONE WHO KNOWS.

"Coded messages. Anonymous tips that don't mean anything." Ricci studied the government office building's flat, concrete backside through the windshield. "I'm sick and tired of being jerked."

"If you ask me, we're lucky just to be in the game," Glenn said, still looking at the LCD.

"I guess." Ricci glanced at the dash clock and saw that it was exactly 10:30. "Be nice if we could figure some of it out before we need to make our move."

Silence. Glenn pursed his lips, gave the phone back to Ricci. "You know, Laurel connects with a long strip of the park called El Prado," he said. "That's the main pedestrian mall. It has lots of recognizable buildings, a big reflecting pond, other stuff."

Ricci looked at him. "You guessing it's where the action might be?"

"I don't know," Glenn said, "but there has to be a

reason the last car in Enrique's cavalcade of stars broke away to head in that direction."

Ricci tugged at the flesh below his chin. "You're looking to set something up, it's always a good idea to pick a spot where there are landmarks."

"Agreed. And tell me this isn't the *definition* of a setup."

"Do we have people sitting on the area?"

"Some," he said. "And we can shuffle more over."

Ricci nodded. "How close are we?"

"A hop and a skip," Glenn said.

Ricci grabbed for the door handle. "Come on, I think we've got ourselves a destination," he said.

"Lucio," Quiros said.

"Enrique," Salazar said.

They shook hands.

It was a few minutes shy of eleven o'clock, and they were standing in the darkened parking lot behind the Spanish Village. Salazar's Caddy on one side of them, Quiros's Fiat Coupé and Lincoln on the opposite side, their bodyguards grouped loosely near the cars from which they'd emerged.

"So," Salazar said. "What now?"

Quiros looked at him in silence a moment, the cool night breeze riffling his lightweight sport jacket around his body. "Now we talk," he said. "See if we can find a way to straighten out our problems."

Salazar tilted his head toward their guards. "We need to give ourselves some room," he said. "Take a walk, air things in privacy."

Quiros nodded. "I propose we each bring one man to

follow behind as a precaution," he said. "Leave the rest here with the cars."

Salazar had to grin. "Sure, a precaution," he said. "Got to make sure we don't kill each other on the garden path."

Enrique looked at him. "I'm glad you're smiling, Lucio," he said.

The balance that Sword's foot surveillance teams generally had to strike was the same balance struck by cops doing undercover work in every major population center in America or for that matter the developed world. On the one hand, there was an appreciable chance that someone would see them—regardless of their skills at camouflage, concealment, and clandestine movement, and also regardless of how derelict, deserted, or remote their area of operation might be. On the other hand, they understood that being seen and being noticed were two very different things, and that being exposed was yet a third thing altogether.

Here and now in Balboa Park, this meant they faced specific limitations in their use of apparel, weapons, and accessories. They could not, for example, wear form-hugging stealth suits, equipment vests, night-vision goggles, and ballistic helmets in environments where there was even the scant likelihood of a late-night stroller mistaking them for terrorist invaders out to lay siege to his home and neighborhood or, worse, of their targets nailing them for the covert personnel they happened to be.

With regard to arms, they were a bit less hamstrung. Full-sized VVRS rifles with their twenty-inch barrels were of course virtually unconcealable and consequently out. The diminutive upgrades most recently trialed by

Ricci's rapid deployment team were in, but because they were still designated as prototypical, they had been issued only to the complement of A-Team Sword ops who accompanied Ricci from San Jose that afternoon. Nevertheless, a fair range of offensive and defensive gear was available to the entire task force, from incapacitant sprays and grenades and less-than-lethal stingball guns to very lethal revolvers, automatic pistols, and compact submachine guns.

Their tactical guidelines were basically low profile: Street clothes were to be donned over mandatory Zylon bullet-resistant vests, weapons had to be easily stowable, and deadly fire restricted to an option of absolute last resort.

The civvies worn by the three-person foot team in the shadows outside the botanical building were sufficiently camouflaging to make the odds of their drawing a first glance quite slim, and sufficiently inconspicuous to make a second glance even less probable, should anyone's eye chance upon them. One of the men had on a black rugby shirt, navy chinos, and black canvas loafers. The second wore a slate-gray sweatshirt, baggy crew pants, and black running sneakers. The female member of the team was dressed in a dark green rigger ensemble and matching jogging shoes. Their Sword identification patches were concealed beneath pull-down velcro flaps.

All three had been plainclothes law enforcement agents prior to hiring up with Sword, and were thoroughly versed in the ins and outs of surveillance.

As they passed under lushly crowned trees and wound through flourishing gardens, they strode casually side by side, one sipping bottled spring water, one unwrapping a stick of chewing gum, another pausing briefly to tie a shoelace. While attempting to remain quiet and keep out of direct light, they avoided letting it become an elaborate production. They did not walk on their tiptoes, dart between lampposts, peek around corners, or freeze in place like window mannequins whenever a head turned in their direction. The idea was to do their damnedest to stay out of view but act as natural as possible if they were sighted.

On tonight's job, their experience yielded valuable dividends. The four Quiros soldiers they had been hastily assigned to follow had exited the breakaway Lincoln behind the Marston House at the far western end of El Prado, advanced across the gardens and meadows to the thoroughfare's north, and then finally taken positions of hiding on either side of a thickly hedged walkway without displaying the slightest awareness that they were being tailed.

Although they couldn't have known they were watching a trap being set for Lucio Salazar, the Sword ops did realize they had stumbled onto something important and quickly radioed Ricci and Glenn with word of their observations and position.

What would soon throw their situation into confusion, however, was the fact that they weren't the only ones doing the watching.

In the Town and Country, the small man at the monitoring station saw Quiros's men slip into the hedges through his optical relay with the shooter on the museum's rooftop, who had noticed their movement while surveying the area through his long-range scope . . . a stroke of good fortune for Lucio Salazar.

Had it not been for that observation, he might well be walking to his death.

• • •

Little was said between Quiros and Salazar as they left the parking area, walking south past the Spanish Village toward the green dominated by the Moreton Bay fig tree, their bodyguards following like unspeaking golems, near enough for their presence to be felt, far enough away for it to be unobtrusive. The few words they did exchange were inconsequential: *Beautiful night, air's nice and fresh, been too long, don't see each other much these days, business, you know.* Even without the duplicitous secrets they concealed, their planned or contemplated treacheries, they would have been disinclined to hurry their conversation toward matters of substance. There was a timing, a restraint, an almost formalized ritual of overtures and preambles to which they were both accustomed and that for men such as themselves was essential to the politics of survival. Talk too soon, and one could look weak or anxious. Too late, and deception or indecision was assumed.

Timing.

At the eastern border of the green, Quiros paused a beat, glanced around as if to gain his bearings, then started briskly onto a path that would take them past the side of the Natural History Museum and into the Plaza de Balboa at the east end of El Prado.

Salazar touched his shoulder, noting his quickened pace.

"Lawn's shorter," he said and waved a hand to indicate the area behind the museum between the big Aussie tree and the village. "If it's okay with you, I'd like to cut across it instead."

Quiros appraised him quietly. He'd heard the mistrust in his tone, seen his reluctance to take the path. "Why not?" he said, inserting a note of hesitancy into his own voice as he moved off the path. "I picked the spot, you pick the route."

Salazar gave him a thin smile. "I hadn't looked at it that way, but it sounds good to me," he said and turned right toward the green.

That was exactly where Quiros had meant to steer him all along, knowing his men were in position at its western side, hidden there in the shrubs that bordered on the walkway leading toward the reflecting pond, lying in wait, ready to spring their ambush.

The squawks came almost back to back, one from the surveillance team that had stayed on Quiros and his walking pal since they'd appeared from behind the Spanish Village, a second from the spotters who'd watched Quiros's soldiers move into hiding in the garden near the reflecting pond. Ricci and Glenn were jogging briskly toward the latter from the park entrance over by the Marston House at Balboa's western extremity, not far from where Quiros's breakaway car had been left.

"What's your take on those sluggers that crawled into the bushes?" Glenn said.

"Same as yours," Ricci said. "Looks like Quiros has something rotten cooking for whoever met him here. . . . What's his name again?"

"Salazar," Glenn said. "Lucio Salazar. At least that's who my people think it is. He and his brothers in Mexico are old-time, all-purpose smugglers and racketeers. Got into dealing dope, hit the mother lode. He's Quiros's chief local competition."

"Maybe not for much longer," Ricci said.

Glenn nodded and ran on in silence a moment.

"At this pace, it'll be a quick shot to that garden."

"You positive we have a vehicle at every car exit?" Ricci said.

"Yeah."

Ricci grunted, hustling along. "Be good to make the action," he said. "Main thing for us, though, is that Quiros doesn't slip away. Because that E-mail we got is looking righter and righter. And I've got a feeling that if we lose him now, we're done."

As soon as they got halfway across the green, Salazar slowed to halt and stood gazing at the Moreton Bay fig. "All those twists and turns, one grows out of the other, you never know which way they're gonna go," he said and indicated the outspread branches and root system intricately silhouetted in the partial moonlight. "I figure it's what life's about."

Quiros made a meaningless sound and waited, concealing his impatience.

Salazar kept staring at the tree. "We should talk about Felix," he said.

Quiros looked at him. This was not how it was supposed to happen. He wanted to get to the damned garden walkway.

"Let's hold off," he said. "The pond is a better place. We can sit there and—"

Salazar raised a hand abortively and faced him. "*Now*, Enrique," he said. "I want to talk about him right now."

Quiros studied his expression. It left no room for argument. *So be it.*

"You had a problem with my nephew, you should have come to me," he said after a minute.

"For what? The problem, like you said . . . it was

never him. He wouldn't have done that job at the tunnel if you didn't authorize it."

Quiros shook his head. "He was on his own."

"No." Salazar's voice was at once weary and bitter. "We came all the way here, might as well be straight."

Quiros inhaled, exhaled. "That's what's been wrong from the start, Lucio. You answering your own questions. Making up your mind before you know the facts. I told you the truth, and you can believe it or not. It doesn't make a difference to me. It isn't even the real issue between us anymore. If you'd given me a chance, I'd have put Felix on the rack, made amends. But you chose otherwise. You took things into your own hands. What you did, how could you think it would resolve anything?"

"What I did—?"

"Killing my nephew. My sister's only son. What were you thinking?"

Salazar glared with anger. "Even here, between us, you're trying to pass off that bullshit—"

He never got to finish his sentence.

There were four simultaneous flashes from four different points above the green, four rifle cracks that merged into one loud, echoing sound that split the night like a thunderclap. Salazar jerked with surprise and confusion as Quiros's head snapped sideways, blood misting up around it and spurting from a hole in his chest, and then his mouth dropped open and blood was pouring from it, too, streaming over his lips and chin. Quiros went down, folded almost neatly, and lay still there in front of him on the grass.

Salazar spun around and saw that Quiros's guard was

also on the ground, his own man standing over the sprawled body.

He looked up at the roof of the museum, at the great fig tree, at the tops of the Spanish Village cottages and saw no sign of the snipers, nothing at all except shadows and pale silver moonlight.

His eyes widened with confusion. He hadn't given the order. What the hell had happened here? *He hadn't given the goddamned order.*

Ricci and Glenn were within fifteen yards of the hedges when they heard the discharge of the sniper guns smack the air up ahead.

Both had slowed to a trot to keep from scaring Quiros's men out of the bushes. Now they came to a frozen standstill and looked at each other.

"Those were rifle shots." Ricci removed his radio's earpiece so he could hear more clearly. "Plural, I'm pretty sure."

Glenn nodded. "I've heard synchronous fire before. You don't forget the sound."

Ricci reached under his sport jacket and pulled his Five-Seven out of its holster. Glenn drew his own piece, a Beretta 9mm.

"Where you think the shooting came from?" Ricci said.

Glenn started to answer, then abruptly tapped his radio earpiece to indicate he'd been squawked, and listened.

His features were stunned as he ten-foured into the unit's neck mike.

"Let's have it," Ricci said.

Glenn looked at him.

"Quiros is down," he said. He pointed eastward beyond the walkway and hedges. "The green, back of the museum."

"*Fuck*." Ricci's breath escaped him in a sick rush. "What about Salazar and his bodyguard?"

"They're on the go."

"Tell our people to stay on his tail, but I don't want anybody trying to take him, not under any circumstances. Those shooters that tapped Quiros have the overhead positions and are going to cover his retreat."

Glenn nodded and conveyed the message.

Ricci was forcing himself to think. "We have to get over to Quir—"

There was a loud stirring of vegetation to his right.

They might have started out of the bushes a second or two earlier, Ricci wasn't positive. In his momentary crushing distraction, his effort to pull his wits together, he could have missed hearing them right off. But he'd heard them now.

He wheeled toward the sound of tossing branches, spotted Quiros's men spotting Glenn and him, remembered a couple of them from the Golden Triangle office. One was the bulky door-opener, Jorge.

Just doing his job, Ricci thought.

And all within a heartbeat he saw the recognition in Jorge's eyes, saw Jorge notice the Five-Seven in his hand . . .

And then Ricci saw Jorge start to point his own gun at him.

Glenn reacted to the disturbance in the shrubbery in near unison with Ricci, pivoting on his heel, whipping his Beretta toward the hitters as they appeared from cover.

"Team One, move in!" he called into his throat mike. They were already moving.

By the time he saw the gun coming up in front of him, Ricci was on automatic pilot: his position, movement, and firing seamlessly integrated, the large figure outlined against the bushes objectified to his trained eye, a target with specific aiming points.

The Five-Seven in a firm, two-handed grip, his arms extended, feet apart, he dropped into the slight crouch of a police shooter's stance and fired three rounds into the darkness, catching Jorge dead on with every one of them.

Clouted off his feet, Jorge collapsed backward, a yawning hole briefly visible in his chest before he crashed heavily down into a clump of shrubbery.

Ricci didn't pause to think. You didn't pause at these moments, didn't think; at these moments you were the tip of an arrow.

Leading with his Five-Seven, he swiveled to the right, where another slugger had advanced from the bushes, his pistol a blur as he brought it up toward Glenn. Ricci took a quick breath, sighted, pulled the trigger on his exhalation. Glenn's Beretta spurted flame at the same instant. The slugger did a grotesque shimmy on his feet, then pitched over sideways.

Ricci sought more movement, listened for more rattling in the hedges. There, over to the left, a third man raised his gun. A fourth beside him.

And then from farther back in the darkness, a female voice called out, "Don't try it! Toss your weapons, hands up in the air. *Now!*"

Ricci focused on the spot from which the command

had been shouted and saw a woman in a rigger's outfit with a semiautomatic pistol in her right hand. The luminescent Sword ID on her breast identified her as one of his own.

A moment ticked by.

Two more figures had rushed out of the night to either side of the woman and formed up in a semicircle around the hedges. Men in dark civvies, firearms held out, glow-in-the-dark Sword insignias seeming to float over their chests.

Ricci kept his Five-Seven on the sluggers, saw Glenn doing the same with his Beretta from the corner of his eye.

Both men waited to see if the sluggers would pick smart or dead, their choice here, no lifelines, no polling the audience.

They dropped their pieces, raised their hands.

Smart.

Ricci sprang out of his crouch toward Glenn, leaving the frisk-and-cuff to their foot team.

"The green," he said. His hand on Glenn's arm. "Take me over there."

Ricci had known Quiros was down but had hoped to a God he'd never been sure existed that Quiros wasn't out. What he found on the lawn would not make a religious man out of him.

One brief glance at the body on the grass was all it took to establish there wasn't a spark of life remaining in it. Whatever part of the head hadn't gotten scattered aross the lawn was a gaping, bloody mess. Ricci guessed it should have seemed odd to him that Quiros's glasses had stayed on his face, that they weren't even askew, but he'd been around violent death enough to know it often had a sardonic touch.

He knelt over the body, searched through its pockets, and found nothing of use. Then he just knelt there feeling numb.

Far across the lawn, he could see Glenn looking up at the tops of the buildings around them, standing with his gun loosely at rest against his leg. The roofs looked empty. The monster tree looked empty. Not much risk to being here, the snipers were probably gone by now. If they were still in place, they weren't a threat. Their work showed they'd been top-tier pros, and the job they'd been hired to perform was finished.

Glenn raised a hand to catch Ricci's eye and signaled that he wanted to do a walkaround, pointing toward the front of the museum. Ricci waved for him to go ahead and watched him turn the building's corner, leaving him alone with the body.

Ricci knelt over it, looked down at it, the night feeling very deep around him, its chill penetrating his clothes.

"You got away from me," he said to Quiros's unhearing ears, his voice flat and husky. "Got away, you son of a bitch. And I don't know what to do."

He never heard anyone slipping up on him. Never heard a sound. Despite his natural alertness, his finely keyed senses, not a sound until the voice spoke out of the darkness mere inches behind his back.

"*Shazam,*" it said.

"Jesus Christ, what'd your guys think they were *doing*?" Lucio Salazar barked into his cellular.

Shaken and baffled, still clueless about why his hired

373

triggers had opened fire, he was speeding from the park in his Caddy, unaware he'd just passed the spot where Sword's roadblock for Enrique Quiros had been lifted moments earlier.

"They fulfilled their assignment," the little man in the control station replied over their connection. "The proof is that you're alive right now."

"Are you out of your mind? I was handling things with Enrique. *Talking* to him. I never gave you the god-damned word—"

"It would be better if you could give me some respect. Quiros had people in the bushes ahead of you. I saw at least one of them holding a gun."

Salazar's brow wrinkled.

"Hold it a second," he said. "Are you sure?"

"I know my job. Should I have waited until you reached those men? Let them make their move? If I'd done that, you'd be the one laying in your own blood right now."

Not quite knowing how to respond, Salazar got off the phone and sat quietly as his driver turned toward the highway. In a way, the brief conversation had left him more confused than before. Looking back upon every-thing that had happened in the past half hour, remem-bering Quiros's words to him, he had to admit that Quiros had seemed to genuinely believe it was the Sa-lazar family that off'ed his *bastardo* nephew. And then there were his comments about making amends, which in hindsight also had sounded like they might have been sincere. On the other hand, Quiros *had* set a trap for him along the path, assuming the sniper boss had been on the level . . . and what would he have to gain from bullshitting about that?

The lines on Salazar's forehead grew deeper. He supposed it didn't pay to start entertaining second thoughts at this late stage. The best thing for him was probably to be thankful he was still in one piece, and move on. But questions of what Quiros had or hadn't known—or done—kept gnawing at him. Because if there was even a speck of truth in the words he'd spoken before he was killed, it would cast serious doubt upon the reliability of Lathrop's information. And then you'd have to start asking how Lathrop could have gotten it so wrong, and wondering about his motivations, his *intentions* . . .

The Cadillac was swinging onto the entrance ramp to I-5, heading north to Del Mar, where the timed explosive charge beneath its fuel tank suddenly detonated with a crumping blast, sending a burst of flame through its interior, its force punching out metal, blowing out both windshields and three of its four side windows, instantly killing Lucio Salazar, his driver, and the bodyguards who had been riding inside with them—leaving Salazar's questions to vaporize in the smoke and superheated air.

But then, in matters of life and death, one could very rarely expect to receice all the answers.

Ricci's hand went to his Five-Seven, drew the pistol from its holster even as he turned fast at the hip and looked behind him.

The man standing there was dressed entirely in black, regarding him with sharp, intelligent eyes. His hands were straight down at his sides. One was empty. The other held a square, flat object that Ricci would have immediately recognized as a CD gem case had the setting been different. In the context of his present situation, it took him a second or two.

He studied the man's face. If the gun Ricci was pointing at him gave him any fear, he showed no sign of it.

"Who are you?" Ricci said.

The man tilted his head up a little, his lips parting, seeming for the briefest of moments to gaze past Ricci into the night sky. Then he locked eyes with him. "One Who Knows," he said. "But I'll bet you already have that figured out."

Ricci's gun was steady in his grip. But it felt suddenly cold. "Tell me what the hell you want."

The man shook his head. "It's what you want that's important, and I've got it right in my hand." He lifted the gem case from his side, held it out toward Ricci. "Take it. Poor Enrique here's a dead end, so you'd might as well. What's there to lose? Maybe you'll feel you owe me one. But that will be up to you."

Silence.

Ricci did not move for a long moment. Then he slowly reached out to the man and took the case from him, keeping his gun trained on his chest.

The man's hand dropped back to his side. "I'm going to steal away into the night now," he said. "Just tell me I don't have to worry about you putting a slug into me for some odd reason."

Ricci was still watching his eyes. "You already have that figured," he said.

The man smiled and dipped his head in a gesture that almost resembled a bow.

"Be careful now," he said.

Then the man turned and walked into the darkness, heading toward a nearby footpath, disappearing into the shadows beneath the trees rising tall on either side of it, leaving Ricci crouched over the body of Enrique Quiros, alone in the silent green, one hand around his gun, the other holding tightly on to a mystery.

TWENTY-THREE

THE CAPACITY TO BALANCE EMOTIONS THAT WOULD seem bound for shattering collision is a wonder of the human heart.

They had gathered in this room more times than any of them could recall. UpLink International was a vast organization with interests in many countries that were only an armed or political power play away from disintegration, and its very presence in those unstable regions often threw it into the center of violent conflict. In this room, they had plotted strategies and determined their reactions to swiftly unfolding crises in Afghanistan, Turkey, Russia, Malaysia, Brazil . . . even to a terrorist strike that had killed thousands in America's largest metropolis. In this room, with its steel-reinforced concrete walls, its embedded sound-masking equipment, its bug detectors, phone and fax encryptors, and myriad other surveillance countermeasure systems, they had felt able to deliberate and exchange intelligence with an unexceeded level of privacy. Reserved for UpLink's inner circle, it had been their closed chamber, their sanctum sanctorum. But, though their minds told them to trust Phil Hernandez's assurances that its security remained intact, their hearts would permit no such confidence. How could they, after a hands-on custodian of their privacy had become their worst betrayer?

In the confines of this windowless room one level below the lobby of their San Jose headquarters, UpLink's inner circle had gathered around Roger Gordian like knights at a modern round table, dedicated to helping him shape his dream of a freer, better world, offering him the sum of their insight, expertise, and counsel at moments of urgent decision. Now his chair at the table was vacant, and their hearts ached from his absence. How could they not, when it was his vision and strength of character that gave them inspiration? Yet somehow the members of this group took comfort in simply being here together, with their wide diversity of backgrounds and personalities, consolidated around a shared goal, determined to prevail over the challenges they faced. And stirring in the hearts of several of them—deeper in some than others—was an embryonic awareness that if the unthinkable did happen to Roger Gordian and his chair were to remain empty, one of their number had the attributes to pick up his fallen standard and guide them on toward the further realization of his dream.

"Now that everybody's arrived, I think we'd better get the meeting under way," Megan Breen said. She looked around the large conference table at Nimec, Scull, Ricci, Thibodeau, and finally at the morning's unexpected visitor. "Alex, it's good to see you back, these god-awful circumstances aside."

He gave her a somber but genuine smile. A lean, fit,

smartly dressed man in his late forties whose corrective laser eye surgery had made his once-familiar wire glasses a memory, Nordstrum had been UpLink's chief foreign affairs consultant before his retirement for personal reasons the year before.

"I just wish I could have returned sooner," he said. "Gord's fighting for his life, and I'm off trekking in Morocco, footloose and oblivious."

"Bad things can happen, Alex," she said, "whether you're here or gone. That's life."

"Maybe," he said. "And maybe I'm finished with being gone."

Megan's was less of a true response than a signal she wanted to get down to business. They had much to cover, and the clock was ticking.

"We've all seen the information on the compact disk Tom brought back from San Diego, and it's an incredible amount to digest," she said. "I'd hoped to organize the material in a report or have something ready on the digital projector. But there wasn't a chance, so I had to settle for an old-fashioned chalkboard and pointer." Megan paused and gestured at the transparent clamp binders she'd given to each of them. "As everyone can see, I did manage to make up printed transcripts of the audio portion of the carousel surveillance and the conversation between Quiros and Palardy."

"We don't need to get too fancy," Ricci said. "With what Nameless gave me in Balboa Park, the threads are pretty easy to follow."

"Some blanks gonna have to be filled in before we can do the boss any good," Thibodeau said. "Otherwise it *une cargaison*. Not a cargo, but a load, y'hear what I'm sayin'."

Alex was nodding his agreement. "It's like what I used to drum into the heads of my journalism undergrads. The six questions that are critical to any story," he said. "Who, what, when, where, why, and how. We've gotten partial answers to most of them. We can make some fair guesses about the rest. But we need to find out more. And decide what needs to be found out *first*."

"No argument from me," Nimec said. "But before that, I figure it might pay for us to go through a quick rundown of everything we know."

"Yeah," Ricci said. "Starting with the blonde."

He motioned toward the green chalkboard on the wall behind Megan.

Written on it in her hand was:

???

↑

Wildcat

↑

Melina Laval aka Alison Kerry aka Janet Cardomon (real identity unknown)

↑

Enrique Quiros

↑

Donald Palardy

Megan went to the board, lifted her pointer, and held its tip to the line of aliases beneath the second arrow.

"The blonde it is," she said. "The digital video we acquired from Nameless, as Tom calls him, establishes that she gave Quiros what Eric Oh believes to be some sort of activator for the viral agent—"

"This is from Quiros-Palardy, correct?" Nordstrum said. He was flipping through his copy of the transcript. "Apologies, everyone, but I'm still playing catch-up . . ."

"Yes," Megan said. "We can guess the conversation occurred when Quiros passed along the activator to Palardy." She had moved her pointer down one line. "Some of our major unanswered questions still revolve around how Roger contracted the dormant virus and who else might be carrying it. Eric's working with the Sobel gene tech people to assure that we'll have a rapid screening test for the germ very soon. It's frightening to contemplate, but virtually all of us could have been infected . . . you being the least likely, Alex, having been overseas. Which I hope won't set you on a guilt jag again."

He produced another wan smile. "And the activator?"

"A separate problem," she said. "Unless Quiros was selling Palardy a complete load, we know they can be designed or adapted for individual targets. There were mentions of an ampule and liquid, so the assumption is that it was dispensed with a syringe. Injected into something Roger ate or drank. It would be a huge benefit to obtain a specimen of the activator Palardy slipped Roger. And we're trying."

"That what those guys in space suits are doing in the boss's office this morning?" Scull said.

Megan nodded. "And in the cafeteria, and kitchen, and anywhere else in the building that edibles and drinkables might be kept," she said. "I had a phone conversation with Eric at the crack of dawn, and he gave me some of the basics of viral biology. Most of it was leagues above my head. This is probably a terrible oversimplification, but from what I gather, viruses infect other living organisms by producing molecular proteins that let them fasten on to and penetrate the outer surfaces of the target cells. Eric thinks whoever designed the bug started out with a hantavirus, or something close, and modified it in important ways. We can't know how many, but one of them allows it to be transmitted to humans by some route other than contact with rodents. Another presumably keeps it quiescent until the activator causes the release of binding and entry proteins. If we determine the activator, the scientists should be able to analyze its chemical makeup and learn what starts the bugs incubating. And how they attack their victims."

"One thing," Scull said. "How do we know Quiros didn't sell Palardy a bill of goods about the activator? Don exposed the boss to it. Now he's history. And the morgue docs haven't come up with any results that show violent death. Or poisoning. From what they've told us, it looks like his heart gave out from the disease—"

"That's only half accurate, Vince," Nimec said. "The investigators know his heart quit on him. Period. There are poisons that can simulate a coronary seizure, and some of them are hard to detect. Especially when the vic's system is already a mess from his sickness. The toxicologists still haven't completed their batteries."

"Even so," Scull said, "if Quiros wanted him out of the picture, he wasn't going to warn him about it. No matter what killed Palardy, the fact is he was infected. It could be that the activator's one-size-fits-all. It could be the *virus* is what changes from person to person. Or could be neither of them does. I'm not trying to get us confused, but we've gotta be careful about our assumptions. It could make a difference, as far as finding a cure for the boss."

Megan nodded. "You're right," she said. "We're not taking anything for granted. On a kind of reverse track, Eric's team has already begun tests on Don Palardy's blood and tissue specimens. And they're working with Peruvian medical authorities to get hold of any remaining samples taken from Alberto Colón. Once they do a comparison study of viruses that infected and killed them—and we're really just speculating about Colón on this one, since there's lots about the circumstances of his death that his government has kept filtered—they'll know more about the processing mechanism that creates the binder cells."

"The blonde," Ricci said. He had been listening silently for a while. "We should get back to her."

Megan turned to him. "Yes, we should," she said. "And not just because she's easy."

They exchanged glances. She wasn't smiling. But the flicker of amusement in her eyes told Ricci the pun had been intentional, and he was surprised to realize it had brightened his mood a little.

"Here's the score," she said, bringing the pointer up to the board again, moving it between the blonde's various chalked-on pseudonyms and Quiros's name. "The Balboa park carousel surveillance obviously ties the woman to Enrique Quiros. But Quiros-Palardy ties both of *them* to Brazil. . . . What's the exact quote in the transcripts?"

Ricci picked up and opened his binder, scanning its pages as he turned them.

"Here, it's in the middle of page thirty, Quiros talking," he said after a few seconds. Then he read: " 'When you wanted money to pay off gambling debts in Cuiabá, you were glad to sell off confidential information about the layout and security of an installation that it was your job to protect.' "

"Quote unquote," Megan said.

"Yeah," Ricci said. "Small world."

Her pointer moved up to the second name from the top. "We know Brazil equals the Wildcat," she said. "That comment alone would give us a clear idea who sent the blonde to Quiros. But we've also got what our computers kicked out on her when we layered Profiler over the NCIC database." She looked at Nimec. "Pete, you were at your computer early doing the search. Might as well give us a summary."

"Our blonde's a terrorist groupie; we all know the type," he said. "Into bad boys and pretty things. She's been detained for questioning by everyone from Europol to the Canadian Duddlies, but nothing's ever been pinned on her. More often than not, she's stayed under the radar. The FBI's tracked her movements with some degree of consistency, but they've kept her dossier restricted. Who knows why. Maybe the usual proprietary reasons, distrust of other agencies—"

"They've shared it with us, Pete," Megan said. "We shouldn't forget that."

Nimec made a slight face. "No, we shouldn't," he said. "Anyway, the feebs figure her for a runner of supplies and messages. When she first caught their eye in '99, she was running with Amir Mamula, an Algerian resident of Montreal who's been connected to the Groupes Islamique Armes, or GIA. That's the same group that did the Air Paris hijack in Morocco a year later, where the Wildcat got vogued by the French diplomat.

After Mamula lost his shine, our gal was scoped loving the nightlife with a parade of other top-dog narcos and terrorists. Changed her hair color, visited the plastic surgeon for some fine-tuning on her facial appearance. Boob job, needless to say. And those pseudonyms on the chalkboard are only the latest in an ongoing series. About a month ago, she went on a romp around the world using the Melina Laval handle. Europe, Latin America, Canada. I should mention that there have been a *lot* of hops to Canada. Eight, ten over the past half year."

"Whereabouts?" Nordstrum asked.

"Mostly western Ontario. Quebec once . . . days before she showed in San Diego," Nimec said. "That's when she dropped off the screen again. Probably also got finished being Melina Laval."

Nordstrum's brow furrowed.

"Tell us what's brewing, Alex," Megan said.

His eyes traveled around the conference table. "Is it fair to say everyone here's thinking we should look very closely at Canada as the site of the bioagent production facility?"

Nods.

"Okay," he said. "Back when I was with the State Department, what made it difficult or impossible to prove foreign governments or militant groups were involved in the manufacture of biological weapons was the dual-use applications of the production technologies. Centrifugal separators, fermenters, freeze dryers, BL4 containment equipment, even known pathogens and toxins, are all readily available on the export market for legitimate medical, agricultural, and industrial purposes. We *knew* who was buying the stuff for the wrong reasons. But you can imagine the problems we confronted trying to argue our case before the UN Security Council, some of whose member nations were among the very ones hiding bioweapons programs."

"Sounds like a joke," Ricci said.

"Yes." Nordstrum shrugged. "It was really a procedural formality anyway. We didn't expect cooperation but wanted our findings on record if we needed to take unilateral action, as in the airstrikes against Osama bin Laden's supposed pharmaceutical plant. And of course we continued tracking the flow of equipment. It isn't too hard. There's a short list of bioprocessing equipment manufacturers worldwide. And that's for materials used to proliferate naturally occurring germs or toxins. With a microorganism that's the product of genetic alteration, the associated technology becomes increasingly use-specific and gets easier to chase. Our government keeps routine tabs on its acquisition and shipment."

Megan looked at him. "*Government*'s a big word," she said. "Can we go to the FBI for the information?"

"They've got the take-charge law-enforcement role in a chemical or biological incident on national soil and would have good intelligence, but it's the Nonproliferation Center at the CIA that's chiefly responsible for gathering the flow data and making it available to the State Department and DOD."

"Can you check out what's been moving into Canada? I mean check right away?"

"I'll try," he said. "You may recall that I've incurred the lasting disfavor of the current White House administration from President Ballard on down. But there are back doors that might still open to an old government bureaucrat."

That, Megan thought, was a curious way for a former deputy secretary of state who'd served as acting head of the department to refer to himself. "Don't hesitate to mention what's at stake while you're knocking on them," she said.

There was a brief silence in the room.

"We should get one of the Hawkeyes into orbital position over our northern neighbor," Nimec said. "If Alex is successful in getting the dope from his contacts, it can help us choose the areas to target for GIS passes."

Ricci gestured toward the blackboard.

"And help Meg work her pointer up to those three big question marks at the top of her list," he said.

She turned to him, held his gaze a moment, and nodded. "That's the idea," she said.

"Alex, your request is *way* out of line. I'm very uncomfortable with this entire conversation—"

"Come on, Neil," Nordstrum said into his cell phone, Neil being Neil Blake, one of his former students and presently an assistant secretary of state, Foreign Affairs Bureau. "Just fax me a copy of that BW tech flow list. You've done bigger favors before. Without blinking."

"That's right. Before. But right now I'm at my desk looking over my shoulder. I swear to God, Alex. If you were a fly on the wall you'd see that I'm serious. Over my shoulder. Somebody overhears me talking to you on the phone, I'm in the shit. At 1600 Pennsylvania Avenue your name is an unwelcome utterance. And will be until the current administration leaves office."

"Because I opted to attend a press conference that the president felt might have stolen some of his bill-signing thunder," Nordstrum said. "Are you listening to yourself? I was a journalist. And I'm still a free citizen. Ballard's executive powers do not extend to canceling my First Amendment rights. I'm surprised he hasn't just ordered me thrown into a dungeon somewhere."

"Let's not get hyperbolic—"

"I don't have to. Or I shouldn't. We're potentially talking about Roger Gordian's life."

Blake sighed. "Nobody holds him in higher regard than I do," he said, easing into a semiofficial tone of voice. "And you know he's got a legion of supporters here in the capital. Give me a day or two. I'll figure out how to handle your request, work it through the appropriate channels."

"What kind of ridiculous phrase is that? It can't wait. Not an *hour* or two. I need what I need. Right away."

"Alex, please, I'm trying to explain—"

"Never mind," Nordstrum kept his voice level. "How's the new bride, Neil?"

There was an instant's silence.

"Cynthia's fine," Blake said, thrown off stride.

"What is it now, a year that you've been married?"

"Yeah. Well, close. We celebrate our first anniversary the day after Christmas—"

"You plan on taking her to that cozy little apartment on Euclid Street for the romantic occasion?" Nordstrum asked. "Or is it still set apart for your independent use?"

This time the silence was much longer.

"How come you ask, Alex?"

"No reason in particular. I just remembered that you never let go of the place. Must have a sentimental attachment after all those good times you had there in the heyday of your bachelorhood." It was Nordstrum's turn to pause. "But listen, you can forget about my request.

I know you're under constraints. I'll try some of my old pressroom cronies at the *Washington Post* instead. You never know, they might have something for me. With them, it's always give and take."

"Alex—"

"I need to hang up—"

"Alex, wait, damn it."

He waited.

"Give me that fax number at UpLink," Blake said.

In his Sacramento office, Eric Oh listened intently as Todd Felson, his colleague at Stanford, offered him the details of the initial tests he'd performed on the food samples taken from Roger Gordian's office.

"You know those wafers we found on his desk? Three of them are impregnated with polymer coacervates in the fifteen to twenty-micron range," he said. "There's a tremendous amount of the stuff."

For the third time in a seventy-two-hour period during which he'd been swept along like a man on a whitewater run, Eric was caught breathless.

"Microencapsulation," he said. "Todd, I think we've found our activator."

"Looks like it," Felson said. "The particle walls are an ethyl cellulose/cyclohexane gelatin. Highly soluble in liquids at body temperature. And very susceptible to breakdown under the high pH levels in a person's digestive system. Or mucous membranes, for that matter."

"Have you gotten to examine the core material at all?"

"Coming up next."

It was ten o'clock in the morning, just two hours after the closed conference room meeting adjourned, when

Megan answered her office phone to hear Alex Nordstrum's excited voice on the line.

"Meg, I've got news," he said.

She sat up straight behind her desk

"I'm waiting," she said.

"I can lay out the paper trail for you later, but the main thing now is that there's a private outfit in Ontario, west of the Hudson Bay, that fits the bill for our germ factory in every way. *Uniquely.* The flow of bioprocessing equipment to it is incredible. I've got listed purchases of regulated biological cultures and growth media, freeze drying and containment equipment, recombinant gene tech . . . it goes on and on. This is a soup-to-nuts bioprocessing facility, and one that was built at great expense. I'd guess the initial cost would total a hundred million dollars. You won't find any other operation like it in Canada, and only a few comparable facilities exist here at home."

Megan took a breath.

"You mean to tell me that nobody in Washington has deemed it in our national interest to investigate what's being developed at this place?"

"I'll share a bit of irony, Meg. We do *business* with these folks. Loads of it. They own agricultural patents that have scored them numerous federal contracts. And they recently won the bidding competition for a huge deal to develop genetically modified strains of *Fusarium oxysporum*—a fungus that's proven to be wholesale murder on coca plants." He paused. "The State Department's been trying to persuade the Columbians and Peruvians to use it against their narco farmers, and it looks like it's going to happen. Chew on that one for a second. Given this company's presumed ties to the Quiros family, which derives its income primarily from the cocaine trade, it's conceivable they're creating a fungus that's specially adapted to wipe out the crops of *competing* growers. And all on our government's tab."

Megan was silent a moment, thinking, the receiver held tightly in her hand.

"Tell me the name of the firm, Al," she said at last.

"Earthglow," he said. "Pretty, isn't it?"

TWENTY-FOUR

REMOTE WAS A RELATIVE TERM NOWADAYS, PAUL "Pokey" Oskaboose was saying as he dipped his single-prop Cessna 172 from the cloud rack. "I read some magazine article by somebody a while back, and I think it said there are something like six, maybe eight places left on the planet where you can spend an hour—or maybe it's a night, I forget—without hearing an engine noise of some kind or other." He banked sharply toward the bunched, snow-draped hills to port.

Seated on his right, Ricci watched the world slant down and away. "How long till we're over the plant?" he asked, his stomach lurching.

"Should be any minute." Oskaboose pointed out his window. A Cree-Ojibway Indian with a wide, bony face and dark hair worn in a buzz cut, he was on loan to Ricci from the Sword watch quartered amid the radomes and communications dishes of an UpLink satellite ground station to the southwest, located midway between the Big Nickel Mine in Sudbury and Lake Superior. "You see the twin rises over there, sort of rounded, got all those wrinkles in them?"

"Uh-huh."

"The local tribes call them *Niish Obekwun*. Means Two Shoulders. Past them's a gap where a stream slices down to the White River. And then that third taller slope. Goes up pretty steep."

Ricci nodded.

"Far side of it, on the west face, is our spot," Oskaboose said. "Go ahead and check the moving map on the instrument panel. Groundhog like you, it'll help with your orientation."

Ricci glanced at the nonglare video display, where a Real Time Geographical Information System map overlaid a live image of the rough, frozen vista below, plotting the airplane's course with a series of flashing red dots, and enclosing Earthglow's position in a bright green square. It *was* helpful, he thought. And precisely matched his recollection of the Hawkeye-I photos he'd seen back in San Jose. With a zoom resolution of under three centimeters, they had afforded detailed aerial close-ups of the custom biological facility and its perimeter defenses. But Ricci had wanted to get a visceral feel of the land that for him would only come with firsthand observation.

Oskaboose leveled the aircraft. "In today's world, Tarzan wouldn't have to worry about being raised by apes," he said. "You've got, what, a couple thousand gorillas left in Africa, that's counting all five subspecies. And they're more used to having their pictures snapped than models and movie stars. Some British kid in knickers being nursed at the breast of a furry mama would be spotted in no time by rich tourists on photo safaris. And brought back to civilization, heaven help him."

The guide's apparent non sequitur drew a puzzled glance from Ricci.

"Another instance of how the wilderness isn't wilderness like it used to be," Oskaboose said, noticing his expression.

Ricci grunted.

"Give you one more example," Oskaboose continued. "People hear the name Tibet, they think robed Buddhist mystics levitating and astral-projecting in transcendental bliss. Or at least I do. But you know, it's become just another getaway for Hollywood stars with personal problems. Donate a million bucks to the temple chest, they'll issue you a wallet card listing the chakras, declare that you're pure of spirit, and initiate you as an honorary monk of the order. I kid you not." He made a sad *tsk*ing sound and motioned out the window again. "We're about to head over the basin. You might want to take a peek."

Ricci looked downward. The folds of the rise they were overflying were thick with pine forest. On the almost perpendicular uplift at the basin's far side, the growth was sparser, clinging to the rock face in stubborn, woolly tufts between wide, white expanses of snow. Directly below them now, the tributary was a crystalline blue ribbon in the midday sunlight.

"That water frozen solid?" Ricci asked.

Oskaboose shrugged his shoulders. "Hard to be sure from up here," he said. "You can tell for yourself that there's a surface layer of ice. But it only takes a little silty runoff for the crust to stay thin in patches. Especially this early in the season, when the temperature can still poke above freezing."

Ricci compressed his lips. "The snow on the slopes. You have any idea how deep it is?"

"The precip hasn't been too bad, so I'd guess about a foot, with drifts coming up maybe knee high." He gave Ricci a quick glance. "Inexperienced climbers have to watch out for cracks in the rock that get covered by bridges of crusted snow. Fall into some of 'em, and you can take quite a plunge."

Ricci nodded thoughtfully.

"Okay," Oskaboose said. "Soon as we cross that next hill, you'll catch sight of Earthglow to your right, down on a ledge near its base."

"We do one pass. That's it. No doubling back."

"Understood." Oskaboose shrugged again. "The point of what I was explaining to you, though, is that the sight of a plane is nothing to make anybody suspicious around here. Pukaskwa National Park isn't too far to the south. Rangers there use fixed wing aircraft and choppers for wildlife observation, search and rescue, and supply transport. Then you have airmail deliveries to townspeople, recreational pilots, and so on. We don't have to be too worried about being noticed."

Ricci kept silent, his pale blue eyes staring out the window.

In a large conference room at the Sudbury ground station, Rollie Thibodeau and the rest of the twenty-four-man RDT were gathered before a flat-panel wall monitor, viewing the same pictures that appeared on the Cessna's video display as it made its flyby.

The Earthglow facility was a low, concrete building backed directly against the almost vertical eastern slope, bounded on its other three sides by a high, industrial chain-link perimeter fence topped with multiple rows of electrical wiring. A sliding gate in the north-facing section of the fence opened onto a two-lane blacktop that curved along the base of the hill and then stretched off eastward toward the railway station at Hawk Junction— about a hundred miles distant, across rolling, heavily forested country. Small guard posts were visible at the southern and western corners of the fence. A third stood outside the gate at the terminus of the blacktop. A network of access roads branched from the gate to various building entrances.

Watching the stream of recon images over his microwave link with the aircraft, Thibodeau muttered unhappily under his breath. He knew Tom Ricci better than he liked—would have *liked* not to know him at all— and could anticipate the mission plan he would present upon returning to base.

What bothered him, in part, was that it stood to be dangerous to the extreme. But the thing that filled him with deepest distress was also knowing there was no workable alternative.

Back at the ground station an hour later, Ricci and Pokey Oskaboose had joined Thibodeau and the others in the conference room. The lights were dimmed around them. On their screen was a bird's-eye color still of the Earthglow building and its surrounding terrain, the key tactical points highlighted with *X*s.

"That high slope behind the building is a natural defensive wall." Ricci indicated it from his chair with the beam of his pen-sized laser pointer, feeling queerly as if something of the wicked Megan Breen's persona had rubbed off on him. "Our pals at Earthglow don't have a guard post there, either on the peak or any of the ledges. And it isn't hard to understand why. It looks like they're unapproachable from that flank."

"Be the reason it's the best way for us to come at them," Thibodeau said. His tone was grimly resigned. "Take advantage of their overconfidence, *soit*."

Ricci nodded and moved the pointer's red dot to the right, focusing it on a small, flat hollow between the northernmost rims of the Two Shoulders hills.

"We can land a chopper here. Off-load our equipment, and one of those radio-frequency-shielded tents that we can use as a command and communications center," he said. "It's a nice pocket of concealment. And as close to Earthglow as I want to set down."

"The RF-secure tents are cold-weather white, and should blend right in with the snow on the ground and slopes," Oskaboose added. "Guess we can hide the copter under some cammo pretty easy, too."

"Sounds good." Ricci's laser dot jumped up and to the left onto the blacktop leading to the facility. "We'll have an escape vehicle ready to roll around this area west of the bridge, not far from where the two-laner swings around the bottom of the hill toward the perimeter gate. My team'll have to reach it on foot once we're out of the building. Then it takes us across the bridge, the chopper picks us up on the other side, and we're off."

"You catch a break, make a clean getaway, sure," Thibodeau said. "But we can't depend on it. Got to figure there might be somebody on your tail wants to stop that from happenin'."

Ricci looked at him. "So your team prepares something to stop them from stopping us."

Thibodeau scratched his beard.

"Yeah," he said. "Suppose I got me an idea or two."

Ricci nodded again. Then he turned back to the photo image on the wall, slid the red dot down onto the icy stream spanned by the bridge, and tracked its course through the basin that divided Two Shoulders from the larger hill.

"Our approach is going to be what's trickiest," he said. "From where we strike camp at Two Shoulders, my insertion team needs to hike to the stream, ski across its banks, then climb the northeast side of the hill and go down the northwest. That'll leave us behind the building. From there we move along its side to the guard station at the gate, take out the sentries, and carry on with the rest of the program." He inclined his head toward Pokey Oskaboose. "I know it seems like you'd have to be a damn spider to make it up that big slab of rock, but Pokey mentioned a couple of things I wouldn't have noticed."

"You and whoever built Earthglow figuring the hill would guarantee protection from the rear," Oskaboose said. "Anybody knows this country could see how it's tough but not anything near the worst. You've got all kinds of plants clumped on its slopes: juniper, pines, spruce, cedar, berry bushes. That means root systems to keep the ground from slipping out from underfoot. Also means plenty of handholds and matted branches to break your fall in case you do take a slide."

Thibodeau gave him a look. "An' you intend on bein' there to point out them mats an' handholds?" he said.

Oskaboose seemed unbothered by his dubious tone. "Let me put it this way," he said. "I usually prefer to get my high-altitude kicks in a pilot's seat, but for special company like you boys, I'm thrilled to make an exception."

That night, before his group set out on their cross-country hike, Ricci emerged out of the metalized fabric igloo tent and stood surrounded by the humped granite rises of *Niish Obekwun,* their furrowed contours other-worldly in the darkness. The temperature had fallen well below freezing with sundown, and continued to drop at a precipitous rate. The wind had also picked up. Swirling into, over, and through the snow- and brush-covered crannies and ledges of the hillsides, it filled the cavity below with a toneless idiot chant, as if the landscape itself was astir with some impersonally menacing ritual.

Ricci stood there, alone, outfitted in a snow cammo shell jacket and pants, a polar liner, his Zylon vest, and thermal undergarments. He carried his baby VVRS on a shoulder sling and wore an ALICE pack on his back. His hands were covered with ultrathin-insulate gloves that wouldn't get in the way of firing his weapon. On his feet were white rubber boots and tapered-tail aluminum alloy snowshoes. His sleekly molded full-head helmet was equipped with an integrated, hands-free wireless audio/video system, its dime-sized color digital camera lens invisible above his forehead, its microphone embedded in the chin guard. Ricci's polycarbonate ballistic visor was pulled down over his eyes-only balaclava and shielded the exposed portion of his face from the fiercely cold air. But he could still feel its bite through his breathing vents, feel its tingle in his lungs with each inhalation. Never in the coldest, bleakest Maine winter had he experienced such inimical cold. No sane human being would expose himself to it without good reason.

Ricci hadn't had any desire to contemplate his own reason. He had simply wanted to be by himself before leaving: to be still, without thought, quiet inside. That was really all.

He turned around now, stepped back toward the tent, and then leaned his head through its entrance flap to signal his men to gear up and assemble. He'd had his moment of solitude and was ready to get under way.

The glazed surface of the stream gave out with occasional complaints as they tramped across its banks, making crumpled-cellophane noises under the glittering snow cover. They proceeded in single file, Oskaboose at the head of the column, followed by Ricci and his Cape Green graduates: Seybold, Beatty, Rosander, Grillo, Simmons, Barnes, Harpswell, and Nichols. Three additions had been made to boost the number of men in the insertion team, a seasoned hand from Kaliningrad named Neil Perry, and Dan Carlysle and Ron Newell, both veterans of the Brazilian affair and recommended by Thibodeau.

Oskaboose kept his eyes downward, wary of thin ice. He would test any suspect area by putting one leg carefully forward, shifting his weight onto it, and pressing in hard with the crampons of his snowshoe, alert for the slightest hint of cracking or buckling or a telltale flit of shadows around the snowshoe's edges that would reveal the movement of water beneath a shallow, weakened crust. Although the group was on a networked communications link, he remained entirely silent, using hand gestures to wave the others forward when he was confident of the footing or to steer them clear of places where its soundness was questionable. Ricci didn't need for him to explain why. It was the habit of someone who had spent a lifetime in this terrain, knew it inside out, and preferred to negotiate it without technological mediation. Who wanted his senses freed up to listen and feel for its hazards.

The cold had seemed to deepen after they left the Two Shoulders camp, but perhaps as a result they only encountered a few potential trouble spots during their crossing of the stream . . . although on a single instance, just yards from its west bank, the ice cracked under Oskaboose's foot with a sound that reverberated between the dark walls of the cleft like a rifle shot. The men started in their heavy packs, Ricci's eyes briefly going to the slope, the buttstock of his VVRS gun raised against his shoulder. But then he heard a splash and turned to see Oskaboose pull his snowshoe out of the break, water gushing up around its frame, droplets of moisture wicking off the leg of his shell pants.

"Sorry, fellas," Oskaboose said over their comlink. They were the first words he'd spoken since they'd trod onto the ice. "Bad step there."

Ricci loosened his grip on his weapon and followed him the rest of the way across the stream without incident.

Ricci's recollections of the climb would later streak together in his mind, staying with him as a mostly random shuffle of images and impressions.

He would remember his men pausing at the base of the hill to remove their snowshoes and sling them over their backs, and then their first adrenaline-charged push up the lower ledges, the group surrendering themselves entirely to forward motion. Remember seeking out

Pokey Oskaboose's ascending shadow, following his lead, trying not to fall too far behind. Remember the feel of coarse, cold stone against his flattened body. And the gusts tugging at him. Snow spilling around him in loose talc-white clouds. Icicles snapping apart under his fingers. His gloved hands twisting into notches, grabbing hold of needled juniper branches, clutching at bare tangles of scrub that grew precariously out of hairline fissures in the rock. And, once, a startled bird bearing aloft with a querulous shriek, its wings flaying the air. He would clearly recall the moment he heard the scuff of Seybold's boots below him and turned to see that he had stumbled, lost traction, and was swaying backward off a ledge, chunks of ice and pebbly material fragmenting underfoot to skitter down the slope. Then reaching for him with one hand, catching his wrist, driving his own feet against the rock as he pulled upward and steadied him. And drawing a long inhalation, and moving on, and on, always with Oskaboose in sight, toiling upward in that fury of wind and billowing powder.

And then finally the crest of the hill was above him. And his right arm was over it. His left arm. His chest. His legs. And almost to his own surprise, he was standing beside Oskaboose, and both were giving Seybold a hand up, the rest of his party appearing in ones and twos and threes, helping each other gain the final bit of ground, gathering there atop the rise overlooking the blockish spread of the Earthglow facility.

They had allowed themselves only a brief period to catch their breath before starting the climb down. Two or three minutes, as Ricci recalled. They had made progress, yes, but that wasn't the same thing as having achieved their objective. Not nearly.

The job they had come to do was still ahead of them, and there was no time whatsoever to lose.

They descended the hill as they had started up its opposite side, in single file, and again the elements proved equal parts advantage and handicap.

Open to the constant force of wind and storm unlike its basin wall, the hill's western slope was almost scrubbed of vegetation and bore the insults of constant battery: crumbling juts of granite, craggy scars and pockmarks, and deep gouges that looked as if they were bites taken out of its stony hide by some great, vicious set of jaws. Any of these could have been serious pitfalls for someone who didn't know the territory. But to Oskaboose they represented options: handholds, footholds, covered niches where his teammates could take momentary respite.

The drawback was that the weather-blasted pieces of hillside had nowhere to go but down, an inevitable consequence of gravity that gave Oskaboose his full share of problems for the last fifteen or twenty yards of the descent toward its base. Picking his steps over and around tumbled boulders, pulverized rocks, and slippery cascades of pebbles, snow, and ice was a strenuous challenge complicated by his mindfulness of having to select a path that would be least difficult for those behind him.

The guide's effort was not lost on Ricci. When his boots touched ground, a glance at the tritium dial of his wristwatch showed that over two hours had passed since his group had left camp. Longer than he'd expected, maybe, but thanks to Pokey Oskaboose, they had gotten this far without a single injury worse than a bump or bruise.

And straight ahead of them now was Earthglow, its shadow deeper than the black of night.

The dangers were supposed to seem real during tac exercises, and indeed they had to an outstanding degree. But there were parts of the mind that refused even voluntary surrender to illusion, and the spilling of simulated blood did not equal loss of life, no matter how true its shade of red.

Pressed against Earthglow's windowless back wall, Ricci watched Rosander nose his telescoping probe around its corner with a powerful sense of déjà vu. Still, he was acutely aware that Cape Green had been little more than a stage set: Africa one day, Balkan Europe the next, Motor City if you wanted it to be. The here and now was what it was, and it never would be anything else, he thought. And this time the men who fell under his watch would not rise to joke, complain, or be chastised about it afterward.

"Picture any clearer on your HUD?" Rosander asked. He fingered a rocker switch on the probe's pistol grip handle to adjust its nonvisible IR illumination level. "I've maxed the output, can't get better res past about ten yards in this darkness."

"It'll do." The image superimposed on Ricci's field of view by his visor display showed a pair of guards in hooded parkas, goggles, and wool scarves taking relaxed strides along their patrol of the building's north side. Their shoulder-slung FN P90 assault weapons fired the same ammunition as his Five-Seven pistol: small rounds, big punch. "Get rid of the sound, though. I don't need to hear their horseshit about boffing townie high school girls."

Rosander pressed another switch to cut his rod's surveillance mike.

"These guys go down fast and quiet," Ricci said. The comlink's acoustical gain was set to output his whisper as a normal speaking voice to his team members. "Can't let them get off a shot. Rather we don't have to, either."

He reached into his belt pouch for the DMSO, looked quickly over his shoulder, then gestured for Seybold to produce his canister.

"On my signal," he said, raising his fist.

Seybold nodded to him, and they edged up beside Rosander.

They waited. The guards appeared to be in no hurry to complete their rounds. Just a couple of gun-toting chums on a leisurely stroll through the meat-locker cold of night in the Canadian Shield.

After what seemed an age, they approached the corner of the wall.

Ricci's arm came up like a semaphore.

Seybold moved with him at once. They rounded the corner and got right in the guards' faces with their canisters, knowing the high-pressure spurts of fluid would not disperse in the wind at close range and that the permeable fabric scarves wrapped around their mouths would do nothing to stop the sedative from acting instantaneously.

Silently and painlessly kayoed, the guards hit the ground unconscious and then were flex-cuffed and dragged into the shadows at the base of the hill. They would be out for hours.

Ricci turned to his men.

"All right," he said. "Let's hit the gatehouse."

• • •

Pokey Oskaboose's guidance had been a blessing for more reasons than his familiarity with the physical terrain. He had also imparted a critical tip about area transport during the mission's planning stage: Pretty well everything that made its way to and from the rest of the world was conveyed three times weekly via Toronto on the wilderness train. A single train. Mondays, Wednesdays, and Fridays. Like other outposts located many miles from the nearest railway depot, Earthglow would need to connect with the station by truck over the Trans Canada Highway. There was simply no other practical means.

Of course, Oskaboose hadn't known the facility's specific shipping and receiving schedules. But that hadn't been necessary. These were the boonies, last stop on the civilization express. Conduct the insertion in the long, murky period that bridged Thursday and Friday—say at two, three, four o'clock in the morning—and you could safely assume that the delivery gate would be manned by a skeleton crew. Warm bodies, if the expression was applicable here at world's end. You could also figure they would go on shift expecting to do little more than gulp coffee and pick their noses. Because not for a million bucks would a driver try rolling his wagon over the frosted local roads at such an hour, especially the black, winding spools of blacktop off the main highway, where painted lanes were nonexistent, and you had to sort of guess whether you were in danger of getting smacked by opposing traffic. Well, maybe for a million bucks, Oskaboose had reconsidered. But far as he knew, nobody had gotten offered that amount yet.

It was now a few ticks of the minute hand short of three A.M., and Ricci was thinking that Oskaboose's skinny had been worth a fortune and more.

The gatehouse was nothing fancy. A lighted, heated modular steel booth designed for a small handful of personnel, it could have been lifted from where it stood and dropped at the entry to any commercial building anyplace, maybe a factory that manufactured fountain pens, or fan belts, or soda bottles, or zippers for ladies' skirts. It was hard for Ricci to imagine it as a breeding farm for a killer germ of a type never before known to man. Hard for him, sometimes, to remember that the shape of evil could be so drummingly bland and commonplace. The devil as the guy next door.

Hugging the north wall of Earthglow about a hundred feet from the gatehouse, his men drawn up behind him, Ricci could see three guards through the plate glass windows of the booth. Two were seated behind a control panel with a bank of video monitors on it, talking, neither of them apparently paying attention to the screens. A third was dozing on a chair behind a desk or counter, legs stretched, arms folded, head tucked to his chest.

Ricci thought a minute. The door was on his side of the booth, a magnetic swipe card reader on the frame. It would automatically lock when closed, but these prefab housings weren't designed to store the crown jewels. He was sure one good kick would take care of it.

He called four men over to him. Grillo, Barnes, Carlysle, and Newell. The rest would stay put. This would have to be perfectly coordinated, and he wanted experience with him.

His instructions took seconds: *Fast, quiet.* The guards at the other perimeter posts had to remain oblivious.

Ricci shuffled forward in a squat, the others close behind him, all of them sticking to the shadows along the main building's wall. At the edge of the wall he signaled a halt. There were ten yards of open ground to the gatehouse. Dark yards. His group would be fine if they stayed low. He gave his command, and they made the stealthy dash.

Out of sight beneath the windows now, pulse racing, epinephrine flooding his system, its taste filling his mouth like he'd bitten into an allergy pill, Ricci waited for his men to hastily take their positions, Grillo and Barnes to the right of the door, gripping their VVRS guns, Newell right behind him on the left side, Carlysle crouched back in the darkness facing the door, ready for the kick.

Three fingers of one hand raised, Ricci drew his expandable ASP baton from its belt scabbard with the other and counted off. Vocally and manually. One finger went down.

". . . two, *three!*"

In a heartbeat, Carlysle sprang erect and took two giant steps forward, his leg thrusting up and out. The sole of his boot hit the door under the handle, and it banged inward.

Ricci rushed into the gatehouse, clenching the tactical baton's foam grip, thumbing the release stud to extend its tubular-steel segments. The guards seated side by side at the control panel twisted around toward the entrance, agape with stunned surprise. Peripherally aware of his own men moving in around him, Ricci saw assault rifles slung over the guards' chair backs: a P-90 for Mr. Left, and an H&K for Mr. Right.

Mr. Right was quickest on the uptake, snatching for his weapon. Ricci went at him with the baton, smashed a blow to the back of his wristbone, and with a continuous movement slid it under his forearm, grabbed hold of the tip so he was holding both ends, and crossed it, applying strong pressure. The ulna snapped like brittle wood. Mr. Right flopped around on his chair and started to scream. Ricci pulled the baton free of his arm and then brought it up and struck his neck sideways at the pressure point below the ear. He made a noise like water sucking down a partially clogged drain and hit the floor motionless, the clouted arm bent at several unnatural angles.

Ricci pivoted toward Mr. Left, the baton arcing in front of him, but his hands were raised in the air, his firearm already taken, Grillo and Barnes jamming their guns into his ribs. Carlysle and Newell had their weapons trained on the guy who'd been caught napping.

Ricci stood between the two captive guards, looked from one to another, then gestured at the control panel.

"Which of you gamers wants to let us in the freight door?" he asked.

Neither of them responded.

He turned to Mr. Left, waved Grillo and Barnes aside, snapped the baton across his face. Blood gushed from his broken nose, and he crashed back over his chair to the floor.

Ricci whirled back toward the now wide-eyed napper, bunched the front of his shirt in his fist, and hauled him to his feet.

"Guess it has to be you," he said.

"You still with us, Thibodeau?" Ricci asked over the comlink.

"Check," he replied from the Two Shoulders camp.

"How about you, Pokey? Everything under control?"

"Yup." Oskaboose's voice now, from the gatehouse. "It's a big mess, though."

"Next time, I'll try to be neater," Ricci said. "Those two guards should be out for a while. Either one starts to squeal, hit him with some more DMSO. He'll conk."

"Got it."

"I don't want you or Harpswell taking your weapons off that third crack lookout. If anybody from the facility radios or approaches the booth, he's your receptionist. Make sure he answers with a smile. And that he doesn't forget what'll happen to him if he says the wrong thing."

"Got you again."

Ricci paused a moment to order his thoughts. Then: "Doc?"

"I'm here." This was the voice of Eric Oh, at the San Jose headquarters with Nimec and Megan the Merciless. "They just patched me into the A/V a minute or two ago."

"Figured you could live without seeing the preliminaries," Ricci said. "The signal clear at your end?"

"It's a little scratchy, but they're working to clean it up," Eric said. "Where are you in the building right now? It looks like a kitchen."

Ricci looked around, his helmet's monocular NVD sight down over his right eye. Minus Oskaboose and Harpswell, his team had made their way through the opened freight entrance and then down a couple of dim and empty branching corridors, seeking the path of least resistance into the main section of the building. The first unlocked door had led them here. And a kitchen it was. A big one, too. Obviously, it produced food for the resident staff. There were heavy steel commercial appliances, walk-in refrigerators, triple-basin sinks, overhead grid hooks hung with cookware. Shelves stocked with seasonings, coffee, and other supplies.

For some incomprehensible reason, Ricci suddenly recalled his father's preferred version of grace at the dinner table: *Good friends, good food, good God, let's eat.* It had been years since that little snippet of his past had crested from the depths of memory.

"Yeah, Doc," he said. "Hang tight, we're moving."

Ricci started toward a tall swing door at the far end of the room, leading his men down the aisle between a long cutting counter and a solid row of ovens, grills, and ranges.

A hurried glimpse beyond the door's eye-level glass pane revealed the darkened commissary on the opposite side: tables and chairs; vending machines; convenience islands for napkins, condiments, and eating utensils.

Mundane. Commonplace. Like a high school cafeteria.

Ricci pushed through the door, his men at his heels, then saw the general employee entrance to the commissary to his left—double-swing doors this time—and hooked toward it.

He paused again at the doors, eased one of them open a crack with his gloved fingertips, and slowly leaned his head through the opening.

A hallway lined with doors stretched to either side. Name plaques on the doors, these were offices. And down at one end, he spotted something that simultaneously quickened his pulse and made his neck hairs bristle.

There were two signs on the wall, one above the other. The bottom sign was a simple arrow pointing to a cross corridor. The top sign displayed the biohazard symbol.

• • •

Ricci rapidly led his team along the darkened corridor and turned in the direction of the arrow marker, aware of the dull, leached-away sound of their footsteps between the thick concrete walls.

At the juncture with the connecting hall was another set of swing doors. Recessed ceiling fluorescents glowed in the passage beyond their windows.

Ricci ordered his men to fan out against the walls, then went to the double doors and carefully looked past the glass. The hall beyond seemed empty. He gently shouldered through the partition into the milky wash of light.

The doors lining the sides of this passage were no longer of the ordinary office building variety. These were metal-clad, bullet-resistant installations, most with swipe readers and entry-code keypads.

Instructing the others to follow close behind him, Ricci moved forward into the corridor.

"You have any pointers, Doc, let's hear them," he said into his helmet mike.

"My guess is you're heading in the right direction. In general, bioengineering firms are laid out like any commercial or industrial facility. According to the stages of production, from start to finish—"

"You don't warehouse the showroom-ready car with the parts that go into it."

"Exactly."

"Okay, what else can you tell me?"

"The absolute best thing for us would be to find actual, preformulated inhibitors for the virus, chemical blockers that would prevent its binding proteins from attaching to Gordian's cellular receptors. Failing that, we'd need to access Earthglow's computerized gene banks to get the data on how the bug synthesizes its isoforms—"

A twinge of impatience. "Closer to English, Doc."

"The proteins or peptides generated by alternative RNA splicing," Eric said. "If we get those coded templates, we can use the information to derive our own inhibitors and stop the virus's progress. But that could take a while, and Gordian's condition doesn't give us much—Wait, slow down, I want a look at that sign to your right."

Ricci turned so his helmet camera was facing it.

The sign read:

FLOW CYTROMETRY

"Okay, thanks, that's not what we need," Eric said. "Back to what I started to explain, the inhibitors would be an end-stage product. Microencapsulated like the triggers that awakened the bug. And probably kept in the same area. Storage wouldn't be complicated. The capsules are designed to have a long shelf life in a dry, clean, room-temperature environment."

Ricci hastened down the passage. "What am I keeping my eyes out for?"

"Signs with terms like *coacervation* or *fluid-bed coating* or *hot melt systems*. The microencapsulation units themselves consist of several large-batch tanks or chambers—usually acrylic, stainless steel, or some combination of the two—joined by pumping systems: ducts, blowers, et cetera. There would have to be a compressed air source. Computer panel controls. The materials used would be—"

Oh suddenly broke off his sentence. From his monitor thousands of miles away, he could see what Ricci had just spotted ahead of him at an intersection in the hall. It had pushed his heart up into his throat.

Ricci knew at a glance that the guards who'd appeared in the passage had better stuff than the perimeter security crew.

They had turned the corner in his direction just as he'd approached it and paused to motion Rosander over with the telescopic probe. Three men in light gray uniforms with submachine guns over their shoulders and the unmistakable look of quality troops.

Before either group could react, they found themselves facing each other across a straight length of hall, separated by four or five yards with no available cover . . . and no choice except to engage.

Swiftly rasing his weapon, its MEMS touch control on its lethal setting, Ricci had the briefest instant to once again recall the Cape Green maneuvers with that strange sensation of events doubling back on themselves.

The thought had not quite fled his mind as he opened fire, ordering his men to spread out and do the same.

The guard he'd targeted was only a little slower to trigger his own gun. He collapsed to the floor, his uniform blouse chewed and bloody, his rifle dropping from his hand.

Ricci saw a second guard train his subgun on one of the men behind him, instantly swung his around, and triggered another burst, a five-shot salvo. But this time, the guard managed to squeeze out a volley before falling onto his back, and he kept shooting even afterward, scattering a gale of ammunition across the hall. Ricci heard a grunt of pain from over his shoulder, didn't turn. Couldn't. He wanted that son of a bitch on the floor finished.

He angled the VVRS down and fired again, and so did another member of the insertion team. Red exploded from the guard's belly, he rolled over and there was red splashed on his back from the exit wounds, and then he flopped a little and lay still.

More gunfire from Ricci's left, more from his rear, and he turned to see the third guard shiver in place a moment and then spill loosely off his feet.

Okay, he thought. *Okay, that's all of them.*

He spun around to see who'd been hit. Grillo. On his back, blood streaming from his throat. Simmons and Beatty were kneeling over him, getting off the helmet, opening the collar of his jacket, but he wasn't moving, and his open eyes had the look Ricci knew came with the touch of death.

Ricci rushed over to his body, crouched, touched the pulse point on his neck, Grillo's blood oozing over his gloves.

He tilted his face up to his men, tried not to let the clenching he felt inside show.

"Nothing we can do for him," he said. "And we have to get out of this damned hallway while we can."

The lightest of sleepers, Kuhl answered the telephone in time to clip its first ring. "What is it?" he said.

He listened to the report from his security officer, then flung off his blanket.

"Where in the building?" he said.

He listened again.

"Send reinforcements to the area," he said. He decided

that he had best notify DeVane. "I'm coming immediately."

"Doc, I've got to hear from you!" Ricci snapped over the comlink. His team was speeding along the corridor, away from the section where the firefight had broken out.

Silence.

"Come on, Doc, I mean now—"

"Tom, listen, it's me."

"Pete, where the hell is he? We're running blind here."

"I know. Eric saw the whole thing. The shooting. What happened to Grillo. He's pretty shaken up."

"Then pull him together—"

"Tom, for God's sake, we know your situation." It was Megan, her voice tense. "Give him half a second—"

"I'm all right," Eric's voice broke in. "Sorry. I . . . I just . . ."

"Later," Ricci said. "We're coming up to another cross hall. A bunch of signs. Can you read them?"

"No, you're moving too fast, the picture's blurry . . . jolting . . ."

"I'm going to stop and let you take a look. But we don't have long. I don't know who might've heard those guns."

"Understood."

Ricci signaled a halt, then craned his head toward the signs, turning it to allow the helmet's digicam to pan across his visual path.

"You see them okay?" he said.

"Yes . . . Wait. The sign on your left. No, the next one over . . . okay, right there."

Ricci's eyes held on the sign. It said:

AQUEOUS PHASE SEPARATION

"Doc?" Ricci urged.

"That's it. A synonym for the gelatin microencapsulation process," Eric said. "The academic term."

Ricci swung his gaze to the left. A steel door barred the way about three feet down the corridor junction. This had a biometric hand scanner rather than the swipe card reader. The level of security was escalating, itself a strong indication he was getting hot. And while he'd expected to encounter biometrics and come prepared with ways to fool them, the deceptions took time, and speed now took precedence over delicacy.

He turned to his men. "They know we're here, no point tiptoeing," he said. "We blow our way in."

Johan Stuzinski was a specialist in the field of bioinformatics—the use of statistical and computational analytic techniques to predict the function of encoded proteins within genetic material, based solely on DNA sequence data. The applications of this discipline in terms of human genome research included the identification of proteins within chromosomes that caused inherited diseases and inherited predispositions toward diseases that might be triggered by environmental, dietary, and other external factors.

The fruits of this research promise to revolutionize modern medicine by helping scientists design drugs and therapies that target these culprit proteins, attacking or even eliminating the causes of health disorders at the cellular—in truth, the molecular—roots. If cures or vastly superior treatments for cancer, diabetes, cardiovascular disease, the muscular dystrophies, Alzheimer's,

AIDS, and countless other maladies that have plagued mankind throughout history are found in the coming decades, it will be through application of genomic discoveries.

The very best in his field, Johan Stuzinski could have lent his expertise to any of hundreds of medical research establishments and pharmaceutical firms performing meaningful work toward improving the human condition in the twenty-first century and beyond. In January 2000, Stuzinski was offered a management position with a generous salary and benefit package by Sobel Genetics, a leader in the search for genome-based therapies. Though he came close to taking the job, Stuzinski had simultaneously received another proposal from Earthglow, a Canadian firm whose goals were considerably more obscure, even a bit irregular, as he chose to think of them. But its hiring executive had promised him various under-the-table, and thus nontaxable, financial perquisites that were communicated with subtle inferences. A nod and a wink, so to speak.

After some consideration, he had called Sobel to decline their proposition, packed his bags for Ontario, and gladly put on his moral blinders. He kept his eyes on his narrow portion of the work being conducted at the facility, rarely allowed himself to consider its eventual application, and very definitely never questioned the presence of the rather menacing armed guards who patrolled certain parts of the facility.

In that way, Stuzinski was exactly like hundreds of other top-caliber professionals who had come to lend their exceptional skills to Earthglow's operations. He was like them in another way, as well: When the sounds of racing footsteps, dull claps that may have been gunfire, and something that could perhaps have been a small explosion distantly reached his apartment in the complex's living quarters in the predawn hours of Thursday morning, rousing him from sleep, he got out of bed only to make sure his door was locked and then somewhat nervously stayed put.

Until and unless it became a direct threat to him, Johan Stuzinski's attitude was that whatever might be happening outside was none of his personal business.

"You six stay here and cover the entry." Ricci motioned to Barnes, Seybold, Beatty, Carlysle, Perry, and Newell. "Watch yourselves. That boom must've set off alarms everywhere. We don't know what kind of manpower's headed this way."

The men nodded in unison. They were standing near the blown, broken remains of the security door in the smoke and haze left by the detonation of their breaching charges.

Ricci looked at their faces a moment, then turned to the other four members of his team. "Okay, here we go," he said and led them through the ruptured entrance.

In Earthglow's main security station, Kuhl studied the flashing light on his electronic display's building schematic. The blast's location supported what he had already construed about the goal of the intruders. And the connection between their goal and identity was like a match brightly struck in his mind.

His eyes went from the screen to his chief lieutenant. "Keep abreast of developments at the penetration site," Kuhl said, thinking of the alternate path he could take to investigate the target area. "I will be in contact."

He did not await the lieutenant's nod of acknowledgment before leaving the room.

Looking up the corridor, Seybold realized he'd not only cut the opposition's numeric advantage but dramatically shifted it to his own band.

It was a thing that gave him some relief, a thing he'd trained for, prepared for. But he was still human, and the violations combat weapons inflicted on human flesh sickened him.

Five or six of the guards were down in grotesque positions, sheeted in blood, the floor around them slick with blood. Some were screaming in pain. Another guard was pinned to the wall like an insect caught on a fly strip, drenched with superadhesive, his limbs tangled by the impact that hurled him against it, strips of skin flapping off his cheek where he'd torn himself from the concrete in a blind panic. Yet another guard stared dazedly on his knees at a baseball-sized hole in his abdomen.

Seybold had a bare moment to register the damage. The rest of the guards were advancing past the sprawl of bodies, their weapons stuttering, and it was his job to stop them.

He took a deep breath of air, slung the Benelli over his back, then gripped his baby VVRS in his hands and fired a tight burst. To his left and right, hunkered close to the walls on either side of the exploded steel door, his companions were also firing their weapons.

More guards went down, and then another came running forward in a kind of wrathful, aggressive hurtle, yelling at the top of his lungs, his gun blazing away. A couple of feet to Seybold's left, Beatty grunted and was slammed back against the wall, smearing it with blood as he sank to the floor. Then bullets rippled from one of the other men's VVRS rifles, and the charging guard spun around in a circle and fell dead, his weapon slipping from his fingers, clutching his chest with both hands.

That left two of them. One dove onto his belly to present a low target, skidding over the blood of his companions, sustained fire pouring from his weapon. Carlysle and Newell trained their guns on him and fired in concert, a brief chop. These were men whose partnership went back, and it showed in their expert performance. The guard jerked once on the floor and then ceased to move.

A single guard remained now, and he was unwilling to commit suicide. He turned down the hall, running, his uniform splashed with blood that may or may not have been his own.

"We gonna let him take off?" Carlysle asked Seybold.

Seybold looked at him. The question had sounded almost distant through the loud throbbing pulse beat in his ears.

"The son of a bitch isn't important," he said. Seybold rushed over to Beatty, on the floor now, propped into a sitting position with his back to the wall. Barnes and Newell were already huddled around him, getting their first-aid kits out of their packs. Perry had raised his helmet visor.

"How bad?" Seybold asked. His eyes went from Beatty's bloodied shoulder to his face.

"Feels like a slug drilled through my arm, but I think I'll be all right," Beatty said. He licked his lips. "Can't say I love it, though."

Seybold breathed and nodded. "We'll get you patched up," he said.

"Wait," Eric Oh said. "That one. No, no, you're pulling the wrong disk. Count two up. Okay, that's it."

Ricci slid the gem case from the cabinet and turned it over in his hand so the print on its index label faced his helmet's digital camera lens.

Silence over the comlink.

"Doc . . ."

"I need you to slip it into your wearable," Eric said. "Send me its contents so I can have a look."

Ricci bit his lip. He could hear gunfire somewhere in the direction of the blown security door.

Reaching down to the miniature computer on his belt, he ejected its CD-ROM tray, set in the disk, and pushed the tray shut. Then he hit the preset UpLink intranet key and uploaded the disk's contents as a wireless E-mail attachment.

Tortured seconds passed.

"Well?"

"The data's coming through now, I'm going to scan it on-line, give me a chance to—"

Ricci's heart knocked. *"Well . . . ?"*

"My God," Eric said. "Oh my God, Ricci, this is unbelievable."

His SIG-Sauer P220 in his hand should the enemy be waiting near its door, Kuhl rode the pneumatic elevator up from the biofarm sublevel. The underground passages he'd taken had enabled him to bypass the breached security entrance on Earthglow's main floor. When the tubular car opened, he would be in the microencapsulation section, a few turns of the hall from the room that was the intruders' certain objective.

He did not know the size of their invasion force or how far they had penetrated. If he determined that they could be prevented from accomplishing their mission, he would. But his survival had always rested on being a swift contingency planner.

The elevator stopped.

Outside in the corridor, Simmons and Rosander heard the whisper of the arriving car and raised their VVRS weapons.

Kuhl caught a glimpse of them before its door fully opened. His edge over them in speed might have been narrow. In his merciless capacity to kill without restraint, he was a creature alone.

Simmons was on the left of the elevator, and as he prepared to give its passenger a warning, Kuhl pivoted toward him, stepped in close under his gun arm, and brought his own pistol up to Simmons's side, pushing the muzzle between his fourth rib and underarm, where he knew the straps of his soft ballistic vest would leave an unprotected gap. Three shots of Teflon-coated .45ACP rounds against his body, three muffled blats of sound as the snout of the gun discharged through layers of cold-weather clothing, and Simmons went down to the floor.

With the man who'd come out of the elevator pressed close against Simmons, Rosander had been unable to do anything but hold his fire, fearing he might accidentally hit his teammate. But as Simmons crumpled, he brought his weapon to bear.

He was almost fast enough.

In a streak, Kuhl spun toward Rosander on the ball of his foot, moved in at him, grabbed his wrist behind the outthrust VVRS, and twisted it sharply around, wrenching it, simultaneously slamming his powerful forearm up under Rosander's chin to crush his windpipe.

His eyes rolling back in their sockets, Rosander sagged back against the wall and fell.

Kuhl crouched to take the VVRS from his hand, heard movement behind him, turned again to the left, in the direction of the laboratory where the inhibitor formulas were stored. His side sticky and wet from point-blank bullet wounds, the intruder Kuhl had shot still clung to life and was weakly raising himself onto his elbows, fingers fumbling for the grip of his own weapon. Kuhl bent, shoved his knee into the man's diaphragm to crush the air out of him, lifted his helmet visor, and, looking directly down into his eyes, finished him with a shot to the center of his forehead.

Rising then, he heard footsteps down the hall.

Another enemy in winter camouflage was rapidly approaching from the lab area, his weapon ready to fire.

Hearing gunshots down the corridor to his right, knowing Ricci desperately needed more time in the room behind him, Nichols turned and rushed toward the sound of the reports.

All at a glance he saw a man he recognized as the Wildcat standing above Simmons's blood-soaked form, saw Rosander slumped near the wall behind them, and with a surge of horror opened fire on the killer.

Cold-eyed, Kuhl triggered the VVRS he had taken

from Rosander, aiming low, a right-to-left sweep of the barrel.

Nichols's legs gave out underneath him, blood splashing from both knees. And then he felt the floor hard against his back.

Kuhl fired three accurate bursts into him, saw the body quiver as fifteen bullets ripped into it, and for an instant considered advancing farther up the hall.

His teeth clicked. Footsteps were coming from the penetration site behind him, four sets, the sound of their heavy boots distinct from those of his own men. His squad had apparently been held off, and he did not know how many more intruders were ahead of him.

Kuhl took an instant to consider and then made his decision.

He turned toward the elevator, pressed the call button, stepped through the opening, and retreated.

". . . oh my God, Ricci, this is unbelievable."

Ricci's face was bathed in sweat.

"Talk fast, Doc," he said. "Have we got what we *need?*"

"We have it, yes. We have it, we have it. Several different types of inhibitors. Stored as computer models rather than pills. Novelty cures for novelty viruses. They had no reason to preproduce them, not physically, and they didn't. But Ricci, what we've stumbled onto is beyond what we expected. There are hundreds, maybe *thousands* of activators. The virus must be infinitely mutable. A potential doomsday bug, and we've found—"

Ricci's attention broke away from whatever Oh was telling him. He'd heard the thud of what might have been pistol shots down the hall. Two, maybe three. A fourth. Fairly close by. Then, perhaps five seconds afterward, several controlled, staccato bursts from a semiautomatic weapon that sounded like a VVRS.

He turned abruptly, ran across the room, through the door, and into the corridor. Looked left, then right.

No sign of Nichols in either direction.

His heart malleting in his chest again, he bounded down the hall, swung a corner past the microencapsulation lab, putting on speed. This was where the shots had come from.

Another turn, and then Ricci was met by the scene near the bottleneck elevator. It was a sight he would remember always.

Nichols was on the floor between him and the elevator door, sprawled on his back. Simmons and Rosander were down at the elevator itself. Seybold crouched over Nichols, cradling his head in his arms, the helmet off. Barnes, Newell, and Perry squatted over the other two fallen men, examining them, checking the severity of their wounds. And then Barnes looked up from the bodies at the sound of his approach, saw the question on his face, and shook his head *no*.

No.

Ricci dashed forward and knelt beside Seybold.

"How bad?" he asked.

Seybold glanced up from the young man in his arms, met Ricci's gaze, held it. His long, pained look told him everything.

Then, weakly, Nichols's hand came up from his side, and Ricci felt its touch on his arm. "Sir ... I ..." The thin, dry sound from his dying lips barely qualified as a whisper.

Ricci pushed his visor up from his face, swallowed, and leaned over him. "I hear you," he said. "Go on."

Nichols looked up at him, his lips still moving, shaping unintelligible words.

Ricci took his hand into his own, bent closer. Their faces were almost touching now.

"Go on," he said. "Go on, I'm here with you."

Nichols grimaced, struggled out a sound.

"Wildcat," he rasped. "Wild . . ."

Ricci felt something turn inside him. Slowly, grindingly. Like a great stone wheel.

He held Nichols's hand.

"Okay, I heard you. Try to be easy now."

Nichols lowered his eyelids but was still trying to talk. "Did . . . did we . . . ?"

Ricci nodded to his closed eyes. "We got it, Nichols. We—"

Nichols shuddered and produced a low rattle, and Ricci stopped talking, pulled in a breath that didn't seem to reach his lungs.

The kid was gone. Gone before the answer to his question had left Ricci's mouth.

"Pokey, you reading?"

"I hear you, Ricci."

"Tell me what's happening at the perimeter."

"It's getting busy near the main gate. Looks like some guards down there, a couple of jeeps. We saw two other cars turn out onto the road, really hauling, I don't know where they came from. Didn't exit through any of the gates, it's like they came right out of the damn north side of the hill—"

Ricci thought a moment, standing over the bodies he

would have to leave behind. *Go far, killer. Go as far as you want, and we'll see if it's enough.*

"Can't worry about them now," he said. "Your status?"

"We're okay. Somebody radioed our booth to order the perimeter sealed. We had the caged bird answer, and Harpswell made sure he sang like we trained him."

"Good. Be ready to open that service gate for us. We'll meet you at the guardhouse, head to the pickup vehicle together."

"Roger," Pokey replied.

Ricci turned to Seybold.

"Let's collect Carlysle and Beatty and get the hell out of here," he said.

There had been eleven of them when they entered. Now there were seven, one wounded, helped along by his companions.

Battered with loss, strong in purpose, Ricci's men left the same way they had come, retracing their steps from lighted corridors to darkened ones, then through the commissary, kitchen, the freight entrance, and, at last, out into the night. The lack of resistance didn't surprise Ricci. For all its malevolence, this was a working scientific facility, not an armed camp. The remaining security would be stretched thin, spread throughout the building or called to reinforce what they thought was a blocked perimeter fence. They did not know how the insertion team had gained access, did not know one of their gatehouses had been seized, and would be searching for a breach in the building's integrity rather than an elevated freight door. But beyond any of that, they were without leadership. Their commander had fled, abandoned them as he'd abandoned his mercenary raiders in Kazakhstan. Brothers in arms.

Oskaboose and Harpswell remained in the booth until their teammates appeared, hit the switch to slide back the gate, and then hurried to join them. The activity inside the main gate had intensified; there were overlapping voices, headlights blinking on, engines thrumming to life.

They scrambled out the gate toward the road and the waiting escape vehicle.

Ricci had raised the driver on his comlink, advised him to be ready to roll, and as the insertion team arrived at the meet spot, the big armored van pulled out of the roadside trees with its rear payload doors wide open.

The insertion team poured inside.

And they rolled.

Crouched in back of the van, Ricci peered through its Level III ballistic cargo windows and saw two pairs of headlights above the black curve of road behind them.

Again, no shocker. There was only the one route across the hills to the highway, and it wouldn't have taken the guards long to notice the open service gate.

"Those jeeps are getting close," he said and snapped his head toward the driver. "How far to the bridge?"

"Less than half a mile," he said. "We'd see it right now if this damned road wasn't so full of twists."

Ricci breathed. The van was powered by a turbocharged V-8, but its heavy, armor-plate hull gave the jeeps the edge in speed, and they were gaining fast.

He lowered the high, fold-down seat mounted to the side of the right load door, got into it, slid open a hidden gun port in the door, and thrust the muzzle of his VVRS through the port. At his nod, Seybold did the same behind the opposite door.

The jeeps were gaining, gaining, their high beams spearing the darkness. The lead vehicle was maybe a hundred yards back . . . ninety . . . eighty . . .

Ricci poured out a stream of fire, Seybold triggered his own gun, the two of them peppering the road with bullets, hopefully throwing some fear into their pursuers.

It worked. The jeeps dropped back, their ineffectual return fire spacking off the rear of the van.

"How we coming?" Ricci shouted to the driver.

"Almost there, almost, almost—"

They swung onto the short, concrete bridge.

Ricci and Seybold kept laying out parallel bands of fire, kept the jeeps trailing at a distance.

"Okay!" the driver called out. His foot tramped on the accelerator. "We're across, we're home, I can see the chopper straight up ahead!"

Ricci nodded, stopped firing, gave the lead jeep a chance to make the bridge.

Its front tires rolled onto the span.

"Now, Thibodeau!" he shouted over the comlink. *"Do it!"*

At the Two Shoulders base camp, Rollie Thibodeau lightly fingered a switch on his handheld remote-firing device, initiating the radio-addressable mines his team had affixed to the bridge support pillars.

Behind the pickup van, the bridge went up with a flash and a roar, its center heaving upward and then disintegrating, an avalanche of concrete that went crashing downward, taking the jeeps and their occupants with it, mangled, burning, tumbling, down and down and down in a great dome of flame to the frozen streambed below.

"Done," Thibodeau grunted.

TWENTY-FIVE

As he reached for the telephone, Harlan DeVane was pleased to note that his hand was not trembling. Perhaps his control was only temporary and would slip once the ramifications of Kuhl's call from Earthglow sank in. Perhaps some part of his mind was still denying that the Sleeper project was finished. He had invested so much in it, made his pronouncements, staked his name on its success. But the inhibitor codes had been expropriated. Seized by men Kuhl was convinced were operatives for Roger Gordian. What was left?

DeVane pressed the "flash" button on his telephone's keypad and listened to a programmed sequence of bleeps go out into electronic space. The codes, too, were out there. Or soon would be. He pictured them as mathematical formulas on little sheets of paper, dispersing in a loose circle that stretched around the globe. Countless hands grasping for them, snatching them from the air. A cure for this one, this one, and this one. It was a vivid image, and DeVane supposed it would grow even sharper as he came to terms with what had happened in Canada.

Yes, DeVane thought, Zeus had flung a thunderbolt, and now his chariot was tumbling to the ground. But not everything was wreckage. Not yet. He could still leave a trail of flame across the sky.

A ringing tone in his ear now, cut short as a male voice answered.

"Yes?"

DeVane held the receiver in his grip.

"Proceed with the backup option," he said.

Steadily.

From the roofs beyond Roger Gordian's window at San Jose Mercy, only a small corner of his bed was visible, and then at a strained and awkward angle. This placement was intentional and appropriate for the stepped-up security around Gordian. As soon as suspicions arose that he was the victim of a deliberate biological attack, the bed had been moved out of line with the window to minimize the threat of outside observation and sniper fire.

The rooftop shooter had his orders, however. Standing at the foot of the bed, speaking to her unconscious husband in soft tones, Ashley Gordian was a clearly exposed target as he made a minor adjustment to his aim.

"You talk to Gord all the time, don't you?" Megan Breen asked her now. She was seated with her back against the wall to the left of the window, a warm dash of sunlight on her cheek. When the first bullet entered the room, it would pass within an inch or two of her ear.

Ashley looked at Megan. They were alone with Gordian except for the plainclothes Sword op—a thin, dark-haired man sitting quietly to one side of the door with his arms crossed over his concealed firearm—assigned to guard the room. All three wore their ordinary street clothes—no protective aprons, no masks, goggles, gloves, or shoe covers. With the discovery that Gordian's symptoms had resulted from his ingestion of a gene-directed trigger, infectiousness had ceased to be a concern.

"I've got a hunch he hears more than you might think," Ashley replied. "We joke about our running commentary on the state of anything and everything. Roger says we should mike ourselves and start our own radio call-in show."

Megan smiled a little. "I can remember a time, not too long ago, when it was torture pulling a single word out of Gord."

Ashley nodded. "He's really opened up over the past couple of years, Meg. Ever since we got past our difficulties. Some days it's nonstop gab, you'd be amazed."

"It must be nice for you. Being so comfortable with each other."

"Yes, it is," Ashley said. "For both of us."

They regarded Gordian, who lay there under his blankets with his eyes closed, his ventilator making its pumping sounds into the silence. A young man in a white intern's coat entered the room, checked Gordian's nutrient IV bag, noted aloud that it required changing, and left. Behind a concrete rampart three hundred yards away, the sniper cradled his rifle in his hands and waited for the signal.

Megan glanced at her watch.

"We've got about an hour before Eric Oh and the

team from Sobel arrive with the antivirals,'' she said, her voice filled with ongoing wonder and admiration over their ability to synthesize them literally overnight. ''How about you let me treat you to breakfast while we're on standby?''

A sudden look came into Ashley's eyes. Sober, knowing. At first Megan wasn't quite sure what to make of it.

Kneeling on his rooftop perch, the shooter watched her turn from the foot of the bed and step in front of the window, dead-center between his crosshairs. His finger was curled over the trigger. One squeeze and her heart would burst in her chest.

''Breakfast sounds like a good idea,'' Ashley said, her eyes still solemn, her voice dropping to a very quiet volume. ''We need to talk in private, and I think it might be the right opportunity.''

Megan gave her a questioning glance.

''Sword business is Sword business,'' Ashley said. ''I don't have to know everything about how you do your work. In many ways I prefer not knowing. It's a part of Gord's life that scares me. And because I think of you and Pete as family, it makes me scared for you, too.''

''But you want me to tell you something now,'' Megan said slowly.

Ashley nodded.

''If men died in Canada so my husband can live, I would like their names and as much information as you're able to provide about the circumstances under which they were lost,'' she said. Her voice had lowered another notch, and Megan realized she did not want to chance it carrying across the room to Gordian. ''Thanksgiving's just a few days from now. I need to call their families . . . express my gratitude and indebtedness. And my sorrow. They should know how important they are to me. That I'll always be available to help them as best I can."

Megan looked at her.

"It's going to be difficult," she said.

"Yes," Ashley said. "I expect it will."

Megan studied her face a moment, then took her handbag from where she'd hung it over the back of her chair.

"We'd better head down to the cafeteria," she said.

Ashley nodded again, and went to the bed table to pick up her own purse, stepping away from the window.

The sniper breathed, gripping the stock of his weapon. There was a point when it took a tremendous act of will to refrain from firing. When everything was aligned, and you knew you had a sure kill, the target was almost inviting you to take the shot. But this wasn't about either of the women. His orders were to wait for the signal.

Ashley had almost moved out of his sight picture when he finally got it.

Three shots, that was how many Megan would remember.

Three, fired in swift succession. She didn't see any muzzle flashes. Didn't hear any audible reports. The room simply appeared to begin exploding around her. But she was fairly certain of the number of shots.

The first obliterated most of the window just as she was about to rise from her chair. Glass pelted over her in a shower of hooks and needles, a large shard cutting deep into her left temple. She dove to the floor, saw Ashley standing frozen in place, looking from the knocked out window to Gordian, plaster spouting from the wall across the room now, bits and pieces of it fleck-ing her blouse, shot number two. "Ashley, get down!" she shouted, blood streaming over her face in rivulets.

Ashley gave no indication that she'd heard her. Eyes wide with shock, she started toward the bed, toward her husband.

"Listen to me, Ash! The bullets can't hit him over there, he'll be okay, please, *please* get dow—"

"*No!*" Ashley screamed, still on her feet, moving over to the bed, not caring about herself, not thinking rationally about lines of fire, knowing only that bullets were flying here in the room where her husband lay helpless and vulnerable, wanting only to protect him.

Even before the third shot came, Megan was scram-bling toward her on all fours. But the guard had already launched off his seat, propelling himself at Ashley, clutching her around the waist, taking her down to the floor, protecting her with his own body.

There was another crash as more jagged fragments of glass blew from the window frame, round number three, singing through the air, impacting the wall inches from the previous shot, punching a wide hole into it.

Then Megan saw the door fly open, and people rush into the room. Sword guards, hospital personnel, maybe eight or ten of them seeming to flood through the door all at once. She didn't know whether it was the gunshots or the closed-circuit television cameras below the ceiling that alerted them, didn't particularly care. She was just glad they had arrived.

Somebody was yelling to move Gordian out, move him *out* of here! Then the shift doctors and nurses crowded around him, hastily detaching his ventilator hoses from their outlets, rolling his bed toward the door, pushing the wheeled IV stands along as they steered him through it. A couple of the guards accompanied Gordian and the staffers to the secondary room that had been readied down the corridor, weapons drawn. A few stayed behind momentarily, one member of the Sword team scrambling toward Megan, a second moving over to Ashley and the guard who'd shielded her from harm, yet another going to the shattered window and taking a position beside it, carefully craning his head to peer out at the rooftops for any sign of the triggerman, staying flat against the wall, using the wall for cover.

"Looks like you've got a nasty cut," the man who'd raced over to Megan was saying. He helped her off the floor, urging her to keep her head below the windowsill. Meanwhile, she could see Ashley being hustled out of the room. "We'll move you out of here, find a doctor to take care of it. . . ."

She wiped a trickle of blood from her face, felt an awful stinging as her fingers passed over the gash.

"That can wait," she said. "I want to make sure the boss is okay."

"Ms. Breen, I'm not sure that's advisable—"

"I'm doing it anyway," she said.

As a youth in South Philly, Pete Nimec had learned how fiercely combative people could be about their turf, and the rough lessons driven home with fists and bats had stayed with him into adulthood. In negotiations to put Sword manpower on someone else's beat, he never forgot the rules of the street. Keep the boundaries in mind. Pay your due respects. Know when to stand your ground—and when to meet your opposite number halfway.

The administration at San Jose Mercy had expressed a slew of reservations about his desire to take charge of Roger Gordian's security on hospital premises, most of which revolved around matters of civil liability. Although they had been willing to tinker with routine security mechanisms, the board members were leery of any perceived attempt to infringe on their responsibility for a patient's safeguard.

Nimec's comeback was to advance a version of the arrangement he'd worked out with many of the foreign nations that played host to UpLink facilities. Absolute consideration would be given to San Jose Mercy's legal and ethical obligations, with all procedures implemented by Sword to be subject to the board's review. His plan had called for a single Sword employee to join the hospital's uniformed security personnel at key entry and exit points, the establishment of a fixed guard post in the corridor leading toward Gordian's room, installation of a Sword-monitored CCTV camera inside the room, and the designation of an additional space to which Gordian could be rapidly transferred in an emergency situation, its location to be known only to top members of his caregiving team. These specifics had been approved without exception. A final request that Sword techies be allowed to conduct a thorough security rundown of the hospital's computer network was vetoed, but Nimec had expected that would be a touchy issue, and been prepared to abandon it for the sake of expedience.

It was Nimec's inability to convince the hospital to let him protect its data resources—this single blanket restriction imposed on him—that gave the infiltrator a soft spot that could be exploited.

In a room just a few turns of the hall from the commotion stirred by the shooting, the man wearing the intern's coat held the intravenous bag he'd readied, and listened as Roger Gordian was delivered to him. Laced in with the feeding solution's carbohydrates, vitamins, and other nutrients was a massive concentration of digitalis—a glycoside effective at slowing rapid heartbeats when prescribed in therapeutic dosages—that was sufficient to bring about full cardiac arrest in the healthiest individual. Given his fragile state, Gordian would be dead within minutes after the drug entered his bloodstream.

It had been so easy, the infiltrator thought. Almost effortless. Hacking into the hospital's computer system. Adding a name to the electronically generated list of staffers who were permitted access to Roger Gordian's room. Then forging identification to match, a laminated card worn on his breast pocket, again nothing complicated. And while there was no official record of an area designated for Gordian's emergency use, the nearness to his room of a conspicuously blocked off section of the ward had marked it as a probable fallback—and the infiltrator's vigilance over the past few days had borne out that suspicion.

Now the sound of movement in the hall grew louder, nearer. Suddenly the door to the room swung open, and Gordian was rolled inside, surrounded by a bustle of orderlies, plainclothes guards, his wife, and the other woman who had been with him when the infiltrator radioed his firing command to the nearby rooftop.

He stepped back from the entry as the bed was pushed through, urgently waved the orderlies toward a nest of monitoring and life-support equipment.

Easy, so easy.

"Over here!" he said, raising his voice above the clamor. "Let's get him hooked up!"

Megan was thinking that it didn't make sense.

She reached the fallback room and was hurried inside by guards and hospital staffers, Gordian's bed wheeled ahead of her, pushed toward the attending intern who'd checked his drip bag right before the gunfire broke out. Somebody in the press of bodies dabbed her open cut with something cool and moist, slapped on a stitch bandage, put a gauze pad over it and a strip of tape to hold the dressing in place, and then left her to join the activity around the bed. Ventilator hoses were connected to pumps in the wall, waiting machines activated, the depleted IV bag unhooked, replaced with a fresh one by the attending, and still Megan was thinking it made no sense, none at all, who had the sniper been shooting at? Gordian had been out of harm's way, she'd been out of sight, and Ashley could have been hit when she was standing in front of the window if she'd been the intended target. So why pull the trigger?

The question gnawed at her as she waited by the door with Ashley, both women standing clear of the busy professionals, watching the handful of guards that accompanied them pour back into the corridor to seal off access, watching the cluster of orderlies dissolve as they completed their tasks, all of them and filing out of the room now, leaving the intern to start the IV. . . .

An image from moments ago suddenly came into Megan's head, came into it in a flash. The intern. Waiting here in the room. Alone. The drip bag in his hand as Gordian was jostled through the door.

Waiting.

She had seen the intern a number of times over the past several days, moving about the corridor with a clipboard in hand, but never in Gordian's room. He was not one of the regulars on his case, she was sure of that. Yet somehow he had known about the fallback, known where it was situated though that was privileged information, and moreover had been the first person inside it, giving orders to the orderlies as they entered.

She looked at him. He had moved the IV stand close to the bed, run the catheter over the safety rail, and was leaning over Gordian, about to work the needle into his wrist.

"Hold on," she said. Stepping toward him. Her mouth dry, her heart pounding away in her chest. "What are you doing?"

The intern turned his face toward her.

"The fluid bag needs to be connected," he said. "It won't take a minute."

She took another step closer to him, another, quickly crossing the room, leaving Ashley standing at the door in confusion.

"No," she said. Shaking her head. "What are you doing *here?*"

He straightened up, looked at her without any response.

His eyes boring into her eyes.

Reading them.

"Ashley," she said. Not turning from him for an instant. "Open the door and call for help, this guy doesn't belong in—"

His hand released the feeding tube, simply let it drop over the rail, and went under his white hospital coat. Megan couldn't see what he was reaching for, didn't need to see, what she had to do was stop him.

She moved in fast, bringing up her hands, ducking her head under his arms, remembering what Pete had told her in the training ring. Her fist jabbed out, aimed at the middle of his chest, her shoulder rolling behind the motion, her entire back in it, her knuckles digging between his ribs as they made solid contact.

He produced a grunt of pain and surprise, doubled over, gasping for breath, his hand appearing from inside the coat, an automatic pistol spilling from his fingers to hit the floor.

Megan heard Ashley shouting into the hallway at the top of her lungs, and a split second later heard the hurried pounding of feet behind her, and a male voice ordering the guy in the intern's coat to stay put, telling him not to even think about reaching for the gun, and he kept hugging himself and coughing, trying to catch his breath. . . .

And then the Sword security team came in the doorway and were all over him.

TWENTY-SIX

"... STIRRING FOR THE PAST HOUR. ONE OF THE nurses on shift noticed ... about to regain consciousness. I phoned you right away."

"I thought it would be yesterday, Elliot. I was sure. He seemed to be trying so hard."

"It helps that you're here. Talking to him. Bringing him along. His response to the inhibitor's been tremendous. . . . You shouldn't be discouraged if it doesn't happen right now . . ."

Gordian opened his eyes. The room was very bright with sunlight. Ashley stood at his bedside, in the brightness, looking down at him. Elliot Lieberman was next to her in his white doctor's coat.

"If what ... doesn't happen?" he asked.

Ashley looked at him, an almost startled expression on her face, and then leaned over the bed rail.

"This," she replied into his ear. "Oh Gord, Gord, this, right here. Right now."

He slowly raised a hand off his sheet, touched her cheek, felt its moistness.

"Knew I had an angel on my shoulder," he said. "Didn't know angels cry."

She kissed his face, kissed it again, and again, and then raised her head, smiling, her fingers clasped around his, her tears flowing freely over the smile, spilling onto their joined hands, tears of gratitude for the blessing she'd been granted, tears of heartbreaking sorrow for those who had paid the ultimate price for it.

"They let us," she said. "One day each year, they let us."

He looked at her. "When?"

"Thanksgiving," she said.

Tom Ricci sat alone at his kitchen table, its surface bare except for the quart bottle of Black Label he had bought at the liquor store the previous night, last sale date before the holiday, a Thanksgiving dinner he aimed to remember.

It was five o'clock in the afternoon, the window shades drawn in every room of his apartment, phone off the hook, and he was about to dive into his liquid meal, swallow down as much forbidden nectar as his belly could hold. One hundred percent malt, twelve-step program be damned.

Yes sir, he thought. *Yes sir, Tom. Gobble, gobble.*

He stared at the bottle, his hand on the table, slowly reaching across it, slipping and sliding across the table to close around that smooth, cool curvature of glass.

Ricci closed his eyes, tightly holding the bottle. In his mind's eye he saw a scale, like the kind you saw in pictures of blindfolded Lady Justice. Nichols, Grillo,

Simmons, and Rosander on one side. Roger Gordian and the rest of the planet on the other.

The whole damned planet, yes. Billions of possible victims of a germ that, in the end, because of the sacrifices of those he had led on his mission, had claimed only one good man in a small corner of Latin America.

The balance seemed to tip lopsidedly in favor of the mission having been a success . . . and for Ricci it would have been no less successful if he himself had perished with the men who had bled out their lives behind the gray concrete walls of Earthglow.

World's end. Last stop on the civilization express.

Ricci gripped the bottle. He could handle the losses, handle giving up the measure of blood that seemed periodically due to keep whatever was good and worthwhile about existence from falling into darkness. Harsh and unfair as he sometimes found the bill was, he'd always made his payments with a kind of bitter, uncomplaining dependability.

The problem for him now, though, was that the scale had been jiggered. Somebody had fooled with the weights, tampered with the balance, thrown the whole damned system of measurement into question.

The killer . . .

Ricci would never again call him by the name Wildcat, would never again lend him the dignity or power that name endowed. . . .

The killer was free, out there somewhere beyond the drawn shades of his apartment, breathing air that his victims could no longer breathe, feeling the sunlight that was warming the ground atop their graves.

The killer . . . and whatever nameless, faceless, taskmaster he served.

Happy Thanksgiving, Ricci thought, and pulled the bottle closer, pulled it right to the edge of the table, right up against his chest.

I start out hugging a drink, three hours later wind up wrestling with one. Like that Bible story, when Christ wrestles with the Devil in the desert. . . .

He looked at the bottle, held the bottle in both his hands, and moistened his lips with his tongue. Thirsty, so thirsty, so eager to wash the grinding pain from inside him.

But the killer was still free. Breathing the air. Out there in the light. Free.

Ricci sat at the table a while longer . . . he wasn't exactly sure how long. Then he sighed, pushed back his chair, rose to his feet, lifted his quart of expensive pure malt whiskey off the table, and strode across the kitchen to carefully set it into the wastebasket beside the sink.

What the hell, he thought. *What the hell.*

He had work to begin after the long weekend was over, work that might finally set the balance right, and it wasn't the sort of thing that would be easy to pull off with a hangover.

Wondering what he was going to eat for dinner with all the supermarkets closed and not a scrap of food in his fridge, Ricci went to the window and opened the shade to let in what remained of the day.

In one corner of Breugel's painting on the main floor of the Prado, a cart ridden by the servants of Death is shown rolling implacably toward a woman who has fallen across the path of its wheels, her hands clinging to a distaff and spindle. These tools of the spinner represent the unpredictable drawing out and twisting of life's threads. They are also symbols of femininity, for in antiquity spinning had been a woman's craft.

Unable to make himself leave Spain without once again viewing the masterwork, Kuhl stood before it now and thought of his lover, of the softness and delicacy of her body, and then sharply recalled their last moments together.

He had not wanted to let go of her.

Hours before he'd taken her to the countryside southwest of the city, they had been pressed together in their hotel room, sharing splendid intimacies behind its closed door. He had touched her eagerly, greedily, wanting his flesh to remember. And then, afterward, he had suggested they take the long drive down into the Castilla y León, where the old churches and castles stood upon the hills.

On a lonely and beautiful stretch of road, Kuhl had pulled over and sat beside her for a long length of time. Then he'd asked her to walk with him under trees brown with autumn, his arm around her waist as they left the car.

It had been an exquisite place for her to die.

Kuhl had done it quickly, not wishing the pain to last, one hand over her mouth to muffle her cries, his other hand tightening on her throat.

He remembered her straining against him, and then feeling the pulse in her neck quiet under his fingertips.

The struggle had been brief.

There had been tears in her eyes, he remembered.

Even after life was extinguished, and her surprise and fear turned to emptiness, there were tears.

Bearing her to a thickly wooded notch in the hills, he had covered her body so the animals would find her before any man ever could. And then he'd left her, and gone back to Madrid.

He had not wanted to let go of her, but she had known too much. He saw that. What if she had been caught?

The danger to him had been great.

Unacceptably great.

Now Kuhl took a snatch of breath, studied the Bruegel painting for a short while longer, then turned away from it and strode down the hall toward the museum exit.

The world offered hard choices, but it was still under his feet.

In the end, for him, that was what truly mattered.

EPILOGUE

HE HAD SPENT MILLIONS. TENS UPON TENS OF MIL-
lions. And every last dollar had been wasted.

Harlan DeVane sat on the veranda of his expansive
Spanish ranch house in the Chapare region of Bolivia,
staring out at the cattle fields in silence, watching his
imported heifers graze on the grass with plodding bovine
contentment. Once, perhaps, some primal forerunner of
the beasts must have had at least a spark of driving fire
in its breast. But that had been bred out of the species
when their free-roaming herds became livestock, their
migrations became limited by the corral fence, and their
inborn fear of the predator was dulled to a birth promise
of certain slaughter.

DeVane watched them, thinking that he could walk
across the pasture to where they were gathered in a patch
of green, put a gun to one of their heads at random, and
fire, and that the others were apt to go on chewing lazily
or produce some lowing sound of momentary bafflement

as the victim dropped in a heap among them with what little brains it possessed leaching deep into the dirt. All of them unaware of the fate that had narrowly missed being theirs. All incapable of appreciating that they lived by a simple fluke.

His eyes at once motionless and searching, his thin features caught in the ever-still space between thought and expression, DeVane suddenly recalled a string of words from an old leather-bound volume in his library: *What mad pursuit? What struggle to escape? What pipes and timbrels? What wild ecstasy?*

He breathed, as always, without a sound.

These were idle musings, and there were far more important matters to occupy his mind. Matters from which he could only divert himself temporarily, for they were bound to catch up with him, tearing at his false peace like the swipe of claws in the night.

The Sleeper virus that was to have gained him a fortune beyond any ever amassed, prestige beyond any imaginable height—given him the power to steer the sun across the sky—had brought him instead to abject humiliation. With the inhibitors now as commonly available as aspirin, his customers had paid vast sums for genetic triggers that were worth less to them than dust. Some had targeted victims by the hundreds, the thousands, and more. He had wanted only the death of a single man, Roger Gordian . . . and none had gotten the thing for which they had put their good money down.

So what was left for him now? What goddamned pipes and timbrels?

Humiliation. Ignominy. Clients who had become enemies by the score.

And because of Siegfried Kuhl's ineffectiveness, his

failure to eliminate Gordian even by brute, overt force of hand, the very strong chance that the careful screens that ensured his anonymity, that allowed him to roam the world free, would begin to be peeled away.

DeVane closed his eyes and slowly, slowly bent his head back so it was exposed in full to the strong, tropical sun. The rays stung his pale, almost colorless skin, and he knew it would not take long before he burned.

He sat there and did not move.